Books by Jill Marie Landis

SUNFLOWER
WILDFLOWER

JILL MARIE LANDIS

WILDFLOWER

JOVE BOOKS, NEW YORK

WILDFLOWER

A Jove Book / published by arrangement with
the author

PRINTING HISTORY
Jove edition / August 1989

ISBN: 0-515-10102-8

Jove Books are published by The Berkley Publishing Group,
200 Madison Avenue, New York, New York 10016.
The name "JOVE" and the "J" logo
are trademarks belonging to Jove Publications, Inc.

PRINTED IN THE UNITED STATES OF AMERICA

10 9 8 7 6 5 4 3 2 1

To Steve—my pirate, my cowboy,
and my knight in shining armor
I love you

Chapter One

The Rocky Mountains   1830

Walls of stone as gray-blue as the underside of a thundercloud rose to form ragged peaks that clawed the sky. The enduring Rockies stood with faces as cragged and worn as an old woman's skin, scarred and gouged by a timeless onslaught of ice and snow. The Indians called them the shining mountains of crystal stones, for their peaks were ever cloaked in shimmering glaciers.

Life crept tentatively upward as far as snow and ice would allow. Fir and spruce banded together to nestle in hollows, while a few of the more brazen and twisted trees fought for life on unprotected ridges. Aspen leaves gleamed like polished gold pieces between the stands of dark pine. They drifted to earth like sunkissed flower petals and formed a lush fall carpet beneath the trees.

Small, quiet valleys lay hidden on the eastern slope of the range the Frenchmen called the Grand Teton. In these gentle places, protected by the westerlies that swept the snow clean off the glaciers, the fir and spruce grew beside the lodgepole pines, tall and straight, unwilling to bow or become deformed by the harsh environment that whipped the others fighting to survive near the snow line.

Life in the hidden valleys and meadows was abundant. Rivers flowed with the beat of it. The wind carried the song of life, and the branches of the trees echoed the words. The men who came to dwell in the valleys soon grew as worn and

1

rugged as the land itself and, in time, as gnarled and bent as the trees. Big Jake Fisher had been one of these men.

In a valley where the wildflowers and the aspen leaves had already yellowed but were not yet crisp with winter's breath, Jake had carved a dugout shelter into the hillside. Hand-hewn logs reinforced the earthen walls and closed off the opening. It was a good abode for a man of the mountains; like the man, the dugout was rough and ragged on the outside, warm and comforting within.

Big Jake Fisher had moved up the Missouri to the Rockies in 1812, leaving his old life behind. He had roamed and trapped, fought and cursed, in a land that few men had ever seen, but having seen it once, seldom left behind.

A stream meandered through the valley. The beavers that had once built dams and tunnels across its rushing water were nearly all played out now. Jake Fisher and men of his ilk—men who trapped and skinned, weighed and sold the "plew," or pelts, that easterners paid dearly for—had all but wiped out the beaver trade. Water in the stream continued to leap and play on its journey downhill as the morning sun traveled across a cloudless azure sky.

But today the creatures of the forest around Big Jake's home were silent. No blackbirds sang in the branches of the stately lodgepole pines. The busy rust-red squirrels that usually hopped from limb to limb or scampered through the scattered wood debris were nowhere to be seen. The pines themselves were silent, the wind still. Not even a slight autumn breeze dared to whisper through the treetops.

Big Jake Fisher had been dead for two days.

A large slab of granite, warmed by the sun, provided a backrest for a huddled, silent girl who leaned against it. Her legs were drawn up, her head lowered upon her knees as she hugged them to her. Her finely shaped features were masked by the raggedly cropped mahogany-colored hair that hung around her face and by the wide-brimmed, flat-crowned felt hat she wore. Well-tanned buckskin clothing hid her narrow shoulders and slender legs while knee-high fur-lined boots hugged her calves and feet.

The girl sat as still as the forest around her, stealing comfort from the sparkling morning sunlight and the warm rock at her back, unaware of the silence that was broken only by the sound of the mountain stream. An inner voice prodded her, urging her to move on. The girl known only as Dani lifted her head and stared through tear-filled eyes at the entrance to the one-room dugout cabin she had shared with Big Jake for fourteen of her eighteen years. Rubble blocked the way into the cabin now, the earth and rocks meant to prevent anyone or anything from entering the shelter. Big Jake's home now served as his grave.

Big Jake had died in his sleep. Stretched out in death, his lifeless body seemed to have shrunk, his facial features stark against the unruly beard and wild, unkempt hair. The once vibrant man whose booming voice could set the timbers shaking overhead had been stilled forever. The fingers of his gnarled, work-worn hands had lain slack against the hide covers. Dani had reached out to touch them, afraid, and yet unwilling to let Jake go without a farewell.

After discovering Jake's lifeless body, she had moved all the goods and equipment outside the dugout, then lined the doorway with gunpowder. She left a goodly measure lying in a pile a few feet inside the opening. Now, as she rose to her feet and tossed in a torch coated with pitch, Dani whispered farewell to her lifelong friend and mentor and watched the gunpowder explode, sealing away her past and forcing her toward an uncertain future.

A warm tear spilled over her lashes and slid down her cheek. Dani drew her arm across her eyes and quickly wiped it away with the sleeve of her fringed buckskin jacket. It wouldn't do for anyone to come along and find her crying like this.

Seems like I ought to be done with crying by now.

Dani knew Big Jake would be furious that she had shed even one tear over his passing, but here she was, crying anyway. Hadn't Jake always said that everything was born dying? He'd told her that death sent men on to become part of the earth, part of the big wilderness all around. With another swipe at the tears on her cheeks, Dani raised her face to the sky and stared into its clear blue depths. She took a deep breath of the dry mountain air, one last look at the heap that had been her home for so long, and then tightened the rawhide strap that held her hat in place.

Already she sorely missed the burly man who had been her constant companion for as long as she could remember. Acting as her guardian, Jake had raised her since she was four years old.

Now she was alone.

Dani had put off leaving for two days to try to adjust to Jake's death, but now the inevitable was at hand. Jake was gone and summer had ended. It was time to push on, time to begin the fall trapping.

She had never imagined going it alone, but trapping was all she knew how to do. There was no one she could turn to now, except maybe Moze Hadley, one of Jake's old friends, but Dani knew it wasn't likely he'd want a partner after so many years of living alone. Still, she had decided she might as well ride past his cabin and ask if she could travel with him.

Her footsteps made no sound at all as she crossed the clearing toward the mule and two horses tied side by side near a border of pines. She would use her own Indian-red pony solely for riding, not packing. The mule was a sight to behold, laden with buffalo-hide bags of beaver traps as well as bundles and packets of goods needed to sustain life in the wilderness. A buffalo-bladder bag rimmed with deerhide, two pairs of snowshoes, and round willow hoops used as frames to stretch and dry the beaver skins—all dangled from the ropes that secured the heap to the mule's back. Dani and Jake had worked all summer to dry and brand the beaver pelts that were stacked and tied on Jake's big sorrel horse. She had plenty of jerked meat and a hearty supply of pemmican, the Indian cakes made of dried and pulverized buffalo meat mixed with ground berries and melted fat.

Dani checked the bindings on the mule and the sorrel once more, then tied the pack animals' tethers to a lead rope. She stood beside her own mount and with an unconscious movement pushed her hat down farther on her forehead before she adjusted her heavy leather belt. Fashioned from dark brown otter fur and snakeskin, the belt served to hold her buckskin jacket closed. A soft, billowy homespun shirt, made for a figure twice the size of Dani's, trailed to a point below her hips. Only the tail of the shirt was visible beneath her heavily fringed jacket.

A bear's head "possible" bag hung from her saddle horn and held everything she might possibly need, which accounted for its name. Dani opened the flap, reached inside for her pistol, and shoved the weapon into her belt.

Digging into the possible bag again, she drew out a bone-handled blade nearly a foot long, encased in a beaded sheath. She carefully slid it into her knee-high ermine-lined moccasin-boots. As her fingers came in contact with the soft, luxurious fur, she remembered the day Big Jake had traded eight prized pelts for them. Dani stroked the boots gently with her fingertips, then pulled them up higher. She wore fringed buckskin britches, well greased and stiffened by many hours of wading in icy streams.

Jake had dressed Dani like a boy since the day he found her. He told her he hoped to "fool the fools" who might make trouble for her if they knew she was female. The two of them had been "foolin' the fools" for years now.

"You're the only white gal this side of the Missouri that I know of, Dani," Jake had said, "and it wouldn't do to have the accursed ruffians out here aware of that fact."

Mounting briskly, Dani hoped that whatever trouble Jake had been avoiding would continue to pass her by.

Her eyes filled with tears once again as she reached down for the powder horn and bullet pouch that hung on leather thongs from the pommel of her saddle. These were the last of the trappings she needed to don. Always, before they had ridden out of camp, Jake had checked to be sure she'd remembered everything that was essential to her survival.

His gruff voice had been no more than a grunt.

"Knife."

"Got it," she would reply.

"Powder horn."

"Got it."

"Bullet pouch."

"Got it."

"Bullet mold."

"Got it."

"Ball screw."

"Got it."

"Ramrod."

"Got it."

"Pistol."

"Got it."

"Teeth and nose."

"Got 'em."

Each time he called out the seemingly endless list of items that hung from belts and straps about her body, Jake would end with a different jest, and their laughter would start the trek off on a joyous note.

Today the memory served only to rekindle her sadness.

Once more Dani's smoke-gray eyes glanced over her shoulder at what had been the door to their cabin.

"Bye, Big Jake," she whispered, her voice choked with emotion. "Rest easy."

She let her thoughts wander disconnected as she made her way through the forest of fir and pine trees, over ridges and across meadows that lay open and spacious, cloaked in verdant hues that would be blanketed in white before too many weeks passed. Before Jake's death, Dani had looked forward with delight and anticipation to losing herself in the heavy work of fall trapping. She hoped the task would help ease her ragged nerves, for something had been nagging her all summer, a feeling she could not describe. For some reason, Dani felt as if she needed to search the hills and mountains until she found what it was she was looking for, knowing it for an impossible task, since she had no clue as to what that something was.

All through the warm summer months she'd felt an unfamiliar pressure building inside her until it simmered just below the surface of her skin. She'd been irritable lately, and as jumpy as a pond frog. If Big Jake noticed, he'd said nothing. Dani wished she'd talked to him about her strange discomfort, but now it was too late.

The sun grew warm as the noon hour approached. The pleasant weather belied the fact that winter was on its way. "Nothin' can hold back the winter," Jake had always said. Those had been his exact words on the last night of his life. Big Jake had seemed less talkative than usual, staring into the fire, drinking his amber jug whiskey before he turned in to the narrow cot drawn up against one wall of the log-lined dugout. The unexplained tension continued to nag at her, so Dani had wandered out into the crisp darkness of the chilly autumn night. The mountains were alive around her, the moon full, and she knew that sleep would not come easily. So she walked. She had not even said good night to Jake. By morning it was too late to say anything to him at all. There was a stillness that was all too prevalent in the tiny cabin, a mournful silence that announced his passing. She knew before she tried to shake him awake that Jake Fisher had "gone under," as the mountain men said whenever one of them died.

Trying to forget the sight of Jake's cold, lifeless form, she concentrated once more on her present surroundings. Veering north and west, Dani watched for signs of the stream that would lead her to Moze Hadley's. Once she made the small tributary, she reckoned it would be another day and a half before she reached the cabin.

If Moze Hadley chose not to accompany her, her destination would be Hump Bone Hollow, a wide, bowl-shaped valley where trappers gathered in the fall. If Jake were still alive he and Dani would most likely have taken the same route and joined the others for a last rendezvous before they continued on alone. Dani looked forward, with some trepidation, to seeing the other men. It was one thing to assume, with Jake's help, her role as a boy, but now she would have to guard her secret all alone. The thought filled her with a mingled sense of anticipation and dread.

More and more often in the past few months Dani had wondered what could possibly be the harm of admitting that she was a girl. When she approached Jake with the question, he had become angry with her for the first time she could remember. "Anger" was almost too tame a word to describe his reaction. He was nearly in a blind rage, as wild as a grizzly cornering its prey. His deep-set brown eyes had burned with fury. His lips, nearly hidden by his bushy gray-streaked beard, had trembled. He'd held his tightly balled fists against his sides as if tempted to strike her.

"You know what you're askin'?" he yelled. "You're askin' for trouble. You seen any other women like you around here? No!" Jake answered his own question. "You want to end up like some man's bought squaw? What about me? What do you think anybody's gonna say about an old man that's kept a little girl with him all these years and not let nobody know?"

"That you're my pa?"

"Ha! Some of 'em's bound to remember when I found ya. They'd know damn well I ain't your pa. It'd be all well and good to keep a boy out here, but not a girl. And certainly not a woman." He had stomped to the door of the dugout, turned back to retrieve his jug, and then thrown the portal open. The sound of the wood crashing against the dirt wall had reverberated in the small room. Before disappearing to drink off his temper, he had turned back to face her. He was a tall, bulky man in filthy, worn buckskins who all but blocked out the light that streamed through the doorway.

"Holy hot shit." He cursed and then spit. "You go right

ahead and announce to the whole goddam stinkin' bunch of heathens in these mountains that you're a woman and I won't be responsible when somebody decides to throw you down right then and there and—"

Jake had stormed out before finishing his dire prediction, leaving Dani to stare after him, wondering why her question had caused such an outburst, wondering, too, what he meant. Two hours later, long after sunset, Jake had returned to the cabin and waved off Dani's offer of food. Instead, he'd shuffled across the room, obviously full of drink, weaving until he fell onto his bunk.

"Come 'ere, Dani." He gestured to her, barely able to wave a limp hand in her direction.

She approached him slowly, trying to measure his mood. Dani hunkered down beside his cot, her eyes level with Jake's. She waited for him to speak, watching as he tried to collect his thoughts and put them into words. His brown eyes were haunted, the lines and creases about them deeper than she'd ever noticed before. In the dim glow of the firelight, Jake appeared old and frail, his face craggy and shadowed. The ragged beard and unkempt hair were familiar to her; so were his greasy, well-worn buckskins. But the aching, worried look on his face frightened her. Big Jake had never shown fear before.

"Dani . . ." He swallowed nervously, trying to clear his rasping voice. "I've made a terrible mistake keepin' ya here with me all these years."

She shook her head to protest, but he waved a hand at her, demanding silence.

"I have. I shoulda taken ya off to St. Louie, tried to find out if you had any kin back in the flatlands. Instead . . ." He took a long sigh and fell back onto the cot, speaking to the ceiling. "Instead, I kept ya. You were so little. I thought at first you would die, but you didn't. Just a mite when I found ya, sick and all with the fever."

He stopped speaking and Dani thought for a moment he'd fallen asleep. She shifted to her knees, but before she could draw his buffalo robe over him, Jake roused himself and continued.

"I made ya into a boy for your own good. Now what kind of a life will ya have? You oughtta be livin' a good life. You oughtta be married by now, wearin' fancy dresses, prettied up."

"No, Big Jake." Tears filled her eyes as she listened to him pour out his heart to her. "You know I wouldn't even know how to act in a fancy dress." Dani envisioned herself outfitted in the only feminine attire she was acquainted with—an Indian gown of finely cured doeskin covered with quills and beads, with long swaying fringe at the hem and shoulders. "And besides, what do I know about being married or living what you call the 'good life'? *This* is a good life, Jake, the best."

The big man covered his eyes with his hand and collected himself.

"That's what I'm tryin' to tell ya, Dani. There's so much ya don't know. So much I never told ya. So much I can't tell ya, not like a woman could." Suddenly he raised himself up on an elbow and stared at her intently. "Promise me one thing, Dani."

"What?"

"Promise if anything happens to me, you'll take my big Bible. There's a letter in there for my partner in St. Louie. He'll take care of ya fair, Dani."

"Aw, Jake. St. Louie's so far off, and I hear it's *flat*, Jake. No mountains, no nothing that I know about."

"Dani—"

"Really, Jake. I've heard the men talk. I don't think I could stand it. Don't make me promise. 'Sides, Jake, nothing is gonna happen to you. Nothing . . ."

Nothing. Dani tried to shake off the memory. She edged her way through the dense growth of willows that lined a wide shallow stream and prepared to stop to water the animals. With a newfound determination, she vowed she would take care of herself. Not one to look on the bad side of life, Dani was certain that Jake had exaggerated the danger of her situation. He'd told her tales of the world beyond these mountains, and none of what she had heard appealed to her. Here she was born and here she would stay, roaming the land she knew, doing what she did best—hunting and trapping. After all, she thought, what could possibly happen to someone who'd been raised to survive?

Dani pushed the scrubby red horse on until the sun had sunk well behind the mountains and the earth, swathed in purple shadows, had begun to grow chill. She chose a clearing sheltered by hills and tall pines, close to the stream she had followed all day.

It took her more than a few moments to unburden the animals and tie them up to graze. Until tonight, Jake had always been there to help. Together they had tended to their chores as soon as they stopped for the night. Tonight Dani noted the emptiness that was her only companion as she accomplished each task alone. Could she stand the silence and loneliness forever?

She laid out her saddle and bedroll near the small fire before she finally took time to prepare a kettle of cornmeal mush and a pot of coffee. Until she reached Moze Hadley's, buffalo jerky and mush would suit her needs just fine.

She set a pot of water near the fire to boil, and from her packs she retrieved an iron kettle, a sack of cornmeal, and another bag of salt. Her precious supply of coffee beans was stored in a tin. She stirred two spoonfuls of salt into a measure of cornmeal in the bottom of the black kettle. A little water splashed in from her canteen made the batter moist enough to run from the spoon. She poured the mixture carefully into the boiling water and then prepared to stir the mush until it thickened.

Rocking back on her heels, Dani looked around the small sheltered clearing she'd chosen as a campsite. The forest about her was dense, the trees looming ominously overhead while the scent of pine hung heavy on the air. The dark, forbidding wilderness was home. The stars overhead offered her comfort, and for a moment, she wondered if Jake was peering down from somewhere up in the heavens. She sure hoped so.

Lifting the sturdy iron ladle, Dani stirred the mush a turn and reached for her packet of jerky. Hot water simmered in a coffee pot resting on the rocks of the fire ring.

A twig snapped somewhere in the forest behind her. Dani froze. All too suddenly the familiar night song of the crickets hushed. Dry leaves that covered the ground in the clearing rustled. Slowly, with easy, calculated movements, she gave the pot one more turn of the ladle before she crept to the right of the fire toward her bedroll and the long rifle lying across her saddle. Her skin began to crawl beneath her clothing, and she fought the urge to pull her collar up around her neck. Calmly, stealthily, she leaned forward to reach for her "Kaintuck" rifle, her arm outstretched, her fingers inches away from the cold metal of the barrel.

Pounding footsteps sounded behind her and without warning, she was thrown to the left, away from the fire. The breath left Dani's lungs and a sharp pain cut into her rib cage as an almost unbearably heavy weight landed on top of her. A hand pressed over her mouth, forcing her head down into the debris-strewn forest floor. She tried to bury her teeth in the intruder's hand, but the strength of his hold prevented success. Wide-eyed, Dani tried to see into the man's face, but the firelight behind him blinded her. She knew only one thing for certain: None of Jake's friends would come upon her this way.

Suddenly the man spoke, but his hushed words surprised her.

"There are some Indians not a hundred yards from here. Don't make any noise and I'll let you up. All right?"

Dani nodded to indicate her understanding and felt the pressure lessen as he withdrew his hand from her mouth. The stranger continued to straddle her slender form as she lay in the fallen leaves of the forest clearing. Panting from fear and exertion, Dani stared up into the man's shadowed face and fought to catch her breath. He was young, far younger than Jake. His clothing was strange, a mixture of woolens and furs. His eyes were hidden in the shadow cast by the brim of his hat. She could not determine their color, but felt them staring at her.

The man grabbed her shoulders, then slid his hands down along the front of her jacket, pressing against the doeskin as he searched for hidden weapons. He stopped momentarily, surprised when he came in contact with the soft rise of her breasts beneath her clothing. He jerked his hands away as if burned by fire.

"My God! You're a woman!"

Angered by his mauling, she shoved the man, hoping to catch him unaware while he gaped at her. As he tumbled backwards, Dani struggled to her feet. Unmindful of the danger he'd warned her of, she stood above the staring figure, hands on hips and shouted down at him, "What in the hell do you think you're doing?"

"Shh!" He scrambled up quickly and faced her squarely, a good head taller than she. "I'm trying to tell you to be quiet. There's a party of Indians not too far off." His voice was a frantic whisper. He waved his hands up and down, indicating that she should keep her voice lowered.

Angry beyond belief at the man's effrontery, Dani let her voice ring out in the open clearing as she boldly ignored the danger that so frightened the big man standing before her.

"I mean, what in tarnation are you doing throwin' yourself on me like that and grabbin' at me?"

Before he could answer, a party of Nez Percé braves stepped out from the cover of the surrounding trees and filed into the clearing. There were at least ten by Dani's count, tall, lean hunters who seemed to appear out of thin air.

"It's too late now!" the stranger yelled. "I tried to warn you." He spun on his heel and faced the ten silent men. The stranger half crouched in what Dani was sure was the most unlikely fighting position she'd ever seen anyone assume. The tall warriors remained placid, silently watching the two whites.

"Come on. Come on." The man shouted at the intruders as he danced from foot to foot. He turned and threw a glance in Dani's direction and whispered over his shoulder, "Troy says they respect bravery. Don't scream, just stand your ground and they won't torture you. It will be an easier way to die."

"Holy hot shit," Dani muttered Jake's favorite imprecation under her breath and shook her head, sidestepping the strange figure crouched beside her. If the Nez Percé had been hostile, both she and the man would have been dead long before now. Only the Blackfoot needed to be feared this far west, and Dani knew it as she walked toward the hunters. Straightening her hat, she raised her hand in a greeting of friendship. Swiftly she persuaded the Indians to subdue the obviously crazy man who'd jumped her.

Two of the long-limbed braves stepped forward, moving past Dani toward the crouching, shuffling stranger. With one quick movement they grabbed the man and led him toward the fire ring. Dani ignored his shouts as she brushed pine needles and twigs from her clothing and straightened the brim of her hat.

"What are they going to do to me?" The white man's voice held a note of desperation. "Listen, lady, how was I supposed to know they were friends of yours? I'm sorry but—"

Dani spun on her heel and moved to face the man who had dared to grab her and, worse yet, was now calling her "lady"! The mere fact that he'd discovered she was a woman unnerved her. Would he set out to tell the world? Her voice low and seething with anger, she whispered to him, "I'll give you just one minute, do you hear, to clap your trap shut before I have my *friends* cut out your waggin' tongue."

She stared up at him, scrunching up her eyes the way Jake used to when he wanted to make a point. This man was an oddity. His clothing was far too neat and clean for him to have spent much time in the hills. He wore a long fur coat that hung open to reveal a woolen jacket and a pair of trousers that actually matched. A high-collared white shirt was neatly tucked into his waistband. Strangest of all, he wore a type of vest the likes of which Dani had never seen. It was made of shiny emerald-green material that reminded her of wet leaves shimmering in the firelight.

Signing to the men who held the prisoner between them, Dani watched while they trussed him up and sat him before the fire, his hands bound behind his back.

"I said I was sorry, ma'am, and I meant it. This was all a misunderstanding, I—"

A short, downward chopping motion of her hand expressed Dani's displeasure, and the leader of the Nez Percé stepped forward and gagged the stranger with a ragged strip of red calico pulled hastily from around his neck.

Dani stared down at the prisoner who sat round-eyed, searching the clearing as if he expected help to arrive at any moment. She would have to remain wary. The blond stranger was tall. He looked to be near six feet, and solidly built, close to two hundred pounds. His eyes were light. She could see, as he sat staring worriedly into the fire, that they appeared to be blue. His face was beardless and his hair was trimmed around his ears. Dani caught him staring at her as she stood trying to figure out what his presence meant. When his eyes lit on hers, she turned away and scanned the clearing. There didn't seem to be anyone else about, but she doubted such a dandy could be traveling alone.

She offered the Indians food and was presented their catch in return as one of them stepped forward with two rabbits. The group set to work to prepare the meal, some working in pairs to collect more wood to build a larger fire, while two others gutted and spitted the rabbits. The remainder began a round of gambling while the game cooked. Whenever the white man began to squirm and grunt in protest, Dani shot him a quelling, squint-eyed glare and he abruptly stopped. The Nez Percé hunkered about the fire, talking quietly among themselves, never sparing the prisoner a glance as they shared Dani's meal.

Supper ended, Dani walked to her gear and wrestled with one of the largest bundles. Within moments she found what she was looking for and rejoined the men around the fire. With great ceremony, just as she'd seen Jake do so many times before, she pulled a long-stemmed pipe from its case. The fringed and beaded pipe sheath was dyed red, the ceremonial color most sacred to the Indians. Sitting cross-legged, she picked up the tobacco tin from where it rested between her legs and opened it carefully. After filling the bowl and tamping down the aromatic leaves, Dani raised the pipe in both hands and offered it to the man sitting at her side. He commanded the group of hunters.

The man reached out strong hands that were as dark and creased as old buckskins. Reverently he cupped the pipe in his palms. He touched the glowing end of a twig to the bowl and pulled on the pipe, then watched the smoke rise skyward. Carefully the Indians passed the pipe from hand to hand, each man taking care to point the stem toward the left while passing it in that same direction, as ceremony dictated.

When her turn came, Dani held the slender bit between her lips and drew in deeply as she'd seen Big Jake do so many times. The tobacco smoke burned its way into her lungs, scorching her throat as it descended. Struggling, she held back a choking cough until tears threatened to stream from her eyes. The tense moment passed and finally, able to breathe freely, Dani passed the pipe on without mishap.

The ceremony completed, Dani watched the men who sat around the fire. They continued to talk and laugh among themselves, their dark eyes flashing, wide smiles lighting features that appeared so fierce when confronted with an enemy. They wore leggins to protect them from the cold, and a few wore unadorned buckskin shirts. All carried some form of covering, either Hudson Bay blankets they had traded for, or heavy, well-tanned buffalo robes.

As she sat in silent observation, Dani realized how much she welcomed the Indians' company. She tried not to think of what might have happened if they had not come along when they did. She stole a glance at the white intruder. What would happen now that he was aware she was a woman? Could she persuade him to keep her secret? She would have to deal with him sooner or later, but tomorrow morning would be time enough. Perhaps after spending an uncomfortable night bound, gagged, and ignored, he'd be more than willing to ride off and forget he'd ever seen her. Dani stretched and yawned, turning her attention back to the Nez Percé. She recognized too few of their words to follow their conversation.

As the hours lengthened, the Indians began to wrap themselves in robes and stretch out around the fire to sleep. The leader of the band, whom Dani learned was called Crooked Hawk, selected two men to watch while the others slept.

She pointedly ignored the stranger who sat drowsing with his chin on his chest. Feeling the need for a moment of privacy, Dani stood and walked across the clearing to check the horses and supplies, then stepped into the forest and sought a secluded spot just beyond the circle of light cast by the fire's glow.

Chapter Two

"Reach for the knife I saw you slip into your boot and I'll cut your throat."

A man's hand pressed over her mouth while his thumb and forefinger held her nostrils closed. Dani stopped struggling immediately and drew a welcome breath of air when he released her nose. His palm ground tight against her lips, his grip like that of an iron trap. A well-muscled left arm tightened around her midsection just below her breasts. She knew by his strength that, with little effort, he could snap the nerve that ran along her spine. Dani stood rigid in his imprisoning hold, trying to concentrate on the deep, smooth voice so close to her left ear. His breath was warm against her skin and caused the hair along the back of her neck to rise as gooseflesh ran down her spine.

So. There *were* others with the crazy man, Dani thought. She had suspected as much, and now she cursed herself for relaxing her vigilance. How many were there? And where were they hiding? Even as her mind asked the question, her assailant provided an answer.

"My men have the camp surrounded. If you don't want to see your Indian friends murdered as they sleep, you will kindly release the prisoner."

Dani tried to nod in understanding. It was a trick, she was certain, for had there been others in the forest, wouldn't the Nez Percé have been aware of them? She had to get this second man to release her and then set the braves upon him.

What was happening to her? Big Jake dead not three days

and already her life had turned upside down. Not one but two men had jumped her within a few hours of each other. She'd been obliged to stretch her supplies of tobacco and coffee to accommodate ten men. If this was a sample of the life she would lead without Big Jake, Dani wondered how she ever dreamed she would survive the winter.

God, Jake, what do I do now?

She let her eyes scan the forest, searching for signs of men hidden among the trees, but saw none. The man's tight hold on her ribs did not ease up.

"I can see you have never heard of Fontaine's Fighting Forty."

That voice again. She tried to shake her head, but he held her immobile.

"Forty of the fiercest, most capable woodsmen and mercenaries in the world. All under my command. They are adept at hiding and then striking when an attack is least expected." He gave her a shake to emphasize his words. "Don't think you can see them in the darkness. Even your Indians are not aware of the guns trained at their skulls at this very moment."

He waited as her gaze frantically scanned the trees, then hissed against her ear again. "Right now I want you to walk back into the camp, release the prisoner, and sit down near the fire. Stay away from your weapons. Tell the Indians anything you want; tell them it was all a joke. I want the man released now. In a few moments, I will join you, and when I do, you will tell them I am a friend. My men won't appear until daybreak. But never forget"—he paused to emphasize his next words—"no one escapes Fontaine's Fighting Forty, so don't try anything. Do you understand?"

Dani nodded. Slowly his hand slipped from her mouth, but his left arm still pressed her tight against the length of his body, keeping her worn leather leggins molded tight against his form. He stayed well behind her, blending into the shadows while he whispered in her ear. His English was laced with the slightest hint of a French accent. Dani knew many men who spoke French, but none had ever whispered in her ear this way before. The feelings that rushed through her as his warm breath raced past her ear were almost overwhelming. She tried to turn and glimpse his face, but he pushed her away from him as he issued a final warning.

"Go. Don't look back and don't draw attention to yourself. I will signal my men and then arrive shortly."

Even though she doubted the man's threats, Dani could not bring herself to risk the lives of the men sleeping near the fire. She crossed the distance and spoke quietly to Crooked Hawk, gesturing toward the blond prisoner with one hand while she spoke and signed with the other. She drew the long, wide-bladed hunting knife from the top of her boot and stepped closer to the white man. Dani stood over him for a moment, enjoying the mounting terror in his blue eyes as he watched her toy with the tip of the blade.

The knife slid deftly through the ragged calico gag and then through the thongs that held the man's wrists and ankles. He rubbed the deep impressions made by the narrow leather strips as he continued to stare at Dani.

When a look of gratitude slowly began to replace his fear, she leaned close and whispered fiercely, "Don't thank me. For all I care they can have you for breakfast. It seems your friends have us surrounded. Be sure they see that you're safe, because I don't want Fontaine's Fighting Forty crashing through the trees in the next minute or two. I've had enough mauling and pawing to last me a lifetime!"

Ignoring the look of relieved surprise on the stranger's face, Dani stepped past him and moved her bedroll nearer the fire. A quick glance assured her the hunters had not concerned themselves in the least with her sudden decision to release the captive, for they rested quietly once again.

Dani scanned the edge of the forest and watched the flickering shadows of the fire rise and fall, pulsating against the trees that bordered the clearing. The flames shed no light on the figure of the man who had forced her to untie his companion.

"Fontaine!"

Dani whirled around at the sound. A dark, solitary figure emerged from the forest, moving out opposite the direction of their brief encounter. After a glance at the men around the fire, her eyes locked with those of Crooked Hawk. The brave watched Dani intently, awaiting a signal. She knew he and the others who appeared so relaxed were coiled and ready to strike. She hesitated and the stranger strode nearer, approaching the circle of light. An uneasy feeling swept through her as she watched the whip-lean figure approach. For some unknown reason, Dani felt that the decision she was about to make would change her life forever. Her eyes scanned the forest once again. If men were lying in wait, hidden in the fathomless shadows beneath the towering trees, she saw no sign of them. Still, Dani could not force herself to gamble with the lives of so many. She knew the odds were uneven, so she made a sign of peace, reassuring the band's leader that this second stranger was a friend.

When no apparent objection came from Dani or the Indians, the blond man leapt to his feet and crossed the clearing to meet the man moving toward the fire. Dani watched in angry silence, wary of the tall, dark stranger. Just who these men were and why they had attacked her, she couldn't guess. The new arrival—Fontaine, the blond man had called him—betrayed no outward sign of cowardice as he quickly motioned his friend to keep silent. Dani fought the urge to collect her gear and ride off, leaving them to their own fate, but years in the wilds with Big Jake had taught her it was foolish to ride out alone into the darkness. She had enough trouble right now without asking for any more.

Instead of leaving, she chose to ignore the two. She gathered her rifle, buffalo robe, and saddle and moved nearer the Nez Percé. She shoved her saddle farther away from the light of the fire and wrapped herself in the thick buffalo-hide saddle blanket the trappers referred to as an apishamore. Dani cradled her Kentucky rifle in her arms and propped herself against the saddle, determined not to close her eyes.

From her vantage point, she silently watched the white men move near the warm, protective circle of firelight. The second man was the taller of the two. His dark eyes caught the glow of the flames and burned in her direction. He didn't take his eyes off her as he carelessly dropped his own gear on the ground and spread out his bedroll. Almost absentmindedly he tossed a blanket at his companion and then without another word, the man called Fontaine lowered himself to the ground. With one smooth movement, he turned his back toward Dani, tossed the end of the blanket over his shoulders, and tipped his low-crowned felt hat over his face.

Dani speculated through the long hours of the night about the stranger Fontaine and his companion as she fought to stay awake, staring at them across the sparking embers. Lost behind the shadow of his friend, the blond man's large frame was only partly visible, so she allowed her stare to bore into Fontaine's back. His long form was stretched out beneath the blanket, and his feet, shod in muddy black leather boots, extended well below the hem of his cover. Unlike his companion's, his clothing appeared well worn, fitted to him for protection against the weather and for ease of movement. He was dressed in natural hides that echoed the colors of the forest—a buckskin jacket and trousers much like her own.

All Dani could see of Fontaine's features, aside from his height, was the wide breadth of his shoulders beneath the blanket and the midnight sheen of his hair where it hung free past his collar.

Bored with staring at the man and finally assured by the steady rise and fall of his rib cage that he was asleep, Dani relaxed and turned her gaze to the smoldering coals in the fire ring. Tongues of blue and white flame licked at the remaining wood, pulsing in a rhythmic dance against the circle of stone. As her eyelids grew heavy, Dani fought a losing battle against sleep. She took one last glance in Fontaine's direction and closed her eyes.

"Damn!"

The barely whispered word escaped Troy Fontaine as he shifted uncomfortably, bone tired of sleeping on the hard ground. Earlier, the rich aroma of rabbit roasting above the fire had been almost overpowering. He was starved.

Going to bed hungry was the last thing he wanted to do after a day of seemingly wasted wandering. None of the rivers he'd followed matched those on the crude, inaccurate maps in his possession. The trails that were supposed to be easily marked had been unrecognizable. Finally, just before sunset, Troy had called a halt to the wandering and decided to set up camp. But for his old friend Grady Maddox, he'd be sleeping on a full stomach now instead of pretending to sleep while he half expected to feel a knife slide between his ribs.

But for Grady . . .

It seemed to Troy his mind echoed that phrase more often of late. But for Grady, he'd still be in Baton Rouge operating his fledgling shipping company. But for Grady, Troy would be at home awaiting word from the man he'd hired to track down his parents' killer.

When Grady Maddox had arrived on Isle de Fontaine and approached Troy with his request, it had been easy enough to turn the man down. But Troy Fontaine had not counted on Grady's dogged determination, or the depth of his own loyalty to his friend. Grady wanted Troy to act as his guide and companion on a journey to the West. A talented artist, Grady longed to experience the unsettled wilderness, to capture its overabundance and untamed reaches on canvas before civilization swept in. He longed to create portraits of the trappers and Indians who peopled the land beyond the boundary of civilization.

Grady had been more than persuasive, and Troy remembered how his own objections had crumbled one by one.

"I have a business to run, Grady," he'd argued. "I can't just leave it and go running off on a whim. Besides, we're not children anymore."

"You have assistants. Besides, this isn't a whim. I've thought it all through, written to men who've been there. I've read all their accounts." Grady had even resorted to a bribe. "I'll even pay for whatever equipment we'll need—and you're right, we're not children, we're nearly thirty. All the more reason to go now."

Playing upon Troy's passion for collecting journals and maps of ancient explorers and travelers, Grady added, "You can have all the maps I've located. I even have copies of reports from Lewis and Clark's own journals."

As Grady had continued, ancient names and places came to mind and Troy thought of Savannah, the fabled "lands yet to be found," once sought by the Spaniard, Coronado; of the Seven Cities of Gold; of the Fountain of Youth; of a waterway across the Northwest. Losing himself in stories of and by explorers helped him forget his own past.

"Your own map collection is already famous," Grady reminded him.

"Hardly."

"Well, it is around here. Would Herodotus have turned down his trip to Egypt? A man who's memorized the works of the world's first historian should show a little more enthusiasm for my idea."

"My having memorized the works of a Greek historian isn't exactly going to help get us across this continent," Troy reminded Grady.

"No, but with the right maps you could do it, Troy. My God, there's not a path, visible or invisible, out in the bayou that you don't know, or all the way up the trace to St. Louis, for that matter. Those wide open spaces should be easy. Would Leif Erikson have turned down a chance like this? Or Cortés, or Columbus?"

Grady's exuberance began to chip away at Troy's resolve. His business would demand nothing his manager could not handle for a few weeks. His grandmother, Leial, still oversaw the house and grounds on the island. Only one thing stood in his way: the ongoing search for the man who had murdered his father and abducted his mother.

Since the day Troy first began to realize a profit from his shipping company, he'd spent every spare dollar hiring men to search for Constantine Reynolds, the man believed responsible for Merle Fontaine's death. Even as Grady had tried to persuade him to leave Louisiana, Troy's attorney, Leverette Devereaux, was sending out yet another man to follow the latest lead in the hunt for Reynolds.

Grady must have read his thoughts, for he had added, "Come on, Troy. Put some miles between yourself and Louisiana. It might help you forget all this for a while."

Troy knew he could never put the past behind him, nor could he ever forget the promise he'd made to himself when he was twelve years old. That was the year his father had been murdered and his mother had disappeared, the same year he was sent away to school in Boston where he had met Grady. He would find his mother or learn what had become of her even if it took all his life to do so, and he would see that his father's killer stood trial.

"Devereaux thinks he has a good lead this time," Troy had said.

"He always has a 'good lead.' What have you got to lose? Take a few weeks off and see the West."

"What I have to lose is time, Grady. If Leverette Devereaux's man tracks down Reynolds, he might move on before I can get to him."

"And it might be another false lead."

Troy had to agree. "It might."

"Even if you find Reynolds, you still have no proof that he killed your father."

"No. But you're forgetting the man may still have my mother with him. She was abducted with my father, and she and Reynolds both disappeared after my father's body was found."

"Did it ever occur to you that your mother might not want to be found?"

Troy had stifled the urge to lash out physically at Grady. Instead, he had held his emotions on a tight rein and ground out his words: "What exactly do you mean by that?"

"What I mean is that maybe, just maybe, your mother left with Reynolds of her own accord."

"Damn it, Grady!"

"Think about it."

Troy had lost control and railed at Grady, "Don't you realize that's all I think about? It wasn't enough that my father was murdered; my mother disappeared at the same time." He had turned his back on his friend and strode to a window overlooking the bayou. "I know she loved my father, Grady, more than me, more than anything. It didn't matter to Jeanette Fontaine that her husband was a wastrel, that he'd gambled away nearly all he'd inherited. She loved him."

"Listen, Troy, I'm sorry for what I just said, but I'm not sorry about trying to get you out of here for a while. We aren't talking about years; we're talking about two months."

In the end, Grady had persuaded Troy to join him in what he referred to as "the adventure of a lifetime." The two months had stretched to four, and "the adventure of a lifetime" was fast becoming a monotonous routine of hours in the saddle, meals that consisted mainly of underdone or charred meat, and nights spent sleeping on the cold, hard ground.

And now, had it not been for Grady, Troy might be enjoying the balmy warmth of Louisiana and the taste of fine French wine. Instead, here he crouched, cold, bone tired, and none too happy with this "adventure of a lifetime."

Except for the brilliantly executed paintings and charcoal sketches Grady had produced over the past four months, the trip west had been one disaster after another. Until they left Louisiana, Troy had not realized that trekking into the wilderness with his only close friend would prove as trying as playing nursemaid to a child. It had been quite obvious as soon as the two left St. Louis and took to the trail that Grady was incapable of doing more than riding along and seeking out subjects for his portraits. Troy finally assigned Grady only two tasks: stay out of the way and try not to get killed.

It had taken Grady a full month to learn to saddle his horse well enough to prevent the saddle from slipping sideways. Once, while they were fording a stream, Troy had glanced back to gauge Grady's progress. He was rewarded with the sight of his friend fighting for balance while his saddle listed to the left side of his horse. Within seconds, Grady was wallowing in the shallow water.

Slipping off a loose saddle wasn't Grady's only irritating habit. Downright clumsiness had accounted for Grady tripping more times than Troy could count. The man could not light a fire to save his life, nor could he stand to gut and dress the game Troy killed. Troy was thankful that he could at least be depended upon to load and fire his rifle accurately.

At first, Grady's exuberance had sparked Troy's own enthusiasm and made up for the artist's bumbling. The two men had traveled over the same route as Louis and Clark, up the Missouri River to its headwaters in the Rockies. Together they had thrilled to the sight of the majestic peaks that pierced the clouds, the deep canyons, the verdant valleys. The pair had witnessed natural phenomena the likes of which most men would never see or even imagine: bubbling hot springs reeking of sulfur; geysers that shot hundreds of feet skyward; unlimited varieties of animals that stood in stark silhouette against the splendor of their natural surroundings. But now, anxious to be home, his limited patience at an end, Troy longed to leave the Rockies behind.

Troy glanced over at Grady. His friend was no longer the pudgy, awkward boy who had been his roommate at school. True, the Grady Maddox who had earlier sat bound and gagged before the fire was still clumsy when out of his element, but at twenty-nine, the man was solid, well built, and decidedly handsome. His fair hair and blue eyes contrasted with Troy's dark features. Grady was all lightness, a sensitive, artistic, carefree soul. He'd spent his life surrounded by the love of his parents and four younger sisters. All doted upon him. Troy, on the other hand, had been raised by his grandmother, Leial, and Venita, the Fontaines' cook. He had no one else he called family, except Grady and Hercules, the manservant he had left behind on the island.

He shook off his reverie and wondered how in the hell Grady had managed to get into this predicament in the first place.

They had become separated during their search for a

campsite, a task that had become a nightly ordeal. To Troy's growing annoyance, Grady insisted that their campsites offer not only shelter but beautiful scenery as well, affording them a clear view of the sunset or sunrise. At the very least, Grady felt they should camp near some natural feature such as a waterfall or tree-lined stream. It was during tonight's quest for "the perfect spot" that they had become separated.

Grady had only been missing for a matter of moments before Troy was alerted to his predicament. By the time Troy found the clearing, Grady had already been hog-tied and surrounded by the hunting party.

Troy shifted uncomfortably. He dreaded falling asleep, and so sleep never came easily to him, not even at home on Isle de Fontaine. Especially not on the island, for the place was too alive with memories. It was there that he had found his father's body hanging from a beam in an abandoned barn. He had only to close his eyes and he could recall the riotous pounding of his heart, the screams he had suppressed so as not to alert his grandmother. Troy would never forget the deadweight of Merle Fontaine's lifeless body as he mustered his strength to lower his father to the floor. Nor could he erase the memory of the feel of the rough rope slipping through his hands. He was thankful that his empty stomach, September's chill seeping up from the ground, and the woman nearby made sleep more elusive than ever.

The entire situation was getting stranger by the moment. What was a woman disguised as a man doing alone with a band of Nez Percé? The shock that had reverberated through him as his forearm came into contact with her breasts had nearly been his undoing. He wished he'd seen the girl more clearly, but he had grabbed her from behind, and now the oversized hat hid her features entirely. Even without seeing her face, Troy could feel the anger aimed toward him. The girl's hostility was nearly a living entity. He had felt it as he entered the campsite and so had avoided staring in her direction.

She was not asleep, either. Although his back was to her, he could feel her gaze boring into him. What, he wondered, had harmless Grady Maddox done to anger her in so short a space of time? He would not even hazard a guess. For now Troy contented himself with recalling her appearance.

He had felt no spare ounce of flesh on her body, and he knew instinctively the girl was no stranger to the rigors of mountain life. No doubt she was in far better shape than Grady. Troy tried to imagine her features. All he had discerned from across the fire was a pair of wide-set, shadowed eyes. Her brow had been hidden by the idiotic oversized hat, and her cropped hair barely grazed her collar.

His body was desperate for rest and so he tried to bargain with himself. *The sooner you sleep, the sooner you'll see her in the daylight.*

Closing his eyes, he smiled, suddenly remembering that forty of the most highly trained mercenaries in the world would protect them tonight.

Chapter Three

Somewhere amid the branches of the pines, a hairy wood-pecker beat out an annoying tattoo as it worked to extract grubs from the tree bark. Eyes shut tight, Dani lowered the brim of her hat in order to hide from the bright morning sunlight. Stretched out flat on her stomach, she groaned and snuggled deeper under her buffalo robe. The thick aroma of coffee eddied about her, teasing her awake, but she fought to slip back into sleep, searching for the place she'd left behind in her dream. Aware of an aching crick in her neck, Dani stirred, pulling one knee up and drawing her robe around her shoulders.

It did not surprise her that she had not heard Jake set the coffee to boil; he always teased her about how soundly she slept, especially out in the fresh mountain air. "A grizzly will climb in with you one day 'fore you wake up." If he'd said it once, Jake had said it one hundred times before . . .

Before . . .

Before he died.

The sleep that had fogged her mind suddenly cleared, and with sharp clarity, she recalled the events of the previous evening.

All of them.

Dani stiffened, suddenly afraid and vulnerable, lying there on her stomach like a snake asleep on a hot rock.

Slowly, trying not to call attention to herself, Dani slipped her index finger up to raise her hat ever so slightly. She opened one eye and peered out from beneath the floppy brim.

27

"Morning!"

The blond man bending over the fire spoke as pleasantly as if he were greeting her over breakfast in a cozy cabin. Dani pushed herself up, first to a sitting position and then all the way, until she stood staring at him across the fire.

His smile was wide and sincere, and he seemed well pleased with himself as she tried to hide her chagrin with a confident pose. Dani guessed that here was a man who found excitement in the dawn of each new day. His eyes were clear and blue, as blue as the still waters of a lake reflecting the sky in its depths. Neatly trimmed, his hair was short by backwoods standards and was the color of grass bleached yellow by the late summer sun. Tall and sturdily built, he was a fine figure of a man, unlike anyone she'd ever seen.

Dani found she'd been correct the night before. His jacket did indeed match his trousers. The entire outfit looked new. He wore pants of a fine light gray wool, the legs disappearing into knee-high black leather boots. Beneath his gray wool jacket she could see the front of a vest and the collar of a white shirt. She caught herself staring at the emerald-green material she'd noticed last night. It seemed to catch the light and bounce it back as he moved.

"It's satin," he explained, pointing to the vest.

He spoke casually, as if nothing untoward had passed between them the night before, as if he had not surprised her by jumping out of nowhere and dragging her down onto the forest floor. The warm smile that showed his even white teeth began to fade as Dani ignored his comment. This man had grabbed her breasts. He deserved no greeting from her.

Last night's scene was again fresh in her mind and she scanned the clearing, searching for the rest of them—the Nez Percé, Fontaine's Fighting Forty, Fontaine himself. Where were they? The Indians were nowhere in sight, and neither was Fontaine. Only she and the blond man remained in camp.

Her worry mounted. Dani ran her hand through her tangled hair and pulled out a few straggling pine needles before she put her hat back on. A quick glance told her that the pack mule and horses remained where she'd left them. The savory scent of venison roasting slowly on a spit above the fire began to mingle with the aroma of coffee. It set her mouth watering. She was suddenly all too aware that she was hungry enough to eat a buffalo.

Dani brushed leaves and dust from her pants, straightened her belt and jacket, and then bent to heft the heavy leather saddle. Without a word, she turned to walk past the man who stood between her and her mount.

"Listen . . ." He extended his hand in an effort to stop her. "I'd like to apologize for what happened. Please . . ."

She halted in midstride and glared at him, her weight on one foot as she held the saddle in both hands.

"Start talking." Dani hoped she sounded as tough as Big Jake. Just in case she didn't, she squinted fiercely.

"First off," he began, "my name is Grady Maddox and I meant you no harm." He held out his hand in greeting, but she stonily ignored it. Embarrassed, he let his hand drop to his side, but continued his explanation. "It was just an accident. I didn't mean to knock you down last night. Troy always complains about my jumping the gun, but . . ." Aware that she was fast losing interest in his rambling story, Grady began again.

"We were looking for a place to camp when Troy—that's Troy Fontaine, a friend of mine who agreed to guide me on this expedition—anyway, we became separated. Actually, I got lost, and when I saw the Indians, I didn't know if they were the friendly ones or not, so I began to run. When I came into the clearing and saw you, I only intended to warn you, but just as I got close, I tripped on a branch or something and plowed right into you."

Dani looked right through him. "That's why you decided to . . . search me?"

"Well, the way you were struggling, I thought maybe you were going to kill me first and ask questions later."

Dani lowered her voice. "I should have."

"Why? I was only trying to save your life."

"I don't need saving." She looked around the camp, unwilling to ask the whereabouts of his companion and just as unwilling to run into Fontaine in the woods. Her anger rose as she became convinced she'd fallen for a ruse. Fontaine's Fighting Forty!

"Listen." His voice held a note of frustration. "I've apologized." He held out both hands, pleading for her to understand. "What else can I do?"

"You can move out of my way." The saddle was getting

heavy, the sun was making its way toward midmorning, and Dani was clear out of patience.

"Here"—he took a step forward—"let me carry that for you." Grady reached for her saddle.

She took a step back. "Stand away from me. I can handle it myself."

A deep, softly accented voice issued from directly behind her. She'd heard it only once before and yet recognized it instantly. It was him: Troy Fontaine.

"Leave her alone, Grady."

When Dani did not turn in response, refusing to acknowledge Fontaine's presence, he continued.

"The only way to earn a wild creature's trust is to leave it alone."

She whirled to face him then and was arrested by the warm, calculating stare that challenged her own. Without his having uttered another word, she felt almost compelled to draw closer to him, but caught herself before she could step forward. Blue-black hair and obsidian eyes suggested an aura of darkness that his mocking stare did little to dispel. The sun had carved a network of tiny lines and creases around the outer corners of his eyes. High cheekbones and dark brows made his eyes appear deep-set and shadowed. She decided his nose, straight and finely tapered, matched his other features well.

His lips were stern, yet he clenched his jaw tightly as if perhaps he held a smile in check. The long, tapered fingers of his right hand rested easily on the butt of the pistol shoved into his belt. He was dressed as he had been the night before, in buckskin. His black hat hung by a thin, rawhide thong behind his shoulders. Fontaine's stance indicated a wary readiness. He was a man always on guard.

Here was a man she could deal with. Unlike his friend, this one belonged in the wild untamed world she knew. This man, this Troy Fontaine, was like her, a survivor.

She caught herself staring up into his eyes, too astounded by her reaction to his compelling looks to move. Before he'd stepped into the clearing, she thought she'd never seen anyone as handsome as his friend—but now, as Dani stood staring up into Fontaine's fathomless eyes, acting as if her will had completely left her, she realized what the word "handsome" truly meant.

"Where . . . where are the Indians?" Dani finally managed to ask, trying to break the spell.

"Gone. They left at daybreak." Although his words were curt, his accent softened them, as did the teasing smile that appeared at the corners of his mouth.

"I'm leaving now, too," she said. As much as she was drawn to Fontaine, she knew for her own safety that it would be best to put space between them. It was what Jake would have wanted her to do, she was certain. Dani wrestled with her saddle once more before heading for her pony. "If you'll just empty out the coffee pot and my kettle, I'll be on my way."

"But . . . you can't just ride off alone," Grady protested, panic in his voice as he stood there, uncertain of what to do next. "Troy, talk to her. We just can't let a *girl* ride off alone, can we?"

A girl! At the sound of the word Dani dropped her saddle beside her pony and spun about to face the men, her fists riding her hips, her eyes pinned on Grady Maddox. Damn the man and his mouth, anyhow. She watched Fontaine, who demonstrated no concern about her departure. He poured hot coffee into two tin mugs and then tossed the remainder across the ground.

"She got here somehow, and she can get back on her own."

The coffee pot clanged against the kettle as Fontaine carried them to her from across the campground. He stopped within an arm's length of her. He did not say a word, just stood looking down at her. The angry words that had welled up inside her, the threats she thought to issue, did not surface. Her tongue failed her. She could read the faintest signs left on the land by wild game, but Dani could not read the thoughts behind his dark, searching eyes. Fontaine seemed to be reaching deep inside her with his gaze, and the intense expression in his eyes made her own shy away.

She knew she was acting as skittish as a new colt, but Dani couldn't seem to help herself. Disgusted with her own lack of courage where this man Fontaine was concerned, she glanced at Grady Maddox and found that he, too, was staring at her. She ran the palms of her hands along the front of her buckskins and tried to remember when she'd ever felt her palms sweat before. If she didn't leave these two soon, Dani was certain she would come down with some curious ailment. She felt so very strange all of a sudden.

Fontaine moved and she started, then felt her cheeks flush with embarrassment. He did not speak, but held out the pot and kettle. It was a moment before she could reach out to take them, and when she did, Dani was careful not to touch his hands. She turned her back on him then, hastily opened her largest pack, and stuffed the cookware inside it. It took her a minute more to cinch the rawhide ties; then she set to work saddling her horse.

It was obvious to Dani, by Troy Fontaine's easy dismissal of her, that he cared little about where she went or what became of her. But Grady Maddox refused to give up. He tried once more to persuade her to stay with them.

"Listen, miss, at least let us escort you back to your people. You must be close to home." He stepped up beside her as she grasped the reins and prepared to mount. "I have four sisters at home and I hate to think of any of them out in the middle of nowhere, riding around alone like this. You don't have anything to fear from me."

"You're right. I don't. 'Cause I'm leaving."

Dani thrust one foot into the stirrup and swung the other leg over the saddle. With the mule and Jake's horse tethered behind her, she pulled the lead rope and nudged the red forward.

Aware of the men's eyes still on her, Dani drew up just as she was about to enter the forest. Glancing back over her shoulder, she avoided Maddox and met Troy Fontaine's stare.

"Don't think you'll ever be able to fool me again," she warned. "I was near certain you were bluffing last night, but I couldn't take the chance." Her face flamed with embarrassment as she recalled the way she'd agreed to his demands, the way he'd tricked her with his tale of Fontaine's Fighting Forty. The feeling made her angry all over again and helped ease any desire to linger. Her eyes narrowed and she vowed, "I'll never be foolish enough to believe you a second time."

Without waiting for their reaction, Dani faced the trail again and pushed on. Her stomach grumbled in protest, and she rummaged around in her possible bag for some jerky. *Damn you, Jake.* She cursed him in her mind as she ripped off a healthy strip of dried buffalo meat and worked it to a chewable state. No, she took it all back. Not "damn you." Dani would never want to send Jack to eternal damnation. But as she started off on her own again, she wondered for the hundredth time why he had to go off and die like that.

To the naked eye, the forest around her seemed empty, but although she felt very alone, Dani knew she wasn't. The woodpecker's knock was fading as she put space between them, but a male mourning dove cooed out his song somewhere up ahead of her. A slight breeze whispered through the upper branches of the pines. She knew that squirrels were scrambling through the branches of the fir trees while deer mice, porcupines, and rabbits scurried through the soft blanket of rotting pine needles that covered the forest floor.

The world was alive with sounds, but Dani heard none of them as her horse plodded steadily toward the gully where old Moze made his home. Melancholy began to replace her resolve to carry on, so she decided to sing. At first it was hard to think of the right song. Without Jake, she faced an uncertain future, and at the moment nothing seemed worth singing about. Still, she owed it to herself to try. If she didn't, Dani knew she'd be crying again in no time. In a halting voice, she sang slowly as she made her way across the hillside: " 'The fox went out on a chilly night, prayed for the moon to give him light, for he'd many a mile to go that night afore he reached the town-o, town-o, town-o. He'd many a mile to go that night afore he reached the town-o.' "

The merry words of the old folk tune began to fill her heart and push aside her sorrow. The song itself seemed most appropriate, for like the fox, Dani knew she had many miles to travel before she reached her destination. Jake had always loved listening to her sing as much as she enjoyed expressing herself in song. Dani remembered how he had requested his favorites and she readily obliged. Music had helped fill the quiet hours of winter and the miles of silence as they traveled across the land. She let the sound swell, trying to send the notes beyond the treetops so that Big Jake could hear, if he was listening.

Troy Fontaine smiled to himself as he watched the slight figure lead the heavily loaded pack animals through the dense forest. *So small,* he thought. She was so small and yet she seemed to fill the already bright morning with sunlight. Last night's darkness had disguised her unkempt appearance, the worn buckskins stained with dirt and grease, her thick hair cut in a jagged wedge just above her shoulders. But even the deep shadows of the forest night had not been able to disguise the way her body molded itself against his and the feel of the firm, generous breasts pressed beneath his restraining arm.

Today, in the sunlight, her gray eyes had trapped him as surely as iron spring-load traps would hold the game she hunted. Silver-flecked, her eyes were round and clear, outlined by thick dark lashes. An intense sensation had tugged at him as he stared down at her, a feeling he could not put a name to, a feeling he'd never experienced before.

Grady interrupted his musing. "I don't think we should let her go off alone."

Troy was thoughtful, his eyes focused on Dani, who was slowly disappearing between the trees.

"No. But we can let her think we are."

Fontaine walked over to the succulent venison flank that was nearly ready to eat. Deftly he turned the strong green branch that served as a spit.

"Grady, go get the horses and the rest of the gear. I left them beside the stream." He pointed eastward and added, "They're close enough that you ought to find them without running into any more trouble."

"Won't she get too far away?"

"With that string of gear she'll be easy enough to track. We'll eat and give her time to put a little distance between us. When she's feeling confident that we're not following her, we'll set out and make sure our little friend gets safely back to her people." As an afterthought he added, "Or wherever it is she's headed."

Making no move to retrieve their goods, Grady kept right on talking. "Those eyes! Did you get a good look at them? I'm still not sure what color they were. Do you think she'd object to posing for a portrait?" He didn't wait for his companion to answer, but asked still another question. "How long do you think it's been since she's had a bath? You don't think she's married to some trapper, do you?"

Troy hunkered down before the fire, slowly turning the spitted meat. The girl had reminded him of one of the street urchins who ran along the levees back home. Her skin was tanned darker than that of many octoroons. Tanned and dirty. He had his own suspicions about her background. There was little chance the girl was still a virgin. There wasn't another white woman around for hundreds of miles, and she had probably belonged to more than one man. For some reason, that thought bothered Troy a great deal. He wondered how she had retained such an innocent, wide-eyed demeanor.

He shrugged, pretending to be unconcerned, and answered Grady's questions.

"Who knows? To answer your first two questions, her eyes are gray, and she probably would object, seeing as how she can't bear the sight of us. In answer to your third, probably not since last summer."

His expression gave no hint of the queries his own mind had conjured in regard to the girl. "She appears to be quite young, but perhaps she is already someone's woman. If you'll stop talking long enough to get the horses, we might for once have a decent meal and then be on our way."

At the sound of Grady's receding footsteps, Troy stood, looped his thumbs in the waistband of his buckskins, and walked on silent feet to the edge of the clearing. He gazed off in the direction the girl had taken. He hadn't expected his body to respond to the feel of her firm thighs pressed against his length as he held her imprisoned in his arms. Why was she dressed like a man? Did her clothing serve a purpose beyond that of convenience? Somehow Troy sensed that the reason was behind her need for a hasty departure.

He realized he didn't even know her name. But Troy Fontaine was a man used to getting his own way. As he stood staring through the thicket of trees, he vowed he would have the answers to his questions and then promised himself he would have the girl as well.

Chapter Four

Dani bent forward and scooped up a handful of water. She splashed it over her face and used the palms of her hands to smooth back her hair. Rubbing as hard as she could, she relied on her fingertips to remove some of the grime that hid her features. The water provided a cool, refreshing shock that made her skin tingle.

How long had it been since she'd had a good wash? She couldn't remember, but decided the rinse would have to do until she reached the hot creek at Hump Bone Hollow. Dani didn't mind getting in water that was good and hot, but plunging into a cold mountain stream was not to her liking and never had been. It was an unavoidable aspect of a trapper's life, though, for beaver traps had to be set in streams fed by snowmelt. Even though she had been setting traps for years, Dani still hated wading into cold water.

Years ago, Jake had insisted she learn to swim, although he could not. He said he didn't want to stand and watch her drown someday, so he devised a way to give her "water savvy," as he called it. The method proved effective, if not comfortable.

Jake had tied a long leather halter around her and tossed Dani out of a canoe into the clear, deep waters of a lake. The first few dunkings had left her sputtering and fighting for air, but Jake always pulled her out in time. Finally, after becoming used to the shock of hitting the cold water and sinking below the glassy surface, Dani soon found a way to move her arms and legs in order to keep afloat. She became adept enough to try it without a halter, and sometimes, in the heat of high summer, she would swim to cool herself off, but those days were few and far between.

High up in the Yellowstone country there were many hot springs and creeks that beckoned to her; the warm water promised to be soothing and enjoyable. Once Dani located a pool that offered her privacy, she never hesitated to enjoy the pleasures a dip afforded. There was a good one waiting in Hump Bone Hollow, but there were miles to cover before she reached it.

This morning, though, she sought only to rid herself of some of the grime that made her feel so uncomfortable. She certainly had had no opportunity to do so the night before. Dani shook her head in wonder, trying to dismiss all that had happened, but it was still hard for her to put aside all thought of the two strangers she'd met—Fontaine in particular. The thought puzzled her. What was it that made him different from other men? A curious feeling overwhelmed her each time she thought of him, even now, after putting a few miles between them. It worried her that this sensation felt like the one that had forced itself on her so often of late. It was the same uneasiness that had sent her out to prowl the hills the night Jake died.

Why Fontaine? What did he have to do with this edginess? After all, she argued with herself, everyone she knew was a man, and Fontaine seemed no different.

She stood and wiped her damp hands against her buckskin pants, refusing to waste any more time thinking about Troy Fontaine or his friend, Grady Maddox. Moze Hadley lived just over the next rise in a shanty well hidden between two hills. It was time she pushed off. A little company was just what she needed. After all, she thought, what had happened to her last night was enough to make the hair stand up on a buffalo hide. Dani was eager to see a friendly face about now and to talk about Jake with someone who'd known him. Maybe she could even make plans for her own future.

Moze was sure to have a pot of something cooking, and she was far too hungry to turn down anything he might offer. Mounting again, she eyed the forest behind her and kicked her horse onward.

"Hello!" Dani's voice sang out across the clearing. "Hey, Moze!"

Seconds passed while she waited for his answering call.

None came, so she stood in her stirrups and leaned forward, watching for a sign of Moze near the shanty at the bottom of the hill. A wisp of smoke escaped the chimney and streamed skyward. Moze Hadley's mules grazed lazily behind the shack, looking no farther than their noses for food. No other sign of life was evident.

She nosed her pony forward, certain the old man must be inside, for where would he go without the string of mules? Dani didn't look forward to telling Moze that Big Jake had gone under. The two men had been friends for as long as she could recall. Still and all, she didn't want Moze to hear the news from anyone else.

As she neared the shanty she called out again. It wasn't wise to come up on anybody unaware, not even a friend.

"Moze! It's me, Dani. Come on out, you old rattler, you."

One of the rags that served as a window covering fluttered. She thought she saw a face at the opening and waved her hand wildly above her head. Moze was certainly reclusive today. He usually waited outside the door, urging them on, shouting his hallo, a wide, toothless smile showing in his long white beard. She hoped he hadn't taken sick. Burdened with this new fear, Dani yanked on the lead rope that held the two pack animals and urged her pony forward.

The old place was so familiar to her that she almost felt as if she were home. The weathered logs of the cabin were sealed with mud. In some places, the hard clay was chipped away. Patching the worn spots was a task Moze obviously ignored more often than not. The door hung on leather hinges, and as in most mountain retreats, the latch was on the outside. Anyone was welcome to use the place; that was an unwritten law among trappers. Today the wooden latch hung unfastened.

"Hallo?" she called again as her Indian red made its way across the littered yard around the cabin. A miniature forest of tree stumps revealed that Moze hadn't cared to haul logs for his crude shelter very far. Empty liquor jugs were strewn here and there amid the discarded antlers and odd scraps of hide. Dani swung her leg across the saddle and slid to the ground. Her soft-booted feet hit the dirt with barely a sound. Tying the pony and the other animals to a makeshift hitching post made of a crooked branch embedded in the ground, Dani sidestepped the hide-scraping frame that stood between her and the door.

"Moze? Come on outta there, would ya?" Listening for a response, she prayed nothing had happened to old Moze.

It was far too late to move when she heard the cold click of metal and recognized it as the sound of a pistol being cocked.

"Stand right there, boy, and don't move if'n you want to see the sun set."

The voice definitely wasn't Moze's.

She stood rooted to the spot, allowing her gaze to slide to the small window just to the right of the door. The barrel of a gun was trained on her. She felt cold prickles of fear run down her spine.

Damn! What next?

"Where's Moze?"

"None of your business. Stay put and hang your hands in the air."

Dani did as she was told, inching her hands slowly skyward.

The door swung open, and mingled odors of stale food and mildew rode out on a current of air. A shadowy figure crouched just inside the threshold. The gun in the window remained pointed in her direction, warning her that there were at least two men inside.

A stooped figure shuffled out of the shack. A ragged red plaid shirt hung on the man's narrow frame. The colorful material did little to hide the hunched spine that forced him to walk with an awkward, stooped gait. His hair was thin and greasy. The shine of his balding scalp showed through the wisps plastered to his head. A long nose as crooked as his back split his face, reminding Dani of a vulture's beak. His teeth were jagged and yellowed, his mouth twisted into a curve that passed for a smile. She shivered.

"Get his gun, Ed."

The gruff voice inside the cabin shouted directions and the hideous little man quickly did as he was told. His stooped figure made him her height exactly, and as he stepped up to stand before her, she was close enough to smell his liquor-tainted breath and stare into the mud-brown pebbles that were his eyes. He slipped the pistol from her belt and then reached out a knobby hand to take her powder horn and shot pouch from around her neck. She ducked her head to aid him, then stepped back away from his gruesome leering grin.

Dani remained silent, unsure of her next move. Her choices were limited by the gun aimed at her from the window. She thought she could overpower the whiskey-soaked hunchback, for even now he fought to keep his footing as he stood before her, but how could she fight against the gun? And how many more surprises awaited her inside the cabin?

If she could keep them from taking her inside, Moze just might arrive in time to rescue her.

If he was coming home at all.

"Get movin', kid. Get inside." The scarecrow figure nodded his head in the direction of the door.

Glancing toward the top of the ridge, Dani tried to delay complying with the order. No one else was in sight. She silently chided herself for expecting to see anyone.

"Move!" The man nudged her forward with a grimy finger.

Stepping gingerly into the dark interior of the cabin, Dani stopped long enough to let her eyes adjust to the dim light. The place smelled stronger than a wolf's den of cured hides and rotten food. The damp earthen floor had its own peculiar musty scent. She knew the one-room shack was beyond cleaning. A good fire was probably all that would rid the place of its vermin. Moze was their friend, but even Jake had refused to sleep in the cabin, insisting that he and Dani preferred the open air.

The man near the window stepped closer to get a better look at her. The taller of the two, he stood in sharp contrast to his companion. Where the other was thin to the point of emaciation, this man was rotund, his belly straining the buttons that fought to hold his long underwear closed. The red undershirt was partially covered by a buckskin jacket that hung open in front. Any hope of it meeting across the man's girth had long since vanished. His eyes, pinched tight in his face and surrounded by fat, glistened like those of a rat. He stood a good head taller than Dani and leaned close to get a better look at her. She saw beads of sweat glistening on his high balding forehead.

"What's your name, boy?" His fat lips worked over the words.

"What business is it of yourn?" she answered cheekily, thickening her speech with mountain dialect. "Where's ol' Moze? This be his lair."

"Not no more it ain't." The fat man stepped closer, threatening. "You gonna tell me your name or am I gonna beat it outta ya?"

"Name's Dani." She ducked her head, dropped her eyes, and looked at the dirt floor beneath her feet. He was looking at her too closely. His scrutiny made her skin crawl. She fought the urge to twitch.

"Danny, huh? Where'd you come from? Anybody else with ya?"

"From just over the ridge."

A sudden thought came to her, and Dani drew herself up to her full height, looking him square in the eye. "Yeah, somebody's with me. I came on ahead of 'em lookin' for Moze. You ever heard of Fontaine's Fighting Forty?" She squinted back at him. Hard.

The man spat and wiped his chin with the back of his hand. She could sense the hunchback moving around behind her and heard his uneven shuffling as he closed the door.

"Nope. Can't say as I ever heard of 'em. Who are they?"

"Fontaine's Fighting Forty?" It gave her intense pleasure to laugh in his face. "Only the fiercest, most highly capable woodsmen and mercenaries in the world. They hide and strike when it's least expected. I'm their scout." She hoped she hadn't forgotten anything. The ruse had worked for Fontaine last night, and it might work for her as well, she reckoned. At least the story would buy her some time.

"And I'm George Washington."

"You don't have to believe me, mister. Wait and see."

"Ed." The fat man threw a glance at his companion. "Get on outside and take a look around. Get that rifle of his off o' his horse, too, while you're at it. I don't believe this liar for one minute, but you better check it out."

"Aw, why me, Abner? I always gots to be the one to do the dirty work," he whined.

Abner pushed his bulk around Dani and grabbed the little man by the front of his oversized shirt.

"You'll do what I say because I'm the brains behind this outfit. Ain't I always knowed what to do? Now, get."

Abner pulled the door open with one meaty fist and shoved Ed outside. "Be sure them mules and horses are tied up. We don't want to be losing no gear."

Abner slammed the door closed behind him and moved back to stand over Dani. He pulled a chair out from the rickety wood table and pointed to it. "Sit."

"I'd just as soon stand."

"Sit, dammit, or you'll be wishin' you had."

Slapping a rough hand on her shoulder, the man shoved Dani into the chair and planted a leather-shod foot on the seat next to her thigh.

"What are you doing here?"

"I told you. I'm scouting for the Fighting Forty. We came to get old Moze."

"Look up at me when I'm talkin' to you, boy."

Abner jerked Dani's hat off and tossed it on the table. He leaned over her, his foot on the chair, one arm across his raised knee. Her position forced her to look straight at the unsightly bulge between his legs. Could she risk slamming a fist into that most vulnerable area? Was she capable of rendering him helpless long enough to make an escape?

She glanced up to find him staring intently at her face. She met his eyes, and in a moment was sorry that she did.

"Hey . . ." His voice was raspy now. "What the hell is going on here?" He held her chin immobile between thumb and forefinger, tilting her face toward the light and turning it from side to side. Dani glowered at him and forced herself to wait for the right moment.

Before she could act, he moved away from her and threw the door open.

"Ed!" Abner bellowed into the yard. "Ed, get the hell back in here!"

Abner left the door hanging open on its leather hinges and walked toward her, stalking her as a bobcat might stalk its prey. He wiped his slack lips with the back of his hand and closed the distance between them.

"What's wrong, Abner?" Ed rushed through the doorway, his eyes wide and unfocused.

Abner's voice was hushed. He continued to stare at Dani. She shifted around on the chair, uncomfortable with the way the man's rat eyes lingered on her face. He was up to something.

"Nothin's wrong, Ed. In fact, things couldn't have worked out better. We got us a place to live, and we got us a woman, too."

Dani's blood ran cold. She asked herself what she'd done to give away her secret. Nothing. There was no way he could know for sure. He hadn't even touched her.

"Look close at that face, Ed. If that face ain't pretty enough to be a woman's, well, it's near enough for me. Either way, we got us some fun here and I'm aimin' to be the first."

"No!"

The ferocity of her own anger surprised her. As Dani stood to face them with fists clenched, the chair toppled to the floor. The two men stared at her for a moment before they realized Dani could do them little harm. She wasn't quite sure what they intended, but she didn't plan to stick around long enough to find out.

"You go around the table and get behind her, Ed. Knock her flat if she tries to run that way." Abner inched forward, his arms outspread, trying to corral her.

Frantic, Dani looked for a way to escape but found none. She would have to go past the big man to get to the door. Leaning forward, she felt the surface of the table for a weapon, never taking her eyes off of Abner's face. She heard Ed shuffling into place behind her.

"Can you reach out and grab her arms, Ed?"

Dani kept moving, trying to keep track of the more formidable Abner while listening to Ed's movements and gauging his position behind her.

"Don't hit her with that, Ed. You might ruin her good looks."

When she whipped her head around to look at Ed, Abner lurched forward and pinned her arms against her body. Dani realized too late that Abner's words were meant to divert her attention from him.

Dani wriggled like a fish and fought to squirm out of his hold. He lifted her off the earthen floor, and she kicked violently, connecting solidly with his left shin. His hold weakened for only a moment before he squeezed her even tighter.

"Let . . . me . . . go!" She struggled for breath between words. "Help! Moze! Help!"

"It ain't no use hollerin' fer a dead man. He's wolf bait by now."

He shook her like a rag doll as he pressed her against his bulk. Stars danced before her eyes and Dani felt her teeth bite into her lower lip. The shaking continued, unnerving her for a moment. She stopped struggling and waited for him to end his violent tossing. He lowered her until her feet hit the floor, and Dani saw her chance. She slammed one knee up between his

legs and heard him howl in pain as she shoved him aside and
scrambled for the door. Ed tried to stop her flight, but she
easily pushed the scrawny drunkard off balance and scratched
at the door in a panic, finally shoving it open. She burst into the
sunlight, her legs shaking with fright, her heart pounding in her
ears. Dani drank in gulps of clean air.

The red horse stood where she had left it, tied to the hitching
post. She lunged for the reins and tried to jerk them free. Too
frightened to look back, she shuddered when she heard the
door bang against the cabin wall. Before she could climb onto
her horse's back, she was slammed against the ground and
found herself looking up at Abner, his bulk looming over her,
blotting out the sky.

She tried to roll to the left, between her pony's legs, but the
animal danced away nervously and Abner threw himself on top
of her. Dani balled her fists and struck out at him with both
hands. Kicking and screaming, she felt his hands tearing at her
clothes and struggled valiantly to break free. Her arms grew
heavy with fatigue; her vision blurred with tears. It was then
she heard the sound of a shot reverberating against the walls of
the ravine. It was followed closely by another.

Abner raised his head and looked around the clearing. A
third shot was fired; the ball lodged in the cabin wall above
him. He lumbered off Dani and ran for the door. A final shot
hit him in the chest and sent him spinning backwards. As he
fell against a log bench, his head hit the wood with the sound
of a cracking melon. Ed cowered inside, his eyes darting to the
hill above them. Taking a chance that the gunmen would pause
to reload, Ed bolted through the doorway. Ignoring his fallen
companion, he scurried around the corner of the cabin. She
watched the hunched figure disappear.

Shaken, Dani struggled to her knees. She drank in air and
forced herself to stand, then leaned against the wall of the
shack. Her horse fought against the reins that still held it to the
post. She called to it with soothing words and it moved toward
her.

Fontaine thundered into the yard on horseback as Dani
finally pushed herself away from the cabin wall and stood on
trembling legs. In one lithe movement he was off his horse and
beside her, shoving his pistol into his belt and reaching out for
her. She felt his strong fingers bite into the flesh above her
elbows as Troy pulled her toward him. Able to do little more

than collapse against his side, Dani was embarrassed by her own show of weakness, yet incapable of resisting his comforting gesture.

"Are you all right?" His dark gaze pierced her own.

"What took you so long?" She barely managed to get the words out.

She heard him laugh then, a rich, deep sound that calmed her racing heart. Before he could answer, Grady Maddox rode into the clearing, and had her nerves not been shattered, she might have been tempted to laugh. Grady clung to the saddle horn with one hand while the other pressed down on the hat that sat askew on his head. His saddle had shifted slightly to the right and he furiously jerked his body to the left in an attempt to slide it back into place without dismounting. She smiled through the tears that threatened to betray her and realized the man was more in need of help than she.

"Are you all right?" Grady called out to her.

Suddenly Dani became all too aware of the fact that she still clung to Fontaine, and she tried to step away, but her knees buckled beneath her. In an instant, he scooped her up and she found herself riding high against his chest. Embarrassed by her predicament, Dani avoided looking at Fontaine. She feared that if she turned to face him, she might find his eyes searching out her own.

He moved without hesitation toward the cabin and kicked open the door, intending to step inside. The rancid smell of the place hit them at once, and Troy carried her a few yards away, then set her down gently on a grassy patch of ground.

"Stay put."

She hardly recognized the soft, caring tone as his. "I'm fine."

"I said stay."

She didn't want to, but she was still shaking so hard Dani doubted she could have even gotten to her knees. Closing her eyes, she drew a deep, calming breath and decided it might be best to stay put. Just for a moment. Just to see how Troy Fontaine handled this mess.

Lordy, Jake, I'm sorry.

I've jumped from the frying pan into the fire, she thought, and shook her head. Dani pulled her knees up and found she'd calmed down some. Hugging her knees to her, she watched while Troy and Grady tramped around the perimeters of the shanty and then converged on the twisted body of Abner lying beside the lichen-encrusted log. When Troy caught the man up by his heels and dragged the body around the corner of the cabin, she dropped her head into her hands and massaged her temples.

"Are you all right?"

Dani started and stared up at Fontaine. She hadn't heard him approach, nor did she know how long she'd been sitting with her head resting on her knees. She tried to smile. "Yep. I'm all right now."

He crouched down beside her, one knee on the ground, his left arm resting on his other knee. His face was inches from hers. Dani found it hard to breathe again and only hoped it wasn't because she had broken something inside her. It was the only reason she could give for the pounding heart and shortness of breath that assailed her.

She wasn't yet sure what the men who killed Moze had wanted from her, but she was certain she would have found out if Troy and Grady had not arrived when they did.

Fontaine brushed her hair back out of her eyes in a movement that seemed so natural Dani felt no need to shy away. The contact, as his warm fingers touched her temple, was a shock. No one ever touched her. Not even Jake. She didn't move a muscle, but tried to sit as still as a rabbit cornered beneath a bush. He stared into her eyes, then let his own gaze play over her face.

"Is she all right?"

At the sound of Grady's voice, Fontaine took his hand away and turned to face his friend. Grady knelt beside them. Dani squirmed at the attention the men focused upon her.

"She seems to be fine. A bit shaken is all."

"Who were those men?" Grady swallowed hard, lifted the brim of his gray hat, and ran a hand through his curls, then settled the hat on his head once more. His eyes were shadowed with concern, but they did not seem to hold the deep, hidden fires that burned in Troy Fontaine's.

"I don't know," she admitted.

"What were you doing here? Is this your home?"

Fontaine let Grady ask the questions while he silently watched her.

She shook her head. "No. I came here hoping to find an old

friend." She swallowed and looked at Moze's cabin. "He's dead now."

"Are you sure?" This time Fontaine spoke.

"Yes. They told me he was." Dani trained her stare on him again. "Did you get the weasely one?"

"No." He shook his head and then glanced at Grady as if to warn him to keep still. "They won't be bothering you again."

"The fat man's dead." She could tell by the way his body lay twisted, his head at an odd angle to his neck.

"Yes," Fontaine admitted. "Grady buried him behind the cabin in a shallow grave. There's no sign of anyone else around."

Dani brushed her hair back away from her face, tracing the same path that Fontaine's fingers had taken earlier. She straightened her belt and then braced her hand against the ground, meaning to stand.

"Here, let me help you up."

Grady Maddox offered her his hand, and she stared at it for a moment, at a loss. Slowly she reached out and held on as he pulled her up. Troy Fontaine stood as well. Neither made a move to leave her side.

"I'm going now." She looked at the ground, then at the sky, then crossed her arms protectively and stared straight ahead. *Here it comes,* she thought. If Grady had been concerned for her safety this morning, there was no way he'd let her ride off after this last catastrophe.

"You can't!"

Grady's protest came just as she had expected it would. And as she had guessed, Fontaine stood silent, offering no objection whatsoever.

"I can, and I will."

Before they could stop her, Dani stepped between them and walked to her horse. With shaking fingers, she untied the knotted reins. The empty scabbard hanging from her saddle reminded her that she had no weapons. When she reached up to push back the brim of her hat, she realized she didn't even have a hat. She couldn't leave until she recovered them. Quickly she retied the reins and tried to ignore the men who stood watching her. Grady was whispering furiously to Fontaine, but she couldn't make out his words.

Casually she sauntered over to the cabin door. She entered the tiny shack and looked around for her hat, which she located beneath the crude log table. After a brief plumping and straightening, she placed it on her head and pulled the rawhide thongs tight beneath her chin. Her rifle stood against the wall in the corner; her pistol lay on the rumpled cot.

Surveying the interior of Moze's squalid cabin, Dani saw nothing worth taking, so she walked out and closed the door behind her. Her steps faltered when she found Troy Fontaine standing beside her red pony.

"Don't you think it's time you trusted someone? After all, we did save your life," he reminded her.

She sheathed the gun. "I didn't asked to be saved." She hadn't meant to sound so cold and ungrateful.

"No, you didn't."

Dani turned away, intending to shove her foot into the stirrup, and suddenly felt the pressure of Fontaine's hand on her shoulder. When she refused to look at him, the strong, lean fingers tightened their hold.

She stalled and he waited.

With a sigh that revealed her irritation, Dani spun to face him.

"What do you want from me, mister?"

Their eyes locked, hers smoke gray and splashed with the sky's reflection, his as mysterious as the depths of an underground pool. A dove cried in the distance.

"I'm beginning to think you really don't know," he said with a shake of his head.

There was something in the tone of his voice, something that the soft, slow accent playing upon his lips did to her nerves that she could not describe. Her stomach sank to her toes and then settled back into place. She began to look away once again and was alarmed by her own cowardice. What had happened to all the bravado she'd shown earlier? What would Jake think of her now?

Dani met Fontaine's gaze, thankful when he released his grip on her shoulder. A searing, tingling heat radiated from the spot where his hand had grasped her. She was awed by the power of his touch and again battled the urge to run away from this man and the emotions he evoked in her. Instead, she reacted by squaring her shoulders. As soon as she looked into his eyes, she realized it was a mistake.

Dani felt herself leaning toward Troy Fontaine and wondered again if she was taking sick. Her knees felt weak. A curious warmth spread through her, invading her even in the private, unexplored regions of her body. In self-defense, she took a step back and found herself trapped against her horse's flank. Finally she managed to speak.

"No." She shook her head. "I really don't know what you want from me."

Troy Fontaine believed her. She had no idea what havoc she played upon his senses. He'd been months without a woman. Now he found he wanted this slip of a girl, wanted her in the worst way. He felt himself harden with desire as he looked down into her wide-eyed stare.

Dani was aware of Troy's hesitation. His gaze never left her face. His eyes drifted to her lips and back up to lock with her own.

He cleared his throat and shifted uncomfortably before he spoke. "Grady's gathering wood for a fire. I assured him I could persuade you to stay for a meal. Unless I miss my guess, you haven't eaten anything today."

She shrugged.

"Have something to eat, rest a few minutes. Then Grady and I will be happy to escort you to your destination."

Destination? She stared at him while her mind raced ahead. Dani plumbed the radiant depths of the man's dark eyes and wondered if she really wanted to be rid of him. Should she tell this Troy Fontaine that she had no one? No destination? What would the consequences be of such an admission?

Though tempted for a moment to put her trust in him, she held back. She didn't really know either of them, but thus far they had proved to be more than willing to help her. Dani admitted to herself that she had never been so elated to see anyone as she was to see them when they rode up to Moze's cabin, pistols smoking. But did she now owe them an explanation? How would she ever rid herself of them once they knew she was all alone?

Troy Fontaine continued to search her face while awaiting an answer. Dani gazed at the toe of her boot, then scuffed the ground. It was hard to admit to herself that she did want to ride a bit farther with them. Fear, she supposed, was as good a reason as any for her change of heart. Fear of another attack. As strangely uncomfortable as this man made her feel, she was still forced to admit that she needed him, if only until they reached the hollow.

Finally she nodded her assent. "I'll wait." She shrugged again, suddenly feeling awkward. "At least until I have something to eat."

"After you." He stepped aside graciously to let her pass.

Dani watched him curiously until she realized he meant for her to lead the way across the clearing to where Grady Maddox was stacking wood for a fire.

"Have a seat." Indicating a nearby stump, Fontaine left her while he went back to their pack mules for supplies. She watched him walk away, noticing every detail of his clothing, down to the scuffed black leather boots much like Grady Maddox's. She shook her head, trying to rid herself of this compulsion to stare at him.

"Sit tight, miss. We'll have some hot coffee ready in no time at all," Maddox called out cheerfully from where he knelt before a low pile of gnarled branches, valiantly trying to strike a flint and get a fire going. She could see it would be a while, the way he was going at it.

It was time to get her mind off of Fontaine anyway, so she began to study his companion. Dani had never seen anyone as clean as Grady Maddox. It was a near miracle, and she was determined to question him about it.

Maddox was nothing like the men she'd grown up around, although she had heard tales of the dandified greenhorns who lived east of the big rivers. She had even seen one at a rendezvous a couple of years back. She was certain Grady Maddox could be called a greenhorn, but she had no easy way to classify his friend. Troy Fontaine did not seem to fit any mold, as far as she could see.

Dani propped her chin in her cupped hand as her eyes sought Troy Fontaine again. He stood near his mules, retying the pack, a coffee pot tucked under his arm. Goods were piled on the ground near his feet.

She would just have to keep an eye on him until she figured it out, she told herself, deciding it was a task that might not prove too difficult at all.

Chapter Five

"Here."

Troy stood over the girl, looking down at the crown of her weathered hat. She sat on a log in the clearing, staring off at the distant mountain peaks, lost in thought. At the sound of his voice, she glanced up quickly and then reached for the tin mug of coffee he offered. He caught a glimpse of the tears that glistened in her eyes before she looked away.

Grady was near the mules, rummaging through the packs for his sketchbook and pens. Until this moment, Troy had left the task of conversing with Dani up to his friend. Fontaine was not one to make small talk, but this strange forest nymph seemed to be much in need of comfort at the moment. He lowered himself to the ground and stretched out casually beside her. He crossed his long legs at the ankles and leaned back on his elbows.

She'd been subdued and silent during the meal, choosing to answer Grady's questions in monosyllables. Now that dinner was over and Grady was off collecting his artist's supplies, an awkward silence hung between them. Troy was astounded at how adept she'd been at avoiding direct answers to Grady's questions. All they knew of her was that her name was Dani and that she lived "back a ways." Who her people were and where she was going remained a mystery. Troy was unwilling to press her, and Grady seemed unaware that he himself was doing so. Now, in the peaceful stillness of the sunny afternoon, Troy found himself wondering what he could say that would offer her comfort.

He would have to begin at the beginning, he decided. He couldn't help her until he found out what was wrong.

"You sure you're all right?" The moment the question was out he thought it sounded stupid. Of course she wasn't all right.

When she spoke, he could barely hear her choked words. "Yeah. I'm about as right as a person can be who's just had two people up and die on her."

"Two?"

Silently she nodded. He looked up to see if she was ready to continue and found himself studying her profile. Her lips were full, almost pouting. He watched them touch the rim of the coffee mug, watched her swallow the steaming liquid. For a moment her lashes rested against her cheeks as if, by closing her eyes, she could block out a painful memory.

"My friend Moze lived here. I was coming by to see if he'd like to hunt with me this season. Those men killed him."

There was nothing he could say, so he waited silently for her to continue.

"Jake died three days ago."

Jake. She offered no further explanation, but the man obviously meant everything to her.

"Your husband?"

"No." There was a slight pause before she continued. "I guess you could say he was my pa."

The word conjured up images of Troy's own father, dark-eyed and laughing, and then, although he fought to dismiss the unbidden memories, he recalled the shafts of sunlight that cut through the dark shadows in the musty abandoned barn. He could almost hear, even now, the slow, haunting whine of the rope as it protected the weight of his father's body. He shuddered and then glanced down at the girl, who was lost in her own thoughts. What could he say to her? What comfort could he offer when he had never found release from his own sorrow?

"It takes time, but the pain will lessen," he said. At least that much was true.

She looked up. "Will it go away?"

He could only draw from his own experience, and he refused to lie to her. "No."

Troy took a deep breath, unwilling to reveal too much of his past. "My father died when I was a boy. It was hard for me at first, but I survived. You will, too. Death is part of life." He glanced off into the distance. Death was a part of life, he thought, but not violent death. Not murder. Troy cleared his throat before he turned to her again. "What will you do now?"

Dani shrugged. Her hands hugged the tin mug in her lap, her thumbs tracing the rim. The expression in her eyes mirrored her confusion as she looked at him. He could feel himself being sized up, measured. He did not press her, sensing that if he was ever going to learn about her, it would not be by forcing her to open up to him. It was obvious that she was confused—confused and hurting.

"I don't know."

Sitting in the middle of the littered yard, she looked small and helpless, clinging to the coffee cup as if it were a lifeline. The oversized clothes only made her appear all the more like some forlorn child lost in the forest.

That's all I need, Troy thought. First Grady, now this.

But she's all alone.

All I need to do is take her someplace where she knows someone and leave her there.

The nearest town was a thousand miles away.

As Troy argued with himself, Grady returned and stacked his sketch pad and pens on the ground, spread his handkerchief carefully on the grass, then sat down on it. Dani watched him in awe while Troy watched Dani.

"I been meaning to ask you something," she said to Grady.

"I'll try to answer." He smiled up at her, eager to please.

She leaned forward and looked him up and down, studying his clothing, his clean-shaven face and neatly combed hair. "How in the hell do you keep so clean?"

Troy burst out laughing, and Dani turned to him with a questioning stare. Grady's face flamed red to the roots of his hair.

"That, Dani, has been the challenge of our excursion," Troy explained. "He has carried along so many changes of clothes that I was afraid for a time we'd need more pack mules just for them. Each night he spends an hour or so washing and mending his shirts. In the morning, he shaves with scented soap."

"What's wrong with taking pride in my appearance?" Grady countered, somewhat recovered from his initial embarrassment and feeling the need to defend himself before Dani.

"Nothing," Troy answered, "it just takes a hell of a lot of time and there's no one out here to impress."

"There's Dani here." Grady smiled up at her again.

She shrugged. "I just can't see the sense in it. You see all this grease on my buckskins?" Dani pointed to the filthy patches of ground-in grime.

A pained look crossed Grady's face. "I've tried not to notice," he said.

"Well, it takes months to build up enough grease to keep the water out of your clothes, at least for a time. Why, I been seasoning these pants for a couple of years now. And"—she leaned toward him conspiratorially—"clean clothes is one sure-fire way to tell the difference between a real mountain man and a flatlander."

Grady looked impressed. "I thought the men out here just adopted the Indian fashions because they are colorful—all the beadwork and fringe . . ."

Dani turned to Troy and included him in the conversation. "Is that why you wear them, Fontaine?"

Troy wondered for a moment why she called Grady by his first name but continued to call him Fontaine. It was as if she wished to keep some distance between them.

"No, that's not why I wear buckskins, Dani," he admitted. "I wear them for the same reasons you do. They are nearly indestructible, and they blend into the surroundings."

"Know why they have fringe?" she asked matter-of-factly, finding an odd sense of power in knowing more than the two men seated at her feet.

"Why?" Troy asked.

"I've always wondered," Grady said, obviously delighted that she was becoming more receptive to them.

"The fringe flicks the water away from you when you walk." She held up her arm and grabbed a long strand of buckskin to demonstrate. "The little drips of rainwater just run right down here"—she waved her arm and set the fringe swaying—"and then get whipped off."

"Amazing."

"Really."

She looked at them skeptically. "You two funning with me, or didn't you even know that?"

"I didn't know it, did you, Troy?" Grady asked his friend.

"No." Troy shook his head, his eyes never wavering from hers. "No. I learn something new every day."

She nodded, satisfied that they were not poking fun at her.

"How'd you two get out here, anyway? Did you sign on as trappers?"

Troy shook his head and Grady explained, "It's a pleasure trip."

Dani looked doubtful. "Nobody comes this far for pleasure, mister. Just living is hard enough."

"I might have come sooner had I realized what pleasures were hidden in these mountains," Troy said softly.

"Huh?" She turned to face him again.

"Troy . . ." Grady coughed nervously. "Actually, Dani, we're just traveling around, seeing the West before civilization crowds in. I'm an artist."

"Oh," was all she said, seemingly unimpressed.

Troy asked, "Do you know what an artist is?"

A moment passed before she answered, "Sure."

Although Dani sounded less than sure, Troy did not embarrass her with an explanation.

"I'd love to paint you, if you'd let me, Dani—"

Before Grady could finish his request, she was on her feet.

"You just try to come near me with any paint and I'll lay you flat, mister. If I wanted to paint myself up like a red Indian lookin' for a party, I'd be ridin' with them and not by myself."

Grady looked to Troy for help, but with a smile and a slight Gallic shrug, Fontaine turned to Dani and tried his hand at setting things right.

"He meant you no insult, Dani. Grady paints pictures of the things he sees here, the mountains, forests, animals, as well as likenesses of people. Perhaps he'll show you some later. For now"—he reached into a rectangular pouch that had been sewn inside his jacket—"you can be of service to us. I'm ashamed to admit that we've become quite lost."

Dani watched him with renewed interest as he pulled out a thick folded sheet of paper and spread it out on the ground near her feet. It was a map of sorts; she could tell by the mountains and rivers drawn on it. She knelt beside him to get a better look.

"I thought we were near here"—he reached out and pointed to a spot near a wide river—"but I can't find any of the landmarks."

She tried to read the words scrawled along the rivers, but the spidery script meant nothing to her. Concentrating on the landmarks sketched on the map, she studied it carefully for a few minutes.

"Which way would the sun move across this?" Her brows knit in thought, she looked at Fontaine and found him disarmingly close. Their shoulders were nearly touching as they bent over the map.

He indicated east to west. "From here to here."

Dani continued to try and recognize familiar signs. She'd never seen a real map before, just directions traced in the dirt.

"As far as I can tell from this"—with her forefinger she traced the river marked "Wind"—"it's in the wrong place."

"Can you show me where we are?"

"Here." Dani pointed with confidence to a spot between the Tetons and Absaroka mountains. "But there's a river that runs more this way." She traced along the correct route. "It's called the Snake. And a mountain pass should be marked here."

Nodding to herself, satisfied she was correct, Dani looked up and found Troy watching her intently. Quickly she got to her feet and straightened her hat.

"Listen," she began, and at the sound of her voice, Troy prepared to do battle with her. He was surprised by her next words.

"I'm going to a place called Hump Bone Hollow to meet up with a passel of other trappers. Since you two are lost, I wouldn't mind leading you there." She turned around to look at Grady in order to set him straight. "If you want to ride along with me, you're more than welcome, but let's get one thing straight: Hump Bone Hollow is the end of the trail for us."

Grady was the first to react as Troy sat speculating upon the girl's sudden decision to include them in her travels. "I know I'd feel a lot better about riding with you, Dani, at least until you reached your folks."

The belligerent stare she turned in Troy's direction led him to believe she would brook no argument. Just as well, he thought; he would let her do it her way. After the past few hours of observing Dani, he knew full well she would never admit she needed them, or anyone else, for that matter.

"Fine," Troy agreed. "From there you can give us directions that will get us through Union Pass and back toward the East. We should start for home before the bad weather blows in."

Reaching behind her, Dani grabbed hold of her own wrist with the other hand and pulled, stretching her arms out behind her. The unconscious motion sent her breasts jutting against the baggy jacket, outlining them seductively and making both men all too aware of her disguised sensuality.

"Well"—Dani dropped her arms and tightened her hat strap—"if you fellas are ready to ride, we'd best be off or we'll never make the hollow before nightfall."

"I'll pack up," Troy offered, more than ready to put some space between them. He moved to the small fire they'd made and began kicking dirt over the nearly burnt out embers.

"Come on, Grady." Dani smiled, her usual good humor somewhat restored by the food and rest. "I'll check that saddle cinch for you. I figure it'll save us some time."

"Thanks." Grady smiled appreciatively, pleased by her sudden willingness to help them. He collected his art materials and hurried to catch up to her as she strode toward her pony.

Troy watched as the two walked toward the animals and was struck for the first time with the idea that Grady Maddox was attracted to Dani, as he had every reason to be. If his friend wanted the girl, Troy knew there would be complications, for Grady was not one to love and then leave. Should the girl give in to Grady's innocent charm, his friend would never be able to leave her behind. Perhaps, Troy thought, that was all the more reason he should give up his own notions of bedding the girl. Troy needed no further complications in his life. He tucked the empty coffee pot under his arm and stooped to pick up his rifle. Straightening, he glanced toward Grady and Dani, who were already mounted and waiting.

Grady was gazing off at the shadowed, blue-tinged mountain peaks in the distance, while Dani sat staring across the clearing directly at Troy.

The trio halted at the edge of a precipice that hung over a verdant valley. Rolling hills edged upward from the valley floor and gradually rose toward the tall, majestic peaks known as the Tetons. The valley had been carved by the river Dani had identified as the Wind. Troy guessed they were not many days' ride from Union Pass. Hump Bone Hollow was perfectly named. The ridges that rimmed and protected the valley were as humped as the ribs—or hump bones, as the trappers were wont to call them—of the buffalo.

A small contingent of tents and tepees filled an open meadow near the river. Randomly situated, the dwellings looked as if they'd been cast down by a giant hand like so many game pieces. Men and animals moved about the makeshift settlement while cook fires sent smoke swirling on upward drafts. The sound of an implement repeatedly ringing against iron filled the air. Farther up the river, steam rose from underground hot creeks and drifted above the treetops.

When Dani turned to face him, Troy was once again treated to the sight of her fine-cut features. Her skin was gilded to a deep tan by constant exposure to the sun, and yet he thought the hue golden and lovely. A finely shaped nose that tilted slightly drew the eye to her lips, and as Troy studied them, his eyes were swift to notice the lush fullness of the lower one. His black stallion stood close beside her red; he and Dani sat nearly thigh to thigh. Troy was arrested by the wide gray eyes that gazed at him.

The sun had dipped low in the afternoon sky, and her eyes had become the color of clouds before a storm, flecked with sparks of silver against the pewter gray. She stared back at him for a fleeting moment that seemed like a lifetime. Troy was tempted to hold the spell forever, but when she spoke the spell was broken.

"We'd best go down."

Without a word Troy nodded to Grady who nudged his mount in the direction of a narrow switchback trail down the side of the hill.

"Wait!" Dani called out to them. Both men twisted in their saddles in order to face her. When she had their attention, she spoke. Halting and unsure, her words betrayed her fear of what their knowledge meant to her.

"Listen . . ." She paused, at a loss as to how to explain. "Nobody down there knows, you know? They don't even suspect that I'm . . . not a boy. I'd be beholden to you if you didn't say anything."

Troy could see how badly it irked her to have to ask for their silence. Her mouth was set in a firm, stubborn line, and although she had asked, she had not begged. Troy knew instinctively she would never plead for anything. He wondered how anyone could have failed to notice her femininity, and he was curious to know what was behind her masquerade.

Grady was the first to reassure her. "You can bet I won't say anything, Dani."

She turned to Troy with a look that dared him to refuse.

"Nor will I," he promised.

"See that you don't. And don't forget. This is the end of the trail for me and you two. From here on out, I go it alone."

It was the first time the two men had encountered such a large group of trappers. Each reacted differently to the sights and sounds of the camp. Troy watched Dani as she rode into the temporary settlement shouting out greetings to the men she recognized.

"Hallo, Jed! Lost your red shirt? Hey, Pierre! Enrique, you old coon-skinner, still cheatin' at hand?"

When the men called out to her in kind, it was more than apparent that all of them thought of her as nothing more than a carefree lad. When asked about her two companions, Dani merely explained that she'd run into them "back yonder," and since the two were lost, she'd offered to lead them this far. Many of the men asked her about Jake, and she told them that he'd "gone under easy," in his sleep.

Fontaine speculated about the man called Big Jake and his relationship to the girl. He could see that having to appear resigned to his death before these men was taking a toll on her. More than once Dani glanced skyward to blink back tears. One thing was quite clear: Except for these casual friends, she was alone now, and the only thing that kept these men away from her was their belief that she was a boy.

The bawdy, boisterous trappers, arrayed in assorted animal skins and Indian apparel, immediately attracted Grady's attention. Troy sensed the man's eagerness to get to work. Before he selected a place to camp, Troy watched Dani, planning to remain as close to her as possible. She rode ahead of them now, moving confidently through the settlement.

"Dani!" Grady called out to her. "Where are we going to camp?"

She whipped her head around to face him.

"*We* ain't campin' nowheres, mister." She lowered her voice and spoke in an angry hush. "Youse can set up anywheres ya wanta."

Her switch to the heavier mountain dialect was so sudden that Troy marveled at her acting ability and watched as she rode away from them, back stiff, eyes straight ahead. Her grammar had been near perfect until they rode into the camp.

Now she was obviously trying to fit in with the rough-and-tumble crew.

Troy's eyes never left the small figure seated astride the spirited Indian mount as she rode toward the edge of the meadow. He raised his hand and gestured to Grady to stop. They would wait until she started her cook fire before they set up a camp next to hers.

Relieved to leave them behind, Dani walked her horses to the farthest edge of the meadow and stopped to make camp. A small hot spring bubbled up from the ground a short hike away; she planned to visit the spot secretly as soon as darkness fell and she was able to escape the eyes and ears of the men.

She stopped and let her gaze travel up the hillside, scanning the thick groves of aspen. The leaves were shimmering flakes of gold dust that danced to earth on a gentle breeze. Far above the meadow the crests of the Tetons were powdered with snow. It wouldn't be long before the white cloak of winter shrouded the meadow and iced the streams and ponds. Already the pelts of the wildlife were thickening in preparation for winter. The hunting season would soon begin in earnest.

Camp set and animals tended, Dani moved toward the center of the portable village, eager to join old friends. The grizzled old-timers reminded her of Big Jake. The younger men, their long hair, beards, and skin wrinkled by long exposure to the sun, seemed aged beyond their years. They offered little threat to her when compared to Fontaine and Maddox. None of these men knew her as anything but Big Jake's boy, and so she moved among them with ease. Now, after having met the two strangers, she realized that none of these familiar faces had ever stirred up the emotions that Fontaine had aroused. It was as if the unsettled feelings she'd had all summer long were set a-jumble just by the sight of him.

Tents and tepees stretched out across the small meadow, and as she passed them, Dani noticed many were inhabited by Indian women and the trappers' half-breed children. Hides in various stages of tanning were stretched out before the dwellings. Women worked over cook fires or sat before the tepees stitching hides together, laying up a supply of winter clothes while the children tumbled over one another and the dogs that ran free about the place.

She stopped to watch a squaw for a few moments as the

woman scraped the back of a buffalo hide that was pegged, fur side down, on the grassy turf. The Indian woman's brown fingers clutched a buffalo-bone scraper by its leather grip. Dani knew from experience that scraping was only the first step in the long curing process. The hide would be greased with buffalo brains, liver, and fat before it was stretched and dried, wrung out, pulled and rubbed again, until it was soft as cloth.

Dani watched the kneeling woman, who seemed oblivious of her close scrutiny, and felt relieved in the knowledge that she'd never be any man's squaw. She performed these same tasks, but she worked for herself. The thought of being subservient to a man, staying behind in camp, and never knowing the thrill of a hunt was abhorrent to her. She looped her fingers into her belt and sauntered on.

Rendezvous also provided a time to repair arms and traps between bouts of gambling, drinking, and hell-raising. Most men carried six to eight traps in a sturdy buffalo-hide sack. The best trap makers were as far away as St. Louis, and so every trapper was careful to keep his metal traps in good working order.

Nearly forty men were camped in the meadow, and Dani knew most of them. She joined a group of ten or eleven gathered about a split-log bar that rested on two tall stumps.

"Ho! Danny boy! Pull up some dirt and 'ave a drink! I 'ere ye've lost Big Jake."

"Ain't lost 'im," she replied. "He's gone under. I know right where he be." Forcing a wide smile, Dani hid her pain, knowing that these men would never show their sorrow at having lost a good friend, and neither should she.

The burly, bald man known to them all as Irish Billy gave her a sharp slap between the shoulderblades that nearly sent her reeling.

Someone handed her a cup of monongahela, drawn from a tin keg of whiskey. The kegs were curved, an innovation that aided their transportation by pack mule.

She refused the cup with a hesitant shake of her head, until Irish Billy, a short, wiry man with a head of wild red hair, explained. "Take it, boyo. It's on the prairie."

Dani recognized the Indian expression that meant the drink was free. Unwilling to refuse Billy's offer, she took the cup and raised it to her lips. The whiskey hit her tongue and worked on all of her senses. Her eyes stung as the bitter watered-down drink slammed into the back of her throat and sent her into choking spasms. At five dollars a pint, she knew better than to waste the precious liquid and fought to keep a firm grasp on the cup even as she choked.

"Been too long without a drink, Dan!" Enrique Dominguez howled, slapping his thighs as he roared with laughter at her plight. All too soon the tables were turned as the men guffawed at the sight of Enrique toppling over into the dirt.

Big Jake had established a routine whenever liquor was brought out: Dani would pretend to drink while Jake downed his share; then he would swiftly trade cups with her, the movement going unnoticed in the ruckus that usually attended such sessions. She had never acquired a taste for liquor or a knack for drinking. It was one experience Big Jake refused her. "It'll only addle your brains," he told her. "One of us with addled brains is already one too many."

Now she was faced with a cupful of the precious drink, and after that first shocking gulp, she found that the warm, pleasurable feeling the stuff gave her was much to her liking.

As she sat listening to the men exchange news and gossip, she savored the drink and felt herself relax for the first time in a month or more. Dani leaned back and listened, learning about the men who'd been "rubbed out" or who had "gone under" since last they all met. The price of beaver was up to six dollars a plew—good news for all. When it came her turn to contribute, she quickly told about Big Jake's passing, and the men sat silent for a moment, staring into the fire, each dealing with his own thoughts on mortality. She was then obliged to relate the tale of old Moze's subsequent death, and that led to her explaining how the two strangers she'd ridden in with had become connected with her. Dani made no mention of the night before. After describing the hunchback who'd disappeared on one of Moze's mules, she sat back and waited for the next storyteller to take over.

Someone passed around a news sheet from St. Louis that was only six months old. Dani declined the pleasure of reading it when it reached her. As the afternoon wore on, the tales became more embellished by the storytellers.

Henry Marker, one of the younger men, sat wrapped in a blanket. Although he had the voice and strength of a young man, his hair was pure white and hung far past his shoulders. A long beard reached the second button on his shirt and his eyes rolled wildly as he related his adventure. During the summer months he had journeyed south all alone, so far south, in fact, that he'd been to the great desert where nothing recognizable grew. At one point he had nearly starved and was forced to eat his own moccasins. Finally he had held his hands in an anthill until they were covered with the crawling, biting insects. He then licked them clean.

"Hell," Henry whispered, embellishing his speech by waving his hands, "I finally ended up lettin' blood from the mules an drinkin' it just to keep alive."

"Shit." The comment was voiced without hesitation by someone in the crowd, and Dani thought it was no wonder that the man's hair had gone gray.

A log was tossed upon the low fire. The afternoon shadowed purple as the sun slipped behind the mountains.

"We got time for a game or two of hand before it gets too dark. How 'bout it, Dani?"

Enrique encouraged her, for Dani was known as the best hand player the men had ever seen. There was a long-standing good-natured feud between the two of them. Before Dani learned the game, Enrique had been champion.

The liquor was already working its wiles on her and although she was relaxed, she also felt a strange euphoria, as if she might win any challenge issued. Boasting, she looked across the short distance between herself and Enrique.

"Only if you go for it first, Rique. I been aimin' to beat you again and beat you bad if'n you ain't learnt a lesson yet!"

Dani reached for the possible bag that hung from her belt. It was made of a red fox pelt, the head adorning the flap that closed the bag. Dani's small bag held her only treasures, a shiny black rock that always looked wet, the cherry stone she used for her hand games, and flint for lighting a fire.

Flipping open the bag, she fished around inside for the cherry stone and withdrew it with her thumb and forefinger. She teased Enrique with a flashing smile. "What are ya plannin' to lose?"

"Wagh!" The swarthy, dark-haired Spaniard, who was sporting a red wool shirt and thick green woolen trousers, stuck out his tongue and wagged his head back and forth much like a woolly buffalo. He wore no beard, just a long black mustache that curved about his mouth, giving him the appearance of a man who constantly frowned. No image could have been more deceptive, for Enrique's white teeth often flashed in a wide smile.

"Play! I'm bettin' my whole stake," he shouted.

The crowd roared and then hushed. Dark-eyed, moon-faced Indian women stood at the fringe of the group, watching eagerly. Many of them were skilled players of the hand game. All waited in anticipation for Dani to begin.

She raised her hands, palms up, to show the stone that rested on her left palm. Pressing her hands together as if in prayer Dani then shook the stone a few times, closed her fists, and separated her hands. One held the stone; the other was empty. Enrique leaned forward to choose. He picked her left hand.

Dani turned her wrist and opened her left hand. The stone was not there.

Twenty men went into boisterous stomping, catcalls, and cheers. Two broke off from the group to dance a jig and swing each other about. Enrique leaned forward. The crowd fell silent.

"Again!" he bellowed.

"You ain't got nothin' left to bet. I jes' took your whole stake," Dani reminded him.

"Wagh!" He repeated his customary head-wagging ritual. "Take my woman, then!"

For a moment Dani was taken aback. What in the hell would she do with his woman? She hid her amusement and started the game again.

And won again.

The crowd went wild.

Enrique held his head in his hands and moaned.

Dani took a liberal drink of her whiskey and waited for the cheering to die down. She waited until all eyes were on her once again.

"One more game, Enrique," she announced. "Winner take all."

His eyes glinted at her in the waning light. Dani shook the stone between her palms, slowing her movements imperceptibly. She put her fists together and stared at Enrique, willing him to choose the right hand. He stared at her hard, then raised his hand to choose one of her fists. His own hand lingered a moment above her left hand, then tapped the right.

Dani turned over the fist and showed the stone.

Enrique Dominguez leapt from his seat, whooping for joy.

He'd won back his traps, mules, pelts, supplies, and Indian woman, virtually all he owned in the world. Dani smiled as she dropped the stone back into her possible bag, then drained the cup of whiskey. When the crowd settled down again, she laughed and said to Enrique, "You owe me one more drink on the prairie, Rique, seein' as how I jes' went from poor to rich to poor again."

He gladly filled her cup from his own jug, and Dani leaned back against a log that had been drawn up before the fire. The men settled down with their whiskey and tales, and in the encroaching darkness, their talk turned to women.

The consensus was that white women were useless, fancified foofaraws who knew little to nothing about the requirements for a mountain existence.

"And don't I know it?" Irish Billy asked no one in particular. "Been married twice't already, and now there's only two things I'm afraid of—a 'decent woman' and bein' left afoot. No." He imparted his wisdom: "Give me an Injun wife and a good whore in town any day."

His comment brought up reminiscences of the Rocky Mountain House Saloon in St. Louis. Dani listened with interest as the men ranked the fancy women there from heaven-sent to "unfit for a drinkin' man to hole up with." It seemed most of the men had been there. Those who had not sought to outboast the others with tales of other whorehouses along the Mississippi. Within an hour, Dani heard all the ways a man could ease his lust on a woman. Thankful for the darkness, she told herself it was only the fire that caused her face to flame. The liquor had numbed her lips and started a strange melted-honey feeling flowing through her.

It was not impossible for her to imagine herself the recipient of a man's advances, but her fantasies seemed incomplete. She looked at the faces around the fire and could not see herself carrying on in ways described with any of the men present. Some she'd known since she was old enough to ride; most she thought of as friends—brothers, in fact. No, she couldn't imagine herself cavorting in the way they described with any man present.

From the talk she'd just heard, it sounded to Dani as if it was up to a woman to pleasure a man, to tempt him with her breasts, her hips, her buttocks, all of which had to be exposed by a minimum of clothing. She'd never seen a white woman in

fancy clothing. Come to think of it, she'd never even seen a
pure white woman, if she didn't count herself. She could
hardly picture the ruffled, shining bits of fluff the men said the
city women called clothes. Such garments were not for her.
Nope. Never.

She drained her cup and looked over its rim. Jet black eyes
bored into hers from across the fire. Beyond the second row of
men stood Troy Fontaine. Watching her. Waiting.

Waiting for what?

Dani's thoughts were muddled, and her cheeks were tingling. She pulled the brim of her hat lower, hiding her eyes. It
did little good, for she could feel him still watching her. Her
stomach growled, the liquor being the only sustenance she'd
had since they had eaten in Moze's clearing.

The urge to leave the crowd began to press upon her. Her
eyelids were becoming heavy; her head had begun to spin. She
needed to feel the cool night air on her flaming cheeks, needed
to be alone, needed a bath. This was as good a time as any to
slip away.

Dani pressed her hands against the log to push herself to her
feet. Blood rushed to her head and she nearly stumbled over
Enrique, who'd passed out beside her.

"All this talk about women too much for you, boyo?" Irish
Billy called to her as she began to move away from the
firelight. "You had a piece of a real one yet?"

Dani hesitated, swaying slightly, and tried to focus on the
fire, only to discover her eyes would not obey. Unable to think
of any retort to his taunt, Dani merely waved and turned her
back on the group. Unsure of her footing in the darkness, she
found that for some inexplicable reason, it was easier to walk
with her arms out for balance. With her gaze intent upon her
destination, she headed toward the stream.

The firelight accented her features, making her eyes huge
against her tanned skin. Troy Fontaine watched in silent
appreciation as Dani drank whiskey from a tin cup with as
much ease as a countess drinking from a crystal goblet. He'd
taken note when her eyes began to glisten with the effects of the
liquor. Her tongue passed between her lips, catching the
remaining taste of the numbing liquid. He'd watched her win
at the hand game, watched her laughing gaily all the while, her

eyes sparkling with mingled pride and mischief. She fit in well with these men, but what would become of her?

None of them made advances toward her for the simple reason that they truly saw her as a boy. He wondered how they could be so blind, and then realized that it was her very familiarity that kept them from discovering the truth. Dani had always been a boy to them. They did not see a woman when they looked at her.

It was all too easy for Troy to imagine her gracing his table at Isle de Fontaine. Any man would be proud to call her his own. Even in the buckskin clothes and with her butchered hair, her radiance shone clear and brilliant. He felt compelled to watch her as he sat on the edge of the crowd, lured by the sight of Dani listening to ribald tales that would have shocked Grady, her expression changing often from curiosity to disbelief.

What had she been thinking when her eyes met his over the rim of her cup? Shortly thereafter, Dani had stood and moved away from the fire. It was obvious to him that she had had too much to drink, for like all those who imbibed too much, she labored overmuch to appear in control.

With a last glance back toward the huddled figures crowded about the fire, Troy Fontaine made sure no one was watching him as he followed Dani. Grady was working steadily off to one side of the group, his easel before him, two oil lamps providing him light. Beside him sat a makeshift table covered with paints and other supplies. A few of the men had gathered around to watch him work, one after another volunteering to pose as models. It was obvious that his friend had momentarily forgotten about the girl, for he was deep into his painting, thrilled to have so many models from which to choose.

Troy kept his distance from Dani, unwilling to alert her to his presence. He knew how she would react; he would not be welcome to join her. Upon arriving at her own campsite, Dani checked her supplies and then spread her bedroll.

Troy hesitated. He had seen her safely home, he told himself. Now he knew he should get out of there while he still could. He wished he could forget about her as easily as Grady had.

Before he could turn away, the girl straightened and looked back toward the fire. Her gaze lingered a moment in his direction, and then she moved northward, toward the trees.

Troy followed her, maintaining his distance, uncertain still whether Dani had seen him. If she had, she gave no indication, nor did she question his presence.

A bright three-quarter moon bathed the landscape in silver-gray shadows. As Dani neared the hot creek, she felt the effects of the whiskey diminish. The crisp mountain air filled her lungs and cleared her head, her steps steadied, her senses became more finely attuned to her surroundings. The sound of the creek moving over the rocks, the strong smell of sulfur that permeated the air, the swirling fog caused by cool air meeting warm water—all were familiar and beckoned to Dani. She could hardly wait to let the water soothe her spirit.

Turning slightly, she studied the trees along the bank behind her. Nothing moved. Not a sound disturbed the stillness of the night. The voices of the men around the campfire had receded as she put distance between them. She was a good half-mile from the rendezvous camp. Dani waited, tensed in every muscle, barely daring to breathe until the feeling that she was being watched left her. She was just jumpy, she told herself. After all that had occurred she felt she had a right to be jumpy. The men who were raising hell around the fire would soon collapse into their bedrolls, if they made it that far. With a final glance in all directions, Dani sat down on a boulder near the stream and drew the long knife from her right boot. She set it carefully on the rock, where it glimmered in the moonlight. Then she pulled off her boots.

Shucking her doeskin britches, she laid them out carefully on the cool surface of the rock and sat down on them. Dani wore no other clothing below her waist.

The figure bathed in moonlight seated on the rock was all too visible to Troy Fontaine. Mist swirled and eddied behind her, a fitting backdrop for the wood sprite so unaware of his observation. Or was she unaware? Perhaps the girl was playing the temptress for his sake. She certainly was in no hurry to undress and be done with her bath.

Her shapely legs were fully visible beneath the oversized shirt and buckskin jacket. Before she removed the rest of her clothing, he saw her pause and run a hand over her thigh and down the length of her leg, all the way to the slim, tapered ankle. What was she thinking? he wondered. If her dallying was meant to seduce him, she could already crow over her success, for the slow ache that had started in his loins as he followed her through the darkened forest was now throbbing through his veins. Still he waited. And watched.

Dani looked down at her legs, stretched them out before her, and tried to imagine them exposed to a man's view. She couldn't. No one had seen her naked for years. Not even Jake. Oh, he'd bandaged a bad slice on her calf a few years back, but he'd never seen her unclothed. Would he have wanted to? The thought had never entered her mind, for Jake was a father to her, and somehow Dani knew for certain that was all he ever needed to be.

But tonight her friends had conjured up images of men and women entwined and grasping, grappling, suckling, and prodding, and Dani found those visions more than disturbing. The tales of the city women were not new to her, for she'd heard the men talk before, but always before, Jake had sent her to her bedroll when the men were far into their liquor. She tried to shake herself from her reverie as she untied her belt.

She pulled the shirt and jacket off over her head in one movement, and as she did the cold night air slapped her skin. She felt her nipples harden in response and slowly, tentatively, pressed her palms against them. Did men really enjoy kissing a woman's breasts? Would a woman enjoy the feel of it? What about the milk trapped inside?

Dani knew that babies suckled at their mothers' breasts. Was it the same when a man did so? Tipping her head back, she swung her bobbed hair and felt it tickle her shoulders.

Troy Fontaine—grandson of a pirate, experienced Creole lover, woodsman, hunter, gambler, entrepreneur—was forced to swallow the lump in his throat as he watched Dani press her hands ever so gently to the taut peaks of her breasts. He called himself every kind of a fool and was ashamed to admit, even to himself, that his cheeks burned with embarrassment. He was assaulted with a picture of himself standing hidden among the trees, watching her like half a man. He realized with a sudden, startling clarity that he had been watching her for two days now. It was not his style to watch. He was no voyeur.

Troy Fontaine began to strip away his clothes.

Hot. The water was as hot as the steam promised it would be—even hotter, a shock to Dani's skin as she gingerly waded into the waist-deep pool. She took care not to slip on the rocks until she was in far enough to glide away from the edge of the stream. Once in the middle, she wallowed in the luxury of the intense heat, which relaxed her instantly. Ducking under, she shook her head until her hair was thoroughly soaked and then broke the surface, brushing the water from her face. Raising her arms skyward, Dani let the water trickle down from her fingertips before she plunged under again.

This time when she rose to the surface she stood and let the water play around her waist. The air was a cool, welcome shock as it hit her skin full force. She was alive and tingling all over. As she swept her hair back off her face and brushed the stinging water from her eyes, she became aware of a slight movement near her. She opened her eyes to the sight of Troy Fontaine standing in the water not a foot away.

Too stunned to react to his appearance, she was almost ready to believe he had materialized out of nowhere. Frozen where she stood, Dani opened her mouth to issue an objection, closed it, then finally found her voice. She could barely rasp out the words. "Get the hell away from me."

Who was she kidding? Troy's finely arched brows drew together above his eyes as he frowned down at her. "I was under the distinct impression that I was invited."

"What?"

Was she unaware of the way she looked standing there, hands on hips, submerged from the waist down, bare from the waist up? Her nipples beckoned him like forbidden fruit.

"I thought you saw me following you," he insisted.

"Yeah, and it's all right to piss upstream."

"You didn't?"

She looked confused. "No. I never piss upstream."

He sighed. This wasn't working out the way he'd fantasized at all. She was supposed to melt into his arms. Silently.

"You didn't see me?" he asked. "This whole show wasn't for my benefit?"

"What show?"

"I think you knew very well I was following you, so you took your sweet time undressing before my very interested gaze."

"Holy hot shit."

"You have a filthy mouth for a woman."

"You have a little brain for a man. I am not supposed to *be* a woman, remember?"

"Well," he began, one brow arching as he contemplated her breasts, "you certainly look like one."

Dani shivered as a breeze wafted along the stream. It was all too apparent to her that he was studying her breasts, the breasts no one had ever seen, the breasts she wasn't supposed to have. God, she was confused. She shook her head, trying to clear it.

"Move aside. I'm getting out."

He watched her cross her hands over her breasts, an overwhelmingly feminine reaction, and somehow found it enticing, and very unlike her. He lowered himself into the water until they were at eye level. He stared at her across the steaming water.

Unbidden pictures of Troy Fontaine rolling and thrashing in the clutches of one of the city women clouded her mind. She frowned. Suddenly it was all too clear to her. What he wanted from her was what all men wanted, what the trappers had described. That was what Troy Fontaine had wanted of her all along. "*I'm beginning to think you really don't know what I want*"—he'd said those words to her just this morning. She hadn't known then, but she knew now.

And what of her? Did women, too, have this urge to mate? Did it come as often to them as it did to a man? Animals all had the mating urge, and animals were something Dani could understand. As far as she knew, she had never experienced such an urge, but perhaps that would explain the strange way she'd been feeling lately. The way Fontaine made her feel when he looked into her eyes.

Dani cursed Big Jake again right then, cursed him for dying and leaving her so ignorant of the ways of men and women. When her body had started bleeding a few years ago, she'd run to him screaming, terrified of the blood that stained her pants and trickled down her legs. With little explanation, Jake had told her it was Eve's curse, told her what to do when it happened, and told her to keep it a secret. From then on, she had hated this woman, this Eve, for putting such a curse on her. That was all she knew.

And now it was not enough. Not nearly enough.

The strange, mellow warmth was beginning to seep through her again. Dani thought the water that bubbled up from the core of the earth was hot, but it was nothing compared to the heat that was radiating from the very center of her being. The man facing her had not moved, but stared into her eyes, waiting.

He didn't look to be a patient man.

"You aren't afraid, are you?" Fontaine asked.

The challenge was softly issued. He knew exactly how the word "afraid" would make her react and was satisfied when Dani tried to stare him down.

"No," she said.

"It's not as if you haven't done it before."

"Of course not." Would he be able to tell? she wondered.

"Perhaps we should move a bit closer together."

"It might be easier that way," she agreed.

Dani eased toward him, amazed to find that her legs had turned to mush. She bridged half the distance, then stopped and waited for him to move toward her.

Troy knew a rush of victory as the girl floated nearer. Slowly, surely, he closed the gap between them and opened his arms to her.

Chapter Six

He was more than amazed when she leapt at him, threw her arms and legs about him, hugged him to her in a fierce bear's grip, and mashed her sealed lips against his mouth. Troy was flabbergasted.

It was a struggle to disengage her, but finally he was able to pry her arms from his waist. Holding her at arm's length, Troy stared down into her upturned, questioning face.

"*What* are you doing?" he asked.

Dani felt like a child caught in some act of mischief. She smiled up at him. "That's how we do it here."

Troy had his doubts about that. His hands fell away from her shoulders. "Well, that's fine, but it's not the way we do it in Louisiana."

"Oh." She was on very unsteady ground and she knew it.

"Perhaps I should show you," he suggested magnanimously. "Shall we try again? A bit slower this time, with a bit less . . . passion?"

She shrugged.

The half-smile on his lips was barely perceptible as he lowered his head and leaned toward her, hands still at his sides. This time she stood immobile and let him take the lead. After all, she admitted, she really didn't know what she was doing. She wished her head would stop spinning. As his lips played against hers, her mind went blank and Dani lost herself in the sensation his gentle kiss evoked. His breath was whiskey-scented, the taste of it tainted his tongue. His lips were warm.

They brushed against her own the way a butterfly brushes against the petals of an open flower.

He teased her with his kiss, and Dani felt her senses dance as every pore of her body cried out with life. She felt his tongue outline the crevice between her closed lips. They parted as if of their own volition, and his tongue slipped between them. When the tip of his tongue, ever so slowly, touched the tip of hers, a moan escaped her, dragged up from some deep inaccessible region inside her.

And he had not yet touched her with his hands.

Without relinquishing his lips, she moved nearer him when she felt she could no longer stand alone. Craving the warmth of his touch, she longed to be enveloped in his strong arms. Locking her arms about his waist, she sought to press her body into his. Dani discovered she could not get close enough to this man.

Troy broke the kiss and stared down at the woman in his grasp. Her skin was alabaster in the moonlight. Dani reminded him of a statue in a fountain, droplets glistening upon the marble surface of her skin. Only her face and neck were tanned.

Dani sought to draw him closer as she pressed her palms against the small of his back. She seemed as hungry for him as he was for her. Reaching down, Troy grasped the backs of her thighs and slid her up the length of his body.

As he lifted her, Dani instinctively wrapped her legs around him. She let her arms drift up his back until she could grip his shoulders and pull herself up, aiding him as he sought to fit her to him. The air about them was cool, and yet Dani found it a comfort. It did little to chill her blood, offering only slight relief from the surging heat that threatened to engulf her.

She could not see that part of him that was below the water, but she could feel it pressing against her, as if seeking entrance to that secret place that seemed to be on fire with need. Dani would gladly have welcomed the sweet intrusion if she had known how to proceed. He was kissing her again, and that was definitely wonderful. It made her head swim, much as the whiskey had earlier. His lips were cool, his tongue a flame that darted between them, igniting her. She gripped him harder with her legs, clasping him to her with all her might. He pulled his lips away and she protested with a moan, then strained to hear his whispered words.

"Ease up a little bit," he murmured. "You're squeezing the air out of me."

She drew back, still riding his waist. Hanging away from him at arm's length in order to see his face. Didn't he desire that intense closeness? "But . . ."

"I know. That's the way you do it out here."

"Yes."

She pulled herself to him once more and hugged him ferociously, her face pressed against his neck. Troy dared to suggest, "You are going to have to let go a little so that I can . . ."

Why did he insist on whispering?

"What?" she whispered back harshly.

"Ease"—he tried to push her hips back with his hands— "off."

The force of his shove and her own sudden compliance combined to throw Troy off balance. Beneath the surface of the water, his left foot slipped down the rounded face of a rock. Before he could utter another word, the two of them toppled over into the stream.

At least the fall broke her desperate grip.

The first to recover, Troy reached down into the water and pulled Dani to her feet. He waited until she brushed the hair out of her eyes and stopped coughing. Then, without another word, his strong fingers still clamped around her upper arm, he led her to the edge of the stream.

"Wait! What are you doing?" Dani tried to stand her ground but was easily pulled through the water.

"I have a feeling we'd be better off on solid ground. You certainly aren't making this easy." Stopping at the water's edge, Troy looked down into her upturned face and asked without preamble, "You haven't changed your mind, have you?"

"No."

Dani answered without hesitation. So far she'd enjoyed herself. This mating business was not so hard after all. In fact, she thought it downright intriguing.

She followed him without further argument as he led her out of the hot creek toward the towering pine grove. The chilly night air caressed her heated skin, teasing every pore and nerve ending. Her nipples stood erect. The cool, crisp air was a relief after the swirling heat of the stream. Dani glanced once over her shoulder, gauging the distance between herself and her clothing. Her possessions lay where she had left them on the rock, the pile appearing as little more than a dark shadow in the dim moonlight.

"Lie down," he commanded.

The hunger in his tone thrilled her.

"You first."

She was surprised when Troy complied graciously, choosing a welcoming spot on the soft, sandy earth between the stream and the pines. He stretched out casually on his side, resting on one elbow as he stared up at her, comfortable with his own nakedness.

Dani feasted upon the sight of him. She had seen more than her share of naked men. The male anatomy was something she'd always taken for granted. Until tonight. He was beautiful. Resplendently clothed in rays of moonlight, Troy Fontaine reminded her of a sleek, well-muscled mountain lion. Sinews rippled when he moved. His skin was as flawless as the underside of a prime pelt. She took her time, allowing her gaze to wander over him until her attention shifted to the strong plane of his chest, down the hard surface of his upper abdomen, past the smooth, slight curve where his hip dipped into his waist.

Then her eyes were drawn to his arousal. She shuddered and looked away, only to meet his dark, mysterious gaze. The look in his eyes calmed her. He remained unaware of the surge of overwhelming fear she had just experienced.

"Never let anyone know when you're afraid," Jake had warned.

Never, she thought.

Slowly she knelt beside him. She wanted this man to admire her skill at lovemaking. *What skill?* her mind taunted. *Who are you fooling?* Stubborn to the last, Dani was determined that before the sun shone, she'd know all about this mysterious experience that had previously eluded her. Staring into Troy Fontaine's obsidian eyes, she took a deep, silent breath and decided to let her instincts guide her. Longing to touch the man's smooth golden skin, she reached out, much as she would reach out to tame a wild animal, and stroked the palm of her hand along his ribs.

His skin quivered beneath the gentle touch of her fingertips, and Dani knew an instant surge of power. She smoothed her hand once more along his chest and then let it slide down to his waist and up over his hip. When she reached his thigh, she raised her hand, intending to repeat the procedure.

He seized her wrist with a grip as strong as an iron trap and pulled her toward him until she rested against the strong wall of his chest.

"You're playing with fire, little pet." His voice was a low, warning growl.

"You're hurting me." Dani found she could barely whisper. He loosened his grip, but he did not release her.

"I'm through playing. Come here."

He pulled her closer until her lips reached his, and then he covered them with his own. Once more the heady rush of sensation coursed through her veins as his tongue played against hers. This time she expected it, welcomed it, and tasted back. This time she was determined to go slowly, to learn all this man had to teach her about lovemaking. Tomorrow he might be gone, and she would have to remember it all.

Dani felt the beat of his heart, hard and steady, against her own breast. His arms enfolded her in a warm embrace, and while never relinquishing her lips, he rolled her to her back in one polished movement. Never had she felt so warm, so alive. His kiss had become the center of her universe. Dani closed her eyes against the moonlight, for even that soft orb seemed too harsh a distraction. With her eyes closed she could dwell in the darkness and let her senses guide her.

His tongue was teasing hers again, and she responded by tightening her hold, pulling him closer. She could feel the hard muscles of his chest pressing against her breasts, the crisp, light covering of hair teasing her nipples until she wanted to cry out in need at the sensations he evoked. Still, Dani could not pull him close enough.

As a low, drawn-out moan issued from her, Troy ended his kiss and slowly lifted his head. He wanted to see her, to study her fine, clear features. Her eyes were closed. The velvet lashes had become dark crescents against her skin. Her lips were full and pouting, inviting him to take more. He nuzzled his lips against her neck and felt her squirm against him. Troy ran his hand lightly along the side of her breast down to her waist and then smoothed her hip with his palm. He covered her lips with his own once again. He relished the feel of her fingertips as they toyed with the hair at the nape of his neck.

Troy moved his lips on hers, slanting his mouth in order to savor the nectar she offered him. Breathless, he pulled away once again and heard her moan in protest.

"Be patient," he whispered.

She lay still and panting in the soft sand beneath him. Troy bent to explore her. He kissed her neck, then slid his lips across her shoulders. He did not stop when he felt her tense as his tongue toyed with one taut nipple and then the other. It was not until she writhed against his swollen member, pressing her hips to his, that he gave in to his own need and a groan was wrested from his throat.

I'm going to die, Dani thought. *Die dead, just like Jake.* While Troy worked his magic on her, Dani's mind flashed fleeting images. *They'll find me in the morning stark naked. Dead.* The most astounding realization of all was that she did not even care. As Dani felt him caressing her hip and then her thigh, as she opened her legs to his exploring hand, she knew for certain all she wanted was for Troy to extinguish the fire he had kindled inside her. Everywhere he touched her, Dani's body awakened to new life. She gasped as his fingers slipped inside her, then cried out in protest as he began to pull them away, afraid he would deprive her of the ecstasy his touch evoked. When he slowly continued to tease her with his hand, she relaxed and let her body ride with the motion. Searching, seeking release, she met his movements by thrusting her hips.

And still she wanted more.

His lips claimed hers again. The universe had divided. His lips and hands claimed equal attention and drove her on until Dani thought she would shatter into countless pieces. She became aware of everything at once. Troy's body steamed hotter than the water of the creek as he lay across her, pressing her down against the earth. She felt every grain of sand on the bank. The breeze gently wafted over them, soothing them as a parent might comfort a feverish child. The fire in Dani continued to build until she waited instinctively for some final act that still eluded her.

She tore her lips from his and grasped his thick midnight-black hair in her hands, pulling his head back until she could stare into the depths of his eyes. She was not unaware of his needs, for his swollen, turgid manhood pressed against her thigh. Suddenly she knew what she wanted. Everything that had once been a mystery was clear to her now.

"I want more," she demanded, knowing full well that he would understand.

Without a word, without taking his eyes from hers, Troy moved to comply with her wishes. He knelt between her open legs as his hands held her shoulders immobile against the earth. When he pressed himself against the warm, wet apex of her thighs, Dani urged him on, writhing against him. Troy lowered himself into her, and as he did, Dani thrust upward to meet his entry, wrapping her legs about his waist, drawing him in. When he tore away her virginity, she cried out, not so much in pain as in triumph. As he filled her during this final act of possession, Dani fully realized that she'd found what she'd been seeking.

When he entered her, Troy swiftly realized he'd gained more than he bargained for. The girl was still a virgin. At least she had been. Until now. Until him. For a moment he was still, sheathed inside this sprite who had tempted him with the mysteries of her body. The implications of the act crowded his mind, threatening for a moment to cool his ardor, until the woman newly made in his arms began to demand more of him. She gazed into his eyes, her own glazed with passion. Clasping his face between her hands, she drew his head down, seeking his kiss. Her tongue moved against his, circling, exploring. Her hips began to swing in circular motions, urging him to respond. She was too much to ignore. *What's done is done*, he reasoned, before he lost himself in her.

Troy rejoiced in her spontaneity. As he thrust against her, answering her demands, she met him with her hips and tongue until the two of them rose together, each following the other's lead. She was moaning now, thrashing against him and driving him to the brink of climax. He was on fire. Troy knew he could not hold back much longer and so buried himself deeper inside her. He smothered her cries with his kiss, and as he climaxed, unable to hold himself in check any longer, Troy felt her hands grasp his hips as Dani clasped him to her. She tilted her hips upward, receiving his seed as if he were presenting her with some sacred offering.

As Troy abandoned himself to his own need, Dani became lost in a celebration of senses, suddenly certain that some release equally as shattering was about to overwhelm her. She let her instincts guide her through the uncharted world of sensation and enveloped him further, hoping to ease the incessant throbbing that had built to a fevered pitch. When her release happened she was taken unaware, and it was so thunderous she feared she might disintegrate into countless, pulsating starbursts.

She shattered, exploded, died, and was reborn. As the sweetly aching pulsations died away, Dani lay beneath Troy and listened to the sound of her pounding heart as it echoed in her ears. He seemed to be resting in silence, his face hidden in the curve of her neck, his body still pressing hers into the sand. Dani tried to think of something to say, but for once in her life, words would not come. Should she thank him? It seemed only fitting. It was proper to thank someone who gave you something, especially something so wondrous. As her fingertips played along his spine, trailing up and down, down and up, she stared at the moon and listened to the soft sound of his breathing and the gentle lapping of the water against the creek bank. He kissed her collarbone, and then she felt him raise his head. His eyes searched hers as if for answers, and before he could speak, she did.

"Thank you."

If he expected anything from her, it was not that. Troy raised himself to his elbow, shifted to a more comfortable position, and stared down into her guileless face.

"Thank you?"

"Yep. That was great." She smiled. "Just what I needed." A calm that she had not experienced for months pervaded her being.

"I might feel flattered, pet, if I knew you had countless males to compare me to, but seeing as how I was the first, I don't think you can really rate me."

"How did you know I never did that before?"

Troy could only stare. This girl lay beneath him, content, naked as a babe, having just lost her virginity to a virtual stranger, and she was not only thanking him but asking him how he knew she was a virgin. He sighed deeply and rolled off of her to lie on his back and stare up at the heavens.

He didn't need this at all.

With all of her survival skills, Dani was even more naive than Grady. And she was alone. Now, by an act of passion, he'd made her his.

No, he didn't need this at all.

When Troy realized she was talking to him again, he gave

her his full attention and tried to sort out what she was saying.

". . . didn't rightly know what to expect. I knew it had something to do with the man putting . . . you know . . . but I couldn't figure out all the kissing and tugging parts the men were talking about. Anyway, now I know." She sat up suddenly and turned to look down at him. A smile brightened her face as she looked at him mischievously and then added, "So, can we do it again? Just to make sure I have the hang of it?"

Troy stared at her in disbelief for a moment, let his gaze roam down the length of her as she sat beside him, then threw his arm over his eyes and groaned aloud.

"You all right?" she wanted to know.

"Yeah. I'm all right. I just can't believe we are having this conversation."

"Well, it sure looks like you're ready to do it again."

He bolted upright in one quick move and began walking toward the creek. She followed him, just as he suspected she would. Troy didn't answer her until they were in waist-deep water. She was nearly hidden by steam when she bobbed down and let the water cover her shoulders. He followed suit and found it easier to talk to her through the mist.

"Dani . . ." God, how could he put this? he asked himself. "What we did was a mistake. We can't ever do it again."

"What?" Dani was taken aback by his words. A *mistake*? "Was I that bad? I know I didn't know what I was doing, and I'm sorry I tricked you into thinking I did, but if you'll give me another chance, I know I can—"

Aware of the hurt in her voice, he stopped her before she could go on. "You were . . . wonderful." Troy did not have to lie as he sought to reassure her. "Really wonderful, Dani. It's just that, had I known you were a virgin, I would not have done it."

"Why not?" she demanded. "Besides, I'm not a virgin. I don't even know what that *is*."

"Dani—"

"I'm a hunter, a trapper, a girl—of course, no one but you and Grady know that—a good rider, but I *ain't* no virgin." She used the word Jake always said was not a word just to stress the point.

"You're not now," he muttered. "Dani, listen to me: All that aside, what we did was wrong for you—and for me. Grady and

I are on our way home. I can't stay here and look out for you."
He fought for a way to explain so that she would understand.
"I can't be your husband or look after you, as Big Jake did. I'm
leaving. And you can't come with me." He stopped speaking
as a sudden thought struck him. Why couldn't she go with
him? He tried to imagine her in Louisiana and then shook his
head. No. It would never do. He had neither the time nor the
inclination to take on a wife. Not now, when Devereaux might
already have located Constantine Reynolds. Once Reynolds
had been brought to trial, once Troy knew for certain his
mother was dead, only then would he allow himself to love.

She was silent for so long that he moved closer to see her
better. Was she crying? He could tell in a glance that she
wasn't, but her eyes shone bright through the mist that swirled
between them. When she spoke it was in a voice so soft he
could barely hear her.

"I just thought . . ."

"Thought what, pet?"

"I don't need a husband, but I thought once I . . .
mated . . . I thought things would be different from then on.
Like the wolves or the beavers. They pick a mate and stay
together. They work together, hunt and fish together, set up a
winter camp." She shrugged. "I guess I don't know enough
about humans, is all."

"Dani, listen . . ." Troy stepped forward, reaching out to
touch her and felt a distinct sense of loss as she flinched away
to avoid his touch.

She'd heard the pity in his voice and wanted no part of it.
Dani forced herself to forget he called her "pet." No one had
ever felt sorry for her, and Jake had never let her feel sorry for
herself. She'd be damned if she would let this man pity her.
Forcing a smile, she tipped her head back and watched him.

"It's all right, Fontaine." She shrugged off his attempt to
comfort her. "I'm wet, I'm tired, and I got a lot to think about,
so I'm going to dress and head back to camp." Turning away,
she stopped before she reached the bank and added, "Tomorrow you just ride on out of here and don't pay any mind to
what I said. It was just a crazy notion I had. It seems I've still
got a lot to learn about this lovemaking."

* * *

It seemed the night would never end. Dani lay awake, tossing from side to side, staring first at the star-spattered sky, then at the moon-washed aspen, then at the campfires flickering in the hollow. It was not the revelry, the boisterous sound of the men across the glen dancing and stomping to fiddle and mouth harp, that kept her awake. She was disturbed by the sound of her own heart. The euphoria and light-headedness brought on by the liquor had ebbed, only to be replaced by a throbbing at her temples. The heat of her body had been replaced by a chill she could not dispel even though she lay on her soft apishamore, covered with a thick buffalo robe.

Troy's words repeated themselves, throbbing against her temples, increasing the ache left behind by the alcohol: *"What we did was a mistake. We can't ever do it again."*

Again.

Again . . .

She rolled over and tried to sleep on her stomach. Pulling the hide over her head did no good. Remorse assailed her, not over having committed the act, but for getting snared like an animal in a trap of her own making. A tenderness at the apex of her thighs served as a constant reminder of their lovemaking. Her breasts ached for Troy's caress.

"We can't ever do it again."

She would leave before morning came, she decided, and felt better for having finally made a decision. Let him wake up and search for her. It satisfied Dani to think of Troy Fontaine combing the camp with no success. She would cover her tracks so well he and Grady would never find her . . . if they looked.

Taken by a fit of temper, she rolled over, threw off the covers, and sat up. A blinding pain behind her eyes forced her to press both hands against the crown of her head. So fierce was the throbbing that Dani feared her skull would crack open.

"Can't sleep?"

At the sound of his voice, she nearly jumped clean out of her skin.

Troy sat not two feet away, leaning back against one of her own packs. The last glimpse she'd had of him was just after he'd followed her back to the campground and bade her good night.

"What are you doing here?"

His voice was deep, hushed. "I couldn't sleep, either."

"What makes you think I couldn't sleep?"

She heard him chuckle. "I figured since that hide came from a long dead buffalo, it had to be you rolling around over here." When she refused to comment, he reached out toward her, offering her a cup. "I've found that a bit of what ails you helps numb the pain."

She sent one quelling glance in his direction, and he lifted the cup to his lips and swallowed the whiskey himself.

"Listen, Dani . . ."

"Where's Grady? Why isn't he here in the middle of the night pestering me, too?" Reaching down, she drew the cover back over herself.

"He's asleep." Troy pointed toward the campfire separated from hers by a few yards.

"Tell him I said good-bye." The words were out.

"Where will you go from here?"

She shrugged, then realized he couldn't see the gesture beneath the hide. "I don't know. Someplace. Anyplace."

"I'm sorry."

"Don't . . ." She held up a hand to silence him. Dani could not bear to hear him say he was sorry for what had been the most memorable hour of her life.

"This has changed everything," he said.

"How?" Hopeful, she faced him, a shadow in the darkness.

"For you. For the way you see yourself." Troy sighed. "Can you go back to being the way you were?"

"How was I?"

"Innocent. Free."

"And now?"

He didn't answer her. She knew the answer anyhow. Beneath the robe, she drew up her knees and hugged them. "I don't know what I am. Not because of you." She shook her head, "It was something starting before Jake died. I . . . I felt something different. I don't know what it was, but when Jake up and died, I didn't have time to think much about it. You two came along and found out about me, then those men at the cabin and Moze getting killed. Now this . . . you, tonight."

Troy moved within reach and drew Dani into the shelter of his arm. She didn't realize until that moment that tears were tracking down her cheeks. Ashamed of her weakness, she wiped at them with her sleeve. She didn't need this man to feel sorry for her.

"Is there no one to take care of you now, Dani? No one at all? I could help locate someone for you . . ." Troy rubbed the back of his neck with his free hand. How did one deal with this? Until now, he'd been involved only with experienced women, women who'd calculated every move of seduction, women he had not needed to feel responsible for. He felt every kind of a fool, sitting here in the middle of nowhere, holding tight to a wisp of a girl who should have meant nothing to him. Yet he couldn't bring himself to ignore her plight. As soon as this was settled, he promised himself, he would head for Louisiana and Dani would take her rightful place in his life—she'd be one more memory, like all the others.

"I'm not asking for your help," she told him, "and I don't need you feeling sorry for me."

"I know that."

"If things get real bad, there's always the damned letter."

"You really should try not to curse, Dani." It was a moment more before he asked, "What letter?"

"The letter to his partner. Jake said to look in the Bible and take the letter to St. Louie."

"Would you care to explain further?"

"Well, every season we send our share of the plew to Jake's partner in St. Louie. Sol credits our account and then sends out supplies with a trader who makes the circuit every season. It always worked that way. Jake preferred not to work for the big companies, but stayed a free trapper. 'Sides, he always said he could trust Sol."

"Have you read the letter?"

She shook her head. "Nope. Nor the Bible, either. Jake always said if I needed to know anything to look in the Bible, but all those little words just look like an army of ants marching across the paper to me."

"Do you still have this letter?"

"Sure. In the Bible."

A glimmer of hope began to shine for Troy. "May I see it?"

"Why?"

"I'm beginning to think you should take Jake's advice."

"I was dead set against going to St. Louie," she said, but she sounded less than sure.

"And now?"

"I don't know what I'm going to do. One thing's certain, though: I gotta get out of here for a spell." *Away from you*.

Silence stretched awkwardly between them. The noise had died down across the hollow and the sun would not be long in rising. Dani stiffened and brushed her hair out of her eyes. Troy withdrew his arm from her shoulders and cleared his throat.

"May I see your letter, Dani?"

"Why? You're just interested in helping me so as to ease your own mind. A body can sense these things."

"To ease my mind, then," he admitted. *If I can*.

"It's in the pack you're leanin' on. Feel around. It's near the right side."

Troy searched blindly through the bundles and tins in the bulky pack until his hands felt a book. Gently he slipped it out from beneath the staple goods and held it up to see it better. The Bible was old and worn, the corners of the once fine Moroccan leather cover now brittle and peeling.

He stood up and looked down at the huddled figure dwarfed by the shaggy robe. It would be easy to slip beneath the cover and take her in his arms to offer what comfort he could, selfishly seeking solace for his own troubled mind at the same time. But it was too near morning and there was far too great a chance that Grady or one of the drunken men would literally stumble upon them and discover Dani's identity and his own indiscretion.

No, it was best that he leave and put space between them, at least until he'd had time to search through her Bible for an answer to his self-imposed predicament.

"Good night, Dani. Try to get some sleep."

" 'Night, Fontaine."

He had not called her "pet."

She rocked back and forth, hugging her knees, and watched him walk toward his campfire. Suddenly she felt tired. Bone tired. Glancing toward the east, she figured there were a few hours left until sunrise. She stretched out again and before she finished tucking the hide under her chin, she drifted off to sleep.

Chapter Seven

The promise of fall whispered on the chilly wind that fanned the luminous yellow aspen, shaking down their leaves, leaving stark branches to stand barren against the landscape. The sky was heavily laden with low-lying gray clouds that hid the crests of the Tetons in the distance. Far below the clouds, the denizens of Hump Bone Hollow were greeting the new day.

Crawling out from beneath his blankets dressed in a long white nightshirt and wool socks, Grady Maddox shook his head and laughed when he caught sight of his friend. "Troy, to repeat a phrase I heard last, 'you look as limp as worn-out fiddle string.'"

"Thanks." Troy couldn't hide a smile when Grady so aptly described the way he felt. He had been awake all night.

Staring across the way at the girl's vacant campsite, Grady poured the last of a pot of coffee into his tin cup and swirled the steaming brew to cool it. "Looks like Dani's already out and about."

Tethered to a nearby tree, her horses and mule stood packed and ready for departure. Dani was nowhere in sight. Troy sat staring into the fire, oblivious of the gray morning and the activity around him. Dani had risen early and packed up her gear as he watched silently. He had pretended not to notice as she walked toward the center of the hollow, apparently bent on some last-minute business with the other trappers. Her rifle cradled in her arm, she left without sparing him even a backward glance. He supposed his sleepless night accounted for the heaviness around his heart.

Grady spooned up a portion of beans and then sat on his bedroll to eat. Between bites, he glanced over at Troy.

"We haven't really had time to talk since yesterday." The metallic sound of his spoon against the tin plate punctuated his words. "I looked for you two last night, but I couldn't find you, so I turned in. Everything all right with Dani?"

"Sure." A sense of unease began to creep over Troy. What was Grady hinting at? Could he know what had happened at the stream?

"That was a great ploy yesterday, telling her we were lost just so she'd let us travel along with her."

"It was the truth. We *were* lost."

"You're kidding. How could we be lost?"

"Just as she said. The map was all wrong. I was lost."

"Is she still intending to go off on her own, or is she meeting someone here?"

Troy shrugged. "I don't know what she's going to do, but there's no one here she plans to trap with."

"She's enamored of you, you know." Leaning forward, Grady helped himself to more beans, then continued. "I saw that right away."

Troy cocked a brow and stared. "What makes you say that?"

Grady smiled, gave Troy a wise, all-knowing look, and then shrugged. "Simple. I'm an artist. It's my business to notice every nuance of expression." He went on to explain. "Dani watches you when you aren't aware of it, and she stiffens up as if she's on guard when she's around you. There are lots of little hints, but mostly I can see her feelings in her eyes."

Amazed by his friend's disclosure, Troy stood and shook his head, then stretched. He bent to pick up the Bible he'd left on the ground near his blankets.

"What about you, Grady?" He flipped through the book as he watched his friend eat. "Aren't *you* a bit enamored of her?"

"Beneath those filthy buckskins is a real beauty, and I admire her courage," Grady admitted. "But you know me, Troy. I'd never stand a chance competing with you for a woman, especially one like Dani. I'd never be able to hold on to her." Without a trace of envy in his voice he added, "You, on the other hand, are just the type of man she needs."

Gravely, Troy shook his head in disagreement. "No woman needs to be tied up with me, Grady. You of all people know that."

"Why not? You're handsome. You have a sense of adventure and daring about you that's no doubt an inheritance from your pirate grandfather."

"My *only* inheritance from him."

"In a few years your business will be thriving."

"You know I can't and won't make any definite plans for the future until the past is settled. Devereaux might have located Reynolds by now." Troy looked off toward the east, wondering what news awaited him. He shrugged as his mouth twisted into a sad half-smile. "Maybe I'm not capable of caring enough to make a commitment to anyone."

Grady slammed his plate down on the ground in a rare show of impatience. "That's the way you see yourself, Troy. I know different."

"The way I see myself is the reality, Grady, not an illusion."

"Why haven't you left me out here and gone home, then? I know you wanted to be back in Louisiana two months ago."

"Don't remind me."

Grady knew enough to change the subject. "Dani's definitely not my type of woman, but I am concerned about what's going to become of her." He stood and began to pile his plate with cooking utensils. "I don't think she'll come with us, but I'm prepared to offer to take her home to Boston with me. My sisters would like nothing better than to take her under their wing."

It wasn't difficult in the least for Troy to imagine Grady's passel of young sisters—a flurry of ribbon, lace, and ringlets—fussing over Dani. What he could not envision was Dani allowing it.

"I think I may have found a solution," Troy began, "if she'll agree to it."

"Ah." Grady smiled knowingly. "The beast with no heart has been up all night seeking an answer to a problem that doesn't concern him." He sat down beside Troy. "I see you've taken to reading the Bible, too."

"Do you want to hear this or not?"

"Please"—Grady waved him on, bowing like a courtier—"proceed."

When Troy shot him a dark look, Grady only smiled evenly in return. Troy lifted the Bible. "It seems as if our little wayfarer's real name is Danika Hope Whittaker. Her birth is the last entry recorded in this Bible. April second, 1812."

"That makes her . . . eighteen," Grady calculated. "I'd have guessed sixteen."

"She comes from a long line of Whittakers, and all of them hail from New York or Philadelphia. Her father's name was Henry Whittaker. Her mother, as far as I can make out, appears to have been from Norway or Sweden. Her name was Inga Jergusen. That would account for the name Danika." Troy handed Grady the Bible, and the big man bent over to inspect the writing on the foreleaf of the book.

Troy continued to unravel Dani's history. "There's no mention of anyone called Jake Fisher, the man Dani told me was like a father to her."

"Do you think we could take her to New York or Philadelphia to search for her relations?"

"No, I don't think we need to go that far, but we can get her to St. Louis where this Jake's partner lives."

Leafing through the book, Troy found and removed a sheet of parchment and unfolded it. The paper was fragile and yellowed with age.

Carefully executed spidery script covered the page, the words a mute testimony to the man who had penned the lines. In silence, Troy listened while Grady read the letter aloud.

" 'To Solomon Westburg, St. Louis. Be it known to you, Solomon, when you read this missive that I'll have passed on to the final chapter of my story. You've served me well, old friend, over these past years, and I know you'll execute this, my final request. Be the bearer of this letter a girl who calls herself Dani, give her all of the holdings I have accrued over the years. I know you'll see she gets her due.

" 'This be the child I wrote you of finding around the year of 1816 or 1817. I look upon her as my own blood and pray that you will, too, being as fair minded toward her as you were to me. With every wish for your continued good health and prosperity, I remain your friend, Jake Fisher.' "

Grady sat back and continued to stare at the letter. "What do you make of it?"

"Just what it says. There's some money held in trust for Dani in St. Louis, probably not much, but this Westburg is a tie to Jake Fisher. I'll bet he'd be willing to help Dani find her family. If you put the information written in the Bible together with the letter, it seems easy enough to understand."

Caught up in the story, Grady expanded upon Troy's

thought. "This Jake must have found her, or taken her from her folks, when she was around four years old and then raised her himself. But what I can't fathom"—he shook his head—"is what she was doing way out here in 1816. It doesn't seem possible."

"Possible or not," Troy countered, "we have an eighteen-year-old white girl on our hands who may or may not have family somewhere who're wondering what became of her. I think she deserves a better existence than this."

Silent, Grady took in the myriad colors in the valley—the red and yellow aspen against the green hills, the blue-gray mountain range beyond the ridge—and then inhaled the clean, dry air.

"Is this so bad an existence?"

"Not for a man, not for a woman with a man maybe"—Troy shrugged—"but for Dani, it won't be easy. It'll be backbreaking, butt-busting work. She'll either give in finally and ride with one of these half-wild crazy men or she'll end up getting killed and dying all alone."

"So we have no choice but to encourage her to join us." Grady looked skeptical.

"Dammit, Grady, I wish to hell we did, but I'm afraid I feel responsible for her." He stopped himself from adding "now."

"No more than I, Troy."

A lot more than you, Grady.

Troy refolded the parchment and slipped it back into the Bible. "It appears Dani's packed up to move out, so I suggest we make ready before she gets a jump on us."

"Troy . . ." Grady stopped him in midstride, and Fontaine turned to face his friend. The heavyset blond's expression was open and honest, as always. "I know you've been ready to head back for a couple of weeks now. You know me; I'd be content to wander around out here forever without sense enough to come in out of the rain. But after the sketches I did last night and the other scenes I've captured, I'm willing to go back, too, and really put them together. My mind's brimming over with scenes to paint."

Waiting expectantly, Troy knew that Grady would eventually get to the heart of the matter.

"I just wanted to thank you, Troy, for putting up with me all this time and getting us through this."

Embarrassed by his friend's show of sincerity, Troy waved him away and turned to collect his blankets.

"We aren't back yet, Grady. There's a lot of tough miles between here and St. Louis." *A lot of long nights to face if Dani comes along.*

Grady took another deep breath before he set to work. "I know everything's going to work out, though. I can feel it in my bones."

"I hope so, Grady." *I sincerely hope so.*

Rendezvous had ended. Tepees had already come down, and a long line of travoises slanted southward, following the Snake out of the hollow. Beneath a sky cast in pewter gray, Dani roamed the campground, saying good-bye to her friends as she made a last bid for trade goods.

This morning she had felt compelled to purchase various and sundry goods she didn't really need but felt she surely wanted. She didn't need the new low-cut moccasins, intricately beaded with an arrowhead design, for which she traded two ermine pelts, nor did she need the extra sack of sugar she bought for two dollars a pound, mountain. But she *wanted* them. Just as she wanted the soft white doeskin garment she now carried carefully rolled beneath her arm.

She made her way to Enrique Dominguez's campsite. As Dani suspected, he, too, was nearly packed and ready to ride out. She stood back and watched the dark-skinned trapper as he cinched tight one of the many bundles of goods he was packing on his long string of mules.

Rumor had it Enrique had ridden into the rendezvous with twenty-two packs of beaver pelts. At over one hundred pounds a pack, he had collected somewhere near eighteen hundred pelts last spring, which made Rique a rich man, for what such wealth was worth in the Rockies.

"Headin' on, Rique?"

He flashed her a wide, toothsome smile and then returned to his work. "Shore am, Dani, and you best be at the same thing. Won't be nothin' left 'round here in an hour but low-lifes that are about as sociable as a bad tooth and too drunk to move. Them, an' the Injuns are lookin' for trouble."

Now that the three-day drunk had ended, the liquor had ceased to flow, except around the camps of the few stragglers. Dani had passed one such group who had induced a few young

Shoshone bucks to perform tribal dances in exchange for liquor. As the whoops and cheers became louder, the gyrations had become wilder and Dani opted to skirt past the group in search of Enrique.

"I need some trap springs and gun flints, if you got any t' spare. The best I can give ya for 'em is these here moccasins or a gold piece." Dani held out the beaded shoes and then tapped the pouch on her belt, which held the coin.

"Seein' as how I got 'bout as much need for the mocs as I do for the gold, how's 'bout I jes' credit them to ya, boy, till next spring?" Rique wandered down the line of mules until he reached the pack that contained the items Dani needed.

She followed close on his heels. "That'd be right generous of ya, Enrique. Unless, o' course, you want to play a fast game o' hand for 'em?" Dani peered up at him from beneath her hat brim with a glint of challenge in her eye.

"Naw." Rique squinted, then spat far off to the right. "Let's just leave it at that an' remember to use the goods as a stake next spring."

As he counted out the items she needed, Dani stared down at his gnarled hands. His nails were ragged, encrusted with years of grease, guts, and grit. She thought of Troy's long, tapered fingers. His hands, too, showed the wear of a rugged life, but his nails were smoothly trimmed and clean, the half-moons visible at their base. Mesmerized, she stood watching Enrique's hands, dwelling on thoughts of another's and what those hands could do to her, could make her do in return.

Dani shook off the memories and lifted her gaze, only to find Rique staring down at her.

"Ya miss Jake, don'tcha, boy?"

"Sure," she admitted, quickly averting her gaze.

"Dani, if ya want to ride along with me, I could use ya."

She knew Enrique was making the grandest gesture a mountain man could offer. A man might condescend to haul along a squaw, but hardly ever did a trapper want to live and work with another man. Winter confined a man to close quarters. It was hard enough to spend the winter with a woman, let alone to endure male companionship. For the most part, the men of the Rockies had come west to get away from the encumbrances of civilization. One had to love to be alone if one was to live for months without seeing another human soul, so Dani knew how much it meant for Rique to offer to put up with her company. It was a show of friendship, but she would not take advantage of him.

"Thanks, Rique, but I'll be tryin' t' go it by myself." When he visibly relaxed at her words, Dani was sure she'd made the right decision.

"Well, then, you take care, Dan, and I'll see you next year, the Lord willin'."

"Same here. Take care, Rique." As she started to leave, Dani turned and called back, "Has Billy left?"

"Irish was up and gone before dawn, I hear. Like I say, Dani, you best be headin' out, 'cause all's that's left is the dregs!"

"Bye, Rique!"

With a wave that was far jauntier than she felt, Dani headed for her own camp. As she drew nearer, she recognized Troy and Grady, still occupying the site they'd claimed the night before, the one too near her own. They looked to be packed and ready to move out, but sat as if waiting for her to join them. Dani wished she'd lit out earlier and hadn't left enough tracks to trip an ant.

Slowing her pace, she tried to act as if she hadn't noticed them sitting there like two puffed toads on a log.

Holy hot shit. Keep walking, she warned herself. *Don't look at them.*

Her hands shook as she tried to untie the pack on Jake's horse. She stuffed her purchased goods inside and retied the heap. Her powder horn and shot bag she quickly slipped over her head. Then, after checking to see if her pistol was secure in her belt, she untethered the animals. Her palms were sweating, her mouth was dry, and there was an annoying itch behind her eyes that threatened to fill them with tears. She rammed her rifle into its scabbard and picked up the reins.

The sound of horses moving up behind her was unmistakable, but, she could not bring herself to turn and bid them farewell, especially Troy. This was the end of it. The end of the beginning. She would never see him again.

"Dani, we have to talk to you."

Naturally, it was Grady's voice she heard behind her, not Fontaine's. She steeled herself and felt as primed as a rifle ready to explode.

"What is it?" She mounted, then turned to face them.

Grady sat his horse squarely for a change, and Dani met his open smile with a nod. He was rigged up in one of his woolen suits—this one was brown—and over it he wore a capote with a fur collar. His gray hat was perfectly formed and seated on the crown of his head. A pack mule laden with art supplies trailed behind him.

It was harder to face Troy. She hadn't seen him since late last night when he'd left her alone in the darkness. The shadow of a day's growth of beard darkened the lower half of his face. His lips were set in a crooked line, a half-smile playing upon them. He stared back at her from beneath slightly arched ebony brows. His eyes never wavered as he met her gaze. The creases around them seemed deeper. He looked tired. Although he was dressed in buckskins once again, he wore a white homespun shirt beneath his jacket.

When the tears that had threatened to fill her eyes did just that, Dani bent over the side of her horse and pretended to adjust her stirrup. Hidden from view, she hastily wiped away the telltale tears.

"I came to return your Bible, Dani."

The sound of Troy's voice and her name on his lips knifed through her as Fontaine sidled up close enough to hand her the book she had nearly forgotten. She stuffed it in her possible with a quiet "Thanks."

"I read the letter and the words inscribed in the Bible," he explained.

Dani stared at him, watching his lips, failing to hear a word he spoke.

"We think it'd be in your best interest if you'd come with us as far as St. Louis, Dani," Grady added.

"*My* best interest?"

"Yes." He nodded. "You may have family in the East who're searching for you. You owe it to them to at least try to locate them."

"I *owe* them?"

"I think so." Grady nodded.

"*I* don't. I don't even know who they are. I don't owe anybody anything." She turned to Troy again as she slowly emphasized her next words, "And I'm sick and tired of you two buttin' into my life and stirrin' me up!"

"Dani—" Troy began to protest, but he barely got her name out before the sound of gunshots reverberated through the hollow. War whoops and hair-raising howls followed, and the trio looked up to find a dozen mounted, none too sober Shoshone headed in their direction.

"Ride!" Troy bellowed, grabbing Dani's reins and pulling her red horse along behind him. Thankful that she'd tied Jake's horse and pack mule to her own, she instinctively ducked and clung to both her pommel and the horse's mane. Hooves pounded beneath her, churning up the ground as Troy led them all down the hollow toward the south. They had a good half-mile lead on the bucks before Dani spun around to see if Grady was still close behind her. Somehow the pack mule trailing him had broken free and Grady had veered off to the right after it.

"Stop!" she called out to Fontaine, but he thundered on. "Troy! Stop!"

Dani managed to yank her pony's reins from Troy's hand. Instantly responding to the commanding pressure of her knees, her pony veered off after Grady. She reached into her boot for her knife and leaned back to slice the rope holding her own pack animals. They could be retrieved later on. Grady's life could not.

Closing the gap between herself and Grady, she called out to him just as a Shoshone brave pulled within gunshot range. As the artist turned at the sound of her voice, she raised her pistol, primed and ready, and took aim. Grady ducked instinctively at the sight of the gun pointed directly at him and the bullet whistled overhead, burying itself in the brave not three feet from them.

Grady pulled his own rifle from its scabbard and, as he did, fell off his horse and landed in a heap on the ground. Dani thundered to a halt and dismounted beside Grady's sprawled form. Tugging on the reins again, she commanded her horse to lie down. Using the animal for cover, she drew her rifle and fired at the four approaching riders.

Another buck fell.

Grady fired and hit a third.

Seeing three of their number lying wounded, the others, even in their drunken state, opted to give up the chase and turned back up the valley with a show of bravado, hooting and calling just out of gunshot range. Within minutes, they, too, had disappeared.

"Thanks, Dani."

She rolled over to face Grady, who was stretched out on his stomach beside her.

"You can shoot," she said, still amazed.

"That's one thing I can do . . . besides wash and paint, that is." Despite everything, his face was lit by his wide smile. Dani found her heart softening toward this kind, open man. They continued to lie there, side by side, chatting amiably as they tried to catch their breath.

"I must say, I'm grateful for your talents, too," he admitted.

Dani sat up and brushed the leaves and dirt off of her jacket. She slapped her horse's rump and it stood up. "What were you going after that cussed mule for, anyhow?"

"It's got all my sketches on it, my paints, my easel."

"They worth your hide?" she wanted to know.

He paused for a moment. "Yes. I think they are."

"If you two are finished chatting down there, I think it's high time you got up."

They looked up at Fontaine like two naughty children. He remained astride his stallion and imperiously stared down at them. Grady and Dani glanced at each other and attempted to hide their smiles.

"Sorry, Troy," Grady apologized. "I got carried away."

"You damn near got yourself killed and her along with you!" Furious, Troy dismounted, his features dark with rage. He strode toward them. "Dammit, Grady. What fool thing are you going to pull next? Look at that saddle!" Troy thrust his forefinger in the direction of Grady's horse. The saddle hung nearly between its legs and even the horse had the good sense to look embarrassed. Grady only smiled from ear to ear.

Dani watched the strange exchange between the two men and wondered who in the almighty heaven Troy Fontaine thought he was, anyway? All the pent-up fury she'd buried, and her jumbled reaction to Troy, boiled to the surface. She stepped forward to challenge him.

"Who in the hell do you think you are, yelling at him that way?"

"I"—Troy jammed his thumb at his own chest— "am in charge of this expedition, and that means *I'm* responsible for *his* worthless life." They stood nose to nose as he continued to bellow down at her. "Therefore, *I'm* the one who charges after him, and *I'm* the one to risk *my* neck to save him, *not you*. *You* are to do as you are told until we get to St. Louis."

"And who says I'm going to St. Louie?" she screamed back at him.

"I do!" Troy bellowed.

"Me, too," Grady added, still smiling at Troy's rage.

"And why is it you're so all-fired bent on taking me to St. Louie?" She had Troy backed into a snare and planned to keep him there.

"Because!" he shouted. "Because—"

"Because we don't know the way," Grady finished for him. Dani blinked. "What?"

"He's right," Troy finally answered in his normal, husky tone. "We're lost, remember?"

"I'll fix your map. You'll be all right." Dani felt her pulse return to normal.

"Oh, sure," Grady pressed, "we'll be all right until we make the first wrong turn."

"I've never been beyond the South Pass, but everybody knows you just follow the Platte from there until you come to the Missouri. Then it's on down the river to St. Louie."

Troy played his last card. "Don't you think you owe it to Jake to meet his partner, Sol, and tell him how Jake died and collect the money he's been saving for you?"

"What else have you got to do this winter?" Grady wanted to know.

"Holy hot shit," she swore softly. There was no fighting these two.

Grady blanched at her choice of words.

Troy knew they'd won.

"What's wrong with you?" she asked Maddox.

"Nothing . . . but I don't think I've ever head a woman say anything like that before."

"You mean to tell me the women where you come from don't cuss a blue streak?"

"I'm afraid not," he admitted.

"It seems they've got a lot to learn."

"Give us a chance to help you, Dani," Grady said seriously. "You can always come back."

Dani knew there was no going back. Nothing could change what had passed between her and Troy Fontaine last night. Could Grady guess what she and Troy had done? She assumed Grady had no idea; at least, she hoped he didn't have. She studied Fontaine's cool exterior and was amazed to see how quickly his temper had quieted after his outburst.

"What about you?" she asked Troy straight out. "How do you feel about having me along?"

"How do *you* feel about it?"

"I'm only going as far as St. Louie," she reminded him. "Then I'll travel alone."

"Only as far as St. Louis," Troy agreed. Weeks on the trail, knowing that beneath her rough clothing her skin was as soft and smooth as silk. Living with the knowledge that she had come to life under him, and that she could again.

Only as far as St. Louis.

And what then?

Grady sighed audibly, relieved that the crisis had passed and they could finally be on their way.

Retrieving her rifle, Dani moved away from the men to collect her horse and pack animals. They watched her move out of earshot. Then Troy turned to Grady.

"What's so damned funny?"

"Nothing." Grady grinned, raising one brow. "Nothing at all. It's just that, for a man who claims he doesn't care about anything, you certainly got upset when Dani was in danger. Better watch yourself, Troy. You might discover something I've known about you all along."

The artist walked away without a backward glance, leaving Troy to stare sullenly after him.

They were on the trail within the hour, having found the pack animals grazing not far afield. Dani followed along behind Troy. Grady brought up the rear, trailing the pack mules behind him. Troy called a halt at the top of the first ridge they climbed, and the three dismounted and stood staring back at the grandeur of the scene behind them.

"We should reach the pass day after tomorrow," Dani estimated, but her mind was miles away, remembering Big Jake and the dugout she'd known as home.

She stared off into the distance, wondering how she could even think of leaving the Rockies. It was all a mistake. Troy moved beside her, touched her lightly on the shoulder, and drew her attention back to the moment. Dani was arrested by the fleeting look of understanding she saw in his eyes. If she could but dare to hope that someday soon Troy might see in her what he sought in a mate, then perhaps that glimmer of hope would carry her through the next few weeks on the trail with him. After all, she admitted to herself with pride, she was a skilled hunter and trapper. Why couldn't she put her talent to work on Troy Fontaine?

Buoyed by the thought of the challenge before her, Dani turned away from the river valley and mounted up.

"At lest we're well protected," she said, calling upon her sense of humor to ease the sadness of missing Jake that lingered around her heart like the clouds that shrouded the mountain peaks.

"What makes you say that?" Grady wanted to know.

"Fontaine's Fighting Forty," she explained.

"Who?" Grady asked.

"Fontaine's Fighting Forty."

Fontaine laughed aloud. At the unfamiliar sound, Dani felt the clouds about her heart begin to lift. Troy went on to explain the trick he'd played on Dani to obtain Grady's release. She then told them how she, too, had mentioned the Fighting Forty when she was threatened by Ed and Abner.

"I was stalling for time, so I told those two men at Moze's cabin that I was a scout for Fontaine's Fighting Forty." She turned a bright smile in Troy's direction and was rewarded by the warm glow of admiration in his eyes. "I had no idea you'd really turn up."

"But we did," Grady said.

"So, like I said," she repeated, "I feel real safe with Fontaine's Fighting Forty riding along with me."

But only as far as St. Louie, her heart reminded her.

Only as far as St. Louie.

Chapter Eight

Hidden in the midst of the Rockies was the Great South Pass, the gateway to the vast prairie. For a time the trio despaired of reaching it, yet each continued to reassure the others that in no time at all it would be found.

Troy swore by the maps and accounts in his possession; the Great South Pass was clearly marked on each. The problem was that it had been placed in a different location on every map, a mere notation made at the whim of the mapmaker. He sat before the fire at night jotting entries in his log and straining to read the words in the various texts he referred to, often quoting Nicholas Biddle's 1814 accounts of Lewis and Clark's journal. In a piece published in 1810, Zeb Pike likened the prairie to Africa. As Troy read the passage aloud, Dani asked if they would pass through Africa on the way to St. Louis. Grady tried to hide his smile while Troy merely shot her one of his dark, silent glances, drew a map of the entire world from his leather pack, and methodically introduced her to world geography.

Dani claimed she held no store by Fontaine's "flimsy, paltry maps," which so far had proved highly inaccurate. When he argued that all the features were indeed noted, she agreed, only to add that they were not likely to be anywhere near where they actually existed.

"I don't know how you ever found the Rockies!" she finally admitted, sorrowfully shaking her head over the map Troy was consulting. "If you're so all-fired worried about getting to St. Louis, it seems to me you'd have sense enough to just follow a river toward the sunrise. You'll likely get someplace. No trick to it. Why, hell's fire," she shouted before she recalled Grady's sensitivity to her cursing, "that danged map by that Clark fella has the Rockies pictured as one big hump. You said yourself it was at least two hundred miles outta place!"

When Dani noticed the worried expression on Grady's face and Troy's look of impatience, she assured them that there was indeed a Great South Pass, but she needed no map to tell her so. She was sure of it simply because Big Jake had said there was one.

Grady, with his usual exuberance, declared at the start of each new day that they would come across the pass by nightfall, and when they did not, he assured them it was probably just one more day's ride away.

Finally they found the pass and left the mountains behind. To Dani it seemed as if the Rockies watched her leave in stunned disbelief until, disgusted, they turned their stark, unyielding faces to the west and silently slipped away.

On the east side of the pass, the land fell away into a deceptive wilderness of broken plains. Buttes and spires carved by wind, gullies and canyons eroded by water, stood in silent testimony to the ravages of time. Dani hated the barren windswept surface of the plain. Compared to the sculptured slopes of the mountains, blanketed with pine and aspen, colored by wildflowers, this place was a wasteland.

The earth was covered with stubborn sage. Dry and brittle, it broke free of the thin layer of soil to run ahead of the constant wind. Each time a tumbling bundle of sagebrush rolled past, Dani imagined it was only trying to escape the tedious sameness of the prairie landscape. She wished she could do the same.

It had become her habit to follow behind the men, her gaze pinned on a point between Troy's shoulderblades. The fringe across the yoke of his buckskin jacket swayed hypnotically, lulling her into a deep reverie. During those times, she was hard pressed to forget the man's touch, the way he had looked, lying naked in the starlight, and the wild, pounding response she had felt the night they joined together beside the stream. Traveling along the trail east was tiring in its sameness, especially as Dani was forced to pass the time staring at Troy and wishing things were different between them, but the days were certainly more to her liking than the nights.

Once, as they slept beneath the stars, Dani had been abruptly awakened by a harsh cry that shattered the stillness. Using her saddle for cover, she had instinctively reached for her rifle and rolled onto her stomach. It was Troy who had cried out, and fear for his safety overrode caution. She lifted her head and tried to see through the firelight.

"Fontaine?"

"It's all right. Go back to sleep."

"Sleep?" Dani was incredulous. "Sleep? You let out a scream that'd wake the dead and then tell me to go back to sleep?" She laid down her rifle and got to her feet. As she crossed the clearing and paused long enough to add a few dry twigs to the fire, she noted that Grady was still sound asleep where he sat, his back against a boulder. It was his turn at guard duty.

"I can't believe he slept through that," she said.

"He's used to it."

She reached Troy's side and knelt down. He sat hunched forward on his bedroll, elbows propped on his knees, rubbing his temples with his fingertips.

She placed a hand on his shoulder. "What is it?"

"Just a nightmare. It's been so long since I've had one, I'd hoped I was over them."

"You have them all the time?"

"Up until a few weeks ago."

"Why?"

"Why do I have them, or why did I stop?"

"Pick one," she said.

He shook his head. "It's nothing to worry yourself over. I'll take watch. Get some sleep while you can. It's nearly dawn."

It was easy to see that he was unwilling to offer further explanation, so Dani decided not to press him. Still, she felt she needed to try. "Troy?"

"Go back to sleep."

"You know, sometimes a man's burdens get lighter when he lets a friend help carry them."

"Is that another of Jake's proverbs?"

"It makes sense, doesn't it?"

Troy shrugged. "I don't know. I'll think about it."

She persisted. "How come you know everything about me and I know next to nothing about you, Fontaine?"

"Look"—he turned on her sharply, his dark eyes brooding in the fire's glow—"I said get some sleep."

Although she stood up and stomped back to her bedroll, it was hours before Dani could shake the memory of his anguished cry.

After that, Dani dreaded the darkness. During the day she was preoccupied with the rigors of the trail, but each evening after the sun disappeared beyond the horizon and the stars huddled in clusters against the great blanket of the sky, the tension grew between her and Troy. He seemed to hold it against her that she had witnessed his weakness, and to Dani, there seemed to be no way to talk to him about it again. Each evening she was forced to spread out her bedroll and sleep alone, staring across the fire at his shadowed form until sleep finally came.

Dani was beginning to feel as if her nerves were as tightly stretched as a piece of rawhide staked on a curing frame. Although Troy seemed to have put the night they mated out of his mind, she had been unable to accomplish the feat so easily. As the days and weeks on the trail mounted, so did her own need for him intensify. If Troy Fontaine felt any such need, Dani saw no evidence of it. He was polite, yet cold and distant toward her. If he was aware of her watchfulness, he gave no sign. Dani began to wonder if she had imagined their night of wondrous lovemaking beside the hot creek, but she knew she had not. Feelings long hidden beneath her boyish disguise, beneath her very flesh, had been awakened. They were feelings so overwhelming that Dani could no longer ignore them. She continually asked herself why Troy Fontaine had to be the one to set them aflame and how he could ignore the tension between them. She felt like a powder keg about to explode.

They traveled along the northern branch of the great forked river known as the Platte until it merged with its southern half and continued on, ever eastward. October became November.

As the cold weather set in, Dani took to sleeping in an easily constructed and comfortable shelter made of willow stakes and hides. Although the low, round-sided cocoon left little room for movement, she welcomed the privacy it afforded.

This morning, as Dani lay inside her shelter, she stared up at the crisscross stitches that held the skins together. Awake before dawn, she tried to force herself to rise, stir the campfire to life, and set the coffee to boil before the men awoke. Instead, she slipped deeper inside the thick, shaggy buffalo hides that served as her bedding. As she lay snuggled in the warm furs, she could hear the shallow water of the Platte as it meandered across the wide, flat prairie toward the Missouri, unencumbered by even so much as a riverbed.

Lately Dani found herself wondering if the river was as lost as she felt. She looked forward with growing trepidation to reaching St. Louis. After all, she reminded herself, she'd never seen an actual settlement, at least not one built to last. Moze's cabin was the only permanent shelter of any kind, besides her own dugout, that she'd ever entered. The thought of moving about in a strange environment scared her nearly spitless. For days now she had doubted her decision to travel with Troy Fontaine as far as St. Louis. More and more often, Dani found herself wishing she'd turned back before they left places familiar to her. But then she would look at Troy and wonder if there would ever come a time when she could just ride away from him.

What's happening to me?

Dani closed her eyes to the morning light creeping into her shelter and hoped she wasn't becoming as needful of Troy Fontaine as some men were needful of whiskey. It worried her that she wanted him so badly, even now, when the man didn't seem to care one whit that she was nearby. And wanting.

Yes, she knew she'd changed, but not for the better. This new Dani scared her, for as they traveled eastward, away from the mountains, she felt herself shrink and diminish, her outside self somehow drawn inward until she feared she would awaken one morning to find that the real Dani had disappeared altogether. Like the Rockies.

Everything she had known stood for little on the open plains. Even the long dried wildflowers of summer were unfamiliar. She thought of Jake and found herself missing him sorely. Would she have been able to talk to him about this muddle she'd gotten herself into? Dani doubted it, but then, had Jake lived, she wouldn't have found herself in such a predicament. Troy Fontaine was slowly driving her senseless, and it was a state she didn't relish being in at all.

With a sigh, Dani shook herself out of her pondering mood and threw back the covers. She knelt, unable to straighten her spine in the tiny tent, and pulled a thick wool Hudson Bay coat over her buckskins. The blanket coats had been a trade item since the fur company began, the style quickly adopted by trappers and Indians alike. She'd taken to wearing one of the gaily striped coats to ward off the icy chill carried on the ever-present wind. Cold weather stiffened her buckskins and caused her very bones to ache. Jake had suffered from the "rheumatiz," as he'd called it. The aches were a hazard all fur trappers faced, the result of time spent wading in the icy waters of mountain streams as they set their beaver traps. She hoped she wasn't coming down with a touch of rheumatiz herself.

"Dani?"

Troy called to her from outside her shelter. The sound of his voice made her start. He rarely spoke directly to her anymore.

"Comin'."

"No hurry. It's getting late and I just wondered if you were all right."

A smile lifted one corner of her mouth as she cocked her head toward the closed flap that was her door. "I'm fine. Just lazy, is all. Grady up?"

"Up and out. He'll be right back. Coffee's on and mush is ready to fry."

"I'll be right out," she called, trying hard to hide the pleasure in her tone. Maybe it was going to be a good day after all.

Dani quickly folded and rolled her bedding, tied it with sinew, and after pulling open the flap, tossed it out upon the frozen ground. She crawled out of the miniature dome and began to untie the ropes that held the semicircular willow hoops taut. In a matter of minutes her makeshift shelter was dismantled and loaded on her pack mule. Walking back toward the fire, she glanced up at the leaden sky and judged the clouds, then blew on her freezing fingers. Crossing her arms, she slipped her hands inside the cuffs of her coatsleeves.

Silently Dani watched Troy as he walked away from the fire to collect eating utensils from his pack mule. Both men had volunteered to cook rather than let Dani burn whatever they were going to eat. Grady had promised and Troy had agreed that if she would hunt, they would prepare the food.

Now, as she watched him gather his supplies, her eyes were drawn to his hair. It had grown longer over the past weeks and now hung nearly midway between his shoulders. It glistened blue-black in the sunlight, thick and luxuriant as the finest pelt. He wore it tied back with a leather thong, and Grady, who of course kept his tight blond curls neatly trimmed, claimed Troy reminded him of a pirate.

"Troy's grandfather was a pirate, you know," Grady had

informed her one evening as they sat before the fire passing the early hours of darkness before exhaustion forced them to turn into their bedrolls.

"How would I know that?" Dani had shrugged before she added, "What's a pirate?"

"A pirate robs ships on the high seas, or sometimes on the rivers—in this case, the Mississippi. Troy's grandfather was one of the best."

Dani remembered how Grady had closed his sketchbook to devote full attention to the story. "Philippe Fontaine built a home on an island in the bayou near Baton Rouge. Isle de Fontaine is still Troy's home. Before the old man had a waterway cut through the bayou leading to it, the island was well hidden and mysterious, a perfect pirate's lair. And an old legend says that a fortune in gold is still buried somewhere on the island."

"What happened to him?"

Grady's easy laughter filled the air. "Something the crusty old sea dog hadn't counted on: He fell in love and gave up being a pirate."

Dani had been thankful for the shadows and orange-gold glow of the fire that hid her sudden blush as her eyes caught and held Fontaine's. She had to agree that he did look quite like the pirate that Grady went on to describe. As she looked at Troy today, she was again reminded of the tale.

A month's growth of dark beard shadowed the lower half of his face, startlingly enhancing his dark, piercing eyes. His brows were straight, even slashes as black as his hair. His lips were nearly hidden by a full mustache, and on the increasingly rare occasions when he smiled, his teeth fairly gleamed, set off by the dark skin and hair surrounding them.

Instead of letting his hair hang free from a middle part as did many of the mountain men, Troy wore it smoothed back off his high, aristocratic forehead and tied, as it was today, in a queue.

It had been so long since they had spoken without using Grady as a foil that she longed to say anything to Fontaine in order to break the barrier of silence between them.

"Looks like there's a storm coming in." As soon as the words were out, she longed to call them back, for they sounded contrived.

"Yes, it does."

As he answered her, Dani was surprised by the unguarded

expression of warmth on his face. When he poured and handed
her a cup of coffee, she was not only surprised, she was
tongue-tied.

Dani let the steam from the rich, aromatic coffee warm her
chilled cheeks and nose before she blew on it. As she took her
first sip, she glanced up and caught Troy watching her. They
both quickly looked away. He moved back to the fire and set
a skillet over the hot coals. She watched as he cut up the
near-frozen slabs of cornmeal mush they'd cooked the night
before and slipped them into the melted buffalo fat in the
skillet. Her mouth began to water as she realized the cold night
had stoked her hunger. An unbidden thought came to mind, a
fleeting picture of Fontaine lying naked beneath the furs, his
warm body pressed against her own.

Dani caught the coffee cup just as it nearly slipped from her
fingers.

"I forgot the sorghum." He nodded toward the mules.

"I'll get it," she volunteered quickly, feeling the need to get
away and collect herself. By the time she returned, the jug of
syrup in her hand, Grady had come back from his morning
walk.

"Did Troy ask you yet?" the artist wanted to know.

"Ask me what?" She glanced at Troy, who was concentrating on the meal.

"We were wondering about the storm that's coming in, and
he wasn't sure whether we should move on or set up shelter
along the river." Grady knelt and poured his own coffee as he
continued, "I told him to ask you what you thought."

"He didn't ask," she told Grady.

Grady looked from one to the other and continued to stare at
Troy.

Troy shrugged. "I was going to." He paused to flip the
mush. It was evenly browned on the underside, and Dani
silently marveled at how he knew exactly when to flip it.

"But then," Troy began again, "I figured we'd have to hear
all about what Big Jake used to say before we got an answer,
so I thought we might just as well eat first."

"Well, in that case," Dani said, not one to ignore a
challenge, "Big Jake used to read bear grease."

Troy groaned none too silently as Grady handed him tin pans
to dish the fried mush onto.

Dani continued despite their reactions, talking as she moved

to sit cross-legged on the ground near the fire. "Big Jake"—
she gave particular emphasis to the name and watched Troy as
she did—"Big Jake used to keep bear fat in a glass bottle in
order to watch the weather. When the fat lay heavy on the
bottom of the jar, he said the weather wasn't likely to change
for two or three days." She looked at Grady and noted that
even though his face showed doubt, he hung on every word.
She leaned forward and used her hands as well, in imitation of
a yarn-spinning session with the mountain men. "When the fat
began to sort of mound up in the center or along the sides of the
bottle, you could expect a storm. If specks of dirt drifted above
the fat it meant wind. Now, just a few specks meant a light
breeze, but if there was lots of dust, it'd more than likely be a
real blow."

"Like Jake." Troy mumbled the words under his breath
before he passed her a filled plate.

"What about winter storms?" Grady wanted to know.

Dani paused long enough to chew and swallow a bite of the
heavenly fried mush bathed in sorghum. "When the grease
froze, you knew it was cold. Simple as that." She took another
bite and swallowed. "I'd say today was one of those days."

Grady's own plate was clean before he spoke again. "Do
you think we ought to travel?"

Dani looked at Troy. "What do you think?"

Glancing up from his plate, he met her eyes honestly and this
time did not shy away. "I think we're close to the Missouri.
I'm for making all the miles we can before a really big storm
hits. So far we've been lucky; we haven't been hampered by
deep snows. The Missouri can't be too much farther. Once we
reach it and begin heading south, we'll be nearly there."

"What do you think, Dani?" Grady asked anxiously.
"Should we go on, with this storm coming or should we dig
in?"

She studied the sky. It looked gray and leaden, heavy
enough to fall on them. The wind from the northwest had
picked up since she'd stepped out of her tent earlier. Dani
scanned the landscape. The Platte was a mile or more wide, the
shallow water little more than mud that slogged around and
past islands of cottonwood and willow trees, the same growth
that lined the river's edge. Toward the east, the land appeared
to rise some, and the bluffs along the banks might provide them
needed shelter.

Dani hesitated to give an opinion either way. She'd been determined to defer to Troy as leader ever since his outburst the day they left the Rockies together. He'd made it clear that he was in charge, and since that day he'd turned a cold eye in her direction. So be it, she thought, the man's mind was as hard to pin down as smoke in a bottle.

She reached out to collect Grady's plate and then bent to grab Troy's. "It's up to Fontaine." Dani shrugged. "We could make for that rise up ahead and see what's on the other side. Might make better shelter than this place, where we're pretty well out in the open."

Troy watched her for a moment, silently weighing her words. "Didn't Big Jake have a saying for a time like this?" he wanted to know.

Dani tried not to smile. She felt a sudden warmth when she realized he was teasing her.

"He did say, 'Once you make up your mind to do something, do it.'"

The warmth was replaced by a sudden chill as she watched Fontaine's expression darken again.

"Let's pack up." He stood and abruptly tossed the words over his shoulder without a backward glance.

Once you've made up your mind to do something, do it.
Jake Fisher's words sounded simple enough as Troy repeated them to himself until the old saying, "Easier said than done," echoed back. He had indeed made up his mind at the beginning of their journey. Troy was determined to put the night he'd made love to Dani out of his mind, but after two months of daily contact with her, he still found the task nearly impossible.

He rode ahead of her and Grady, scouting the trail, while his imagination teased him with fleeting remembered visions of Dani, her vibrant smile, the smoke-gray eyes that appeared almost silver whenever they shone with merriment.

"It's the way we do it out here," she'd declared the night she'd thrown herself into his arms. Troy knew he would never forget her spontaneity and unbridled enthusiasm for lovemaking, nor would he soon put the feel of her against him out of his mind, but he was determined to convince Dani that he had done so.

For her own sake.

Dani had been subdued and thoughtful lately, but during the first few weeks on the trail, the girl had remained undaunted. Nothing Troy had said or done could dampen her spirit. She loved to regale them with mountain lore. On the upper plains, just beyond the pass they sighted a time-worn peak jutting out above the landscape. Even before Troy could locate the landmark on his maps, Dani recognized it.

"I know about this!" she'd shouted in delight, pointing to the distant bluff.

As Troy made a notation of the location on his own map, Dani wove the colorful story of how the bluff had been named.

"Now, I'm not certain, mind you," she said, looking every bit the authority as she sat astride her red pony, head cocked to one side, silver-gray eyes focused on the bluff. "But I'll bet you a bundle of plew that's the very place where they found Hiram Scott's bones."

"His *bones*?" Grady looked at the wind-ravaged precipice with new respect.

"Yep. Hiram Scott took sick travelin' east with a party of trappers about two years back. It seems they left him here and kept right on goin'. Well, old Hiram managed to crawl to the base of that rock and there he died." Dani was silent a moment as she recalled further details. "On the way back, the trappers found his bones and named the bluff after him. I remember all the chaff spread around about it a couple o' years back."

That night the wayfarers had camped beneath the bluff. It had been a moonlit night, the stillness almost thick enough to cut with a buffalo knife, until a coyote shattered the eerie silence with a chilling howl. Troy remembered how Grady had nearly come out of his skin at the sound, but Dani merely laughed.

"You think that might be old Hiram Scott howling, Grady?" she'd teased.

"That's not funny." The artist shivered visibly.

"Is there anything you're afraid of, Dani?"

Troy could not resist asking, for the girl seemed to delight at any brush with danger. She claimed it did her heart good to dance around against her ribs once in a while, and then, her thoughts seemingly disconnected, she said, "Lizards. I hate 'em."

"Lizards?" Both Troy and Grady found it hard to believe that the girl would fear such a small harmless nuisance.

"I hate them," she repeated, shaking her head. "They aren't natural. More like a deformed frog, or a snake with legs . . . And those bugged-out eyes. Yucch!"

Troy smiled even now as he remembered her dramatic imitation of rolling lizard eyes. He halted his mount in order to wait for Grady and Dani to catch up to him. A light but steady snowfall had begun, the large, dry flakes sticking, but not yet covering the ground.

"Starting to snow," Grady commented unnecessarily when he reached Troy's side. "Think we should stop?"

Troy nodded to the rise just ahead. "There's an indication of a knoll. We could always hope for a ridge." He looked back and took note of Dani's position a few yards behind. She indicated with a wave that they should ride on ahead and not glance back for a time. It was a system they'd arranged so that she could see to her private needs. Troy waved to her in response and then turned to Grady.

"Ride up ahead. I'll lag behind and wait for her." He watched Grady's horse and pack mule amble past. Grady trusted no one else to lead the animal that was loaded down with his art supplies. The legs of Grady's easel protruded at odd angles from where it rode atop a mountain of bundled goods on the back of the mule.

Troy smiled and shook his head, reminding himself not to look back in Dani's direction. What a pair you've hooked up with, Fontaine, he thought as he stared ahead at his friend. His thoughts turned to Dani. He could not imagine traveling without her. Her presence was so natural, it seemed she had been with them since the beginning. She had yet to complain during the rigorous days of riding and the endless tasks required of her each evening as they set up camp. At first he'd waited for her to break down under the strain of the journey, until he realized that Dani's life had never been any easier. She expected nothing less than bone-wearying, muscle-straining work from dawn to dusk.

The girl had changed physically since he'd first seen her. She kept her face considerably cleaner now that she was free of the fear of discovery of her gender. Dani had taken to scrubbing her face every morning in the icy river water, and her skin was aglow with a healthy radiance. Her hair had grown, too. A rich mahogany color, it was tinted with sun-lightened red tones that sometimes appeared streaked with gold. Grady had offered to trim the uneven ends one day as he carefully groomed his own hair, but Dani had vehemently refused.

"Any cuttin' to be done on me, I do it," she warned.

Grady had not asked again.

Dani seemed to be filling out some, as well. Her already feminine curves were even more apparent when she bent over in her tight buckskins.

He watched for signs that she might be carrying his child, but guessed that her woman's time had come shortly after their first month together. Dani had been unusually cross and irritable, wandering off the trail more often in order to see to her needs. One evening, noting the shadows of fatigue etched beneath her eyes, he had longed to ask if she needed anything, but held back, knowing Dani well enough to realize it was best to let her tend to herself. Troy was certain that calling attention to her feminine needs would only serve to embarrass and irritate her more. He rested easier then, knowing she was not with child and yet somehow experiencing a fleeting sense of loss. Nothing bound him to her now except regret. That, and a deep, aching need.

Troy scanned the rise that was just ahead of them now. The snow was still falling steadily, thick flakes that clung to his eyelashes and the collar of his jacket, where they soon melted and ran down his neck. One hand on the reins, he used the other to free the heavy wool coat that was rolled and tied to the pommel of his saddle. Careful not to spook his horse, he drew his coat slowly over his shoulders and slipped his arms into the sleeves. He then pulled the brim of his hat lower on his forehead and turned up his collar. Reaching into the pocket of his coat, Troy pulled out the fur-lined mittens Dani had made for him.

As he drew on the mittens, he thought of the night ahead and knew they would be forced to sleep in their tents. The feeling of disappointment he experienced surprised him, and with it came the realization that he had become used to the peaceful nightly routine the three of them had so easily assumed. Somehow they all meshed together during the dark hours of early evening, absorbed in their own tasks as they shared the fire's warmth. Dani always seemed to have unending hours of handiwork to perform. She braided lariats from long lengths of dried deerhide, and she stitched pelts together into simple but effective mittens. While she mended and repacked her supplies, she sang or spun long nostalgic tales of Big Jake, Enrique, Irish Billy, Old Moze, and countless other mountain men she knew. In the beginning her tales had seemed to ease her grief at the loss of Jake Fisher and the way of life she'd left behind. Through her storytelling, Troy began to know the man Dani spoke of so often, and he soon admitted to himself that Big Jake must have been an extraordinary figure. Fontaine found that he regretted never having met the man who'd taught Dani so much.

Grady used the evening hours to sketch and sometimes to paint. Dani had become a great source of encouragement to the young artist. She often slapped her hands against her thighs and exclaimed with delight over the sketches he produced of the men and Indians he and Troy had encountered. One evening, as she looked through his sketchbook, quietly lost in thought, Dani had come up with a question: "Do you think you could make a likeness of Jake if I was to tell you what he looked like?"

For three consecutive nights, the two of them had worked with heads together in the dim firelight. Dani described Jake as Grady drew, then told him how to alter the sketch until she was satisfied with the result. Troy had watched in silence when Dani's eyes misted as she gazed down at the picture in her hands. The next morning she looked at it again, then carefully folded it. She carried the drawing safely tucked inside her jacket.

As Troy watched Dani and Grady working together to compose the sketch, he had realized how well the girl and the artist were suited to each other. Grady was sincere and sensitive, and Troy guessed he was attracted to Dani. Troy knew for certain that Grady's family was warm and welcoming. His sisters would love Dani just as she was, and at the same time they would help make a lady of her. From that night on, Troy had become even more determined to discourage Dani's affection, hoping to turn her heart in Grady's direction.

At first, it had been hard for Troy to maintain his stony silence, especially in the face of Dani's lightheartedness. Lately, though, she had become withdrawn, her spirit visibly dampened. Troy was not certain whether she was reacting to his icy demeanor or to her own anxiety as they grew nearer to St. Louis. Instead of feeling relieved, he found himself growing miserable with his own success.

The cold, austere attitude was no longer hard to maintain, for as the number of days and nights on the trail in Dani's company mounted, so did his own tension. He longed to experience again the splendor he'd known the night he had initiated Dani to the art of lovemaking. Unbidden images and feelings he sought to ignore plagued him. The forced intimacies they shared on the trail only made him all the more aware of the near-impossible task he had set for himself.

Somehow, he vowed, he would manage to keep up the ruse, to keep his eyes off her, to keep his hands from reaching out to her, and most of all, he'd try to quell the deep longing that was becoming an all-consuming ache within him.

Aware that the snowfall had grown heavier in the last few moments, Troy pulled down his hat to shield his eyes from the swirling flakes. He called out to Grady who had already reached the slight rise.

"I'm going to bring Dani up closer," Troy shouted to his friend before he turned and rode back to collect the girl, who had fallen behind. "We need to stop and set up shelter!" he shouted.

"What?" Dani called out before she realized the blurred figure she saw through the falling snow was riding toward her. Her voice carried on the still air, although it seemed as if the words should have been muffled by the heavy, swirling flakes. Instead, sound was intensified. Her leather saddle creaked with each rocking movement of the horse, the pans and other metal equipment hanging from the pack mules clinked and clanked continually. The animals' hooves struck the earth, beating out a tattoo that had lulled Dani into a trance until she saw Troy approach. During the last few hours the world had changed from a panorama of color to a landscape shrouded in white. The sky seemed to be nearly upon them now, as soft, swirling snowflakes came at her from every direction but up. Troy reached her side and turned his mount in order to keep pace beside hers. His eyes held the only sparkling warmth in the bleak whiteness, and Dani found herself longing to lose herself in his heated gaze.

"I said, we need to pull up. What do you think?"

For a moment she was surprised that he had sought her advice.

"I think you're right. The sooner the better." Dani strained to see the trail ahead. Grady had disappeared over the slight rise in the land. When she looked at Troy, she found that although he was but a few feet from her, he'd become barely visible. She glanced back in the direction from which they had traveled, then nudged her red horse forward, picking up speed.

"Where's Grady?" she asked as she pressed ahead.

"I called out to him to wait," he answered. Then there was a brief lull and Dani knew that Troy was searching for some sign of his friend. "Grady?" he shouted.

The voice that answered sounded even more distant.

"Where are you two?"

They heard Grady's voice, a disembodied sound that drifted to them over the snowy landscape.

"Stay put!"

"Don't move!"

Dani and Troy called out together, then glanced at each other again.

"What?" Grady called back.

The sound came from farther away.

Troy stood in his stirrups and bellowed. "Stop!"

When they reached the top of the rise, they were unable to see how high it rose above the riverbank. The snow was a thick blanket of white that enfolded them and hid Grady from their sight.

"Hey, where are you two?"

Grady's voice was growing fainter, and could have come from anywhere.

Troy tugged at Dani's arm to get her attention as she sat intent upon gauging the direction Grady had taken. Squinting, straining to see through the dizzying snowfall, she had little success. When she looked at Troy, she read the fear and concern shadowing his expression.

"Stay behind me with the mules." His words were a sharp command.

"We ought to stay by the river." She knew as long as they kept the river to their left they would have a point of reference. "We should stop and set up camp."

"We have to find Grady first."

"What we're going to do is get us all lost. Look around you, Troy. There aren't even any tracks left."

She waited for realization to dawn on him. There were no longer any signs that would help them locate the artist.

Troy raised his face to the sky. "Grady?" he called again.

This time there was no answering call. Dani's stomach felt as if it had dropped to her knees and was slowly crawling back up again. She could not bear to look at Fontaine, but knew she had to.

This time Dani issued her own command. "Head to the left, toward the river. There'll be enough deadwood along the bank to build some sort of a shelter." She turned her horse in the direction of the Platte and waited for his response.

"What are you doing?" His lips were taut with anger, his eyes disbelieving. "We can't move away from Grady."

"He's already out of shouting range. We can't save him if we lose ourselves." She tried to see again in any direction and found herself defeated. "Listen, we're lucky there's no wind; the storm could be worse. As it is, the clouds are low and holding in some warmth. It might stop snowing any time now, but I suspect it won't clear till morning." Dani took a deep breath and continued, "If I know Grady, he's moving around out there, more than likely getting himself more lost. We don't need to be doin' the same."

Troy cursed silently to himself, staring off in the distance. As he sat weighing her words, Dani tried to locate any sign in the snow. When she moved away from Troy's side by only a few feet, visibility became so diminished that she was forced to return to him.

"Surely he'll set up some sort of shelter. He has his gear. We'll find him tomorrow morning, I just know it." She smiled as she tried to reassure Troy. "That's when the real cold will set in, when the clouds lift."

"I should have called him back before I turned around."

Dani felt the hurt mirrored in his eyes and knew that if anything happened to Grady, Troy Fontaine would never forgive himself.

She tried to lighten his mood.

"Shoot," she declared, "Grady knows he can't find his way out of the open end of a rifle barrel. He'll stop and set up for the night." When there was no response from Troy she added, "Come on, Fontaine. He'll be all right. You'll see."

Troy followed Dani as she moved nearer the Platte. He stopped on occasion to call out to Grady. She prayed they'd hear the man's answering shout.

There was no response.

Chapter Nine

"Here, take this."

Dani extended a steaming cup of coffee heavily laced with Jake's jug whiskey in Troy's direction. They'd worked without respite for over an hour to construct an intricate shelter that would keep them warm and dry.

It was an unspoken agreement that the shelter would house both of them, and although neither had said so, the need to stay together in light of Grady's disappearance was evident to them both. Dani suggested they make use of the willow saplings that grew in abundance along the edge of the river. She tossed a looped rope into the topmost branches and pulled it taut, bending one sapling after another to form a crisscross frame for the hut, a larger version of the one she'd built for herself previously.

Troy stacked their supplies behind the shelter and then hobbled the pack animals, allowing them to forage in the snow for the abundant buffalo grass. Dani gathered dry wood, dug into the deepening snow for buffalo chips to use for fuel, then built a fire and started the coffee brewing.

Finally, their tasks accomplished, Troy and Dani found themselves ensconced in a shelter of mismatched hides and blankets, a domed, cavelike dwelling that neither could stand erect in, but in which they were able to sit comfortably, shielded from the elements.

The fire crackled, the drier pieces of wood splintering and popping as the flames licked the life from them, turning them to white-hot ash.

"Here," Dani repeated, this time reaching out to touch Troy's shoulder with her free hand.

Shaken from his thoughts, he looked up as if surprised to see her, then reached out and took the cup of steaming, heady brew. As his fingertips brushed hers, Dani felt a tremor snake up her arm. Quickly she turned her back to him and concentrated on the fire.

"We shouldn't have left him." His tone was filled with bitterness and self-recrimination.

Dani twisted around to face him again after setting the pot of coffee back on the hot stones that rimmed the fire.

"He'll find us . . . or we'll find him." She nodded toward the open door of the hut. "He might even see the fire."

Troy had refused to let her drop the door covering in the hope that Grady might be attracted to the camp by the sight of the fire's glow. Snow still sifted down from the sky as the weak light of dusk ebbed into darkness.

"He won't find us." Troy continued to stare into the fire as he spoke. "You've said it yourself often enough—Grady couldn't track a fat squaw through a snowdrift. He can't start a fire, and he's out there without food or shelter."

"Listen." She sat cross-legged beside him, holding her cup as she leaned toward Troy. "The man's not an idiot, Fontaine. Give him a chance. He's got horse pistol flints, and with any luck he'll think to fire them into a pile of buffalo chips. Grady doesn't ever do much around camp because you and I do it for him. That doesn't mean he isn't able if he wants to."

Ignoring Dani as easily as he disregarded the cup resting between his own palms, Troy stared out into the night. Dani watched the emotions play across his face, highlighted by the dancing flames. The ebony depths of his eyes flared with each quiver of firelight. Dani watched him raise his coffee cup to his lips and savor the warm, strong brew. The tip of his tongue appeared as he traced the taste of the drink along his lips. His innocent movement stirred Dani so that she was forced to look away.

The weight of emotion caused by Grady's disappearance pressed down heavily upon them in the oppressive silence of the crude shelter. Troy downed the rest of his coffee and then tossed the cup aside, startling Dani with his sudden movement.

"My God," he said aloud, his emotional outburst shaking Dani to the core, "if anything happens to him . . ."

This was a side of Troy Fontaine she had never thought to see. His usual self-assurance was crumbling. In place of the arrogant woodsman she saw a man who was hurting deeply, a man who felt he had let his best friend down. Dani ached to comfort him. She called upon her own strength and instincts to guide her.

"Troy, no use lookin' at things on the dark side. We'll find Grady and we'll find him alive."

"What makes you so sure?"

"What makes you so sure we won't?" She met his unwavering stare.

He shrugged. "Things don't always work out for the best."

She nodded. "That's true, but till they work out for the worst there's no sense in thinking they might. You have to think of things the way you want 'em to be, and more than likely they'll come out that way."

He started to smile, then shook his head and looked away.

Dani leaned forward. "Life isn't as serious as you make it, Fontaine."

Troy turned his gaze away from the doorway. "Oh?"

"No, it's not. I been studyin' you and Grady, and from what I can see, we all three got different ways of looking at the same picture. Grady, now, he sees everything as beautiful, like he's always thinkin' of ways to paint things using soft colors and light. That's the way he sees life. Me"—she shrugged—"I guess I tend to see things the way Jake showed 'em to me."

"I have a feeling this is leading somewhere." He allowed himself a smile. "And what of me, Professor?"

She took a deep breath. "You, Fontaine, don't have any happiness in your soul. How many times have you really let go and laughed? None that I can recall. For some reason you been walkin' around with all kinds of shadows over your head. I don't know why"—she shook her head—"but I do know if it was me, I'd try lookin' at the good side of things 'stead of the bad once in a while."

Troy continued to stare. Dani's own gaze did not waver. He seemed about to speak, about to comment on her suggestion, but he remained silent. She wished he would say something, anything, to let her know what he was thinking. Instead, he remained silent. Finally, he turned away.

He did not seem to notice when she set her cup down near the fire. Nor did he move when she pressed close to him, so close that their buckskin-clad thighs touched. When she slipped her arm across his shoulder, paused to touch the silky, midnight braid and run her fingertip along it, then let her hand smooth and rub the tension from his shoulders, Troy finally raised his head and looked at her.

It was a new experience for Dani, this need to offer comfort through touch. In the warm, close air of the hut they'd built together it seemed only natural for her to share her strength of spirit with him. She met his eyes and looked past the worry she saw reflected there and recognized a deep hunger that matched her own.

Troy stared back. He let his gaze roam over her and fought against the emotions warring within him. Her wide, honest eyes were no longer silver but a deep, smoky gray, as open and translucent as shimmering jewels.

For two solid months he'd lived with the desire to hold her just as she was now holding him. He'd lived with the guilt of wanting her again. Now, while he wrestled with his conscience over Grady's disappearance, Troy tried to stand by his earlier decision, but he felt his resolution waver as the heat mounted in his loins.

"Dani—" His voice was a husky whisper.

"No." She stopped him with the touch of her free hand, pressing her fingers softly against his lips. "Don't say it." Dani closed her eyes and let her fingertips play over the smooth contours of his warm mouth. The silken feel of his ebony mustache teased her sensitive fingertips. He kissed them lightly and Dani drew her hand away.

Troy did not dare touch her.

"This isn't what I wanted to happen, Dani." His face was inches from hers, his eyes boring into her own. "It's been so hard."

She shook her head, willing him not to speak.

"This is what *I* want," she told him honestly. "I want to feel what I felt before." Dani slowly drew her arm from about his shoulders. "I want to feel you inside me again."

She was flushed, suddenly overheated in the close air inside the hut. She pulled away from him long enough to rise to her knees and untie her belt. Tossing it carelessly aside, she then shucked off her buckskin jacket before she knelt close to Troy once again.

Dani whispered, "I want to forget that Jake is dead. That I

left behind everything I love. I don't want to think about
heading God knows where, toward something I don't know
anything about at all."

She drew the oversized homespun shirt over her head and
watched the fire flair in Troy's eyes as he gazed down at her
exposed breasts. When he reached out to gently cup them in the
palms of his hands, she drew in a sharp breath. His hands were
rough, calloused, but his caress was gentle and sure. As if he
had never touched her, Dani continued to whisper, this time
reaching for Troy as she spoke, working her hands beneath his
jacket, urging him on. "I want to forget that Grady's lost. I
want to forget that you told me what we did before was
wrong."

None too gently, Dani took hold of his linen shirt and tugged
it from beneath his waistband.

"I want you to make me forget."

Her hands found the ties at his waistband, loosened them,
and slipped inside his leather pants, hesitantly searching for
that part of him she desired. She was not disappointed.

Troy groaned deep in his throat and rose to his knees when
she touched him, mirroring her posture. He felt her hands
move away to ease his buckskins off his hips. He drew her
close, pulling her tight against his chest. Burying his face
against her shoulder, he tongued her ivory skin, kissing the
throbbing pulse point at the base of her throat, his hands
playing at the small of her back until his fingertips slipped
inside the waistband of her buckskins.

With her act of natural seduction, the chains of his own
making suddenly fell away. Unfettered, Troy's longing over-
came his determination to hold himself aloof. His long, sure
fingers deftly released the rawhide thongs that held her
waistband. Hooking his thumbs inside the small band of leather
that encircled Dani's slender waist, he shucked the buckskins
down past her hips until she knelt before him, her pants
gathered about her knees.

As her fingertips continued to tease his rib cage, Troy
pressed her close against him. His hands rode her hips, pulling
her nearer. He was consumed by the need to feel her pressed
against his fevered length.

She watched him intently, her eyes shining with the same
hungry expectancy he suspected was mirrored in his own gaze.
Her ripe lips were parted, inviting, offering him everything.

He, too, had things to forget, including the fact that he could not offer to make this woman his own forever. But for tonight . . . tonight she was in his arms, warm and willing, and he was consumed by a passion that strained to be released.

Dani heard him murmur as his mouth moved against hers and she was overcome by a heady sense of power. She knew an ecstatic rush of joy and for a moment was motionless. Her hands stopped their exploration of him, her concentration centered upon the feel of his warm, whiskey-scented lips as they moved over her own. Troy's tongue teased her lower lip, slipped past her teeth, and without hesitation began to delve into the heated depths beyond. Dani imitated his kiss, returning all he gave until she was forced to clasp her arms tight about him. Her mind spun with a delirium of pleasure.

The rough texture of his clothing as it brushed against the tender, blooming tips of her nipples nearly drove her wild. At the feel of his arousal straining against his tightly molded buckskins, Dani experienced an overwhelming need to know his bare flesh against her own. As Troy's hands continued to roam her heated skin, she moaned in protest. The driving force of Troy's mouth as it moved against hers, the stimulation of his beard against her skin, were not enough—she wanted it all. Mustering her will, Dani pulled away, openly staring into his eyes. She knew another rush of power when she recognized the deep hunger burning within the dark depths of his gaze.

"Take 'em off," she demanded. She pulled on the hem of his shirt, lifting it along the length of his upper torso. He raised his arms obediently and the linen she had gathered in her hands slipped over his head, pulling with it the open jacket. Dani dropped his clothing to the ground where it was immediately forgotten.

She surged toward Troy again, sliding against the hard length of him, meeting the sculptured, well-defined planes of his form, fitting her own finely molded figure to his. He met her halfway, and as they clung together, Dani knew that whatever the cost, she wanted this man and the feelings he evoked in her to last beyond this one night. She wanted him forever.

As Troy held her firm buttocks and pressed her against him, he drove hard, seeking entrance to that secret place he had awakened within her. Dani found it impossible to grant him admission in their awkward kneeling position. The buckskins gathered about her knees prevented completion. For a moment, she became so lost in the tantalizing tease of his lips upon hers that she almost forgot her predicament.

"I . . . I can't move," she managed to whisper.

When Troy drew back and stared down at her, Dani shrugged and closed her eyes, hoping to escape further embarrassment. She spoke softly again, praying he would not think her awkward and inexperienced. "My pants are wrapped around my knees."

When Troy failed to respond, Dani glanced up and found him watching her. His eyes were still aflame with passion, but his lips now quirked in an amused half-smile.

"So are mine."

Cupping her face between his hands, Troy stilled further words with a quick kiss before he wrapped an arm about her shoulders and slowly descended with her until they lay upon the pile of discarded clothing.

He covered her face and then her neck with kisses, lavishing them upon her. He felt the erratic pulse beating so close beneath the silken skin at the base of her throat. He allowed himself to tease her breasts with his tongue, lapping at the erect, open buds of her nipples, circling and teasing them until he heard her moan low in her throat. It was a seductive, animal sound that sent his own blood pounding that much faster.

She thrashed. She writhed against his strength as he lay across her, exploring the uncharted mounds and hollows of her perfectly formed body. Troy carefully noted each response he evoked just as expertly as he had made notations on the maps he valued so highly. These reminders were etched deeply in the secret recesses of his mind, and unbeknownst to Troy, upon his very heart.

His explorations continued lower down her body, and he allowed his warm breath to sigh across the contours hidden beneath the soft, silken curls at the apex of her thighs. When he pulled away from her, Dani cried out and he glanced up long enough to find her tossing her head from side to side, her lips parted with each panting breath that escaped her.

Quickly, almost irreverently after the pleasure he'd already given, Troy rose to his knees and pulled off her boots and tossed them aside. As soon as he slid her buckskins off, Dani spread her unencumbered legs wide in an act so instinctive, so natural, that Troy realized she had never learned to effect the cool reserve that hampered the lovemaking of other women he'd known intimately.

He tore off his own boots and pants, anxious to dip himself inside her and appease his raging need. Easing his weight atop her, Troy did not hesitate, but plunged and, as he entered her, was reminded of the warm, refreshing waters of the hidden pool on Isle de Fontaine.

He burrowed deeper and she cried out, not with pain, but with pleasure, and then he heard his own name echo on the air about them. Dani chanted it as part of the litany she panted with each thrust.

"Oh . . . Troy . . . please . . . don't stop . . . please . . . don't . . . ever . . . stop . . . Troy please . . ."

As the words escaped her, Dani was certain of one thing: She was fully alive as Troy rode inside her at last. Her world had dwindled to this one moment in time. With this one man. She knew that whatever the cost, she wanted Troy and the feelings he evoked in her to go on forever.

Eyes closed, inundated by the quicksilver feel of him as he plunged and withdrew, descended and pulled away, Dani begged Troy never to stop, even as she fought her way upward toward the pinnacle that would bring them the completion their bodies longed for. Each time Troy began to withdraw, she followed him. Fear as well as longing drove her on. Would this be the last time? On the morrow, would he once again wear the heavy cloak of regret and silence?

Don't think.

The warning came to her, fighting its way through the passion in which she was enmeshed.

Don't think about tomorrow. Don't think past this one moment.

Dani let herself ride upon the waves of sensation; she rode hard and fast and free until she sensed new, frenzied energy in his thrusts. She met those, too, until she found herself lost in a pulsating reverberation that began deep inside, then spiraled up and outward. She cried out again, this time with release.

It became suddenly clear why the coyotes called to their mates, why the wolves howled in the night, why the cougars screamed and wailed during mating season. She smiled a secret smile. No matter what Troy Fontaine might insist, Dani knew mating with him was good. It was true and right. Nothing bad could carry her so close to heaven.

Dani felt as if she'd turned to honey. She was amazed to find she had the strength to raise her arm. Troy lay across her, his labored breathing slowly calming, his manhood still inside her. He was quiet now, somehow vulnerable, and at peace. Her fingers slipped beneath the thick queue at the nape of his neck and released the slender thong that bound his hair. She spread her fingers wide and gently combed them through the midnight silk. It barely reached his shoulders. Troy sighed and Dani felt his warm breath play against the hollow above her collarbone. She feared he might move, or speak and break the spell. But her fears were groundless, for he remained there, imprisoning her with his weight until his breathing became deep and even.

Dani held him as he slept.

Although the fire had burned itself to ashes, it was not yet cold. The smoldering red embers winked alive in the darkness. Troy gingerly eased his weight off the sleeping woman beneath him and sat back on his heels, relishing the frosted air that chilled his heated skin. He raked his fingers through his hair and vaguely remembered Dani pulling out the rawhide tie that bound the unruly length. He felt around, searching through the pile of haphazardly strewn clothing and finally found the thong.

Dani stretched in her sleep and rolled to her side, drawing her legs up toward her breasts, obviously missing his warmth. Troy studied the graceful line of her hip where it rose gently before tapering sharply to her trim waist. She was lovely. A treasure hidden beneath rough clothing, a gem he had discovered but was unable to keep. Or did he dare do so? For the first time tonight, he had been able to put the past behind him. When he thought about it, Troy realized that lately he'd spent little time dwelling on the events of the past. Should he dare to think of making a life with her? Troy decided time would tell. Right now, his concern was Grady Maddox.

He turned away from the sight of Dani's ivory skin, aglow in the weak light of the fire, and found a robe stashed against the wall. Drawing the heavy buffalo hide over Dani, he reached for a wolf pelt and draped it around his shoulders. Without making a sound, he placed a few buffalo chips upon the glowing embers and blew on them gently until the flames leapt to life again.

Troy knew instinctively that if he crawled beneath the hide

with Dani, he could once again rouse the fires banked inside her. Instead, he sighed with regret, pulled the wolfskin pelt tighter about his shoulders, and took up a position near her. He reached out and touched the thick red-brown hair that teased her cheek. Troy knew full well that his worry and fear over Grady were only part of the reason he had taken refuge in Dani's arms.

What excuse would he find next time?

Sitting cross-legged, Troy stared out into the night waiting for the light of dawn when they could finally go in search of Grady.

Dani dipped the soft linen square into the warm water once again and then reached for the bayberry-scented soap ball that Troy had left her. He'd awakened her before dawn's first light, thoughtfully providing her with warm water for washing, a cloth, and one of Grady's precious soaps before he excused himself and left her alone.

Happier than she had been in days, Dani ran the cloth over her body and marveled at the way she felt this morning. Her mind seemed clearer. No longer did she carry the burden of fear and rejection that had weighed so heavily upon her over the past few weeks. She felt alive again, brave enough to face whatever lay ahead, and she was ready to set Troy Fontaine straight before they lit out looking for Grady.

After she had washed and dressed herself, wrung out the cloth, and set the coffee boiling, Troy returned. He ducked into the entrance of the hut and paused for a moment to stare at her. Through the open doorway behind him, she could see the first fingertips of light inching their way up the sky. Their eyes met and held across the fire and then he looked away as he was forced to crouch and negotiate his way into the hut.

As he busied himself with the coffee and jerky, Dani laid out a hasty meal. While he wrapped extra strips of the dried meat for travel, she watched him from beneath lowered lashes. Troy looked different this morning. Perhaps he felt the same changes she had experienced. He certainly was not wearing the heavy expression of regret that had marred his handsome features of late. It was then she realized why he looked so different.

"You shaved off your beard!"

Troy turned at the sound of her voice and smiled. "It was a long night. I was looking for things to do."

"It looks good." She complimented him easily, open and honest as always. "I'd almost forgotten what you looked like."

He was the most handsome man she had ever seen, and as much as Dani wanted to spend the morning staring at him, touching him, she was as anxious as he to begin the search for Grady.

Dani followed his lead and ate sparingly, wrapping food for later. The search might take hours, or even days. Within minutes they were ready to leave the warmth of the hut and saddle the horses. Dani was equipped with her pistol, rifle, powder horn, and flint, her deadly buffalo knife once more in place in its sheath inside her boot.

"Ready?" Troy wanted to know.

"As I'll ever be."

He turned his back to her, preparing to leave the hut first, but Dani's next words stopped him.

"Troy, wait."

It felt strange to call him Troy. She had used his name on only two occasions, when she lay in his arms. Usually she called him Fontaine out of vexation, knowing that it irritated him somehow when she did so. But now she had called him Troy, and as he turned around to face her, Dani watched his expression soften. Perhaps last night meant more to him than he let on. She knew by now that Troy would never voice his feelings, but that knowledge would not keep her from explaining her own.

Dani took a deep breath, sat up as straight as she could in the low-domed structure, and faced him squarely. "I don't expect anything from you," she began. She watched his features darken as his brows knit together above the obsidian eyes.

"What are you talking about?"

Undaunted by the intensity of his gaze, she continued. "The last time this happened," she said, waving her hands in the direction of the hides where they had been together, "I assumed that it bound us somehow, that you and I would be . . . well"—she looked away, searching for the appropriate words—"tied. Obliged."

"Married?"

She nodded. "I just want you to know that I don't consider you beholden to me for what happened. And I'm not beholden to you, either. And . . . if it happens again, well, that's another time and another place. You still won't owe me anything, nor I you." She pushed a strand of hair back off her face and watched him intently. "Do you understand what I'm trying to say?"

Troy nodded, and a warm, thoughtful expression crossed his features. It was fleeting, and was soon replaced by one of dark intensity. "I know what you're trying to say, Dani, but what you don't understand is that where we are going, a decent woman doesn't enter into that sort of bargain."

"Decent?"

Troy glanced over his shoulder and watched the sunlight strengthen with each passing moment. Grady was out there somewhere, and if he was still alive and waiting to be found, every moment counted. Still, there were things here that needed settling. Troy paused long enough to set his saddle on the floor of the hut and assumed a more comfortable position as he spoke to Dani.

"There are many rules where we are going, so many that it would be impossible to explain them all to you. To make it as simple as possible, there are three types of women where I come from. One kind makes love to a man for money, not because she loves him."

Dani nodded, spellbound.

"The second type has numerous affairs." Again he was forced to search for words she would understand. "Such a woman takes many lovers, not for money, but for power or possessions or merely for the sport of it. She is looked upon in much the same way as the whores, the ones who do take money.

"The last type of woman is virtuous, decent. She remains a virgin until she is married. She is then taught the art of lovemaking by her husband, and she enters into that act only with him for the rest of their married lives. People admire her. That type of woman is the ideal."

Troy glanced toward the burnt-out embers of the fire. Because of him, Dani was no longer a virgin. Far from it. The girl delighted in the act of lovemaking.

"So"—Dani toyed with the fringe of her jacket as she tried to sort out all he'd said—"as I see it, you are trying to figure out just what sort of woman I am, just where I'm going to fit into this society that seems to run things where we're going." She looked up and leaned forward. "I think you best let me worry about that, 'cause until I've been there and seen for myself, I don't know if what you are telling me is true or if that's just the way it appears to you. I might want to decide for myself what type of woman to be."

"But don't you see, Dani, after what we've done, you aren't going to be one of the virtuous women? And that's all because of me."

"Hold it right there, Troy Fontaine." Her eyes began to flash with fury. Dani fought the urge to shake sense into him. "I don't need you walking around carrying the burden of guilt on your shoulders, thinking you are the reason I'm not one of these highly prized virgins. As a matter of fact, I don't see the virtue in it at all." She jabbed her thumb at her chest. "I happened to enjoy what we did last night, and if you weren't so all-fired bent on seein' the gloomy side of life, you'd admit that you did, too."

He opened his mouth as if to protest, but she would not give him a chance.

"I've been tied up in knots the last few weeks, what with everything happening at once. Holy hot shit!" She spat out the words and felt a rush of pleasure at having done so. She watched Troy flinch and was happy to have gotten a reaction from him at last. "Jake up and dies on me, I tie up with you and Grady, light out for parts I've never seen nor cared to . . . Why, I was beginning to feel like the inside of me, that part that keeps me going, was being left behind, a little piece at a time with every mile we rode away from the mountains.

"Now it's back. I don't know how to explain, maybe it's because of what happened last night. Maybe it's because talkin' about the way we all look at life sort of straightened out my own thinkin'. I realize now I let myself start fearin' the unknown 'stead of seein' this trip east as the adventure it is. I'll tell you one thing, Fontaine, I'm not gonna start being afraid again'or worryin' about what's up ahead on the trail. And I sure ain't gonna be afraid of what a herd of folks I don't even know or care to know are thinking about what kind of a person Dani Fisher is."

She took a deep breath and tried to still her pounding heart. Leaning forward, Dani stared at him with enough intensity to drive her point home.

"I can't stop being what I am, Troy, and you are just going to have to let me be. I never again want to feel like I was feelin' yesterday. Like I'm an animal about to curl up and die. Fear does funny things to a person and I don't ever mean to be afraid again. And," she warned, "if you are about to tell me one more time that this lovemakin' is wrong, well . . . I'm going to have to hit you up side the head with your own fry pan."

She reached down for the battered hat that lay beside her and rammed it on her head, then tied the rawhide thongs beneath her chin. "Now, let's go find Grady. He's going to be dying to wash up by now."

Speechless, Troy gathered up his saddle and weapons and moved aside. He turned away from her, for he couldn't help but smile and was amazed when he found he wanted to laugh out loud. He even found himself entertaining the thought that it might indeed be just as easy to assume Grady was alive as it was to give up hope. Why not? he thought. Troy shifted the weight of his saddle as he turned to follow the girl out the door.

Watching Dani crawl through the opening, he was treated to the sight of her derriere outlined by the tight buckskins. He shook his head in mute resignation. If the woman had to have him, there wasn't much he could do about it, except to make sure she was happy.

Chapter Ten

The horses moved slowly through the snow, their warm breath fogging on the cold air as they snorted and pawed their way across the land. Dani and Troy separated, riding abreast but yards apart, their eyes scanning the vast, open land along the river. The sky was cloudless, a limitless expanse of blue lit by a bright sun that speckled the snow with flashing crystals of light.

"I'm going to ride along the riverbank," Dani called out to Troy, her voice muffled by the wool collar of her Hudson Bay coat. She reined in her pony and peered out from between the brim of her hat and the coat collar that covered her nose. Only the gray-brown trunks of the willows and cottonwoods stood out in relief against the stark white of the snow.

A horse whinnied in the distance. Troy's, she thought, then realized that the sound had come from across the river. Dani strained to see over the shallow water and held her breath in anticipation. When she saw a flicker of movement between the trees, she stood in her stirrups, raised her rifle in salute, and shouted to Troy, "I see something on the other side!"

Dani did not wait for him to catch up to her, but plunged ahead, urging her horse across the Platte. They were at a narrow point, the water no more than a yard deep in the center of the river. Fording it took little effort. Weaving her way along the shoreline on the other side, Dani stayed hidden behind the trees until she located the horse and identified it as Grady's. She flicked the reins, hurrying her pony on until she reached the place where Grady's gray stood tied to a fallen log.

Throwing her leg over her mount's back, Dani jumped to the ground, sinking into snow up to her knees.

There was no sign of Grady Maddox.

"Grady!" she called out as she turned full circle, watching for some sign of him. Dani cupped her hands about her mouth and yelled again, louder this time. "Grady!"

Only silence answered her.

She could see Troy closing the distance between them. Dani steeled herself to tell him there was still no sign of his friend. Then she heard a muffled scrape and glanced toward a fallen log a few feet away. There was a small but definite hole in the drift of snow on the river side of the log. Dani wasted no time in struggling toward the spot. She began to dig, frantically pawing the soft, fresh snow away from the log.

"Grady!" Disbelief rode heavy on her tone. "Holy hot shit, Grady, if you are under there, for land sakes, *say* something!"

Her mittened hands scooped and shoveled, tossed and heaved the snow aside. Finally, Troy reached her and joined in the task.

"Is it him?"

"I don't know. But I can't imagine who else might be layin' here in a hollowed-out log next to Grady's horse, can you, Fontaine?"

Ignoring her comment, Troy continued to brush away the deep snow until they reached a layer of debris, thin branches of cottonwood, and long tufts of dried grass.

The muffled sound of Grady's words, weak but lucid, sounded from beneath the woven branches. "While you two are arguing, I'm freezing to death. Stop cussing, Dani, and get me out of here."

They combined their efforts and moved faster, tearing away the debris that covered their friend until they exposed his heavy form. Dani worked to dust off the remaining snow, grass, and earth. Grady had wrapped his coat around the upper portion of his body, shielding his face from the cold. Troy slowly opened the frozen fur to reveal Grady's face, colorless except for the deep blue of his eyes.

"What took you so long?" Grady whispered. The words were followed by a deep, hacking cough that racked his frame.

Troy glanced at Dani, shame and relief mingled in his eyes.

Feeling as guilty as Troy at the moment, Dani tried to explain. "We stopped to set up camp, Grady. It was snowing like hell. We figured it would be impossible to find you till it was light."

Grady smiled weakly at them both. "I was only teasing. I knew . . ." He paused and struggled for breath. "I knew I'd gotten myself good and lost this time. So . . . I tried to think . . ."

"Don't talk now, Grady." Dani motioned to Troy, who went after Grady's horse, although he seemed hesitant to leave his friend's side. She reached for Grady's hands. They were encased in the mittens she'd made him. "Can you feel your hands? Your feet?"

"My feet hurt, but my hands are warm. Thanks to you. Do you know what, Dani? I tried real hard . . . to think of what Big Jake might have done . . . I knew you'd have a tall tale ready about something like this."

"You did just fine, Grady. Real fine. Jake would have been proud." She nodded her approval as she marveled at the fact that he had improvised by burrowing into the open side of the log and covering himself with branches in order to stay alive.

"You'll be all right now." Dani met Troy's eyes as she held tight to Grady's mittened hands, rubbing them between her own. The words were meant to reassure Troy as well as Grady.

She watched as Troy helped Grady to his feet, then slung him over his shoulder. Troy struggled under the weight of the heavier man, and Dani moved to assist him as he lifted Grady up toward the saddle. Somehow, the artist managed to find the strength to grab the pommel and hang on as the other two lifted him upward. Troy swung up easily behind him, wrapped his arms around his friend, and took the reins from Dani.

She stood beside Troy's horse and laid her hand on his knee. Troy looked down at her touch. Concern for Grady was etched deeply upon his features.

"He'll be all right," she said softly. "You'll see."

"I'll meet you back there."

He turned his horse and nudged it slowly toward the river.

Except for Grady's labored breathing, the air inside the hut of hides was thick, silent, and warm. Exhausted, Dani propped her elbows on her knees and massaged her temples with her fingertips. It had only been a few hours since she relieved Troy of his vigil and insisted he get some sleep. Nearly a week had passed since they found Grady in the snow, and during that time his condition had deteriorated. His lungs were congested, filled with fluid that rattled with each breath he took. Earlier he had become delirious with fever, his skin hot and dry to the touch. Dani had boiled dogwood bark in water to make a syrup that would loosen his cough. They tried to force the syrup down Grady's throat, but they were fearful of choking him to death. All they could do now was wait to see if Grady would live through the night. Dani watched for any sign of hope.

Troy had spent hours at Grady's side, talking the man through his pain and frustration, soothing him during the long hours when Grady's mind wandered. While Troy talked to Grady of their adventures at school, Dani was enlightened about the men's years together. The two had been friends since boyhood. She learned that the bond that bound them was forged by respect and love.

Dani rubbed her eyes and longed for fresh air. Reaching out, she laid a gentle hand on the plaster she had applied to Grady's chest. The idea had come to her in the night, and she had immediately rifled through the healing herbs she always carried. She had mixed equal parts of flour and dried mustard and spread the paste between two pieces of linen.

She lifted a corner of the plaster and found that the skin on Grady's chest had already reddened. His breathing had become less labored in the last few moments. Dani glanced over to where Troy slept, exhausted, across the room. The blue-black stubble of his beard once more shadowed the lower half of his face. He had taken little care with his appearance since they had found Grady in need of such intensive care. Troy deserved to sleep, and so, as bone weary as she was herself, Dani rested her head on her folded arms and fought to stay awake.

"Dani?"

Grady's voice was a harsh whisper. She turned to him, fully expecting to see his eyes glazed with delirium, but she met a fully lucid gaze.

Lifting the man's limp hand, she bent closer to him and whispered, trying not to awaken Troy.

"I'm here."

"Did Troy find my mule?"

"Not yet, Grady."

He turned his face to the wall.

"Grady, listen to me." She tugged on his hand, demanding his attention, knowing full well the paintings on the mule meant everything to him. As far as she was concerned, they were not worth his life.

"You still have your sketchbook. We found it in your saddlebags. You can do all the paintings again once you get home."

She tried to share his pain as she watched his eyes brim with unshed tears.

"But the colors . . . all the colors of the mountains, the sunsets, the clothing. I captured them all." His voice faded as his spirit lagged. "Now they are all gone."

Dani reached out and felt his forehead. She found it much cooler to the touch. Beads of sweat outlined his upper lip. She pulled off the plaster and drew the heavy buffalo robe over the angry red patch of skin on his chest. He lay staring up at the ceiling, his mind drifting away from her. Dani cupped his chin in her hand and forced him to face her.

"The colors aren't gone, Grady."

He shook his head, but she insisted he listen to her as she struggled to spur his will to live.

"Why, I can see it all as clear as if I was standing below the Tetons lookin' up at them right now. The trees are so thick and green that in some places a man on horseback can't pass through. There's the green of wild grass in the meadows and the green of the moss and ferns that grow along the streams. Then there's the green that looks to be nearly black, the kind that colors the pines that hug the mountains as far up as the cold will allow.

"Think of the icy blues and grays. Sure, the mountains are made of rock, but I tell you, Grady, they are as alive as you and me. And where the clouds touch the mountaintops? Do you remember how their undersides are stained with the same hazy blue, except you can see through it. You can see them now if you think hard enough, can't you, Grady?"

When she looked down at him, he was staring up at her with new hope, and something else, something vital and alive in his eyes.

"Keep talking," he whispered before he broke into a fit of coughing that sounded as if it would burst his lungs.

Good, she thought. The congestion was loosening. Suddenly her exhaustion fell away as she used words to paint the images Grady needed to remember.

"Did you ever see the frost come in?" Dani asked.

He nodded affirmatively.

"Remember how it fringed the blades of grass and every leaf on every tree? You'll never forget that, not if you really think about it, not if you see it in your mind." She squeezed his hand. "Why, you haven't lost anything, Grady, but a few bits of canvas and some pots of paint"—she smiled and smoothed his thick blond curls off his forehead—"and one ornery old mule. It's all right here." She touched his temple. "All you need to do is close your eyes and it'll come right back to you."

When he squeezed her hand with what little strength he had left, and smiled up at her, Dani knew a surge of pride. She had done it. He would sleep soundly now. The fever had broken and Grady Maddox had reason to recover. He had pictures to paint.

"Will you sing for me, Dani?"

She'd taken to singing while she sat beside him. It helped to fill the hours, and Troy did not seem to mind, either, although he usually pretended he was not listening.

"Which song would you like to hear? You aren't thinking of dancing just yet, are you?" she teased.

"How about 'My Days Have Been So Wondrous Free'?"

"Were you awake all the time?" She wondered how he knew she'd sung the song to him many times already.

"In and out," he admitted. The words brought another smile to her face.

Dani stretched her legs out from their cramped, crossed position and lay on her stomach on the cold ground alongside his bed of hides. Her elbows braced on the floor, she rested her head in her hand. Thankful that he could rest comfortably enough to gain the rest his body needed to heal itself, Dani closed her own eyes and began to sing: "'My days have been so wondrous free, the little birds that fly with careless ease from tree to tree were but as blest as I, were but as blest as I . . .'"

Troy lay perfectly still, feigning sleep, delighting in the sound of Dani's sweet, lilting voice as she sang. He had eavesdropped on their conversation, listening as she encouraged Grady, amazed at the poetic pictures she painted so deftly with words. As she spoke, Troy had felt not only the power of the mountains but the sense of loss that Dani suffered for the land she had left behind. "*My days have been so wondrous free . . .*"

It occurred to Troy as he let the sound of her voice flow around and through him that lately his own days, too, had been "wondrous free." Astonished, he realized that during the past week he had not thought once of Louisiana, his shipping business, Devereaux and what news might be waiting in Louisiana. Exhaustion and concern for Grady were but part of the reason his thoughts were unburdened from the weight of the past. It was Dani who accounted for much of the change.

She had worked selflessly, helping him care for Grady, trying one herbal remedy after another, sponging the big man with cool water when he raved out of his head with fever, singing softly to soothe him whenever he slept uncomfortably, and now even providing the artist with hope.

Dani's voice slowly hushed until Troy heard it no longer. He stared across the space that separated them. Through the hazy, smoke-tainted air, he saw that Dani had fallen asleep stretched out on the cold ground beside Grady's pallet, her head resting in the crook of her arm.

Soon the fire would burn low, allowing the night's chill to invade the shelter. Troy knew the girl was so exhausted that she would sleep on, oblivious to the cold. He was tempted to share the warmth of his bed with her, but not for a moment did he delude himself into thinking he could do so unselfishly. It would be enough just to feel her lying next to him. A week had passed since they found Grady, a week since he had felt more than a passing touch. Still, he was at peace within himself now, and had been since the night they made love. The constant tension of their early days and nights on the trail was no longer present.

Troy dared not guess what the outcome of his relationship with Dani would be; he only knew that where before he had told himself "never," now the words "what if . . . " had crept into his thoughts. What if he gave this overwhelming attraction a chance to grow into something more? What if he allowed himself love, to think that he might eventually share his life with someone?

Before he knew what he was doing, Troy crossed the hut and gently scooped Dani into his arms. He held her close, pressed her against his beating heart, and dipped his head to smell the wood smoke and herbal scents that lingered about her.

"Hmmm?" She stirred but slightly, turning her face into his shoulder as he carried her across the shelter, reminding him of a sleepy child.

Troy placed her on the far side of his pallet of hides and slipped in beside her, drawing the heavy buffalo robe over them both. Wrapping his arm about Dani's shoulders, he drew her close as she nuzzled against him, burrowing instinctively toward the warmth he offered. As Troy drew her nearer, he reminded himself to awaken before dawn, before Grady found them together this way. His eyelids drooped with exhaustion, and as he fell asleep, Troy gently placed a kiss on the crown of Dani's head.

The earth trembled beneath them. Dani awoke with a start, wide-eyed and facing an equally bewildered Troy Fontaine. He glanced quickly in Grady's direction and was amazed to discover that the man slept on although the ground continued to shake mightily with a force that grew stronger by the moment.

Dani threw back the heavy hide before she knelt and faced Troy long enough to admit in a hushed voice, "I don't know how I ended up here and I won't bother to ask."

"Thanks," he whispered back, then looked at the domed ceiling, half expecting it to come tumbling down. "What in the hell is that?"

"Buffalo." She kept her voice low even as she scrambled over the end of the pallet and moved quickly across the room. "If we're lucky, they'll stop someplace nearby and we'll have fresh meat."

"How do you know they aren't about to trample us here and now?"

"Believe me," she tried to reassure him, "you'd know. You think this is bad, you should be right next to them. Some herds stretch fifty miles. From the sound and feel of it, they are most likely still across the river. Slowin' down some, too."

"Thank goodness."

He knew better than to ask what she thought she was doing as she shoved her arms into the sleeves of her jacket, dusted off her hat, and shoved it on her head. Troy watched in silence as she tied her jacket closed, slung on her powder horn, hooked her shot bag into her belt, and crawled back over to his side of the hut, where she stripped the hide covering from his bed and rolled it up.

"Would it be too much to ask what you are doing?" he inquired as he lay back, fully dressed, propped up on his elbows in what had once been a warm, comfortable bed.

"Nope."

Troy waited patiently for an answer until he realized that in Dani's mind, she had given him an accurate response, at least one that suited her. He sighed heavily before admitting defeat.

"What *are* you doing?"

"Goin' hunting."

"No, you're not."

She stopped in the middle of her preparations long enough to stare at him in mild disgust.

"Oh, yes, I am."

"Oh, no, you're not."

Her disgust turned quickly to defiance.

"I am, too. Grady's taken a turn for the better and he's going to need rich red meat and broth. Some good marrow isn't gonna hurt him, neither."

"Then I'll go and you stay with him." Troy shrugged.

"Simple as that?" She was glaring now, but couldn't check herself. The nerve of the man.

"Simple as that." Troy started to rise.

"*You*," she emphasized by pointing a finger at him, "are staying with Grady."

Troy didn't like the authoritative tone in her voice. Not one little bit. No more than he cared to acknowledge the overwhelming feeling of protectiveness that was suddenly overshadowing his reason.

"Why should I stay with Grady?" She spoke in quieter tones after having glanced at the sleeping man once again. "I'm the more experienced hunter. You ever shot a buffalo before?"

"No. But I imagine it's not that hard. What if something happens to you?"

"Do you think Jake followed me around everywhere?"

"No, but he should have," Troy barked at her. "If you insist on going, I'm coming with you."

"Oh, fine and dandy! You plan on leaving Grady here all alone? What if something happens to him?"

It seemed simple enough to Troy. "Then you stay."

"Do you know how to butcher a buffalo?" she countered.

"I've seen it done."

"Great. Seein' ain't doin', and I've done it plenty. Do you

know how to take the tongue out first? Or how to make an incision along the spine and peel away the skin to use as your catchall?"

As her anger rose, her mountain dialect thickened. Troy knew an impending disaster lay ahead if he continued to press her. She was furious, still spouting facts, and he watched her with a bemused, albeit angry, smile.

"I suppose you're an expert on takin' the boss off the back of the neck," she chided, knowing full well Troy did not know the mountain term for the fleshy hump on the buffalo's back. Dani tilted her head back, openly defiant now, her temper raging. "You plan on using the thighbone to crack open the other bones and dig out the marrow? Or hadn't you thought of that, Mr. Flatlander?"

"No, but after that most thorough lecture, I think I could manage."

By now she was crouched in the doorway, rifle in hand, and Troy knew he had lost the battle.

"I'm goin'," she stated clearly, daring him to object again. "Grady needs the meat and I'm wastin' time chaffin' 'bout it."

Before he could reply, Dani lifted the flap and was gone. Troy watched as she disappeared, then shook his head.

"I might have died in the night, but it would not have mattered," Grady volunteered from where he lay unnoticed, propped up on one elbow, obviously having enjoyed listening to the heated exchange, "because you two were arguing loud enough to raise the dead."

Rubbing his eyes, still weary but somewhat rested, Troy turned his attention to Grady. "Feeling better?" he asked his friend.

"Yes, much, but when I first woke up this morning, I thought I was having a hallucination."

Troy was thoughtful for a moment before he asked, "How's that?" Grady's pointed stare gave Troy a moment of unease. "Because I saw you and Dani sharing a bed."

For the first time in his life, Troy felt his face suffuse with color and he dropped his gaze. There was not much he could say in his own defense. "So you weren't asleep earlier?"

"During the stampede? No."

"Oh."

"What are your intentions, Troy?"

"Intentions?" Shaken, Troy looked up at Grady again. "You sound like an irate father."

"Or older brother."

"Or jealous suitor?" Troy countered, but as soon as the words were issued, he retracted them. "I'm sorry, Grady. I haven't been thinking straight lately."

"I can certainly see why not. Has this been going on long?"

Silence yawned between them for a time until Troy spoke again. "No, only twice, and last night was perfectly innocent." He then took a deep breath and admitted openly, "I don't know what I'm going to do, Grady."

"Do you love her?"

"Love?" Troy shrugged. "How would I know, I told you before, I'm not exactly an expert on that subject. I care about her, certainly."

"What about Dani? What has she got to say about this? If I know her, she does have an opinion."

"Of course," Troy admitted, "and of course she's expressed it quite clearly. She says I'm under no obligation to her whatsoever."

Grady pressed Troy upon hearing Dani's side of the affair. "And are you happy with that—being totally free to walk away from her?"

"I will leave her if I have to."

"Have to? Meaning what? What would ever make you give up someone like Dani?" Grady could not hide his disbelief.

"You know the answer to that better than anyone, Grady." Troy gazed toward the door, his mind lost in the past. "If and when Devereaux's men track down Reynolds, I'm going after him, regardless of my feelings for Dani or anyone else."

"Then I hope you won't mind if I try to pick up the pieces," Grady said softly, his tone laced with heavy disappointment at his friend's lack of judgment.

Feeling a need to escape Grady's intense regard, Troy saw to his friend's comfort before he excused himself and left the shelter. The cool, frosty air outside was a welcome relief. The past week had been unusually warm until today, and the snow had melted except for a few stubborn patches. Troy walked to the water's edge and stared down into the swift-moving shallows.

Damn. He was embroiled in exactly the kind of situation he had sought to avoid. Somehow he had to guard Dani's best interests, no matter how casually she claimed she regarded their relationship.

He found he had a hard time dealing with the accusation in Grady's eyes, and he became even more determined to keep his hands off Dani. Accomplishing that feat would be easier now with Grady once again an able chaperon . . . wouldn't it?

Across the river, massive brown shapes milled about. A herd of buffalo that numbered in the thousands was spread out along the prairie for mile upon mile. They seemed, for some instinctive reason, to have chosen the opposite shore as a grazing place. They fed on the short grama, the tough, nutritious grass that carpeted the open stretches. Troy knew the shaggy beasts, with their awe-inspiring bulk, were a sight that Grady would relish seeing.

Troy turned away from the scene, determined to mend the rift between himself and his friend, and to make amends for the disappointment he'd seen in Grady's eyes. If Grady expressed the least interest in watching the magnificent woolly beasts across the river, Troy would offer to carry him outdoors for a look.

Dani stared up at the open blue sky and knew a sense of ease. Tumbling white clouds pushed their way across the vast expanse like so many travelers on a carefree journey. It was good to be in the open air again, to feel the wind playing about her, to smell the clean scent of the damp earth beneath the melting snow. Seated astride her well-trained pony, she quickly worked her way downwind of the massive buffalo herd, intent upon her mission.

Four hours later she arrived at the hut, exhilarated by the success of her hunt. Although she had killed only one cow, it was a prime specimen, heavy with winter fat and covered with a thick hide. She'd taken extra time to skin the animal, a feat not accomplished easily due to the bulk of the cow.

As Dani swung her foot across the saddle to dismount and let her feet hit the ground, she thought of Troy and wondered for a moment why he had taken her into his bed last night. The tender act was unlike anything he had done for her before, and it set her to speculating. Could he be changing? The door of the hut was open, and she could hear the men talking inside. Tying her horse and the pack mule, which was loaded down with fresh meat, to a sapling nearby, Dani moved toward the door and, with an effortless motion, ducked inside.

"Good Lord!" Grady cried out upon seeing her.

"What happened?" Troy jumped to his feet only to ram the crown of his head into one of the support poles of the shelter. He crouched low once again.

Dani stared at both of them, bewildered. "Why? What's wrong?" she wanted to know.

Troy grabbed her wrist and pulled her nearer, twisting her about in order to examine her front and back. He was more furious than she'd ever seen him, and to avoid angering him more, she remained silent.

"You are covered with blood. I knew better than to let you go out alone. How did you get back?"

Dani tried to contain her laughter, but it welled up inside her and soon bubbled over. She was sorry that Grady had gone a shade whiter than the clouds she'd seen earlier, sorry, too, that Troy was so angry. Obviously, they both thought she'd been maimed.

"What are you laughing about?" Troy demanded.

"I forget how you two seem to have an aversion to good healthy muck, or I'da washed up before I came in."

Rummaging through the pile of goods Dani kept near the far wall, Troy came up with her Hudson Bay coat and extended it to her at arm's length.

"Get outside and strip. Put this on." His eyes blazed with anger. The tone of his voice brooked no argument this time, but Dani could not still her tongue.

"No."

"Do it," he seethed from between clenched teeth. "Leave your dirty clothes outside and put the coat on. I'll wash them while you prepare the meat."

Rather than submit quietly, Dani wrenched the coat from his hands and huffed out the door, satisfied that when last she saw Troy Fontaine, he was gingerly examining the crown of his head with both hands.

Within moments she reentered the hut and glared at Troy. "Happy now?"

Dani glanced down at her boots, the only apparel she wore besides the oversized blanket coat, which she held clutched closed. Without a word, Troy brushed past her and stomped out the door.

"There's some warm water in the wash pan, Dani, if you'd like to wash your face and hands," Grady said gently, reminding her she was not alone.

Dani bent low and crossed the room to his side, then knelt down and pressed a hand to his forehead, checking his temperature before she spoke.

"Feeling better?"

He nodded. "Troy even took me outside for a while to see the buffalo."

"Troy." An angry sniff accompanied his name and she shook her head.

Grady sat watching her intently. Too intently, Dani thought, and so she turned away and reached out for a cloth to dip into the warm water. "Guess I look pretty bad."

"I think you nearly frightened Troy out of a year of his life."

"He didn't seem so frightened to me. He seemed mad as a frog on a hot skillet."

She couldn't help but smile when she heard Grady laugh as she continued scrubbing her face.

"When Troy is frightened, he hides behind his anger, Dani."

Thinking about Grady's statement for a moment, she was forced to recall the day she'd gone after Grady and his mule during the Indian bucks' attack. Troy's furious reaction came to mind. Had he been frightened for her safety that day? It was something to ponder.

"You love him, don't you, Dani?"

Grady's openly honest question startled her.

"What?"

"You love Troy. I saw it in your eyes long ago."

Love? Dani had never put the strange, needful feeling she had for Troy Fontaine into words before. She turned to face Grady once again, the washcloth forgotten in her hand.

"I guess I might at that. I never knew what to call it."

"It won't be easy for you, Dani."

She tried to interpret the look in Grady's eyes. Was it sadness that lingered there, or pity?

"What makes Troy the way he is, Grady? I tried to figure it out, even talked about it to him—"

"I would love to have heard that," Grady interrupted.

"You and me, well, we say what we mean and mean what we say. With Troy, I'm always guessing, wondering what I did wrong, and most of the time I haven't done anything at all."

"Troy hasn't had an easy life, Dani."

"Who has?"

"I'm sure your life hasn't been easy, but I can tell by the way you speak of Jake, the respect you have for him, that he did a fine job of raising you. He did the best he knew how, and he loved you, too. And me, I've got both parents and a passel of sisters to look after me." Grady paused long enough to shift to a more comfortable position on his pallet. He was sitting up now, leaning toward Dani as he spoke, his voice low.

"But when Troy was twelve years old, his father was murdered. Troy found the body hanging in the barn behind their house. His mother was abducted at the same time; she was never found, nor was Constantine Reynolds, the man who took her. It seems he tried to extort money from Troy and his grandmother."

"Money?"

"This man believed the Fontaines had a fortune in gold on the island, but what he didn't know was that Troy's father had gambled away what little they had. Troy and his grandmother, Leial, went to their so-called friends and neighbors, begging for help, but no one would lend them a cent. Everyone was afraid that it was another of Troy's father's money-making schemes. When Merle Fontaine was found dead, many of them believed his plan had failed and that he then killed his wife and hanged himself.

"Troy was sent away to Boston to boarding school. That's where we met. His grandmother hoped the separation would help him to forget the murder, but of course Troy never forgot. He vowed to find the man and his mother, if she's still alive."

"He's been searchin' all these years?" she asked.

"At first Troy thought he could find Reynolds himself. But he'd been away at school for six years. When he returned to the island, he found his grandmother with barely enough money to survive. He went to work, trying to salvage the one holding the family had left—his grandfather's shipping business. He gave up trying to trace Reynolds himself, but Troy used every spare penny to hire a lawyer to continue the search.

"Reynolds left Louisiana after the murder and went to France. It's a mystery where the man is now, but supposedly Devereaux, the lawyer who's been conducting the search, thinks it's just a matter of time until he has definite word of Reynold's whereabouts. I had a hell of a time persuading Troy to leave Louisiana and travel with me." He reached out for her hand and held it gently. "Dani, Troy won't be free until he finds this man Reynolds and sees justice done. He's determined to find his mother or to learn what's happened to her."

Dani shook her head and frowned. "The night you were missing I accused him of always expectin' the worst. I can see now there hasn't been much reason for him to think otherwise."

"He's a hard man, but a fair one," Grady admitted. "He's been a good friend to me and has always done right by his grandmother. Troy might only allow himself to show his anger, but I know he cares for you. I think he might be trying to deny that to himself and that's what's making him so damned irritable lately."

"You think Troy'll ever open up enough to tell me any of this himself? Shoot, Grady, I'm one of the best trackers east or west of the Rockies. If Troy wants this man found, why, I'd be more than happy to go with him and flush the snake out of hiding."

Grady shook his head. "I'm sure that's the last thing Troy wants or needs. If I were you, I wouldn't let on you know anything about this. If and when Troy's ready to open up to you, he will." Grady smiled. "You wouldn't want to scare him off, would you?"

Dani stared back into the honest blue depths of her friend's eyes and respected his confidence. She knew all he'd told her was true. Dani squeezed his hand, smiling in appreciation.

"Grady, I can stick to a trail that would make a mountain goat nervous, so don't you worry about me."

Grady Maddox smiled and reached out to tousle her wild, uncombed hair. "If you ever need my help, Dani, just let me know and I'll be there."

"You and all the rest of Fontaine's Fighting Forty, is that right?"

"That's right," he laughed, before he burst into a fit of coughing. Once Grady caught his breath he added, "I'd almost forgotten about them."

Chapter Eleven

"This place smells like a piece of rotten meat," Grady Maddox mumbled from behind the freshly washed and scented handkerchief he pressed to his nose.

Troy turned to his friend and stated dryly, "One would think, Grady, that after all you've been through, your sensitivity to . . . unpleasant odors . . . would have dissipated."

Dani silently stared at the sights and sounds around her. The riverfront teemed with life as flatboats, keelboats, pirogues, and canoes vied for dock space with the heavily loaded steamboats crowded against the muddy shoreline.

Never before had she seen so many varieties of life in one place. Yankee peddlers and farmers, soldiers and Indians, trappers and traders, melded together in a city nearly overrun by boisterous boatmen. She wondered what awaited them once they ventured up the cobblestone street toward the heart of the settlement. From the rail of the steamboat that had carried them down the Missouri she had seen the large, imposing homes built atop the hill above the more crowded section of St. Louis near the river.

Now she stood gazing about at the men pushing hogsheads filled with cargo, watched the carriages and wooden-wheeled carts that arrived empty and departed loaded to bursting with goods, listened to the various accents that colored the men's voices, and lent part of her attention to the men at her side.

She turned to stare at them. What a pair of yellow-rumped warblers they looked in their flatlander clothing. They needed a good ribbing as far as she could see, especially after the argument they'd forced her into earlier that morning.

" 'Sides, Grady, that stink is just the pure rotten smell of poorly cured hides. Shoot, the Indians aren't opposed to eating meat that smells gamier than that."

Grady groaned. Troy merely smiled at his friend's discomfort and then glanced back toward the *Mighty Liberty*, the steamboat that had transported them downriver. They were awaiting the unloading of their horses, a task that seemed to be taking longer than necessary.

"Wait here," Troy announced suddenly. "I'm going to see if the captain will have our horses liveried nearby. There's no sense in us standing out here in the cold while it gets later by the moment." He glanced toward the west and the quickly setting sun. "We need to find lodgings before it gets dark. Then we have to locate Solomon Westburg."

A knot formed in Dani's stomach as she watched Troy walk away from them. She concentrated on his appearance rather than on the coming meeting with Jake's partner. She wondered if Troy was still angry over her outburst aboard the ship this morning.

Their final weeks' journey along the Platte had been slow and tedious, as Grady's weakness had forced them to rest for longer periods and travel fewer hours. The first settlement they reached was below Council Bluffs on the Missouri, and there they had sold their pack mules as well as Jake's big sorrel horse. Troy made immediate arrangements for their transportation, arguing with Dani, who nearly refused to board the lumbering, steaming contraption.

"If God meant folks to float down the river like that, he'd a made us smokin' ducks," she protested, but Grady's hacking cough and the dark circles under the artist's eyes forced her to realize he would be better served traveling in comfort.

She spent most of the days aboard leaning against the rail, watching the land along the water's edge. Tall bluffs had been carved by the water's path; roots and stumps of trees reached out from the sandy riverbanks like ravens' claws clinging to what was left of the bluffs high above the river.

Dani noticed a change in Troy and Grady as the ship neared its destination. They became excited, eagerly anticipating the day when the *Mighty Liberty* would dock in St. Louis. As eagerly as they looked forward to arriving, just as dismally did she await the same event.

Her nerves had been stretched nearly to the breaking point when both men entered her tiny shipboard cabin that morning to win her approval of their newly spit and polished appearances.

"What do you think, Dani?" Grady asked, turning full circle to show off his finery.

She could only stare, for her attention had been centered upon Troy. Grady had always taken care with his appearance; he was forever washing himself, combing his curly white-blond hair, shaving his beard and upper lip. But not Troy. On the trail he'd often let his beard grow in and then shaved it off. Days would pass when he would seem to forget about the tedious process, allowing the dark shadow of stubble to spread across the lower half of his face. He had continued to wear his hair in a queue, and he never exchanged the worn buckskins for other clothing.

But earlier today, when he walked into her cabin with Grady, Dani had been stunned into speechlessness at the sight of Troy Fontaine. His face was clean-shaven, and his heavy mustache was missing, affording her a clear view of his inviting lips. Missing also was the thick, silky mane of black hair. Troy now wore his hair neatly trimmed just above the high, wide collar of a chocolate-brown coat she had never seen before. A flowing white scarf that Grady called a waterfall cravat was tied about Troy's neck. Grady was dressed in a similar coat of deep forest green, but even her untrained eye could see that the lines of Troy's finely molded body were better suited to the fitted coat than Grady's.

Both men wore long, tapered buff-colored trousers that were strapped beneath the instep of their shining black leather boots. To add to the spectacle, they carried gloves and tall beaver hats. Grady even sported a brass-knobbed cane.

"Where did you get the clothes?" she had asked, forced to say something when all she really wanted to do was stare at Troy.

Grady explained. "They were in our packs. We've had them hanging in our cabin since we came aboard so the wrinkles would fall out."

"Oh."

Troy pulled the cuffs of his coat down and avoided her stare.

She wondered if he took offense at the way she looked now that he had regained his civilized trappings.

"Dani, if you'd like to freshen up, we have plenty of clean shirts," Grady offered. "Wool pants will have to do until we dock. I could trim your hair evenly for you and you can order another bath."

She had thought one was enough. It was obvious they were no longer satisfied with her appearance, for there was Troy, once more as silent as the granite face of the Tetons, not even caring to look at her.

"I . . ." The words choked her and she fell silent.

Finally Troy raised his dark, unfathomable eyes in her direction and spoke in the low, resonant voice she'd grown to know so well, "We asked the captain if he had any dresses among the cargo, but he didn't, so you'll have to wait until we get to Saint Louis."

She choked again. "Dresses? A dress?"

They both nodded.

Her voice rose. "You expect *me* to wear a dress?"

They nodded again, looking to each other for support. Troy seemed to have been the one elected by silent agreement to speak.

"Dani, everyone wears dresses in St. Louis."

"You don't."

She could tell he was fighting to remain calm.

"I don't have to remind you that we are men."

"And I don't have to remind *you* that this is all I ever wear."

"She's getting up a head of steam," Grady whispered to Troy; the words were just loud enough for Dani to hear.

"You bet I am! If you two traitors think I'm going to walk into a place I know nothin' about dressed in somethin' I never wore before, lookin' like a fool an' actin' like a bigger one, then you both got holes bored in your heads."

"Listen, Dani . . ." She could tell that Troy had lost the tight rein he had on his temper.

"Listen nothin'," she had shouted, then pointed icily toward the door. "Get out!"

Without waiting for further argument, Troy marched out the door, but Grady had stayed a moment longer.

"Dani, you really should think about dressing up properly. After all, we aren't in the mountains any longer. We are about to arrive in civilization, and for what it's worth, it does offer certain comforts."

But now, as she stood on the riverbank, stubbornly dressed in her well-worn buckskins, staring at the milling, bustling humanity moving about in the waning light, Dani wondered what the comforts of civilization might be. At the moment, she was highly uncomfortable.

As the driver maneuvered the hired carriage through the traffic and mud, Troy turned his attention to the shops and stores along the narrow street and wondered what Dani might be thinking. She sat nervously poised on the edge of the seat between him and Grady, having announced that she would "just as soon walk." Grady had been willing to debate the advantages of riding. Troy had not.

It had been obvious by the way her smoky eyes widened at the sight of the closed carriage, slung high and creaking upon its iron frame, that she was afraid. He knew that she would never admit as much and that the argument might proceed for an hour or more. Grasping her firmly by the elbow, he had propelled her forward until she was forced to step into the conveyance. Thus far, Dani had not uttered a sound, but seemed to be growing accustomed to the bouncing ride, even daring to turn her head from side to side to look at the sights Grady pointed out to her.

"Why did they cover this trail with rocks?" Dani asked, grabbing for her hat as the carriage jolted, nearly knocking her from the precarious perch on the edge of the padded seat.

Troy turned his attention back to the girl at his side and attempted to relieve Grady from the endless round of questions she had begun to ask. He noticed that her hands clutched the seat and she kept her knees pressed together as if to prevent them from knocking. All he could see as he gazed down at her was the top of her ridiculous floppy hat; the wide brim hid her features from view. He felt an urge to reach beneath it and tip her face up toward his so that he could see her expression. It would help to put an arm around her, to try and alleviate her fears, but Grady's presence kept Troy from doing so. Besides, he'd promised himself not to touch her or give her cause to misconstrue any of his actions.

"This trail is called a street, and it is *paved* with stones so that when the weather is rainy, or when sleet is falling, as it is now, the streets won't be so muddy that carts and carriages cannot move about easily."

"Oh."

"Look, Dani." Grady pointed out of the window on her left. "That's a cathedral. The Cathedral of Saint Louis. If we get a chance, I'll take you inside. It supposedly houses ancient embroideries worked in gold, and original paintings by Rubens and Raphael."

"They always build places that big for hangin' paintings?" She bent forward and craned her neck, attempting to see the top of the cathedral spire.

"A cathedral is a church, Dani," Troy explained. "A place of worship where people go to pray."

Grady tried to clarify. "God's house."

"God *lives* there?" Turning to Troy for verification, Dani became brave enough to lean across him and thrust her head through the window for a better look at the building they had already passed. "I can't hardly believe *that*! How does he get in and out? God's bigger than the world. God is nature and air and time and water, and he's in all living things." She shook her head, rejecting the notion. "If there's somebody in there sayin' he's God, then he's got a lot of city folks fooled."

Troy slowly raised a brow as he caught Grady's eye. "I think she has a point."

The carriage stopped before a three-story stone building with even rows of windows and five chimneys visible from the street. Rolling clouds of bilious smoke poured from the chimneys.

"This is the Republican Hotel." Troy explained the stop to Dani as they waited for the driver to open the carriage door.

Dani stepped out first and found herself standing on the walkway before the imposing building. Dani knew that Troy would brook no argument, so although she would rather have slept outside, she followed the two men up the steps. When they stood aside to allow her to pass through the doorway before them, she planted her feet and shook her head.

"I'm not going in there first."

"It's a form of courtesy to let a lady pass before a gentleman." Grady bowed and waved her on.

Dani froze. "I'm not going into *that* again. I won't walk in there first."

Troy sighed and walked past Grady. "Let's not debate this

issue again. She's as stubborn as a country mule, Grady. Give up." He reached for the door handle and pushed his way inside.

The words stung. So did the sight of Troy's broad shoulders disappearing into the lighted lobby of the hotel. Taking a deep breath, Dani squared her shoulders and silently swore beneath her breath. "Damn you, Jake Fisher. Look at the fix you got me into here by up and dying. I'm dead center in the middle of St. Louie, about to walk into a building twice the size of a stone mountain, in a town where they claim to have God locked up in a house with a pointy roof. Holy hot shit!"

The cold stone exterior of the building was nothing compared to what awaited her inside. Dani halted as she crossed the threshold. The large, open room was lit by what she could only describe as a hanging fountain of crystal and candles. She stared up at the dancing flames that reflected off teardrops of shimmering glass.

When two couples descended the narrow staircase to her left, she stared in awe at the women, unable to take her eyes off creatures so vastly different from herself. Was this what Troy expected her to become? Both the women possessed skin as fair and white as the first winter snows that frosted the mountains. The taller of the two wore a floor-length cape that swirled dramatically around her tiny feet. The man beside her reached out and raised the hood that hung down behind the woman's shoulders. Pulling it up carefully, he covered the intricate coils of blond hair piled high on her head.

The other woman was dark-haired and smaller than Dani. Her blood-colored cape hung open to reveal the gown beneath. The shining buttercup-yellow silk shimmered like sunshine on moving water as it caught the light from the fountain of crystals. The swell of the woman's breasts held Dani's gaze.

What made them sit up there all perky like?

Like the blond woman, the dark one wore tiny shoes the same color as her dress. The shoes looked flimsy and unsuitable for outdoor wear, but the couples crossed the room toward Dani, apparently intent on going outside. She found herself blocking their path as she stood gaping in the doorway.

Dani moved forward and gingerly stepped on the carpet, then crossed the room toward Troy and Grady. The couples turned to stare at her, and for a second she halted in her tracks. The women studied her with unabashed curiosity, their eyes sweeping her from head to toe. Dani stood her ground for a moment before moving on. When she heard one of the women giggle, she dipped her head and kept walking. What were they thinking?

She glanced down at her hands, at the tanned skin and the uneven, broken nails. What must Troy think of her when he compared her to other women he had known?

Dani tried to shake off the dark doubts as she joined the men. They stood beside a tall counter engaged in conversation with a gangly young man dressed in black. He acted as if he were peering down at them from some great height, although he was much the same size as Troy.

"You are lucky that we have even one room left. The holiday season is beginning, sir."

His hair was parted straight down the center and greased into place with some sort of shining ointment. When Dani moved to stand beside Troy, the clerk paused long enough to return her stare.

"As I was saying"—he turned back to Troy—"we have only one room left. You will all have to share it." So saying, he pinned Dani with his stare again.

To irritate him, she stared back, leaning both elbows upon the slick, polished surface of the counter. She began to drum her fingertips on the wood. The man looked as if he'd swallowed a swig of lye soap water. She squinted, daring him to speak to her.

"Is *this* the third member of your party?" he asked Troy.

Troy acknowledged Dani with a nod.

The man crooked a brow. "I don't see any problem. A cot can be arranged for the boy."

A few hours ago Dani would have been pleased that the man had taken her for a lad. Just now she was not sure how his assumption made her feel.

"Fine."

Dani heard the hesitation in Troy's reply. "I suppose we'll have to work something out."

"Rest assured, I'm not exaggerating, sir. Still, if you care to let the room go while you inquire elsewhere?"

"No. This will be fine."

Troy and Grady exchanged looks as the man pushed a large open book toward Troy. Dani watched as he dipped a long quill pen into a pot of ink and wrote something in the book. The man studied the words Troy had written until he was satisfied; then he pushed a key toward them.

"Room two-oh-seven." He pointed toward the stairs.

"Our baggage should arrive shortly."

"We'll see it delivered to your room, Mr. Fontaine."

Grady, who had been watching the exchange, suddenly spoke to the proprietor. "Perhaps you can tell us where to find a merchant named Solomon Westburg?"

When she heard Grady mention Jake's partner's name, Dani was reminded of the reason for her journey to St. Louis. Perhaps the men were anxious to be rid of her and be on their way. After watching Troy intently for a moment, she turned to Grady. There was nothing different in their demeanor, and yet she wondered just what they would say when they all reached the end of the journey and safely deposited her with this man, this Solomon Westburg.

Would Troy be able to walk away from her without regret?

Perhaps he might even be relieved. It was a thought she did not care to contemplate just yet. If ever.

The man behind the desk was staring at her again. Dani nearly breathed a sigh of relief when he denied knowing Westburg. Before she turned away to follow the men, she glared at him once more for good measure and strode toward the exit.

Supper was a hurried affair in a small café near the waterfront. Grady called it shabby, Troy said it was adequate, and Dani watched a look pass between the two men that worried her some until she concentrated on the plate of food set before her. She did not recognize any of it, but it tasted palatable enough. It took an hour to locate someone who could direct them to Solomon Westburg, but when Troy learned the man owned a dry goods emporium on a street near the levee, he insisted they seek him out immediately.

Dani felt more at ease and confident in the strange surroundings once darkness shrouded the city streets. Her appearance mattered little then, for there were few women to compare herself with. She delighted in the sights as they walked together through the darkness. Light spilled out from various open doorways, and Dani paused long enough at each one to peer inside. Most were establishments filled with men, some dressed in buckskins like her own. They hoisted frothing mugs of ale as they shouted and sang to fiddle tunes that floated upon the air. Dani longed to wander into the warm surroundings and enjoy the easy camaraderie she had shared with the mountain men.

More than once she fell behind the fast pace the men set until Troy retraced his steps and led her by the elbow along the street. At last she found herself standing beside Troy before Solomon Westburg's shop. Grady stood just behind her. A slender cord set a bell ringing inside the darkened building that housed Westburg's Dry Goods Emporium.

When there was no response, Dani hoped the inevitable moment would have to be postponed.

"Well"—she turned to Troy, straining to read his expression in the darkness—"looks like we better come back here tomorrow. Anybody for going inside one of those saloons?"

Grady cleared his throat. Troy ignored her and reached up to yank the bell cord again before he loudly knocked on the door.

The soft glow of a candle bobbing toward them from the rear of the shop caught Dani's attention. She felt her heart sink to her toes. All of a sudden the confidence and determination she had regained vanished. The candle was moving closer, its halo throwing the stooped figure that carried it into relief against the shadows. The light shone off a bald pate surrounded by a frizz of hair. As he neared, she saw that he wore spectacles perched on the end of a long nose. His shoulders were stooped with age. The candle grew nearer still, and finally the diminutive old man reached the glass-paneled door.

Dani took a deep breath and watched the door open a crack. The merchant peered out as he raised the candle higher.

"Solomon Westburg?"

The rich timbre of Troy's deep voice caused Dani to start. This was real.

It was all happening at last.

Behind the barely opened door, residing with this elfin creature, was the secret of Jake's past, and perhaps her own.

"How may I help you?" Westburg's voice was strong for one so old.

"We've come with news of Jake Fisher. We have a letter written by him." Troy reached inside his coat and pulled forth Jake's yellowed letter. Dani did not know he had brought it along until now.

"Jake Fisher?"

The door opened wider as Westburg peered at them over the rims of his glasses. He studied the three of them intently for a moment, his eyes lingering upon Dani. Then, stepping aside to allow them to enter, he said, "Welcome."

When Troy politely gestured to her to walk ahead of him, she moved into the warm store quickly, afraid she would lose her nerve and bolt headlong down the street into the darkness.

Chapter Twelve

The old man led them through the shop. Shadows loomed around them as the dim glow from the candle vaguely illuminated walls lined with shelves that were crowded from floor to ceiling with shoes and boots, tins and boxes. Ghost-like, their reflections were mirrored in the glass-fronted display cases that ran nearly the length of the narrow room. They followed him as Solomon Westburg moved through the dark-ened store with the familiarity of long occupancy, past crates and barrels, past the iron stove in the back of the shop, which had long since grown cold.

Dani started up the stairway, watching the old man's scuffed leather shoes as he climbed each step ahead of her. At the top of the stairway they found themselves in a small room so crowded with Solomon Westburg's furniture and necessities of life that Dani wondered where they were to stand until the man shuffled to the dining table that occupied the center of the room and indicated the straight-back chairs around it.

"I'm sorry things are in such a state." He shrugged, smoothing his palm across his shining pate as if he possessed hair. "I have little company, and when one is as old as I, one cares little how things look. Sit, sit." He began lifting stacks of books and papers off one of the chairs and indicated that Dani should take a seat. Troy and Grady cleared places of their own, taking care to move the piles of clothing and books to a side table. As the men made themselves comfortable at the table, Dani stared around the room.

Aside from the dining table and the bed, the only other large piece of furniture was a desk, which stood between the two tall windows that faced the street. Long, limp curtains hung at the windows, pulled closed to shut out the cold air of December that played against the cracks and windowpanes.

"So . . ." The old man's voice drew Dani's attention, and she looked across the table at him. The eyes that met hers over his spectacles were alive and sharp. She knew that although Solomon Westburg's body might be bent and frail, his mind was still as sharp as a wolf's teeth.

"What can I do for you, or for my old friend Jake Fisher?" He leaned forward, hands and forearms braced on the table.

"Mr. Westburg"—Troy indicated Dani with a nod—"this is Dani. Danika Whittaker." He went on to introduce himself and Grady and explained briefly how they had met Dani in the Rockies.

When the merchant stared at Dani, trying to see beneath the shadow cast by her hat, Troy reached over and removed her headgear so that Solomon was afforded a better view of the girl. She shot Troy a murderous glance before she returned the old man's stare.

The old man's voice became a whisper in the still, darkened room. "Jake's girl." His eyes became alight with interest. "And how is my old friend?"

"He's—"

Troy cut Dani off before she could blurt out the truth. "The fact is, Mr. Westburg, I'm afraid we have some sad news." Troy extended the letter, but the man did not move to take it. It lay unopened upon the fringed tablecloth.

"Jake?" Solomon's eyes dimmed with sadness.

"He passed on, Mr. Westburg," Grady explained, his voice softened with sincerity as he watched the little man's eyes flood with tears. "Dani said he died peacefully in his sleep."

For a moment Dani thought the old man would break down and cry, but instead, he drew a rumpled linen kerchief from his back pocket. He slowly, almost painfully, removed his glasses, wiped his eyes and the spectacles, blew his nose, and then replaced the glasses. He shook his head.

"Who would have guessed that Jake would go before me?"

"Had you known him long?" Troy asked.

Westburg's eyes took on a faraway glow, and he spoke as if he could see into the past. As he began speaking, Dani tried to imagine Jake—bluff, burly Jake—and this little bird of a man becoming friends.

"It was around eighteen years ago, in 1812, to be exact," he began, "that I met Jake Fisher. We were on a flatboat traveling down the Ohio River. Jake had just lost his wife. He'd lost a son earlier. They had farmed the 'hills of Kaintuck.'" He shrugged. "We were the only single men in a small party of travelers. The others were moving their families west. We had no one.

"It was my dream to open a store of my own. Always before, I had worked for others." He leaned forward to emphasize his point. "I had saved and saved until I could afford to set up my own place.

"But Jake . . . he was heading west to see the open places that were still wild. He said Kentucky was getting too crowded for him. I could see by the hurt in his eyes that he could no longer live where he thought of his wife and son with each passing day."

Dani found herself barely able to breathe as she listened to Solomon tell Jake's story. Never once had Jake mentioned a wife. Or a son.

Solomon continued. "Jake had a notion that he wanted to become a trapper. He'd heard the animals out west practically laid down and begged you to take their hides, but he didn't want to deal with Hudson Bay or any other fur company. He wanted to keep the money he earned—if there was any to be made." Westburg leaned across the table toward them and whispered, as if he were telling a secret. "And there was. Lots of it."

"So you and Jake struck a bargain?" Troy tried to keep the man from digressing too far from the point, hoping they would learn something of Dani's past before morning.

"Yes. He hunted and I became his broker, selling the furs once they were delivered to me here in St. Louis. For the first three years, Jake came to St. Louis in the spring with his haul. Then, as he traveled farther west each year to find beaver, he began sending his share in with men he could trust to deliver the pelts to me. I would broker his furs, make certain he was not cheated, and then bank his share of the money—seventy-five percent for Jake, twenty-five percent for me.

"Jake never returned to St. Louis, but he sent a letter each year. That's how I know about Dani here, and that's how I kept in touch with Jake. I would send him the money he needed, which was next to nothing." Sol stood and made his way slowly to the desk, pulling papers out of the pigeonholes until he located a neatly bundled stack of pages. "I've saved every letter of Jake's over the years. They're all yours now, Dani."

Shuffling back across the room, he tried to hand them to her, but her hands remained in her lap. Dani stared down at the letters the man held in his thin, blue-veined hand.

"I can't read."

Troy reached across her. "I'll keep them for her. Thank you, Mr. Westburg. I'm sure Dani appreciates your kindness in giving them to her. She's been a little distraught."

Dani turned to Troy, ready to protest that she had never been distraught in her life. Well, almost never. But he silenced her with a quelling glance.

Grady asked, "Did Jake tell you anything at all about Dani's past, Mr. Westburg?"

A frown furrowed the man's brow. He looked at Dani as he lowered himself slowly onto his chair once more. "You mean Jake never told you the story?"

Dani shook her head, afraid to hear what the man might say and yet curious to know what type of people might have been her parents.

"I'm afraid it's another sad story. It's all in the letters, but I think I can tell you in a few words."

Troy had serious doubts that it would take "a few words," but he was as anxious to hear the story as Dani and Grady were. He shot a sidelong look at Dani, wondering how she was faring, knowing full well that she would not show her true emotions. He wanted to reach out and touch her, to show her that she was not alone, but his inexperience with tenderness held him back. How would it look to Westburg if Troy were to reach out to Dani? Or to Grady, especially after he'd promised his friend he would not lead the girl on? When the old man began speaking, Troy was forced to ignore Dani and listen.

"Dani, Jake came upon your papa living with the Mandan Indians on the upper Missouri. Jake had been trading with the tribe when the chief mentioned a white man and woman who had been living among them. They had come to teach the Mandan about the white man's God. Both had recently taken a fever, and the woman had died shortly before Jake arrived. The man, it seemed, was already near death."

"Do you remember the year?" Grady asked.

"Eighteen seventeen. When Jake entered the Indian hut, the sick man thought he was dreaming. Then, when he found Jake was no vision, he claimed his prayers had been answered. His name was Henry Whittaker, and he knew he was dying. He told Jake that his family in New York would pay a king's ransom if Jake would take his little girl back east. She was four years old and sick with the fever herself. An Indian woman had taken her in and was caring for her.

"Whittaker gave Jake his family Bible and begged him to take the girl." Westburg sighed, tiring. "Well, as you know, Jake did take the child from the Indians, and as time passed, he wrote fondly of the girl—Dani, he called her—and of the joy she brought him."

Dani stared hard at the rough plastered wall behind the old man's head. She would *not cry*, she swore to herself. Not in front of Troy and Grady. Not in front of Jake's friend.

" 'I may be doing wrong, keeping her,' Jake wrote in one of his letters," Solomon said, " 'but I can't bear to give her up.' Jake felt that God must have given him the girl to replace the boy he lost. His son only lived to be twelve."

When Troy heard Dani clear her throat, he realized she was trying desperately not to cry. Reaching out beneath the tabletop, he rested his open palm on her thigh.

As Troy's warm, reassuring hand touched her leg, the feeling nearly became her undoing. Blinking furiously, she tried to sneak her right hand up to wipe away the embarrassing tears. Listening to the tale of her own past, she realized how much she had meant to Jake and, at the same time, experienced the intense reaction Troy's touch evoked. Emotion welled up inside her and she fought the urge to run. Instead, she did the only thing she could to relieve some of the tension: She pushed Troy's hand away.

"And so," peering at Dani over his spectacles, Westburg concluded, "it seems that I have lost an old friend and you have lost a father. I wish I were young and spry enough to take you back to your family in New York, but as you can see"—he shrugged in his characteristic manner—"I can barely navigate my own stairs anymore."

"I don't plan on going east, Sol," Dani said, suddenly feeling close to the man who'd remained Jake's friend over the years.

He lowered the glasses on his nose as he stared intently at her, his bright blue eyes missing no detail of her determined expression. "No?"

"No."

"I see."

"I don't think you need to decide your future tonight, Dani," Troy interjected.

She heard a cold reserve she had not heard for weeks in his voice. How had she angered him?

"No deciding to it," she countered. "I don't know these Whittaker folks. They don't know me. My parents are both dead. Jake was my father, as far as I'm concerned. No need to go runnin' after trouble's tail."

"But, Dani, the Whittakers are your family," Solomon reminded her.

"I've got all the family I need, Sol. I got my horse, my gun, and the mountains."

"But what about love, Dani?" Sol asked her sagely.

"From what I've seen, it can be quite a hindrance at times, Sol. Sort of a bother." She stared pointedly at Troy, and Grady had the good grace to look away.

"Well, Dani, no matter what you decide"—Solomon rose and walked to the desk again, this time returning with a ledger—"you have quite a bit of money accrued in Jake's name. I'm sure he would want you to have his share."

"That's what this letter states. It's Jake's will, addressed to you, Mr. Westburg." Troy pushed the letter across the table. Solomon picked it up, read it, and then handed it to Dani. "Just as I thought. Now, let's see . . ." He turned through the pages of the large ledger, searching for the last entry.

"I've kept a close accounting of Jake's funds over the years. Some years were good, some were poor. But that's life."

"I don't need much," Dani told him. "Just enough for coffee, shot and powder, and maybe a new hat. I can make my own clothes." Again she threw Troy a blistering glance, reminding him she had no intention of ever submitting to his wish that she wear a dress.

Jake's partner chuckled, the action shaking his thin shoulders. "Oh, I believe you will have enough to buy a little coffee, Dani. Let's see." He slid the glasses back up his nose and scanned the page, his gaze moving up and down the long columns. "At last tally, there was one hundred twenty-four thousand, five hundred and two dollars and twenty-three cents in Jake's account in the Bank of St. Louis."

"Is that a lot?" Dani, who was used to dealing with no more than five dollars at a time, wanted to know.

Grady laughed out loud and Troy shifted uncomfortably.

Sol turned his gaze to Dani. "That's a fortune, my dear."

"Why don't you just keep it?"

For a moment, Sol was too stunned to speak. "Because I don't need it, Dani. I've made quite a lot of money on my own. Oh"—he waved his hand, indicating the crowded room— "you can't tell by my surroundings, because my tastes are simple, but I have more than I need. Jake's money is yours."

"What'll I do with it?" Dani leaned her elbows on the table and began to massage her temples with her fingertips.

Oh, Jake. What another fine mess.

"Dani." Troy leaned toward her, unable to sit by while she was so obviously distressed, shaken by news that would have elated anyone with more sophistication and knowledge of the world. "You don't have to make any decisions tonight. We'll come back and see Sol tomorrow. I'm sure things will be clearer then."

"You are more than welcome to stay here, Dani," Sol volunteered.

She smiled, knowing the man had little space in the crowded room, but still had been kind enough to offer.

"No, thank you, Solomon." She indicated Troy and Grady with a nod. "I best stick with these two flatlanders. You see, I got them here safely, but there's no telling what kind of trouble they might get into if I leave them on their own."

"May I count on seeing you again tomorrow, Dani?"

"You can bet on it, Sol, as sure as the Mississippi out there flows south."

Troy glanced over his shoulder. Dani lagged behind a few yards as the three of them moved down the darkened street on their way to the hotel. She had paused long enough to bid Solomon Westburg good night and reassure the old man that she would return upon the morrow to visit.

Grady coughed. The loose rattling sound had plagued the artist since his illness. Suddenly aware of the frosty December air, Troy watched as Grady pulled his traveling cloak tighter. Fontaine surveyed the deserted street with little hope of locating a carriage for hire. It was well after nine o'clock, and they were still too near the waterfront to encounter any decent conveyance.

"I can't believe it," Grady said, keeping his voice low. "Dani's come into a small fortune."

"I can believe it." Quickly glancing back over his shoulder, Troy made sure that Dani was still out of hearing distance before he returned his concentration to the sidewalk. "We've had nothing but trouble since we met her."

"That's not true, Troy." Grady defended the girl. "What trouble has she been, really? She's a bit willful, but you have to admit, she certainly livened things up."

Thinking that Grady was referring to his sexual encounters with Dani, Troy halted in midstride, his expression darkening.

"What do you mean by that?"

"*That's* not what I meant," Grady explained hastily, "and you know it. I'm trying to forget about . . . what happened between the two of you."

"I am, too, but I can tell you it's damned hard, Grady, especially with her under our noses day and night. Now it looks as if she's still our responsibility."

"Why do you say that?"

Their boots pounded against the uneven boardwalk as they matched pace with each other. Rounding a corner, the men moved on, lost in conversation. There was a little more traffic about them now, but still no sign of a carriage for hire.

Troy was in a mood to argue. "Look, we brought her as far as St. Louis in order to locate Jake Fisher's partner. We assumed he'd be able to shed some light on Dani's past, and I hoped he would want to take responsibility for her."

Grady waited for a coughing spell to subside before he commented. "And didn't we just find him?"

"Yes, we found him, but can you see Dani staying here, content to live in that crowded little shop? She'd suffocate within the week. And the man's too old to take on such a big responsibility. He can barely walk. Give her two weeks alone here and she'll head back to the mountains, this time without anyone to protect her."

"But she has money now, Troy."

"Exactly. That's what makes this all the more complicated," Troy pointed out. "She has no idea how much money she has. Anyone could dupe her out of it."

"What about her relatives?"

"Should we put her on a stage bound for New York? Just hand her a ticket and big bag of money and wave good-bye?"

"No, but—"

"What if her family turns out to be disreputable? Besides there may be no one left in her family. Dani refuses to adapt, Grady. She won't even wear a dress! St. Louis is one thing—no one here even notices a boy in buckskins—but can you really see her in New York?"

"Can you?" Grady asked quietly.

They were within a block of the Republican Hotel. Troy turned to look at his friend. "What did you say?"

"Can *you* see Dani in Philadelphia or New York? Can you imagine her anywhere out of your sight, Troy?" Before Troy could respond, Grady answered for him. "I don't think you can. This situation is complicated only because you want it to be. I can easily accompany Dani to New York. She is welcome to live with my family while we search for hers. You need not feel this heavy burden of responsibility for her any longer."

Even in the darkness, Grady could see the angry frown that marred Troy's features. "No," he continued, "I can't imagine you would go blithely on your way home to Louisiana and let Dani travel east with me. I know the reason, too, even if you won't admit it to yourself."

"And what, Mr. Philosopher, is that reason?"

Grady halted outside the door to the hotel. "You care too deeply for her to leave her."

Troy was silent for a moment as he stared at Grady. Muted light passed through the frosted glass of the double doors, bathing them both in a golden glow.

Troy could not for the life of him envision Dani in New York with Grady. For the first time he realized it was impossible to imagine because he could not bear to think of her away from him. Had he merely fooled himself, telling himself that he was protecting her, that he was responsible for her, when all the time he should have been guarding his own hardened heart?

"Troy!"

At the sound of panic in Grady's voice, Troy turned his attention once more to his friend.

"What?" He glanced back, following Grady's stare. The sidewalk loomed dark and deserted behind them.

Grady whispered softly, "She's gone."

Chapter Thirteen

Lively, tantalizing fiddle music floated upon the air and wrapped itself about her, luring Dani toward the light and sound that spilled out of the open doorway and onto the sidewalk.

Troy and Grady had kept up a brisk pace as they walked ahead of her through the streets of St. Louis. Within moments, they had become separated by a city block. Turning off onto a narrow side street, she had let the music lead her into the shadows just beyond the well-lit doorway. She glanced around behind her. There was no sign of Troy and Grady. Good. Dani needed time alone, time away from them both. There was no challenge, she knew, to finding the hotel again. She would merely use the river as a starting point and head away from the waterfront.

Two burly figures walked out of the light and came toward her, their silhouettes looming large in the doorway. The men were laughing, deep rolling belly laughs, as one pounded the other on the back. To Dani's delight, both men wore buckskins. The swaying fringe waved as if in welcome as they moved their arms about. One wore a coonskin cap much like the one Jake had always worn, while the other had a bearskin hat atop his wild mane of hair. Both sported long, shaggy beards. Pleased with herself for having located fellow trappers with so little effort, she stepped forward into the shaft of light.

"What sort of place does this claim to be?" she asked, lowering her voice and assuming a masculine stance.

"Well, son," the heavier one began, "this here establishment"—he was weaving as he threw his arm out to indicate the place—"be the Rocky Mountain House Saloon."

The other trapper pulled impatiently on his friend's arm, guiding him down the sidewalk. Dani blinked as her eyes adjusted to the light within and she stepped over the threshold.

The place she'd heard of so often around rendezvous campfires was crowded with men and tables. The entire floor of the room overflowed with shouting figures. Dani slipped inside the doorway and kept to the wall, moving toward the long, highly polished bar that ran along the side of the room nearest the entrance.

Mirrors covered the wall behind the bar. Not the small, often distorted mirrors used for trade, but clear, shining mirrors that doubled the size of the room, the crowd, the colors, and the light within the saloon.

Thinking to stand by unobserved, Dani leaned back against the bar and watched the various scenes that unfolded before her.

At a table close by, five city men were engaged in a game of chance with cards. Some of the men had discarded their coats, which now hung neglected on the backs of their chairs. Across the room, a group of trappers stood around the fiddler, stomping their feet, clapping their hands, and swilling ale from large mugs.

Near a high platform draped with blood-red curtains, a trapper arm wrestled with a keelboatman, each contestant ringed by his own throng of supporters. The wood hues of the trappers' clothing were outshone by the white muslin shirts, blue woolen trousers, and bright red sashes the bulky rivermen wore. The boatmen's heavily muscled arms were hardened and defined by endless miles of poling the keelboats upriver against the current.

"What'll it be for you, boy?"

"Huh?" Startled, Dani turned and found herself facing the bartender. The potbellied man's bulk was nearly hidden by the tall bar. His faded blue eyes shone back at her from behind his sallow skin and bored expression. For a moment she was arrested by her own reflection and stared into the mirror over his shoulder.

"Order up or move on."

"Oh." Dani looked about, wondering what the standard fare was. "What's best?"

"New to St. Louie?"

"Yep."

"Then you best try the beer. We make it right here in the city."

"Beer it is."

She dug deep into the small possible bag at her waist and pulled out the one coin she possessed. The twenty dollar gold piece glinted in the light as she pushed it toward the barkeep.

He slid her a frothy, golden drink topped with bubbles that tried to escape over the rim of the glass. Dani held the brew to the light and watched the dancing bubbles until she heard the clink of coins on the wooden surface of the bar behind her.

She stared at the pile of money.

"Your change." The bartender nodded.

"Thanks." She smiled, pleasantly surprised as she scooped the coins into her hand and placed them in her bag.

The beer had a bitter taste and a stench that was not to her liking, but she raised the glass high and drained the golden liquid as she'd seen the others do. Afterward, Dani knew a strong desire to belch.

"Another?" The bartender appeared out of nowhere.

"Whiskey."

"Didn't care for the beer, son?"

"Not much," she admitted.

The glass he brought was only half filled with whiskey and was much smaller than the glass containing the beer had been. The price was higher, too. Still, the stuff kicked like a cross-eyed mule, and by the time she had drained the whiskey from the tiny glass, she was feeling happier than she had in days.

The warm, comfortable saloon, redolent with the smell of leather and wool, appealed to her; the smoke that clouded the air was not scented with pine, but it reminded her of her past all the same.

Dani crossed her arms beneath her breasts and leaned against the bar. When a man dressed in tight woolen trousers with stirrups beneath his highly polished boots stepped from behind the plush red curtains on the wide platform, the noise in the room gradually hushed. The men elbowed one another into silence and faced the stage. Soon only the sound of chair legs scraping across the floor broke the hush as the men turned toward the curtains. Dani watched the man on the high platform above the crowd as he stepped forward and spread his hands wide with a flourish. She felt drawn to him, for in many ways, he reminded her of Troy.

His hair, like his eyes, was dark brown and shone in the light as if it had been greased. His build was not unlike Troy Fontaine's, but where Troy's dark features were often shadowed by his mysterious silences and faraway look, this man's expression exuded gaiety and expectation. Dani felt compelled to watch and listen. Her surroundings forgotten for the moment, she was entranced by the scene upon the strange platform rimmed with tin-shaded candles.

"Welcome, gents. Welcome. It's time once again to *introduce* another of the Rocky Mountain House Saloon's famous *songbirds* for your *listening*, and *visual*, pleasure! At this time . . ." He paused, allowing the anticipation to build, glancing around the room to make certain all eyes were focused upon him. "At this time," he repeated, "we present, Miss . . . Glory . . . Hallelujah!"

Thunderous applause accompanied by shouts and foot-stomping reverberated on the air. Dani found herself joining the throng, clapping enthusiastically, awaiting the announced appearance of Miss Glory Hallelujah.

The handsome man who'd introduced Miss Hallelujah disappeared through the break in the center of the curtains. The cheering and shouts subsided until there was not a sound in the warm room. Dani found herself holding her breath. When the curtains drew apart, as if by magic, opening to reveal a vision in gold standing in the center of the platform, Dani straightened and stared.

The woman was unlike anyone Dani had ever seen or imagined. She figured this one must be some sort of a queen, so wondrous was the shining golden gown she wore. Her skin was as white as the pure linen of Troy's finest shirt. Her cheeks were tinted like ripe apples, her lips pursed into a small heart-shaped bow that glowed redder than hot coals.

Dani found herself most amazed by the woman's hair. It was of a glorious red-gold color, and it hung free past her waist. Shorter curls framed her face, ethereal wisps that gave her an unearthly quality.

"Glory Hallelujah!" Dani whispered. She waited spellbound to see what Miss Hallelujah would do next.

The woman raised her hand, brushed aside a wisp of long,

glorious hair, and took a slow, sensuous step forward. The men burst into raucous applause.

That's it? Dani wondered. *She just stands there and the men act as if they're weak north of their ears?*

Miss Glory raised her dainty white hand again. This time the movement reminded Dani of the soft flutter of a butterfly's wings, and as if under the spell of an Indian shaman, the men quieted again.

The fiddle began to play. A piano—an instrument Dani had not seen before, but recognized from stories she'd been told—sent tinny-sounding notes into the air.

When she realized the apparition on the platform was about to sing, Dani took a quick breath and watched the pursed carmine lips open. Out trilled the sound of Glory's voice, high, pure, and clear. She sang at a pitch much higher than Dani would have guessed possible to achieve: " 'In Scarlet Town where I was born, there was a fair maid dwellin', made every youth cry, "Well-a-day," and her name was Barb'ry Allen.' "

Dani found herself mouthing the words to one of the first songs Jake had ever taught her. She could not take her eyes off the golden-haired singer until the song had ended and the saloon patrons erupted into wall-shaking applause. Scanning the tables, Dani could not help but notice the awe and admiration in the eyes of the men as they gazed up at Glory Hallelujah.

And to think, Dani mused in wonder, all the girl had done was open her mouth and sing.

Oh, it was true, Dani admitted to herself, Miss Hallelujah was beauty itself standing there with her waterfall of hair that held all the colors of a flaming sunset. Her gold dress revealed the pure white skin of her shoulders, and her breasts were shoved up so far they might have been a ledge, but it was the high, pure sound of the notes she sang that Dani admired most.

I can do that.

The unbidden thought struck her as swift and fast as a lightning bolt, and Dani burned with the energy it produced. She whirled around and signaled to the barkeep, who kept her waiting impatiently while he drew beer from an oak keg. Finally, the man ambled in her direction.

"Another whiskey, son?" He had to shout over the turmoil caused by the men's reaction to Miss Glory's song.

"No," Dani yelled back. "I want to sing, like Glory Hallelujah."

"What?"

"I said—" She started to shout just as the crowd quieted, eagerly awaiting another song. Dani lowered her voice to a whisper that carried across the bar. "I want to sing."

"Go right on ahead, boy, but do it outside the doors. Sing your lungs out." The man started to turn aside.

"Wait!" Dani called out sharply. To avoid a scene, the man returned. "I want to talk to that dark-haired fella that was up there."

"Won't do you any good."

Dani pinned him with a threatening squint-eyed stare and growled, "Now."

"Johnson's backstage." The bartender nodded toward a side door near the far end of the room. "You make any trouble, boy, and we have plenty of meat just itchin' to toss you out on your skinny ass."

Dani did not hear the threat, for she had already turned and begun to shove her way through the crowd standing near the bar. The men were unaware of the slight disturbance she caused as she jostled past. They were all staring starry-eyed at Miss Glory Hallelujah.

"I'm taking you back to the hotel," Troy announced when Grady broke into another fit of coughing. He used Grady's brass-handled cane to tap the ceiling of the carriage and alert the driver. When the vehicle halted, Troy called out instructions.

They had searched for Dani for over an hour with no luck. Rousing Solomon once again, they disturbed the old man with the news that Dani was missing. He had not seen her.

"I'll do better alone, Grady. You stay at the hotel." When his friend appeared about to refuse, he added, "Dani may return and take off again in search of us. One of us should wait there for her."

Deep shadows purpled the skin beneath Grady's eyes as fatigue and worry worked to weaken him.

"All right, but, Troy, take my cape and my pistol. No telling where you might find her."

"Meaning . . . ?"

"Meaning I have a feeling you should probably look for the

place most likely to harbor trouble of some sort. Dani will probably be there in the midst of it all."

The cape and pistol exchanged hands and when the carriage stopped before the hotel, Grady was slow to alight. He stood in the dim light and raised his hand in salute, listening as Trey directed the driver to return to the waterfront.

"Is this a joke?"

Joe Johnson stared down in disbelief at the youth eagerly pleading for a chance to sing. "Those men out there don't want to hear a boy sing—or look at one, either."

The dressing room backstage was a cramped space with barely room for the two of them to stand. A table stood against one wall, a mirror speckled with age spots hung in a chipped gilded frame that had begun to tarnish. Brushes and jars lined the tabletop; long, colorful plumes from birds unidentifiable to Dani hung from hooks against the wall as did dresses of shining material that glittered in the lamplight.

She stared around the room, remembering the sound of Glory's voice and the awe reflected in the men's eyes as they listened to the golden-haired woman sing. Taking a deep breath, she found she had to force the next words from her throat. Dani prayed she was not making the biggest mistake of her life.

"I'm not a boy."

She never thought to hear herself admit it out loud under such circumstances, especially to a stranger.

He was not easily convinced.

Dani pulled off her hat and faced him, tossing back her barely shoulder length hair while raking her fingers through it.

Joe Johnson reached out and tilted her chin toward the lamplight with his fingertip, turned her head back and forth, and inspected her like a man buying a mule. He stared into her smoke-gray eyes.

"Well, I'll be damned."

The sound of a woman's lilting voice floated in from the doorway. "You will be damned, Joe Johnson, if Olivia doesn't show up again tonight. I *refuse* to perform every show."

Dani turned toward the woman framed by the doorway and found herself face to face with Glory Hallelujah.

Up close, the woman was even more exotic, her features outlined with paint like an Indian's, her hair long and lustrous.

Glory moved into the room with slow, calculated motions that reminded Dani of a snake.

"What's this?" Glory stared back at her, wrinkling her upturned nose in distaste.

Dani clenched her fists.

Joe Johnson stepped into the space between them. He could ill afford to see one of his songbirds maimed.

"This"—he indicated Dani with a nod—"could be the answer to our prayers."

"Remind me to quit praying," Glory quipped.

To Dani's amazement, the young woman then turned her back to Johnson and demanded, "Unbutton me."

His fingers nimbly began to unfasten the long row of buttons that ran nearly the length of the golden dress. "Seriously, Glory," he explained as he bent over the task, "the kid says she can sing. Olivia hasn't shown up yet and she's due to go on in thirty minutes. I'd say it's a safe bet that Olivia's not coming at all."

"My voice can't take doing all three shows."

"That's what I'm sayin'." He indicated Dani. "We've got the Rocky Mountain Maid here raring to sing."

Glory turned and inspected her with a critical eye.

"*Can* she sing?" Glory arched the fine line of her painted brow.

Dani finally found her tongue. "You two are talking about me like I'm not even here. Where I come from, that's not good manners."

"Manners?" Glory scoffed, her gaze sweeping Dani from head to toe again.

"Sing something," Joe demanded.

"Like what?" Dani shrugged.

"Anything you want."

She searched her mind for a melody to match the one that Glory had sung and decided upon the very same tune. Without preamble, Dani closed her eyes and let the music flow through her.

When the song ended, she opened her eyes once more only to discover Glory and Joe both staring at her, dumbfounded.

"Can you do something with her?" Joe asked Glory.

Once more Dani stood forgotten as they talked around her. Glory slipped the glorious golden gown from her shoulders, and for a moment Dani held her breath. Would they ask her to wear it? Glory tossed the gown over a nearby chair.

Dani could not help staring at the other woman's figure. She was bound up tight, tied into a long contraption that narrowed her middle and pushed up her breasts to form the intriguing shelf of flesh that her gown had done more to emphasize than to hide.

"Hand me my robe," Glory imperiously commanded Joe, who sidestepped Dani and pulled a flowered gown off an open dressing screen in the corner. Glory slipped it on and loosely belted the silk robe before she walked over to Dani and reached out to touch her thick sun-lightened brown hair.

"Nice texture. Needs to be combed." She turned Dani's face as Joe had done earlier. "Pretty short. We'll have to sweep it up off her neck."

"Take off your jacket," Joe ordered.

"No."

Puzzled by Dani's affronted attitude, he asked, "Why not?"

"Why should I?"

"If I'm paying you good money to sing, I'm looking over the merchandise."

"You'd *pay* me to sing?" Dani was incredulous.

"Take off the jacket."

Dani took it off.

"Now the shirt."

"No!"

"I can't tell what's under that rag."

Dani stepped forward threateningly. "Take my word for it—*me! I'm* what's under here."

Without warning, Joe put his arms around Dani and pulled on her shirt from behind until it hugged her breasts.

"Bigger than Olivia," Glory stated objectively, "but I think I can squeeze her into the red dress."

"Okay by me," Joe agreed. "I'm counting on you, Glory girl. You've got twenty minutes."

Glory smiled for the first time, and Dani marveled at the way the woman's beautiful features lit up.

Dani stood watching the smiling couple. Would Troy ever smile at her that way? What would he think if he knew what she was about to do? The beautiful Glory certainly appeared to be respectable enough. Perhaps she was one of the society women Troy had lectured Dani about. Dani wished he could be there, watching her from the audience with the same awe she'd seen in the other men's eyes as they watched Glory sing.

"Are you sure I have to go out there all geegawed up like this?"

"That you do, sugarplum. That you do." Glory leaned down to dab a last bit of rouge on Dani's cheeks. "Those men buy plenty of beer and whiskey while they wait for us to sing. We gotta keep 'em happy."

As she stared into the speckled mirror, Dani wondered who it was that stared back. She had almost stalked out of the dressing room earlier when Glory insisted she wear a gown.

"Do I have to?" Dani moaned.

"Why wouldn't you want to wear a beautiful gown like this?" Glory wanted to know as she held up a red gown of the same shining material as her own gold dress.

"To tell you the truth, Miss Hallelujah, I never even had a dress on."

The brilliant blue eyes widened as Glory's lips formed a perfect circle. "Oh . . . ? Never?"

"Never."

"Well, then, what a treat for you, hon. The very first dress you'll ever wear is one you'll probably never forget. Now, get those things off."

Dani had been pushed and prodded, poked and painted, until she no longer recognized the girl who stared back at her from the tarnished gilt-framed mirror. Her wide smoke-colored eyes were outlined with dark kohl.

"Why?" Dani had asked when Glory applied the black lines above and beneath her lashes.

"Your eyes will show up all the way to the back of the room."

"Why?" Dani asked again as Glory painted her mouth crimson red.

"Same reason. Besides, the men love it."

Glory brushed Dani's hair and twisted it into a knot atop her head. Pins were gouged into the mass until Dani swore so vehemently that Glory stopped poking them in. Donning the whalebone corset nearly forced Dani to come to blows with the singer, but the equally strong-willed Glory warned that Olivia's dress would never fit if Dani did not "suck in her gut" another inch. It took all of Dani's willpower to keep from staring at her own breasts. They jutted up and nearly over the top of the corset.

"You've got nice ones," Glory complimented. "Be proud."

The dress slipped easily over Dani's head as Glory admonished her not to "ruin" her hair. The satin slid effortlessly over Dani's shoulders, whispered down the length of her body and over her hips.

"Where's the rest?" Dani wanted to know, hiking up the bodice. The red satin failed to expand. Glory ignored her.

Black silk stockings and the same silly cloth slippers Dani had seen on the hotel women soon adorned her feet and legs. Dani wished fervently that Troy could see her now, even though the dress was a strange one. The front of the skirt was slit high up on her thighs to expose the tapered length of her legs while the back shimmered along the floor in a wide, swooping train.

"There's no time to practice walking, so when the curtains open, *don't move,* for God's sake," Glory warned, "or you'll end up on your pretty painted face."

Dani jumped when a sharp rapping sounded upon the door. Glory called out a warning, "Just a second." She turned to Dani and took her by the hand. "Stand up, honey. Let's see what Joe thinks."

Glory swung the door wide, and Joe stood flabbergasted, staring at the transformation.

When Dani took a deep breath, both Joe and Glory held theirs in fear. Both pairs of eyes focused on Dani's breasts.

"For heaven's sake, don't do that on stage," Joe admonished with a crooked smile. "It might start a riot."

When she realized what he meant, Dani stared down at the generous display of flesh that threatened to spill out over the top of her borrowed gown.

"You might rip the dress, so move as little as possible," Glory warned for the third time.

"Can you do anything about her neck?" Joe asked.

Dani twisted, trying to catch a glimpse of her neck in the mirror, and felt the seams of the dress strain. She quickly straightened. "What's wrong with my neck?"

"There's a definite color line where your skin's been exposed to the sun," Glory explained, rummaging through the boxes piled beneath the dressing table. "Here," she called out. "This should do the trick."

"There's not much time left. At ten-thirty, they expect another show," Joe warned.

Glory fastened a wide strip of lace about the column of Dani's throat. "Better?"

"Elegant," Joe said. "Now, how about her hands?"

Glory snapped her fingers. "Gloves!" She grabbed a pair of fingerless lace gloves from the clutter on the tabletop and helped Dani slip them on.

As the golden-haired woman took in the final results of her handiwork, Dani felt the first qualms of doubt assail her.

"You look beautiful, honey," Glory admitted. "A real showstopper."

"What's your name again?" Joe asked.

"Dani."

"Danny? That'll never do." He shook his head and began to pace, a nearly impossible move in the confined area. "You're from the Rockies?"

"Yep."

"Rocky Mountain Maid? You said that before," Glory reminded him.

"Too flat. Sounds like she's been off milking cows." Joe paced two steps and turned. "Do you speak any French? Most trappers do."

"A little. None of it polite." Dani thought of Grady.

Joe snapped his fingers. "Can you imitate a French accent?"

Her mind was blank for a moment and she wondered if the corset had stopped the flow of blood to her brain. Suddenly, a French trapper known as Laframboise came to mind. She tried to remember the way he spoke.

"*Oui*. Eez ziss ze accent zat you are theenking of, me-shuh?"

Delighted, Joe Johnson clapped his hands. "Perfect! I'll introduce you as Danielle, the Mistress of the Mountains. If you want to say anything between songs, just whisper sort of huskylike and use that accent. You'll do just fine, Danielle. How's that sound, Glory?"

He whirled around. The motion set his long coattails flying.

"Sounds great, Joey. And it sounds as if you are going to have a riot on your hands if you don't go out and quiet them down. Come on, Danielle." Glory stepped behind Dani and gathered the wide train over her arm. "I'll help you up to the stage."

Chapter Fourteen

Her heart was pounding so loud that Dani barely heard the applause which began to swell as Joe slipped between the tightly closed curtains to announce the Mistress of the Mountains. Vaguely, she felt Glory squeeze her hand before the older woman left her standing alone. Dani stared at the tattered lining of the curtains that hid the room from her view. Joe reappeared all too quickly and gave her a wink before he, too, left her all alone. She took a deep breath, then remembered the precarious condition her breasts were in and quickly released it. As Joe manipulated the backstage ropes, the curtains parted and the barroom crowded with men was exposed to Dani's view.

Every eye in the room was focused upon her, every ear straining to hear the sound of her voice. For a moment, Dani was paralyzed. Her heart continued to pound and a sharp, metallic taste she feared was blood sat upon her tongue.

How did Glory make standing before such an unruly throng appear so effortless?

Breathe.

Dani tried to remember every detail of Glory's act. She pictured herself leaning against the bar in her friendly, familiar buckskins, watching this new Dani . . . this Danielle.

Slowly she raised one gloved hand to the lace collar that banded her throat.

The crowd hushed.

The delicate piece of lace was too constricting, tightening against her vocal chords and threatening to stop her breathing. As her fingers made contact with the lace choker, Dani tugged lightly, pulling the piece free. Dropping her hand to her side, she opened her fingers and let the lace drift to the floorboards.

The crowd went wild.

Her eyes widened as she watched the reaction of the men. They stomped and shouted. High-pitched whistles shrilled, slicing the air. A few men in the back of the room were now standing on their chairs.

What would Glory do?

Dani smiled.

Slowly, seductively, she raised her hand again. Unconsciously, she gave the Indian sign for silence and was understood by most of the men in the room.

The quiet that ensued was more deafening than the applause.

A heady sense of power swelled up inside Dani and she found herself bursting to sing, to entertain, to delight these men who waited spellbound for her to begin.

If only Troy were here to see me now. Grady, too. For once, they'd be so proud.

Dani dropped her hand to her sides and lifted her chin. When she opened her lips to sing, the sound came out true and clear as always. Just as Joe Johnson had promised, the piano and fiddle player picked up the accompaniment: " 'As I went out walkin', upon a fine day, I got awful lonesome, as the day passed away. I sat down a-musin', alone on the grass, when who should sit beside me, but a sweet Indian lass.' "

Gradually relaxing, Dani soon found she was enjoying herself. The men—trappers, gamblers, boatmen, and farmers—gazed at her in rapt attention. She allowed herself to look around the room, making eye contact with as many individuals as possible, and watched them smile in return. Almost before she was aware of it, the song had ended and applause nearly deafened her once more.

As pleased with the audience as they were with her, Dani waved at the crowd and then signaled them into silence again. It was as if she knew them all intimately at that moment.

Four songs later, Dani felt just as elated, when out of the corner of her eye, she caught a signal from Joe. "One more," he mouthed the words. She noticed Glory standing beside him, this time costumed in a violet gown covered with frothing lace. Nodding in understanding, Dani took another breath and began to sing the song that was Grady's favorite: " 'My days have been so wondrous free . . .' "

She let her gaze roam the room and was pleased by the men's response to the song. Most were smiling; many were staring with faraway expressions as the music carried them to other places and other times: " 'Ask the gliding waters if a tear of mine increased their stream, and ask the breathing gales if ever I lent a sigh to them . . .' "

Her attention was drawn to a tall figure standing near the edge of the stage cloaked in a forest-green cape. The notes of the song faded away, the last line remained unsung as Dani found herself staring into familiar obsidian eyes that burned with suppressed fury.

Beyond the footlights, Troy Fontaine stood glaring up at her.

He took two slow steps forward until he stood at the very apron of the stage.

"Get down, Dani."

His voice was a hushed whisper, but the anger in his tone could not be disguised. Tears pooled in her eyes, and Dani furiously blinked them away. For a moment the men in the room sat stunned and unmoving as they watched the scene being played out before them.

Please don't be angry. Dani could only shake her head, rejecting Troy's demand.

"Sit down, mister, and let the lady sing!"

The furious shout came from a barrel-chested boatman who shoved his chair away from the table and stood with fists clenched in anger. Harsh comments of agreement followed.

Dani could feel the sudden, hostile change in the crowd and knew instinctively that they were slipping beyond her control. Thinking to protect her, the men were ready to attack Troy. Dani refused to let that happen; the odds were against Troy escaping with his life if the men grew angry enough. She could see by Troy's dark, furious mood that he was willing to challenge them all.

She had to act and act fast.

Stepping forward, Dani tried to attract the attention of the crowd, but found herself hobbled by the train of her skirt. As she fought for balance, Troy leapt up on the stage and quickly crossed to her side. He held a pistol in the air, threatening anyone who dared approach them. His hand grasped her waist, and she winced at the strength of his fingers as they clasped her side.

"The *lady*, gentlemen, is through singing for the evening."

His voice carried over the sound of the frustrated, angry murmurs of the saloon's patrons.

Dani could not believe what was happening, but she found herself mesmerized by the power of command that radiated from Troy. Not a soul in the room moved to stop him as he held her pressed against his side. The pistol, primed and ready, was now pointed toward the crowd to hold the men at bay.

He leaned toward her and whispered in her ear, "You had better warn your backstage friend that I won't hesitate to kill him if he raises that gun."

Joe stood in the wings, armed and ready to stop Troy if he had to.

"It's all right, Joe," Dani called out.

A slight movement to the right of the stage alerted Troy to impending danger, and he took aim at a tall, thin man who was slowly approaching the stage.

"Stay put, mister, if you want to live to see tomorrow. The same goes for all of you," Troy called out. "I'm taking the girl with me, and if you're wise, you'll all sit tight and finish your drinks. This place," he added in a tone that brooked no question, "is surrounded, and will be until we're well clear of here."

"He's right!" Dani shouted, acting out of fear for Troy's safety. "He's the leader of forty of the most highly trained mercen—oof!"

The wind was forced from her lungs as Troy slung Dani over his shoulder and slowly walked toward the edge of the stage. As his feet hit the floor and his shoulder gouged into her rib cage, she gasped in pain.

Rear end in the air, head dangling, Dani managed an exit that was far more dramatic, if not as polished, as her entrance. Troy kept his back to the wall and worked his way slowly to the open doors of the saloon. Dani could see nothing as she hung over his shoulder except the floor and the backs of Troy's legs. She felt the shock of the cold night air when Troy moved through the doors and out onto the street.

He threw her onto the floor of a carriage and instructed the driver to whip the horses as if the devil were after them.

Dani hauled herself up to a sitting position, but was unable to move any farther and remained on the floor. The train of the gown was wound about her legs and pinned beneath her.

Furious with the ominously silent figure who comfortably

occupied the carriage seat alone, Dani refused to speak until Troy did. With an indignant huff, she crossed her arms and sat staring at the stars beyond the carriage window.

Empty moments of silence stretched on in the small interior of the creaking carriage. Dani was beginning to shiver with cold by the time the vehicle stopped outside the hotel.

Without a word, Troy flung the door wide, descended the steps, then reached in and grabbed Dani by the wrist. She tried to twist out of his strong grasp but found his fingers clamped about her with the strength of steel bands. She had no choice but to obey as he pulled her out of the carriage and stood her none too gently on the sidewalk. Still he held her wrist in his fierce grip.

With his free hand, Troy flipped a coin to the driver, and the carriage rattled away until it became a dark shadow that disappeared down the street, the sound of horseshoes clattering against the cobblestones.

Tugging at the long ties that held the cloak about his shoulders, Troy freed the wrap and whipped it off. The heavy woolen cape flared before it settled upon Dani's shoulders. It covered her to the ankles, concealing the vibrant crimson dress, except for the cumbersome train that spilled out beneath the cape's hem.

As if he had practiced the task hundreds of times, Troy looped the train over his arm and placed his free hand on Dani's shoulder. Silently, he propelled her forward, forcing her to walk as his fingertips bit into the sensitive muscle across her shoulder.

The lobby was deserted. When they reached the second-floor landing and turned the corner to enter the long, carpeted hallway, the sour-faced man who had assigned them their room nearly ran headlong into Dani.

Bug-eyed, he lost no time taking in her hair, the heavy makeup, and the long train draped over Troy's arm.

"Mr. Fontaine," the fragile excuse for a man sputtered, "this just isn't *done* at the Republican."

With an icy stare, Troy crooked a brow and dared the man to delay him further. He brushed past the gaping hotel clerk and stopped before a tall green door that looked no different from the twelve others that lined the hallway.

Troy twisted the knob and the door opened inward to reveal

Grady, still fully dressed, resting against the headboard of the widest, tallest bed Dani had ever seen.

Troy released his death grip on her shoulder, and immediately thereafter she felt his hand against the small of her back. He pushed her forward before him into the room.

Yanking the cloak from her shoulders, Troy tossed it over a chair near the door. When Grady straightened, stared, and then exclaimed, "Holy hot shit!" Dani knew she was as deep in trouble as a mule in a bog.

"Sit." Troy pointed to a chair near the bureau.

Dani sat.

Troy paced.

An undercurrent of silence charged the room with an almost visible tension. Grady stood up, straightened his cravat, brushed imaginary wrinkles from his trousers, and stared at them both before he said, "I think I should leave."

"No!" Dani implored just as Troy commanded, "Stay."

Grady sat.

Troy continued to pace. And fume.

Dani ignored them both and stared at her legs, exposed by the slit in the skirt of the red gown and encased in black silk stockings.

"Would either of you like to tell me what happened?" Grady asked.

Neither deemed it necessary to answer him.

"Fine." Grady drummed his fingers on the bedside table. The silence stretched on, the only sounds in the room those of Troy's boots ringing against the polished oak floorboards and the tapping of Grady's fingers. Occasionally Grady coughed. He alternately stared in shocked disbelief, then looked away from Dani.

Finally Troy halted his pacing and stood before the bureau, staring at the bottle of brandy Grady had purchased earlier to help relieve his cough. Troy poured himself a liberal amount, quaffed it quickly without regard for the rich, heady quality of the liquor, poured and downed another, and then poured a third, only to set it aside as he turned and pointed at Dani.

"I found her," he began at last, the words forced from behind nearly clenched teeth, "singing on the stage at one of the more disreputable saloons in St. Louis."

A smile twitched the corners of Grady's lips. "Dani *is* a fine singer."

"I found her standing in the center of a stage before a hundred men, dressed in that . . . *that*"—he pointed furiously at the red gown, at a loss for words—"looking like a French whore." His voice rose uncharacteristically on the last word.

Grady moved from where he had lounged against the cherrywood headboard. "Troy, calm down. There's no need to use that language in front of her."

Dani jumped up, unwilling to have Grady defend her. "Forget it, Grady. You don't have to speak my piece for me, and you certainly don't have to defend me. Not to *him*." She nearly spat out the word as she faced Troy square on. "He's nothing but a damned hypocrite." Dani felt her temper rise as the humiliation Troy had forced her to feel earlier subsided.

"Hypocrite?" Stepping closer, Troy towered over her, pinning her with his brooding stare.

"Yeah. You think I don't know what the word means, don't you? Well, even where I come from, we've got hypocrites. It means two-faced, forked-tongued. It means you say one thing and do another. For days you've been trying to get me to put on a dress." Hands on hips, Dani refused to back down before Troy's fierce glare. "And when I do, you act like you got nothing under your hat for brains except hair."

For a moment Troy did not move, so stunned was he by her logic. To Dani, a dress was a dress. She obviously felt perfectly justified in her actions. Never mind the fact that she had paraded around half naked before a roomful of the horniest, orneriest men he'd ever seen. Troy stared down at Dani, missing no detail of her appearance. Her rich reddish brown hair was still pinned atop her head. One heavy lock had fallen to dangle against her right cheek. The dark kohl outlined her eyes, enhanced and enlarged them, turning them into deep pools of silver.

Her smooth cheeks were highlighted with rouge; his fingertips ached to stroke them. Her lips were glossy red, like lush, ripe fruit; he could almost taste them. Her breasts strained against the gown's low neckline; his palms itched to cup them. Troy found himself being lured toward her, leaning forward like a willow bending with the breeze. But he had never bent before, and he refused to bend now.

Troy straightened and shook his head, disgusted with

himself. He had almost succumbed to the lure of her innocent seduction again.

Dani read the changing expressions on Troy's face, first anger, then hunger, and now disgust. The last struck her as hard as if he had slapped her full force. Troy was disgusted with what she had done, with the way she looked, with her.

She backed down, backed away from Troy and the pained look on his face. Dani turned and fought to hide the tears she was suddenly powerless to halt.

Troy thought her move just another act of defiance. Still angry with himself, he turned to Grady and sought to vent his fury.

"You should have seen her, Grady. It was priceless." Troy reached out for the brandy and swilled it down. He rammed the empty glass down on the bureau with such force that Grady winced. "Hypocrite? I'll tell you about a hypocrite, *pet* . . ." Troy did not see Dani flinch.

Grady did. "Troy . . ."

But Troy Fontaine would not be stilled. "She won't wear a dress when *I* ask her to. Oh, no. But when some two-bit saloon owner asks, she not only wears a dress, she lets them paint her up like a china doll."

Dani continued to face the wall, refusing to look at him. Troy crossed the room and stood behind her. She could feel the hot anger radiating from him.

"Why? That's all I want to know. Why did you do it?" His long fingers bit into her shoulder as he whirled her around to face him.

Her cheeks were streaked with tears. The realization that she had allowed herself to cry shocked him more than the grotesque trail left by the watered kohl.

Gasping, she inhaled a deep, shuddering breath. "I on . . . only . . . wanted to . . . s . . . sing."

Troy stood immobilized by her tears.

Grady walked to the washstand. A tall porcelain pitcher stood inside a matching washbowl. He splashed water into the bowl, then pulled a linen towel off a rack attached to the side of the stand and dipped a corner into the tepid water. Sidestepping Troy, he handed the towel to Dani.

"Wash your face, Dani. And you leave her alone, Troy."

The force behind Grady's command surprised both Troy and Dani. They turned simultaneously to stare at their usually unassertive friend. Dani reached out with a shaking hand, took the towel, and began to rub the tears and makeup off of her face.

"Now—" Grady began.

A forceful knock on the door interrupted his next words. The tall blond man reached back and opened the door, only to find the gangly hotel clerk staring back at him.

"Mr. Fontaine," the clerk demanded Troy's attention.

Fontaine turned and acknowledged the man without a word.

The clerk's gaze roamed the room as he spoke, taking in Grady, Troy, the rumpled bed, and Dani's disheveled appearance. The men's baggage as well as Dani's pile of pelts and hide bundles were still stacked against the wall. He cleared his throat; his Adam's apple jumped and then fell back into place.

"Mr. Fontaine, it seems an extra room has become available. A guest departed quite hastily." The clerk shot another wild glance in Dani's direction, then held out a key to Troy. "As I said before, *this*"—he raised his eyebrows accusingly at all three of them—"just *is not done* at the Republican. The empty room is across the hallway."

Troy took the key with a curt nod and then slammed the door in the man's face.

"As I was saying," Grady began again, "I'd like to know what happened tonight, and I would like to have it explained to me in as sane a manner as possible . . . Well?" Grady waited for either of them to speak.

Toweling her face one final time, Dani peered over the cloth at Grady as he waited, leaning against the bureau. Troy had crossed the room to stand near the window and stare out at the darkened street below. As stubborn as they both were, Dani knew it would be morning before Grady gave up or Troy gave in.

She was bone-tired. The corset was so tightly laced that she could barely breathe. Dani handed Grady the limp, discolored towel.

"I wanted to sing." She shrugged, speaking softly to Grady, all the while watching Troy's reaction to her words. "I heard the fiddles, followed the music, and then a girl named Glory Hallelujah started to sing."

Her eyes took on a glow with the recollection, and Dani was carried away as she related her adventure. "Oh, Grady, you would have loved seeing her. She had wondrous hair that

ripples and curls down to her knees. It's the color of a
November sunset. And she wore a dress of gold. She sang like
such an angel that I expected to see Jake come flyin' out and
stand alongside her."

Dani sank to the chair behind her and leaned back with
closed eyes. She continued her story.

"I drank a beer." Her eyes flew open and she gave Grady
a mischievous half-smile. "It was awful. And I watched the
men enjoyin' Glory's songs. I thought, now *here's* somethin'
you know about, Dani, somethin' you can do. So I asked
the man in charge could I sing. He had me sing to him
first, and then he said"—she paused long enough to look at
Troy and then lowered her voice—"he said the men wouldn't
pay to see me sing dressed like a boy.

"I wanted to be up there so *bad*, Grady. More than anything.
That's why I let 'em put on the dress and paint me up. I didn't
know it was wrong."

Grady looked down at her, understanding reflected in his
eyes. "I know you didn't, Dani."

"I just wanted to surprise you . . . both." Her gaze moved
to Troy who still had not turned around. "I wanted to make you
proud. I'm sorry if I caused you worry."

"Don't think about it anymore, Dani. You're safe now, and
that's all that matters." As Grady looked at Troy, who still had
not moved away from the window, the artist was taken by a
sudden violent fit of coughing, harsh enough to cause him to
double over with pain.

"Grady!" Dani jumped to her feet to assist him. When he
heard the urgency in her tone, Troy bolted to his friend's other
side. They supported Grady between them and moved slowly
toward the bed.

"I'll be fine," Grady managed to gasp. "Troy, will you see
that Dani gets to her room?"

Troy shifted uneasily. His eyes met Dani's across the bed
before they dropped to take in the deep cleavage exposed by
the shimmering gown.

She scooped up the train of her gown, tossed it over her arm,
and marched to the door. Dramatically, she flung it open and
turned to face Grady.

"Good night, Grady. I hope you feel better."

"See you tomorrow, Dani."

"'Morrow." As she stepped out into the hallway, Grady called out after her.

"Dani?"

"Yep."

"I wish I could have heard you sing."

Unbidden tears bathed her eyes again, and she turned away, blinking fiercely.

There was no warm cloak about her shoulders this time as Troy stood behind her in the hallway. He brushed against her as he inserted the key in the lock of the room across the hall, and Dani hastily stepped aside. The door swung open. Light from the hallway revealed a room much like the first. Troy lit the oil lamps, one on the washstand and another on the bedside table.

Immediately after completing the task he turned and left the room, not even bothering to close the door behind him. As she reached for the knob, the sound of Troy's footsteps sounded again in the hallway. Carrying her possessions in his arms, he walked wordlessly to the far side of the bed and dumped them unceremoniously on the floor. As he passed by Dani again, she watched him pause for a fraction of a second, hesitating. When he moved to leave, Dani called him back with a hushed whisper, "Fontaine, wait."

She hated having to ask this man for anything. But unless she intended to spend the night trussed up in the uncomfortable corset and dress, he would just have to help.

Troy stopped dead still. When he slowly turned to face her, Dani tried to read the shuttered expression in his dark eyes. She nearly gave up the idea of asking him to help her, for she could not bear his touch now, but the discomfort caused by the ill-fitting dress outweighed any distress his nearness might bring. Calling upon her strength, she behaved in the same haughty manner Glory had displayed. Dani turned her back to Troy and announced coolly, "Unbutton me."

When he did not begin the task immediately, Dani was tempted to look over her shoulder. Then she felt his fingers slowly working the buttons free. Clutching the front of the gown to her breasts, she held the dress up as the back slowly opened. His movements stopped at a point near the small of her back.

Without being asked to do so, he reached inside the open

back of the red gown and untied the laces of her corset. Dani let out a deep sigh of relief, but refused to turn and face him.

"Good night." She dismissed him curtly, the coldness in her tone belying the heat she felt along the path his fingers had traced down her spine. The door latched behind her. Dani did not turn around again until she heard him cross the hall and close the door to his own room.

Only then, when she was certain Troy was gone and could not see the tears that had once more started to flow, did she turn and face the door.

Chapter Fifteen

Inside room 207, Troy found Grady amazingly recovered, and pouring himself a liberal splash of brandy. A long white nightshirt had replaced his clothing and as Grady combed his already neat hair, Troy's expression became one of cynicism.

"I see you've recovered remarkably."

"Quite remarkably. Did you apologize to her?" Grady asked.

"No, and if that was the reason you came down with that violent attack of consumption, you wasted your strength."

"She made a mistake, Troy. Haven't we all at one time or another? You don't realize what a madman you must have seemed to her tonight. I never thought to see Dani break down and cry the way she did."

Grady finished the brandy and crossed the room. He lifted the bedcovers and slipped between the sheets. "Why did you rail at her like that? You said some pretty rough things."

"Why?" The anger lashed out of Troy again. As he recalled the scene in the saloon, he experienced the same overpowering emotion that had nearly blinded him earlier. "Because I was furious. When I found that saloon, the last of a string of disreputable waterfront establishments I visited, I walked in and saw her on stage, made up like a barroom whore, being ogled by some of the most questionable specimens of humanity ever to walk the earth."

As he spoke, Troy worked loose his carefully tied cravat and slung it over a chair. His coat followed, and he then began to unbutton his shirt cuffs.

"You were jealous," Grady said.

"No. I was furious. She should be locked up for her own good."

Grady shook his head, ignoring Troy's outburst. "You *are* jealous. Dani knew exactly what she was doing. She wanted to sing, and the owner wouldn't let her unless she wore that dress. After eight hours in civilization, do you think she is any type of expert on fashion?" His smile faded. "Think about it, Troy. We've been on her for days now about changing her appearance. Didn't you hear her say she only wanted *us* to be proud? *You* to be proud?"

Troy pulled off his shirt and let it fall across the chair. He knew his friend was right, but he stubbornly refused to admit it.

"Make me out to be the villain."

"No need for me to do that," Grady said all too cheerfully. "You've done a fine job all by yourself."

Grady turned down the bedside lamp and left Troy standing in semidarkness. Pulling the covers up beneath his chin, Grady settled down on his side of the bed. Troy blew out the remaining lamp and removed his boots and trousers. He stalked to the bed and climbed in beside his friend.

Not surprisingly, sleep eluded them both, but neither spoke. Troy stared at the ceiling, trying to convince himself he'd done the right thing when he carried Dani off the Rocky Mountain House stage. The only clear thought in his mind as he grabbed Dani and flourished the pistol at the crowd was that no man should look at her half-naked body. Except him. No man should even think of touching her. Except him.

As his anger cooled, Troy found himself smiling in the darkness as he recalled the way he must have looked to the crowd.

"She'll never speak to me again." Without intending to, Troy spoke the words aloud.

Grady was still wide awake. "She will. Knowing Dani, though, it will take a week or two." There was a pause before Grady asked, "Was she that bad?"

"Oh, no, but I lost control completely, jumped on the stage, threatened the crowd with Fontaine's Fighting Forty, and carried Dani out over my shoulder." Troy's words were followed by a groan of embarrassment as he realized fully the outrageousness of his actions.

"Your grandpapa Philippe would have been proud."

"Thanks."

Quiet settled around them again until Troy spoke.

"Grady, will you do me a favor?"

"That depends on what it is."

"You owe me one."

"I owe you many," Grady agreed, "but I want to know what I'm letting myself in for."

"I want you to lie," Troy said.

"To whom?"

"To Dani."

"No."

"Hear me out, Grady. I need more time with her. You were right earlier when you said I couldn't see myself without her. But that leads me back to my original dilemma."

"The manhunt. Your obsession with revenge. Your stubborn death wish."

"Call it anything you like, but I can't let go of Dani. Not yet." *If ever*, he thought. "I want you to insist on traveling to Louisiana with me, for your health. Tell her you need to be in a warmer climate in order to recover fully. I'm sure you'll have no trouble playing the part, if tonight was any example."

"What is all this supposed to accomplish? As I see it, you will only end up hurting her more deeply."

"I hope not. I want her to see Isle de Fontaine. Maybe she can adapt to life there. If she is as uncomfortable in Louisiana as she is here, I'll let her go. But I can't just let her walk away until I've seen how she reacts to my home."

"And what of the search for the man who murdered your father? What of Constantine Reynolds?"

Troy was not able to answer immediately without being dishonest. Finally he answered with his heart.

"I'm not sure what I'll do. Besides, there may never be any word concerning his whereabouts."

"And if there *is*?"

"If there is, *then* I'll have to choose."

The silken material of the crimson dress slipped coolly through Dani's fingers. It made a familiar whispering sound as she folded it carefully and placed it atop the corset and stockings, gloves and slippers that were piled neatly on the chair near the window.

Gone was the girl she had seen in the gilt-framed mirror at the saloon last night. This morning, the face that peered back at her from the looking glass above the washstand was her own. Her round wide-set eyes were no longer rimmed with kohl. Today the smoky silver depths sparkled with inner fire. Lush lashes of rich sable outlined the silver-flecked eyes, eyes that showed little evidence of the few tears of self-pity she had allowed herself to shed last night. Dani's mouth was set in a determined line that narrowed the fullness of her lower lip. A flowing white shirt, collarless, the neckline slashed open, set off the golden tone of her deeply winter-tanned skin.

The shirt was one Jake had purchased from an Indian woman but had never worn. As she leaned toward the mirror, the buttonless front of the shirt gapped open to a point just below her breasts. Dani pulled the collar together and tried to think of some way to hold the baggy shirt closed. A large needle and a slim rawhide thong would work. She decided to lace the shirt closed.

The buckskins she'd donned were still soft and comfortable despite their tight fit. She had made them over a year ago, but had never found good reason to break them in. Her others had suited her well enough until she left them behind in the saloon last night. The ones she wore now were snug through the hips and buttocks, a sign of just how much her body had changed. Unseasoned by grease or water, the material was still soft and smoothly textured. It felt as if she'd donned a second skin.

Dani ran her fingers through her hair, trying to undo the tangles that were the result of the savage way she'd extricated the mass of pins Glory had used to create the upswept style. She shook her hair out about her shoulders and wondered if she should cut it to just below her ears, the length she had always worn it. Gathering the heavy mass in both hands, she pulled it back and held it bunched there. A couple of swift slashes with her well-honed buffalo knife would rid her of the bulk of it, but as she remembered Glory's long, luxuriant tresses, Dani let it go, and it swung against her shoulders. It had never been this long before, and for some reason Dani enjoyed the feel of it as it moved around her neck, bounced, and came to life whenever she turned her head.

Today she would ask Grady to return the borrowed clothes to Glory, for she sensed they were worth quite a lot to Joe and the missing Olivia. She would not, she decided firmly, ask Troy.

How could he possibly return to the Rocky Mountain House after last night?

Worse still, how could she face him?

As she searched through the unrolled bundle of goods she'd spread across the bed, looking for a needle and sinew, the sound of a key turning in the lock diverted her attention. Had Troy locked her in? The lock clicked with a metallic sound, followed by two raps on the door.

"Who is it?" Dani called out, fighting to keep her tone flat and disinterested.

"Grady."

"Come in, then."

Dani continued to search through the scraps of material, her extra bag of shot, spare locks and flints, a cloth-wrapped bundle of tobacco, until she found the weasel-skin packet she'd made to hold the needles she used to stitch hides together.

Grady moved quietly into the room and gently closed the door. He stood awkwardly just inside the threshold, waiting for her to acknowledge him.

Dani did not look in his direction, and let the fall of her hair shield her face from his view. Did he hate her as much as Troy did for what she'd done last night?

"How did you sleep, Dani?"

"Fine, considering I kept waking up, afraid I'd fall out of this bed and kill myself." Sleeping in the high four-poster bed had been quite an experience. She had found the sheets so smooth and crisp, the mattress so plush, that sleep had eluded her for hours. "He locked me in?"

Grady cleared his throat. "It was for your own protection. I kept the key."

Dani unrolled the pack of needles. She didn't understand.

"Dani, I have a favor to ask of you." Grady followed his words with a weak cough that finally drew her attention.

"What is it?" As she looked across the room at her friend, she noticed the toll illness had taken on Grady. His eyes were shadowed with fatigue, and he leaned against the door frame as if he felt too weak to stand alone. Immediately Dani moved to clear the borrowed clothing from the spindly-legged chair. "Here, sit down before you fall down." She pulled the chair closer to where he stood. "What favor?" she asked again once he was comfortable.

"I'd like you to go with us to Louisiana."

"Lou-what?"

"Louisiana. To Troy's home."

She stiffened noticeably at the mention of the other man's name. "Why?"

"I want to see that you find your family, Dani, but in my present condition"—he limply raised his hand as he shrugged—"I need rest and a warm climate. It's warmer in Louisiana. Once I've had time to recover, I'll be proud to assist you in finding your family."

"I don't plan on goin' any farther east, Grady. I came this far to see Jake's partner, and I've seen him. I think it would be better if I just went back on home." *And left Troy behind. And tried to forget.* She left the sad thoughts unspoken.

Grady did not speak for a time, but Dani could feel him watching her. She toyed with the pack of needles and then tossed it atop the pile of goods.

"What home?" He spoke softly.

What home?

Dani turned away, walked toward the mirror, and caught a glimpse of herself before she turned back to face him.

"The mountains."

Grady took a steadying breath, as if he were about to plunge into deep, cold water. "What about Troy?"

"Troy hates me now, Grady. That's as plain as the nose on my face." She smoothed her palms against the soft buckskin that encased her thighs and then crossed over to lean against the bedpost at the foot of the bed. "I don't even know what I did wrong last night, and I'm beginning to not even care. Troy and I are just too different, Grady. I'm not like either of you, and I don't think I ever will be. I do know I liked being up there on stage, having folks admire me for what I *am*, instead of pestering me to be something I'm not."

"So you say you're going back to the mountains. You no longer care about Troy or about finding your family or about the money Jake left you? But, Dani, what exactly are you going back to?"

"What do you mean?"

"You met us just after Jake died. You have no idea what it will be like to be truly alone in the mountains. Have you ever thought of that? It's December, Dani, nearly January. You'll have to cross the plains again. Alone this time. It will be spring before you get back."

"So?"

"So why not wait until spring to return? Give yourself a little more time; give me time to rest. I'll go east in a few weeks and try to locate your family." He paused long enough to give her a level stare. "Give Troy time."

"Time for what?" His demand stung her. She was the one who'd been hurt. "Time to grow to hate me more? Time to become even more disgusted with me?"

From the startled look on Grady's face, she knew he was genuinely surprised.

"Disgusted?" he asked, still bewildered.

"I saw it all over his face last night."

"He was hardly disgusted, Dani. Worried, yes. Jealous, very. But not disgusted."

It was her turn to experience bafflement. "Jealous?"

"Think of how Troy must have felt when he saw you up on that stage entertaining all those men, having them see you half dressed. You wouldn't even consider wearing a gown when Troy asked you to."

"Is that what he thought?"

"I think so."

Mulling over Grady's words, Dani tried to see the episode from Troy's perspective.

"Then why the hell didn't he just *tell* me that?" she wanted to know.

"I told you before, Dani. All of these feelings are new to Troy."

As if they aren't new to me. She slapped one hand against the bedpost. "Wait a minute . . ." Her eyes narrowed in anger. "Did he send you in here to speak his piece for him?"

The ensuing cough forced Grady to hide his mouth behind his hand. His shoulders shook weakly.

"Not at all. It was my idea. I can't bear to think of you turning back alone. I'm very curious about your family, even if you aren't, and I hoped you would stay with us in Louisiana until spring." He stood weakly and crossed the room to tower over her. "Troy's grandmother runs her home with an iron fist, Dani. You'll be well cared for there, and you needn't worry that Troy will take advantage of you."

I'm more likely to try to "take advantage" of Troy.

"What does Troy think about your idea?" Dani found herself

holding her breath. Her heart jumped against her rib cage while she awaited his answer.

"He agrees with me. Neither of us wants to see you go off alone until you've at least made an attempt to find your people and collect what Sol saved for you. Obviously Sol can't help you any, and I'm in no condition yet. Troy needs to return to Louisiana; he does have a shipping firm to run." He reached out and took her hand. "So it seems, if you will agree, you're stuck with us for a while longer."

Yesterday the thought of being "stuck" with Troy awhile longer was a dream she longed for. Today, given the present tension between them, Dani was not certain if remaining around Troy Fontaine would lead to good or ill. She thought over all Grady had proposed as she continued to lean against the bedpost. Grady looked down at her as he awaited her decision.

Troy . . . jealous? She doubted it. Worried? Maybe. He wore the burden of responsibility for her like a heavy bearskin rug. Why hadn't he come himself to propose the journey to his home? The turbulent events of last night were still jumbled images in her mind, images laced with feelings of humiliation, embarrassment, disappointment, and sadness. Not to mention the anger she felt this morning. Perhaps this whole idea was something Grady had conjured up in hope of closing over the deep rift between his two friends. She felt him squeeze her hand, reminding her he was still waiting to hear her decision.

"Why didn't Troy come to ask me himself?" she asked.

At that point, the warm timbre of Troy's own deep voice filled the silence in the room.

"Because I was downstairs ordering you some breakfast and trying to find the right words to use to apologize for the way I acted last night."

He was carrying a tray laden with food, so he closed the door behind him with a nudge from his booted foot and tried to ignore the fact that he'd seen his friend holding Dani's hand when he first came through the door. He shot Grady a dark glower, and the artist coughed weakly and moved away from Dani. Grady took hold of the back of the chair for support. He exchanged a brief glance with Troy and then abruptly excused himself, after assuring Troy that he'd be back in ten minutes. Another dark expression colored Troy's features. He was not in the mood to have Grady play chaperon this morning, although he knew his friend only had Dani's best interest at heart. Still, since his recovery, Grady had dogged his every move.

It all happened so smoothly that it was a moment or two before Dani realized she was alone with Troy. She watched as he set the tray on the washstand and then turned to face her. The enticing aroma of bacon filled the room, but her appetite was suddenly gone.

Troy was dressed in a rich brown suit that reminded her of the heady smell of coffee emanating from the tray. His coal-black hair was swept back off his forehead, his skin smooth-shaven, his eyes sparkling and alive in the bright morning light. Her gaze fell to his lips, caught, and held. It was a moment before she realized he was speaking to her.

". . . came to apologize. I'm sorry."

The bedpost was hard and unyielding beneath her fingertips, so very different from the pliant, buckling sensation that swept from her heart to her knees as she tried to concentrate on Troy's words.

No one had ever apologized to her before. *What should I say?* She stood silent. Watching him.

Troy mistook her silence for anger. "You have every right never to speak to me again."

She focused on his lips.

"I wouldn't blame you if you shot me," he added.

Her silver eyes found his obsidian ones.

"I said, I apologize," he repeated.

Her mouth felt dry. She flicked the tip of her tongue across her lips.

"For God's sake, Dani, say something!"

He reached out and grabbed her with both hands, pressing his strong fingers into her shoulders. She let go of the bedpost and swayed into him.

"Say what?" she whispered.

"Say you forgive me. Say you'll go with us to Louisiana. Say anything."

"Kiss me."

She stood on tiptoe and raised her lips to his, expecting a gentle meeting. Troy's fingertips dug deeper into her shoulders as he pulled her closer. His mouth came down on hers, warm and coffee-scented, and his lips parted. There was no apology in his kiss, only raw, aching need and a silent, persistent demand that Dani met and returned until, breathless, they parted.

Troy released her shoulders, but could not move away. A head taller than she, he stood looking down at her and only then realized that the firm well-rounded breasts, open to his view by the gaping front of her shirt, had been exposed to Grady as well. A muscle tensed in his cheek, and he tried to put the thought out of his mind. He pulled the front of her shirt together and then took his hands off her before it was too late.

"I'll go," she said, unable to find the strength to do more than whisper, "till spring."

"Good." Troy smiled into her eyes, his heart suddenly free of the burden that had weighed heavily upon it through the long hours of the night.

"Eat some breakfast," he said. "Then pack up and be ready to go in a few minutes. We'll stop by Sol's and then book passage on the next steamboat headed downriver."

Troy turned to leave, knowing full well that if he was alone with Dani for too long, her watchdog, Grady, would be pounding on the door.

"Troy?"

He stopped as his hand reached the brass knob.

"What?" Had she changed her mind?

She placed her hands on her hips and tipped her head cockily to one side. "Where the hell *is* Louisiana?"

Chapter Sixteen

Grady did not leave them alone during the entire six-day riverboat voyage down the Mississippi. At first Dani had been thankful for his presence, for she was not certain Troy had recovered from her appearance on the stage. But as the days wore on, Dani realized Troy's temper had cooled and he was not going to rail at her again. She began to long for a moment alone with him. Often she thought she saw that same need reflected in his eyes, but they found no opportunity to be together. Grady was as tenacious as a hound dog on a hot trail.

At night, Dani often found herself staring at the dark riverbank or at the star-strewn sky, wishing Troy would leave the cabin he shared with Grady. But he never came to her. Finally, on the evening of the sixth day, as dusk approached the river and daylight waned, the riverboat moored at Baton Rouge.

Excited over the prospect of reaching Isle de Fontaine, Dani awoke early and was fully dressed by dawn. As sunlight began to chase the shadows from her cabin, a barely audible tapping sounded on her door. Without hesitation, Dani answered it.

Troy stood just beyond the threshold, a half-smile teasing his lips. He held his shotgun in his hand. "Come with me," he whispered.

Dani glanced over her shoulder. Her gun and bundles—everything she owned—was inside the cabin. "My things . . ."

"Leave them," he said.

Dani met his eyes and stepped out of her room. He closed the door behind her without a sound.

"Where's Grady?" she whispered.

"Still asleep. I left him a note with instructions to hire a flatboat and bring all our things to the island."

"Where are we going?"

He was silent until they neared the end of the swaying walkway. She caught her breath as he reached toward her, thinking he intended to take her in his arms. Instead, he straightened her hat. "I want to introduce you to my world by myself, without Grady watching us every minute."

"Oh."

He stood so close she could feel the warmth that radiated from him. Troy smiled and reached for her again. This time he kissed her. It was a light, teasing kiss, one that urged Dani to stand on tiptoe and lean toward him.

"Again," she said when the kiss ended.

He flicked his tongue across her lower lip, then dipped his head and pressed his mouth to hers. Moments later, breathless from the kiss they had exchanged, Dani pulled back.

"I take it you're not mad anymore," she said.

"No."

"Good." She reached for him again and Troy hugged her tight.

He whispered in her ear. "I'd like nothing better than to keep this up, but if we don't leave soon, Grady might wake up and find me gone. You don't want him stopping us, do you?"

She shook her head. "Let's go."

He pointed to a long sleek canoe tied to the dock and directed her to take the forward seat.

"Is it yours?" She looked around the deserted landing.

"For now."

"Fontaine—"

"I paid to use it."

She stepped aboard gingerly and lowered herself to the wooden seat, then glanced back at the riverboat. "You sure Grady knows what to do?"

Troy stepped in and carefully set his gun inside the pirogue, then took up one of the paddles. He handed her the other. "I'm certain. He's done this before." He balanced his paddle across his thighs. "Are you afraid to be alone with me?"

She met his intense stare and shook her head. "I'm not afraid of anything."

"Except lizards."

She smiled and nodded. Troy smiled back at her, and Dani felt her heart trip over itself. She watched as he freed the rope that held the craft to the dock, then turned away and dipped her own paddle into the murky water.

They paddled for a time in silence. Troy guided the pirogue along a bayou that led away from the river until the swamp closed in around them. When her upper arms and shoulders began to ache from the exertion, Dani paused long enough to reach overboard and trail her fingertips in the water.

As the long cypress-wood pirogue slipped silently through the still water, Dani found herself becoming entranced with the ethereal surroundings. The surface of the swamp was as still as solid earth, unrippled, covered with a thick emerald carpet of duckweed.

"Keep your hand out of the water." Troy's warning tone broke the silence. "There are too many poisonous snakes for me to name. Besides, you never know when a 'gator might be hungry." She pulled her hand out of the water and took up her own paddle, once again sensitive to the man seated behind her in the canoe. Dani thrilled to the fact that they were alone, surrounded by the eerily silent world of the swamp. She bent her back to paddling, matching him stroke for stroke, and felt a heated tension building inside her as they worked together, their movements rhythmically timed to propel the craft through the water. Although she could not see him, she could feel his presence clear through her buckskins. As he stopped to stab his paddle straight into the water and guide the pirogue along its course, she almost glanced over her shoulder. But just to prolong the tension between them, she kept reaching out and downward, pulling water with the flat blade of the paddle.

". . . besides, your life may depend on it."

He was speaking again, and as the words registered in her mind, Dani began to listen, hard-pressed not to drift off again to more pleasurable thoughts.

"When we reach the island, don't go out on your own. What looks like land oftentimes is really bog or marsh. You can sink in up to your neck without warning. Poisonous snakes can kill you before you even see them."

"This sounds like the type of cheerful place *you'd* call home, Fontaine."

"One can respect and even love the swamp, Dani, but one

can never really know it. Be wary. That's all I'm trying to say."

Suddenly a bird of giant proportions flew overhead. It landed gracefully a few yards ahead to stand on spindly legs and probe the thick undergrowth along the edge of the marsh with its long beak. The bird was white, poised in stark relief against the emerald background of green ash trees and palmetto leaves.

"What's that?" she whispered, half turning toward Troy.

"Egret," he whispered as they slid silently past.

They reached an open area where the duckweed had not yet meshed across the surface of the water. The trees on either bank formed a loosely woven canopy above them, allowing sunlight to stream down and around. The rays cast their intense light in a fan of filtered sunbeams. Here in this primitive world draped in close, thick air, Dani felt she was traveling through a place older than the mountains, perhaps older than time.

"What's that hanging from the trees?" she wanted to know.

"The French explorers named it after the Spaniards' beards, *barbe espagnole*. Over the centuries it has come to be known as Spanish moss."

"Spanish moss." She nodded, certain that whenever she looked at the long, gray-green stuff trailing from the trees, she would think of an old man's beard.

"Do you see that stand of trees up ahead?" he asked. "The ones growing up out of the water?"

Dani nodded, maintaining her silent respect for the bayou.

"Those are cypresses. They're surrounded by stumps called 'knees,' or *boscoyo*. Even the water will not decay them. We call a forest filled with them a *cyprière*, a cypress forest."

"Know what they remind me of?" Dani asked him and heard him chuckle.

"I would not even hazard a guess. What do they remind you of?"

"The knees look like a lot of small, pointy-headed children standing around their mother, poking their heads up through the water."

They moved on and an eerie silence prevailed, draping itself about them in much the same way the gray-green moss draped itself from the trees. Dani shook herself free of the spell and glanced over her shoulder at Troy. His eyes met hers, and his cocky half-smile brightened his expression.

"I never dreamed a place like this could exist," she said. "I can see why you love it here."

"Did I say I love it?"

"You didn't have to. The way you feel about the swamp colors the way you speak when you point things out to me. Maybe that's why you were so all-fired bent on sneakin' away from Grady this morning."

"Maybe." Although she could not see his expression, Dani heard the smile in his tone and it warmed her.

They traveled in silence, content to listen to the sounds of the swamp and the soft splash of the glistening wooden paddles as they cut the water. Dani smiled to herself, her heart soaring as high as the clouds that moved above them. Troy had sought her out, wanted to be alone with her to introduce her to his wilderness. She thought back to the morning and recalled how he had summoned her just as the sun changed the blue-black night into the hazy gray of dawn. He wanted this time alone with her, and although she was eager to reach the island and see his home, part of her wished this time alone with Troy could go on forever.

Dani stared ahead, wondering how much farther it might be to the island that Troy called home. So far she saw no land that looked habitable. "Tell me about your grandmother," she said.

"She reminds me of the cypresses; she's survived the swamp, just as they have. My grandfather, the pirate Grady told you about, literally carried her away from her family and brought her to the island. They lived in a house that was no more than a hut while my grandfather's slaves cleared the land he owned along the river. Little by little, the sugarcane he planted thrived. They became wealthy, with an army of slaves to work the fields.

"Grandmother had four children, but only one survived the fevers that plague those who live in the swamp. That child was my father, Merle Fontaine. He became a gambler who cared little for the land. When Grandfather died, my father's gambling was out of control. He lost thousands in one night, and because planters have little ready cash, he began to gamble away the land up and down the river, and he lost the slaves as well. By the time he died, we were nearly penniless, except for the island and the house servants."

There was no sadness in Troy's voice. He talked matter-of-factly, as if he spoke of another family.

"My grandmother has worn black since the day my father died," he continued. "She's held on to the island by sheer force of will, coupled with the fact that no one wanted it enough to call in any of my father's debts. The place is dilapidated, but as the shipping business grows, I hope to be able to restore the house and grounds to their original beauty. Grandmother says it was something to see."

"Is it far?"

"Not far now. We're nearly there."

Dani felt her apprehension mount. What would Troy's grandmother think of her? Suddenly it was very important that his only living relative think highly of her. She wondered when he might bring himself to speak of his father's death and his mother's disappearance, then put the thought aside. The fact that he'd mentioned any part of his past proved one thing: He was changing. That was enough for now.

Relaxed, content to skim the still surface of the water in the pirogue and let Troy skillfully guide them along, Dani found herself not a little disappointed when she caught a glimpse of a tall white house through the trees. Without Troy's having to say so, she knew they had arrived at Isle de Fontaine. An uneasy quiver started in the pit of her stomach and threatened to rise up and close her throat. She took a deep, calming breath and tried to make out the shape and size of the house as the canoe slipped ever nearer.

The stream that wound itself around the swamp seemed to fan out as it converged with a wider artery that connected the island with the Mississippi. A boat was tied up at an ancient dock that bobbed and floated on the water's surface. It was a small boat, wider than a canoe, and equipped with two oars. Dani glanced at Troy as their own craft gently nudged the dock. A frown creased his forehead. Dani's stomach jumped again.

It was enough that she had to meet his grandmother. She certainly did not welcome any complications the second boat might signal. Perhaps it was not the sight of the boat that worried him. Perhaps he was having second thoughts about bringing her to the island. The idea was not impossible to comprehend, for after all, she was harboring such doubts herself. Refusing to walk into a situation unarmed, Dani did the only thing she could think of to clarify it. She asked a question.

"Is that your boat, too?"

"No. It belongs to Leverette Devereaux. He lives upriver, in town."

Dani sensed Troy's reluctance to say more and fought against her own growing tension. On the trail along the Platte, she'd made a promise to herself: She would never cower in fear; that was not her way. She'd nearly forgotten that promise in Saint Louis the night she let Troy reduce her to tears. She did not intend to break it now. In order to be true to herself, to face this new situation without fear, Dani had to know if he still wanted her here.

He heaved himself gracefully out of the craft and lashed it to the dock. Dani watched Troy's strong, lean hands perform the task with ease. Within seconds he was reaching toward her, offering to help her stand in the wobbly pirogue, inviting her to enter his territory.

"Are you sorry you brought me here?"

The words were out before she could stop them, but once they were issued, she was swept with relief. She could deal with the truth; it was the doubt that frightened her.

He pulled her up as she braced a foot against the dock, refusing to release her hand until she stood so close to him he could see the silver flecks that danced in her gray eyes. The scent of her was unlike the heavy, cloying perfumes worn by other women. It was a natural essence of wood smoke, the outdoors, and woman, and it assailed his senses. Troy glanced back over his shoulder for a moment, gauging the distance to the house and the view through the trees.

Damn Devereaux. Damn them all. Damn the thousand and one promises he'd made to himself not to touch her again. They were impossible promises to keep, and he'd known it even as he made them. She was his, by her own admission. He'd be a fool not to want her. Troy watched her closely as he lowered his head. Her eyes remained open, wide and trusting, as she stared back at him. He brushed her lips at first, her smoke-gray eyes blurring out of focus as their lips met and held, but he could sense that she still watched him. He deepened the kiss, wrapped his arm around the small of her back, and pressed her against his length. The soft, feather-light brush of her lashes against his cheek told him she'd closed her eyes and surrendered to the kiss. He meant to make certain Dani knew he still wanted her on his island.

As he answered her question with a kiss that thrilled her to her toes, Dani's heart sang. He wasn't sorry. The dark look that had marred his features when he saw the other boat had nothing to do with the way he felt about her being here. The heated kiss ended all too soon, as far as she was concerned, and yet it had served its purpose. She was no longer uncertain about whether Troy really wanted her on his island. She would have to wait to discover the reason for his concern.

His hands were on her shoulders. He stared down into her eyes, and for a moment Dani thought he was about to kiss her again, so intense was his expression. Troy turned and stepped aside, indicating with a wave of his hand that she should proceed before him along the shell-strewn path that led away from the dock and curved around a stand of moss-draped cypresses. The thick undergrowth beneath the trees hid the grounds from view. All Dani could see of Troy's home was a patch of white through the slightly swaying branches and moss. She gave him her most dazzling smile, straightened her shoulders, and stepped off the dock and onto the pathway.

The house was not as large as the Republican Hotel, but to Dani it seemed just as forbidding. The place rested upon pillars as wide as tree stumps. She guessed immediately that they served to hold the house safe above the waters of the bayou if they rose over their banks. A wide-open gallery embraced both levels of the two-story building, door after door opening onto it. The second-floor rooms were shuttered against the afternoon light, and as Dani stood staring up, she thought she detected a slight movement behind a corner window.

They reached the wide veranda, and before Troy could knock, the heavy door swung inward to reveal his imposing manservant. The man was a spectacle, a giant of immense proportions who towered over Troy's considerable height. The servant's skin was as black as the darkest ebony. Muscles bulged when he so much as raised his arm to swat at a pesky fly. A wide halo of tightly frizzed hair stood out at least a spread hand's width about his head. A small golden ring pierced his ear, not through the lobe, but higher, just below the wild shock of his hair. Pants tighter than a second skin covered him from waist to ankle. Sandals protected feet that looked to be as tough as shoe leather. Dani found herself staring at his red silk shirt. Her eyes were level with his midriff.

The man looked down at her from his great height, allowing her only a cursory glance before dismissing her. He spoke directly to Troy.

"Mr. Grady arrived with the baggage, Mr. Troy. I put your things away in your room. Mr. Grady say you be bringin' in a guest, so I give him the room across from Mr. Grady, 'cause it have windows all 'round like the rest of y'all have. Mr. Grady's upstairs restin', but he says you should wake him when you get here."

"Thank you, Leze." Troy nodded. It wouldn't do to protest Dani's sleeping at the opposite end of the upstairs hall, so Troy let stand the arrangements Hercules had made.

"Leze . . ." Troy took Dani's hand and drew her forward until she stood beside him. "This is my guest, Miss Dani Whittaker. She's a trapper we met in the West. Dani, this is Hercules. If there is anything you need, let him know."

"Anything?" she whispered as her eyes dropped to Troy's lips.

"Within reason," he whispered back.

Once again Dani watched the giant turn his gaze on her. This time his eyes widened perceptibly as he took in her hat, her hair, and her buckskins with a critical eye.

"*Piégeur*?" he asked, using the Louisiana French word for trapper.

"*Oui*," Troy answered.

"Am I going to have to talk French?" Dani demanded of Troy, obviously startling the servant as she faced Fontaine with her hands on her hips.

"No."

She pointed to Hercules. "He can understand me?" She looked skeptically at the black man who stood with his arms folded across his chest. She could barely understand him, even when he spoke English.

"Yes."

The servant nodded.

"Good." Dani nodded. "I'm not too keen on havin' to squawk like a damn Frenchie."

Hercules reared back and laughed loud and long with a sound that rumbled forth from his toes. He grinned down at

Dani and, pleased with her ability to make him laugh so heartily, she returned the smile.

"Mr. Troy, we got other visitors, too. Mr. Devereaux an' his sister are here for the evenin'."

Troy showed no reaction to the news.

"Where is Leverette?"

"Last I saw of him, he be in the kitchen havin' some tea and pound cake," Hercules volunteered. "The ladies be restin'."

"Take Dani up to her room and see that's she's comfortable," Troy directed. "Then you can tell Grady I'll be in the library with Devereaux."

The servant stood his ground and studied Troy's apparel with outright disgust. "You goin' to be changin' outta them ragtag animal-skin clothes first? I got some nice things all laid out proper for you on the bed."

Dani tried to hide her smile. It seemed this big man was afraid of no one, not even his employer.

"In a while, Leze, even if these buckskins do upset your tender sensibility to style. Take Dani upstairs." Troy laughed as he strode down the cool hallway toward the back of the house and, Dani assumed, the kitchen.

"Come on, Miz Dani." Hercules led the way up the staircase to the second story. "I put your things in the nicest room we had left. Mr. Grady say you'll be stayin' a spell, so I put Miz Erantha in one of the middle rooms. They got less light, bein' as how they only got windows on one side."

Dani remembered the dark interior of the dugout she'd been raised in and could not see how light might make a difference. As long as the room kept her dry and warm, she did not care in the least how many windows the place had.

Hercules fell silent when they reached the top of the stairs. He pointed to a closed door on his right and whispered, "That's Miz Leial's room; she be asleep this time o' day." The room on the left belonged to Troy. Next to Troy's room was the one occupied by Devereaux's sister; the one directly opposite it was for Leverette himself. The two end rooms, their doors opposite each other, belonged to Dani and Grady. She followed Hercules silently through the open doorway of the room meant for her.

It was more spacious than the hotel room, but that was not the reason Dani felt immediately comfortable. The bedroom was decorated with materials that reminded her of wide open meadows. Faded floral print coverings hung beside the long windows that appeared to be more like doors. Hercules crossed the room and opened one of the windows, and Dani followed him to discover they opened out on the covered balcony above the veranda on the floor below.

"All the upstairs rooms be connected by this balcony," he explained over his shoulder as he walked back inside.

Like an excited puppy, Dani followed him. The bed was high, similar to the one at the Republican, but this one was draped with sheer netting, creating a misty world inside.

"Why the tent?" she asked.

"*Barie*," he corrected. "Keeps off the mosquitoes." He moved to tie it back on both sides. "You won't need it now, though, not like in summer when the bugs is swarmin'."

She took in the rest of the furnishings—a low dressing table and mirror, which reminded her of Glory Hallelujah; a tall free-standing closet that Hercules called an armoire; and, near the windows on the east side of the room, two small upholstered chairs with a table between them.

Hercules turned to face Dani. "You'll be wantin' a bath, so I'll send Neola up with some water for you." He paused for a moment as he swept his eyes over her clothing much the way he'd sized up Troy's apparel. Dani did not give in to the urge to squirm under his inspection. "We dress for dinner here."

We dress for dinner? What did he mean by that? She was dressed as far as she was concerned. Dani nearly refused the bathwater, but thought better of it. Perhaps meeting Troy's grandmother called for a little more care on her part than she was usually wont to exercise.

Hercules glanced toward Dani's bundle of possessions and the long Kentucky rifle propped against the wall. He raised his brows in surprise and looked down at her suspiciously. "You *do* got a dress, don't you?"

This time she did squirm before she put her hands on her hips and squinted up at him. "Of course."

He nodded in response, although his eyes revealed his doubt. "I'm gonna be trimmin' Mr. Troy's hair some. You want I should trim yours, too?" He scowled at Dani's thick, uneven hair. "It ain't none too straight, although it be a mighty pretty color."

She marched to the dressing-table mirror. The shoulder-length mass was more than "none too straight." The ends of her hair rose and fell like the ragged top of a mountain range.

"Well . . ."

"It won't hurt none. 'Sides, it'll make all the difference in the way your hair hangs."

She stared up at the wide wild halo of his own hair.

"How do you know?"

"I been cuttin' Mr. Troy's hair for years, and I trim Miz Leial's hair, too, and Neola's and Venita's. I'm the only one what's not scared stiff of *her*."

"Scared?"

He walked to the open door and closed it gently, then returned to Dani's side of the room. In a hushed whisper, he began to explain.

"Venita be the cook here, and *old* . . . that woman is so old she probably know Moses. She been here the longest. Venita talk to the spirits. She know the *voudou* tricks. That one powerful—that she is." He glanced over his shoulder at the closed door and then continued. "Venita, she come here straight from Africa. So do her daughter—believe in the voodoo, that is. But Neola and Neola's husband, Maurice, they was born here on the island. They work in the house and on the grounds." He leaned closer to emphasize his next words. "But Miz Leial, she ain't afeared of the voodoo, an' she ain't afeard of Venita."

Silent with awe, Dani stared up at the man who seemed to be speaking another language. She had only a vague idea what he was talking about.

"Anyway," he rambled on, "Venita an' Miz Leial been at each other for sixty years or more, an' I swear, one's near as bad as t'other. Trouble is, both of them is as hard as the cypress wood outside, and neither of 'em will bend. But me, I'm not scared of 'em. No, suh"—he shook his head—"not Hercules. But, Miz Dani, if I was you, I'd let me trim up that hair, an' then you put on one of your finest dresses 'fore you go sashayin' down to meet Miz Leial."

Dani swallowed hard. That last part was easily understood. She had to pass inspection, and Miz Leial seemed to hold more power here than Dani had realized.

"Yes," she agreed, "maybe you should come back later and trim my hair for me." Dani reached up and ran her fingers through the hair at the nape of her neck.

"I'll do that, Miz Dani. You jest leave it to me."

He left the room with surprisingly little sound for a man so large. Dani turned to face her bundle, which was lying on the floor. With a silent curse, she wished she'd kept Olivia's red dress, but it was too late for regrets. Besides, Troy's last reaction to the red gown assured her that he would not tolerate her wearing it in his house. She had one card left to play. Hastily she unwrapped the thongs that held her parcels together. She unfolded the soft white doeskin garment she'd purchased on her last morning in Hump Bone Hollow—the beaded white Indian dress. Slowly Dani unrolled it and spread it out on the peach-colored spread that covered the bed.

Smoothing it with her hands, she ran her fingertips across the shining glass beads and porcupine quills that decorated the bodice. Long fringe fell from the shoulders of the sleeveless dress and graced the hem as well. Tanned to a rich, pure white, the doeskin was as soft as cloth.

We dress for dinner.

Well, she decided, this *was* a dress, and it was her finest. Buying it had been a whim. Wearing it would be a challenge. Dani took a deep breath and began to put her other possessions inside the armoire.

Chapter Seventeen

"I think you might be right about that dress after all, Miz Dani."

Reassured, Dani nodded at Hercules's reflection. He stood behind her, working a brush through her clean, neatly trimmed hair. "And I have to admit you were right about the haircut." Dani swung her head from side to side and watched the blunt, even ends of her rich red-brown hair fall neatly back into place. The candlelight in the room set the golden highlights of her hair to glistening. She was more than pleased with the results of Hercules's labors.

She'd bathed and dressed, then admitted him to her room. The servant had expressed disapproval of her choice of gowns, then had been stunned when she confessed that it was the only one she possessed. Shaking his head, he had turned her around and surveyed the Indian dress before he volunteered to go and find a suitable replacement among the many that had once belonged to Troy's mother.

"I *can't* wear another gown, Hercules," she groaned. "You don't understand. I've been fighting Troy for weeks, refusing to wear a fancified dress." She thought of her humiliating experience in St. Louis, but refrained from telling the huge man about that disaster. "No. This will have to do." Dani smoothed her hands down the sleek skirt that hugged her hips.

"Got yourself backed into a corner, Miz Dani?" he had asked before he set to work, resigned to her decision to wear the Indian gown or none at all. Hercules had then covered her shoulders with a lined dish towel he'd confiscated from the kitchen and trimmed her hair before the mirror. Dani had watched his every move while she listened to his ceaseless chatter.

"Mr. Troy was bent on comin' up to see how ya'll liked the room, but I tol' him you was bathin' and would see him at dinner. He looked a bit peeved 'fore he mumbled, 'Hope I don't have another watchdog on my hands.' But I think now I understand, seein' as how he thinks ya'll probably planned to show up in them buckskins. I 'spect this dress'll be enough to give Miz Leial apoplexy, but nowhere near as bad as them pants would have."

"What's wrong with it?" Dani had demanded. "It's made of the finest tanned piece of doeskin I've ever seen. The bead-work is perfect"—she ran her fingertips over the red, yellow, and blue arrowhead design—"and I'm covered from neck to ankle."

"I cain't argue with that." Hercules stepped back and studied his finished work. "But it needs somethin' more."

"Shoes would be nice."

"Lordy, gal. You ain't even got no shoes?"

"Nope," she admitted easily, not the least bit daunted by his show of dismay. Dani was becoming accustomed to his theatrics. "I have those boots." She pointed to the knee-high brown riding boots the men had purchased for her in St. Louis. "And Grady rescued my fur-lined mocs from the saloon—"

"Saloon?" His eyes widened.

"That's another story."

"I'll be right back."

True to his word, Hercules was back in moments. Dani had heard him moving about on the floorboards directly above her, but until then, did not realize there were any more rooms in the house. Upon his return, she asked where he'd been.

He pointed up. "Mr. Troy's mother's clothes are all in a trunk up in the attic. See if you can get these on. The ladies call them *savates*."

He extended a pair of soft white silk slippers. Dani turned away from the mirror long enough to slip them on her feet and tie the long, wide ribbons that held them closed. They were a tight fit, but they would do.

"I brought you a nightgown and a dressin' gown, and this here comb, brush, and mirror. You can use 'em if you want. By the looks of the dresses in the trunk, you're a far sight bigger'n Jeanette Fontaine was."

Jeanette Fontaine. Troy's mother. Another time, Dani promised herself, when she was free to dawdle, she would ask Hercules what he knew of Jeanette Fontaine.

She looked up and caught him staring at her hair. Self-conscious, she raised her hand and smoothed it again. "What's wrong?"

He stepped back, walked in a half-circle around her, contemplated her hair awhile longer, and then broke into a wide, pleased grin.

"You got any more of these *fanfreluche*? Any more beads or trinkets?"

"Why?"

Hercules stepped back, one hand on his right hip. "Don't be worryin' about why, Miz Dani. You got any or not?"

"I think so." Dani crossed the room and opened the armoire where her things were stored. She retrieved a small packet of beads, bells, and feathers used for trade and presented it to Hercules.

"Sit back down. You got ten minutes before dinner and I'm gonna make you look jes' fine!"

The stairwell loomed dark and ominous before her. Hushed conversation drifted down the long hallway and up the stairs. Dani could not make out the words, for many voices seemed to be talking at once. Delicious but unidentifiable aromas wafted on the draft of cool night air. When her stomach rumbled in response, Dani pressed her palm against it.

As she moved down the stairs, the voices became clearer. She listened for Troy's but could not distinguish it from the others. *What are you doing?* she asked herself as one slippered foot followed the other down the stairs.

You're doing what you want to do: You're going after the biggest catch you ever made. She had known long before the kiss they had exchanged in the hotel, or the one he'd pressed upon her willing lips this afternoon. She had known long before they eased each other's pain on the prairie. Dani had known on the night when Troy first taught her the art of loving. She had known then, for well and for certain, that she would have him. All she had to do was convince him that he wanted to be caught. And held. Forever.

At the bottom of the staircase she turned and followed the sound of voices to the sitting room. Hercules had told her it was at the end of the hallway. The door stood ajar, light from within the room spilling out into the dim, drafty corridor. She paused for a moment and the hushed whisper of the long fringe that swayed about her slowly ceased. The beads and bells Hercules had woven into the strands of hair closest to her face clacked and tinkled faintly, so faintly Dani hardly heard them herself. A silk ribbon banded her forehead, holding her hair away from her face, the long ends trailing down her back. The headband had been an "inspiration," Hercules claimed. He had pulled it from the neckline of her borrowed nightdress. Of the purest ivory, the ribbon complemented not only her exotic gown but the honey gold of her complexion as well.

She heard Grady's voice above the others. "I wonder what's keeping her?"

She took a deep breath and walked through the open doorway.

"Nothing's keeping me. I'm here."

The soft tinkle of the bells and the gentle clack-clack of the wooden beads in her hair were suddenly as loud as thunder in her ears. Silence fell over the group assembled in the small room, and as she stopped dead still just inside the doorway, Dani quickly surveyed the scene before her. Jake always said that it never hurt to know exactly what you were up against.

Although she spotted Troy immediately, Dani would not let herself meet his gaze, afraid of what his reaction might be. Instead, she studied the equally tall man standing beside Troy near the fireplace. Leverette Devereaux. Both men held squat, half-full glasses of a dark honey-colored liquid. Leverette wore a well-cut blue wool suit with matching trousers and, like the other men, a shining waistcoat over a white linen shirt and a cravat. Dark brown hair, nowhere near as raven black as Troy's, was cut straight across his forehead. It hung in a thick patch above heavy, straight brows. His eyes were small, but quick and sharp. Dani watched them flick over her from head to toe. Devereaux hid a smile by lifting his glass to his lips, but his eyes could not lie. He was watching her with unabashed amusement and admiration.

Two women sat at the far side of the room. Dani recognized Leial Fontaine immediately. The woman's black eyes, straight, finely tapered nose, and full lips were exactly like Troy's. The gown his grandmother wore was high-collared, edged with lace, and as black as midnight. Silver-white hair, braided and wound around her head in a tight coronet, contrasted with the austere black of her clothing. Dani was reminded of the shadowed figure she'd seen in the window as she approached the house. The woman's shining eyes focused on Dani. She sat ramrod straight on a settee, arrested in a half-turn toward the young woman seated beside her. Leial Fontaine's expression was unfathomable, closed and guarded, just as Troy's so often appeared.

Unable to hide her surprise, the woman beside Troy's grandmother was gaping open-mouthed, a teacup poised and forgotten just above a dainty china saucer. She wore her blond hair parted and pulled back into a tight chignon at the base of her neck. Her skin was as pure and white as Dani's dress. Erantha Devereaux. Petite, timid, and lovely in a pale pink dress with wide puffed sleeves and a full skirt that draped about her legs, hiding all but the tips of violet slippers. She was everything Dani was not.

Only Grady, dear kind Grady, was gracious enough—or perhaps brave enough, to step forward and greet her. She rewarded him with her most dazzling smile, and for a brief moment wondered why it could not have been Grady who sparked the fires of passion within her. Life would have been so much less complicated.

Dani fought to keep her gaze from drifting across the room to the tall figure lounging against the mantel. She had felt Troy's eyes on her from the moment she entered the room, and she sensed his surprise.

"You look marvelous." Grady bent to whisper in her ear and then took her by the hand. "Allow me to make the introductions."

Had his feet been nailed to the floor when Dani first appeared in the doorway, Troy could not have been more effectively rendered immobile. Regal in her bearing, she surveyed the room with the practiced eye of a hunter. He had involuntarily clutched his glass of bourbon tighter and, without thinking, raised it in a silent toast to her before he touched it to his lips.

She had never been lovelier. The burnished mahogany hair fell perfectly even to her shoulders. It had been brushed to a high shine and styled with beads, bells, and white feathers that teased her cheeks and moved with her every breath. Troy imagined himself removing the adornments one by one, then teasing her flawless complexion with kisses.

The lamplight cast her skin in a golden hue that was enhanced by the dove-white gown. He felt a slow, upward lift at the corners of his mouth when he realized the shoes and the hairstyle were Hercules's handiwork. Troy had long suspected his burly valet secretly longed to play lady's maid, but he had to admit the man's eye for fashion had paid off well in this instance.

Dani's dress fit her like a second skin, without being vulgar. But it was definitely seductive, though, and enticing enough to cause the man beside him to stiffen to attention. Out of the corner of his eye, Troy unobtrusively watched Leverette react to Dani. His friend's attraction to her was more than obvious, it was downright annoying. As he stole a second glance at Devereaux, Troy felt an unbidden surge of jealousy, but he could not very well challenge his friends for admiring Dani, for she was stunning.

Unable to keep his eyes away from her for long, Troy watched her assess the occupants of the room. First, Leverette, then Leial, and finally Erantha. Thus far, Dani had refused to meet his gaze, and for that Troy was thankful. He was afraid that if she were to stare across the room with the least hint of longing in her eyes, he would find himself carrying her away again, this time up to his own bed where he would appease her hunger much to the delight of his own. The others be damned.

She's not wearing a damn thing under that dress.

That fact became obvious as Dani moved a step farther into the room. The revelation, suddenly made clear to Troy by the sensual slide of the material against her skin, nearly caused him to loosen his hold on his empty glass. Carefully, he placed it upon the mantelpiece and moved across the room to sidestep Grady, who looked as pleased as an early bird about to pounce upon a juicy worm.

Suddenly, Dani felt a presence beside her as Troy stepped between her and Grady. Her hand was given over to his grasp. She wondered at the warmth of his palm against her own cold fingertips.

"I'll handle this," he told Grady.

Dani fully expected him to whirl her about and remove her from the scene. Instead, Troy gave her hand a gentle, reassuring squeeze before he crossed straight to Leial and formally began the introductions.

"Grandmother, this is Danika Whittaker."

Dani looked up to him for direction, and their eyes met and held. For a moment she was afraid he'd forgotten his grandmother's name. "And Dani"—he cleared his throat—"this is my grandmother, Leial Fontaine."

Uncertain, Dani did not speak, but waited for some sign from Troy. Leial interceded in her grandson's behalf.

"How do you do, Danika?" Leial offered in a tone that could be measured somewhere between frigid and chilled.

"I do just fine, Mrs. Fontaine. How do you do?"

Leial met Dani's thin smile with a level stare. "Troy tells me your family is from the East."

The girl shook her head and felt Troy draw and hold his breath. "I don't know my family, Mrs. Fontaine, except by name. I was raised by a man named Jake Fisher."

"I see." Leial studied the beaded gown for a moment, giving Dani ample time to add to the strained conversation. When no words came, Leial spoke again. "That's an unusual dress, Danika."

"The style is fairly common where I come from . . . ma'am."

Troy shifted uneasily. Dani's hand was slowly rendering his fingers useless as she squeezed the life from them.

"Oh, really?"

Dani merely nodded and let the other woman's remark pass. As if Troy sensed that her newfound reserve could not last long, he tried to steer the conversation to Erantha, who sat smugly watching the exchange.

But Dani had found her tongue at last. "Mrs. Fontaine?"

"Yes, Danika?"

"My friends call me Dani. I'd appreciate it if you would, too."

"Appreciate it, or prefer it, Danika?" the older woman asked.

Demand it, Dani wanted to shout, but instead she sneaked a glance at Troy and then took a deep breath. "Appreciate," she said.

"Well, now that you're here"—Leial rose from the settee

with surprising agility and took command of the room—"it is far past time we sat down to dinner."

At Leial's reference to her tardiness, Troy linked Dani's arm through his own and pulled her nearer. He smiled down at her and shook his head, dismissing his grandmother's comment.

"Troy, introduce Danika to Erantha and Leverette so that we will not be delayed any longer."

Dani glanced up in time to see Leial watching Troy as he held her close to his side. The woman then moved past them, gliding across the room, with a slow, aristocratic tread, toward Grady. He offered Leial his arm, but not his usual charming smile.

Erantha stood awaiting an introduction. The two women merely exchanged silent nods. Just as Troy was ready to lead Dani toward Leverette, who was still leaning casually against the mantel, Erantha spoke. Like Leial's, her tone held the caustic sting of a whip.

"I've been wondering, Dani, just what are you supposed to be?"

Dani took a deep breath and smiled. "I'm trying *real* hard to be patient, Miss Devereaux, but my patience is runnin' a bit thin in the face of all this downright rudeness."

Dani turned away from the pretty girl and found Leial, still holding on to Grady's arm, awaiting them in the doorway. The woman's dark eyes, so much like Troy's, locked with Dani's before Leial turned and passed through the doorway. Grady paused long enough to send a backward glance to Dani. He rolled his eyes toward the ceiling, then sent her a swift smile of encouragement.

Quickly Troy introduced Dani to Leverette, who caught her hand, intending to plant a gallant kiss there, but Dani would have no part of it and whipped her hand from his grasp before it reached his lips.

"Any kissin' to be done, Mr. Devereaux, I already have in mind who'll be doin' it," she warned.

Troy laughed at Dani's response to his lawyer's attempt at chivalry. "So do I, Leverette," Troy added as he smiled down at Dani and ushered her toward the door.

Leial Fontaine sat alone in her darkened room, surrounded by the familiar objects of her past and present. The worn *berse*, or rocking chair, on which she sat, had been her mother's. She preferred it to the ones that lined the veranda. She tipped the chair back and forth and listened to the soft, comforting creak as it protested every move. She was dressed for bed, but knew from experience that sleep would not come to her for hours. As the years passed, she needed less and less sleep, but wakefulness afforded her too much time to think. Far too much time to remember.

She often asked herself if she would have lived her life any differently; the only answer she received tonight was the monotonous tick of the clock on the mantel. She tried to see it through the darkness, but could not make out the hands on the face that stood out white against the shadows. Instinctively, Leial knew the chimes would soon strike, signaling half past one.

Time passes, she thought, *without our seeing it go. It moves on silently, like a thief, stealing life bit by bit until there is nothing left but a tired body and an equally tired spirit.* She studied the room again. Although the furniture and bric-a-brac that surrounded her were merely shadows looming in the darkness, she knew all of the items. They were old friends, most as aged and tired as she. There was a fireplace to help fight the winter dampness and mildew. Hers was the only bedroom equipped with one. By rights, the room should belong to the master of the house, but it had been hers for sixty years and would be Troy's soon enough.

As they did so often, her thoughts turned to her grandson. Tonight she had observed in his eyes an emotion she had given up all hope of seeing. Love smoldered in the usually brooding depths each time he looked at the exotic creature he had brought home with him. Troy had kept the girl protectively close to his side all evening, fending off Leverette Devereaux's obvious advances and ignoring Erantha's outrageous attempts at flirtation. His eyes had brimmed with undisguised hunger as he watched Dani bid them all good night and walk from the room. Only after the girl had disappeared upstairs did the all too familiar expression of preoccupation darken Troy's features and cause him to knit his brow in thought.

Leial had waited until the other guests excused themselves for the evening, eager to have a word alone with her grandson. For a time he had talked only of the expedition to the West. Leial waited patiently until he mentioned the girl. She found him as direct as always.

"Grandmother, don't be hard on Dani."

"What do you mean?" she had asked, knowing full well what his answer would be.

His lips eased into a half-smile. "You have a way of testing everyone, dear Grandmama. It's been known to send grown men quivering out the door."

She crooked a brow and fought against a smile of her own. "And why should I treat this girl any differently?" She watched him drain a glass of brandy and set the snifter on a side table before he answered.

"Because I care about her. I don't want to see her hurt."

"Do you intend to marry her?"

"Always direct and to the point." Troy shook his head and shrugged. "I find myself wanting to say yes, and that in itself is a shock to me. But"—he paused and toyed with the crystal snifter on the table—"you know as well as I why I can't make any promises."

"Troy—"

He read the protest in her voice and cut her off before she could begin. "Let it go, Grandmother. There's no way I'll give up the search for Reynolds and my mother. And after today, it is unthinkable that I should do so."

"Today?"

"Today Leverette told me he's located Constantine Reynolds."

"How lucky for us all that Devereaux chose to visit on the very day of your arrival."

"He's known for a month," Troy had added, a note of frustration in his voice.

"I wish you had not come back yet, then."

"But I *am* back, and I am going after Reynolds."

She had raised a hand to protest, but the right words eluded her. Troy crossed the room and dropped down on one knee before her. He reached out, lifted her hands to his own, and met her gaze. "I have to do this, Grandmother, so don't beg me not to. You, above all others, know I can't turn my back on Reynolds after all these years. I have to find him in order to discover the truth."

"Where is he? Where are you going? And when?"

"To the Caribbean. I'll be leaving as soon as I can set the business to rights and arrange passage. Three weeks at the most."

"And what of the girl?"

His fingers tightened on hers. "I will leave her in your care. Yours and Grady's. I'm leaving Leze behind, too. If Dani decides not to wait for me, or if I should fail to return—"

"Don't speak of it."

"I leave her in your care. Do what you think best, but please, Grandmother, treat her gently."

Leial sighed, the sound heavy on the still night air, and turned her thoughts to the girl. She smiled into the darkness as she recalled the way she had tried to nettle Dani into an argument. Philippe would have been enamored of Dani's natural cockiness. The girl was full of spunk, and uncommonly beautiful, but she was like an uncut gem in need of polishing. A fine match for her grandson. If only he could put the past behind him.

As she fought against closing her eyes, Leial rocked forward and stood. Without the need of a light, she crossed the familiar space and climbed into the bed she had once shared with Philippe Fontaine. She had become used to sleeping alone these last thirty-five years, but she had never learned to enjoy it. Still, she was strong-willed enough to live for a while longer before she joined the pirate who had stolen her heart.

Now there was a task at hand: She had to make certain the girl her grandson had chosen was worthy of his love. She would live to welcome Troy home from his mission of justice. God had taken far too much from her already. He would not dare take Troy, too.

The sheets were cool and crisp, the bed ropes tightly turned. Leial sighed again. For a time, Troy was home and she was burdened with a task that needed the attention only she could give. Leial closed her eyes to sleep and, for a change, eagerly anticipated the morning.

Chapter Eighteen

Dani stood staring down at the night-shrouded swamp as unsettled feelings kept her pacing the darkened bedroom in the silent house. She still wore her beaded dress, the white muslin nightgown clutched in her hand, forgotten.

Dani sighed, tossed the nightgown on the bed, then moved silently to slip the bolt on one of the tall windows that opened onto the balcony. Cool night air swept about her, carrying with it the close, heavy smell of dampness and earth. The scent of the swamp permeated the house.

Rubbing her bare arms with her hands, she stepped out onto the gallery and crossed to the wooden railing. An animal screamed in the darkness from some distance away. A big cat, puma or panther, perhaps. She turned toward the sound and listened attentively, but it did not cry out again. Dark, humped shadows against the black backdrop of cypress and oak were all that was visible of the small cluster of slave cabins behind the house. Everyone slept, but Dani could not.

Dinner had been a disaster.

The strained introductions in the sitting room had been but a foreshadowing of what was to follow. Troy had remained beside her throughout the evening, but his attention was occupied elsewhere as he alternately glared at Leverette Devereaux whenever the man dared to stare heatedly in her direction, and answered questions his grandmother put to him regarding his journey west.

Erantha, seated beside Grady, monopolized the artist's attention throughout the meal, laughing coyly, batting her eyelashes, using the strange Louisiana French that peppered much of the conversation. She had not fooled Dani one whit, for between the pouts and giggles, Erantha had slyly glanced at Troy. Although he took no notice of the girl's obvious display, Dani's temper had simmered at the way Erantha flirted. More than once Dani fought the urge to hurl her wine goblet across the table.

The thought of Erantha's actions still piqued her as Dani leaned against the low rail and stared out at the bayou. The slightest hint of a breeze tickled the Spanish moss. She rubbed her arms again and turned around to step inside.

She knew now that her beautiful dress was all wrong for this place, although no one but Erantha had been rude enough to say as much. Troy's compliments had helped ease her discomfort, but Dani had felt near naked when she noted the detail of the other women's gowns and saw that their arms were not bare, like her own.

"Elle est méchante comme une taïque," Erantha had whispered to Leverette in passing, loud enough for Dani to hear. She had not recognized the word *taïque*, but later in the evening had asked Troy the meaning and learned it was a Choctaw word for squaw—"She's as bad as a squaw." Dani thought of the Indian women she'd known—trappers' wives, loyal, sturdy, and fine. All of them more honest than the hostile girl she'd met this evening. Still, the comment found its mark and hurt.

There were no stars out tonight. Low-lying clouds shrouded the sky, so thin the moon peered through. In the muted moonlight, Dani could see the moss moving as if it were alive, like long, searching arms waving gently in the slight breeze. After sunset, the air had grown cooler. Dani found it impossible to compare the beauty of the dark swamp, with its shadowed variations of gray, to that of a snow-covered mountain meadow sparkling in the moonlight. Turning away from the scene, she crossed the gallery and went back indoors. Her dress slipped easily over her head, setting the beads and bells to dancing in her hair. Nude, she walked to the armoire and carefully hung the doeskin inside. She threw the voluminous borrowed nightdress over her head and fought her way toward the neck opening and sleeves. It was made of soft, comfortable white muslin, loose and carefree. *Une blouse volante*, Hercules had called it. The full sleeves reached her wrists and warmed her immediately.

Dani looked forlornly at the bed. It was far past time she tried to sleep. Her head ached terribly, but it was not nearly so uncomfortable as her stomach. For a few moments during dinner she had been certain they were trying to poison her, but the others ate with gusto, as if the hot, overly spiced foods were delicious. Dani could do little more than follow Troy's example and partake of the meal.

Leial, seated at the head of the table, was on Dani's left. The older woman was kind enough to explain the contents of each dish to Dani, who was busy watching Troy, attempting to mimic his use of eating utensils. An army of forks and spoons seemed to surround her plate. Red beans and rice, sweet potato pone, and croquettes accompanied ham and roast duck. A thick soup they called gombo z'herbes—made of bacon, greens, vegetables, and crawfish—was also served. To please Leial, Dani ate far more than was necessary, but still succeeded in relishing the dessert—colle, a cake made with black molasses and pecans. Café brûlot was served last. Dani found that the thick black coffee, heavy with sugar and laced with cognac, was much to her liking—then. But now she realized it had only added to the indigestion brought on by the strange foods. She was used to far plainer fare—roast game and little else.

A gauzelike drizzle began to fall without a sound. Dani moved to close the jalousied shutters, but stopped as soon as she recognized the touch of the warm hand that reached in through the open doors to clasp her wrist and the hushed whisper that played about the contours of her ear.

"May I come in?"

Her heart jumped at the sound of his voice, and she answered in the same hushed tone. "What are you doing here?"

"I couldn't sleep. I see you can't, either."

"No." She strained to see his handsome features in the darkness. "Will you sleep here? With me?"

Dani half turned toward the bed, her voice playful yet laced with hope, although she knew what his answer would be.

It was a long time in coming, as if Troy wrestled with the words. Dani felt him stiffen, then sigh. Unable to hold himself away from her, he drew Dani into his arms, warming her against the chill as they stood in the open doorway.

His right hand strayed to the adornments in her hair. He lifted a feather to his cheek and then brushed it across his lips. When the piece of white fluff dropped back into place, he lowered his head. She could not see him clearly, but felt his lips when they touched hers. They were warm and dry, scented with coffee and cognac. Delectable. She let her tongue slide between his lips and savored the familiar taste of him as she slid her arms up under his and pressed her open palms against his broad, tightly muscled back.

She heard him moan, a deep growl that made her want to smile at this newfound power she held over him. Dani pulled away from the kiss, but still safe within the circle of his embrace, she leaned back and stared up at his night-shadowed features.

"Is it so wrong for you to hold me, Troy?"

"When I feel this way, I don't believe it's wrong at all."

With just the slightest pressure of her hands, she pulled him toward her, meeting him halfway. On tiptoe, she melded against him. The soft muslin presented little barrier between them. Dani could feel the urgency of his hardened shaft straining against his trousers. She kissed him again, slowly, languorously, the way he'd taught her. She could feel him losing control as she lured him into the trap. It was so simple, it was almost unfair.

"Would it be wrong if you were to hold me all night? Only that, and nothing more?"

"Not wrong. Impossible, maybe," he whispered.

Coyly she asked, "What do you mean?"

"What do you think I mean?"

"I wouldn't mind if *that* happened again." She paused long enough to press closer, to be certain he was still fully aroused and yielding to the power of her nearness. "But I know you would care. Especially here, in your grandmother's home. Please, Troy, will you just lie down with me until I fall asleep?"

"Is this a trick?"

"Not at all," she lied.

"Are you certain?"

"Are you afraid, Fontaine?"

"Not at all," he lied.

"Then come." She took his hand and led him toward the bed. Troy stopped to close the door and remove his boots while

Dani pulled back the bedclothes. A blurred form stood out in shadowed relief against the sheet.

"What's this?" Dani whispered and reached forward.

"Don't move!" Troy was beside her in an instant, pausing long enough to light a candle. The ring of light illuminated a strange pile of bone and feathers tied together.

"What is it?" Dani asked again.

Troy reached down and picked up a chicken claw, some feathers, and a few bleached bones. He turned them over in his hand and then set them on the bedside table.

"Voodoo charm. Some call it a gris-gris, some say *owanga*. It is supposed to cause you to go shrieking off into the night."

"Voodoo?" She recognized the strange-sounding word Hercules had used earlier.

"Venita's handiwork."

"The cook?"

"Exactly. What I can't understand is why she'd want to drive you away."

Still perplexed, Dani climbed into bed and moved over to make room for Troy. "A couple of feathers and some old bones are supposed to scare me off? How?"

"Magic. Hercules would be halfway to New Orleans by now if she had put them between his sheets. I'll have a talk with her tomorrow."

"No," she shook her head, insistent. "Let me talk to her. I can look after myself, Fontaine. 'Sides, I want to see what this voodoo woman is like. Can we just forget about that for now? You promised to lie here until I fall asleep."

The mattress dipped with his weight as Troy slipped in beside her, fully clothed. Dani relaxed against him, aware of the crisp, clean feel of the sheets, Troy's warmth alongside her, and the contentment she experienced. More tired than she had guessed, Dani let the softness of the down pillow lull her into a gentle quietude until all too soon, despite her longings, a full stomach and exhaustion wrapped her in the arms of sleep.

Lying stretched out beside her, Troy fought to keep from exploring the perfect shape beneath the sheer *blouse volante*. He listened as her breathing slowly deepened and she drifted to sleep. The little minx. He smiled into the darkness. It seemed the huntress had caught herself in the trap she had set for him.

He held Dani close, staring up at the canopy formed by the *baire* tied overhead, and tried unsuccessfully to avoid thinking of his conversation with Devereaux earlier in the day. After tracking down word of Constantine Reynolds, following evidence of his having lived in Paris, London, and Belize, Devereaux's agent had finally located Reynolds on the Caribbean island of Tobago. Owner of a well-established sugar plantation, Reynolds was so confident of his complete disappearance that he used his own name instead of an alias.

Troy let his fingers play over Dani's upper arm as he held her close. For a brief moment he had considered paying Leverette for the information and then turning his back on the whole affair. The woman in his arms was real and warm and willing to share her love with him. Why should he leave her behind to chase after the ghosts of his past? The question had answered itself. Because those ghosts would haunt him for the rest of his life if he did not exorcise them while the opportunity presented itself.

Still, he did not relish leaving Dani behind. Nor could he tell her where he was going. Perhaps he would not even tell her he was leaving. It would be easier that way.

But didn't he at least owe her an explanation?

Tired of wrestling with his thoughts, he closed his eyes and pressed his lips against her temple. In sleep she turned toward him and snuggled deeper beneath the sheet. Without disturbing her rest, Troy pulled the coverlet higher over them both and tried to sleep.

"Mr. Troy? 'Less you want your grandmama to remove some of your most precious private parts, you best creep on outta there and git away along the gallery, 'cause Miz Leial, she headed down the hall with a cup o' somethin' for Miz Dani, lookin' to have a li'l chat."

The deep rumbling whisper startled Dani awake. She sat bolt upright and stared, first at the massive bulk of Troy's servant, leaning over them, then at Troy, who threw back the covers and stood up in his stocking feet beside the bed. Hercules disappeared around the corner of the gallery, Troy's boots in hand, as he led the way to safety. Troy, feeling like a fresh-faced schoolboy caught with his first woman, turned to Dani with a quick shrug and a smile of apology before he followed.

Dani grinned openly at his discomfort and whispered, "Thanks a lot, you two," at their retreating footsteps. She straightened the sheets rapidly when she heard a tap on the door. She pulled the pillow up against the headboard and, thus ensconced, called out, "Come in."

Leial Fontaine entered, followed by the Negro woman, Neola, who carried a tray laden with china cups, saucers, and a pot of café au lait. The tall, striking older woman's presence filled the room as she took command, ordering a small side table and ornately carved chair pulled up beside Dani's bed.

Uncomfortable as she watched the silent procedures from beneath the covers, Dani asked, "Should I get up?"

Leial glanced up from the task she'd undertaken, pouring the steaming cream-laced coffee into a wide saucer-shaped cup, as if surprised to find Dani in the room.

"Of course not. Please stay where you are."

The woman smoothed out her wide black skirt, settled herself in the chair, and waved away the servant who hovered behind her.

Dani guessed Neola to be around forty. Medium in height and build, she wore a simple homespun dress; her hair was hidden by the kerchief she had tied about her head. Neola's skin was far lighter than Hercules's, and Dani was arrested by the yellow-gold of her eyes. This was the daughter of Venita, the cook. Dani tried to remember the woman's husband's name . . . Maurice. The gardener and stable hand. Although she wished she could ask the woman about her mother's voodoo charm, Dani remained silent and waited to see what Leial would do next.

Leial took in Dani's appearance, the tousled, sleepy-eyed look, the imprint of another's head on the pillow beside the girl, and surmised correctly that her grandson had spent the night in this room. The doors to the gallery gaped wide, obviously forgotten by Troy in his haste to escape. Leial, choosing to ignore the open doors for the moment, pulled her shawl tight about her shoulders to ward off the chill and handed a cup of aromatic, heavily sugared coffee to Neola. The woman moved forward and presented it to Dani.

"Neola, close the doors and then please leave us," Leial directed.

Dani watched Leial, suddenly feeling cornered and defenseless. The woman was up to something. Dani recognized the look in Leial's eyes. A cougar took on the same hard stare when it cornered its prey. Wary, Dani let Leial make the first move.

"So, Dani, you are in love with my grandson."

Dani masked her surprise easily and, unafraid, met Leial's stare. "Yep. Seems I am. You unhappy about that?"

Leial took a sip of coffee and carefully centered her cup on its saucer before she spoke. "To be truthful, I am not sure of my feelings in the matter. Do you think my grandson loves you?"

Dani mirrored the woman's actions perfectly. Stare, sip, settle the cup. Then she answered, "I think he does. He brought me this far."

"He's never said he loved you?"

The query hurt, but Dani did not falter. "Not in so many words, but I figure he doesn't know his own mind yet."

"My grandson has made love to you, has he not?"

"Yes."

"Last night?"

"No," Dani answered with her usual candor. "Before. On the trail."

"I see."

They were silent again, biding their time as they drank their coffee without tasting it.

So, it had gone that far. Leial, aware of the girl's natural beauty and her feelings for Troy, found it no wonder that her grandson wanted Dani. The girl was young, though. Leial assumed that Troy had taken her virginity. She knew he would feel responsible for his actions, but the expression she read in his eyes surpassed mere responsibility. He loved the girl deeply, whether he knew it or not. All that was left was to determine how strong-willed this Dani Whittaker was, and whether she was worthy of Troy's love. Could this girl stand up to the challenge she would face?

"You realize, don't you, Dani, that you are not at all what I had in mind for my grandson?"

"Yes, ma'am, I think I do. But if Erantha is the kind of woman you have in mind for Troy, I think you're like a coon dog barkin' up the wrong tree."

Leial hid a smile behind the rim of her cup. Erantha. The backwoods girl was right on that score. The simpering Miss Devereaux was not capable of holding a vital, intense man of Troy's ilk. Erantha had no backbone, no fire.

Leial could not resist seeing just how far Dani could be pushed. "Troy is no fool, Dani. He is fluent in English, Spanish, and French and well versed in ancient history. He was schooled in one of the finest universities in the East. And he has had the foresight to develop a steamboat company that stands to make him a fortune. I wonder what you have to offer such a man, besides momentary pleasure. How do you intend to keep him from becoming bored with you once your novelty wears off?"

Carefully, with slow, calculated movements, Dani rose from the bed and walked toward Leial with the quiet, sure strength born of stubbornness. She placed the empty cup and saucer on the tray, then straightened and crossed the room to the armoire. Reaching inside, she drew out her buckskins and bent to pull them on, all the while aware of the old woman's eyes on her. Once the pants were drawn up to her waist, Dani pulled the nightgown over her head and threw it into the open closet. She found the linen shirt that had been Troy's and pulled it on, then sifted through her possessions for a belt.

She carried her boots to the bed and sat down to pull on one boot and then the other, all the while allowing her anger to build as she stared at Leial. Finally, she stood up and spoke.

"I don't intend to let my novelties wear out, ma'am. Nor do I intend to let you or anybody else scare me off. I'm here 'cause Troy asked me to be. I'll stay till he tells me to go. And don't be surprised"—Dani picked up her shot pouch, powder horn, and rifle—"if I stay here a bit longer than you reckoned I would."

It wouldn't hurt the old lady none to hear some good stiff mountain talk, Dani thought as she continued to lace her speech with the familiar twang Jake so often assumed.

"Now"—Dani straightened up, armed and ready to hunt— "if you'll tell Troy next time you see him that I've gone out to see if a little huntin' will clear my head, I'll surely be obliged." Dani took her buckskin jacket from a hook behind the door and then turned the knob.

"Oh, I almost forgot," Dani added, "thanks for the talk."

The door banged shut behind the girl. Leial stared at it for a moment and then smiled.

The faint sound of a footfall caused Troy to glance up from his paper-strewn desk. He paused for a moment to listen as

someone moved stealthily along the narrow corridor outside
the small library that served as his office. Thankful for the
distraction, he pushed his chair away from the desk and crossed
the room.

When he opened the door he was treated to the sight of Dani
in her buckskins, rifle in hand, stealing toward the back door.

"Dani, wait. I'd like to speak to you for a moment." He
watched her stop in midstride, saw her shoulders slump in
defeat, before she turned and headed in his direction like a
wayward child caught in an act of disobedience. "Come in."
He ushered her into the library and closed the door softly
behind her.

She stood staring uncomfortably around the room. Books
and rolled pages filled shelves along one wall. Troy's books.
Books he had read, books filled with knowledge that was now
in his head. Books filled with things she would never know.

Almost fearing her response, he asked, "How'd it go with
Grandmother?"

"I don't like her."

Troy stepped toward her, his brow knit with worry. So much
for asking Leial to be patient with the girl. "I'd hoped you two
would get along."

"It's all right. She hates me, too." Dani shrugged with
feigned nonchalance, determined not to let one old woman get
her down for long.

Troy resisted the urge to take her in his arms and comfort
her. "Pretty strong words," he said instead.

"You weren't there."

"No, I wasn't. I'm sorry, Dani." *Damn Grandmother! How
much would it hurt her to leave the girl alone?* He decided to
speak to Leial again before he left.

Hoping to cheer Dani, he led her to the desk and rifled
through the pages that littered its cherrywood surface. "I'll be
going to Baton Rouge tomorrow," he said, still sorting through
the papers. "My shipping business has been left untended far
too long, but I hope to be back here within two weeks. I hope
you and Grandmother will be able to make peace during that
time."

He looked up in time to catch her startled expression before
she masked it with one of cocky self-assurance.

"Two weeks?" She knew her tone was far less confident

than her demeanor, but it was hard to hide the loss she was already beginning to feel.

"I'll be back before—" He cut himself off before he disclosed his plan to go after Reynolds.

"Before what?"

Troy hid his own concern with a smile. "Before you miss me too much."

Dani smiled crookedly, warmed by his teasing words. "Not a chance."

"Here it is," he said, having found the paper he was looking for. Troy motioned her forward and Dani approached the desk as if it might take on a life of its own and lunge toward her.

"What is it?"

"I'm going to open an account for you at the bank in Baton Rouge. The funds Jake entrusted to Sol Westburg will be held there in your name. All you have to do, should you need money, is write out the amount and sign your name. The banker will match the signature to the name you sign on this form."

She glanced up at him, her steel-gray eyes mirrored wariness. "Sign my name?"

He nodded.

Silence stretched between them in the cluttered room, and Troy took the moment to measure Dani against the alien environment. The library had always been a place of solace and peace for him. It was untidy at his request; he found it more comfortable to live amid the piles of books and sheaves of paper than to have Neola straighten up and disrupt his work. If he allowed her to organize the room, he might never find anything again.

His treasured collection of books and maps, journals and reports, filled the shelves that ran along one wall. As in every other room in the house, one door led to the hallway and another to the gallery that overlooked the bayou. The desk was covered with papers and ledgers he had had sent from Baton Rouge in order to arm himself with the current status of his company's resources before he met with its manager. The room was cramped and cluttered, yet it served his purposes.

But his retreat closed in around Dani like a prison. He had a fleeting memory of her standing in the open against the backdrop of the Rockies, and he wondered now if he had acted wisely in bringing her here. She had the look of a trapped animal seeking escape. He watched as she glanced down at the paper in his hand and cursed himself. If she could not read, it was highly likely she could not write her name.

He laid the carefully written directions to the bank on his desk and found a blank sheet of paper. "Here, I'll teach you how," he said softly, hoping to draw Dani to the task.

She hesitated a moment and then stepped forward. "I can write my name."

"Good." He nodded.

"I think," she said.

Dani rested her rifle against the desk and took up the quill Troy offered. She bent her head to the task and, with her upper lip drawn between her teeth, set to work. He watched in silence while she printed out DINA.

Troy cleared his throat, half afraid to comment.

She stared up at him. "Well?"

"That's very good," he said, searching for the right words. "You have all the letters properly formed."

"But . . . ?"

"But you have two of them in the wrong places." Dani stared down at the letters on the page. "I do?"

"You do."

She squinted. She turned the page a quarter turn to the right. Then she shrugged.

"It says Dina," Troy offered.

Dani laid the pen down and picked up her gun. "I won't be needin' money anyway." She stalked toward the door.

"I never knew you to give up so easily. You think you can't learn to write your name?"

She stopped with her hand on the doorknob. Slowly she turned to face him. "Is it so important to you?"

They locked eyes across the room, and Troy nodded nearly imperceptibly. Dani remembered Leial's earlier words: *"He was schooled in one of the finest universities in the East."* She shrugged again and sighed dramatically. "Let's get it done."

Troy worked with her for a quarter of an hour, forming and reforming the letters and having Dani copy them in the correct order. Soon she was confident enough to reproduce her name on a blank page and then on the official letter to the bank. Proud of her efforts, Troy smiled and threw an arm about her shoulders. He squeezed her, drawing her close.

"Good work," he said softly, staring down at her lush mouth.

"You can kiss me, Fontaine," she whispered.

Unwilling to disappoint his guest, Troy bent his head and let his lips play over hers. Dani remained still, eyes closed, reveling in the taste of his lips on hers.

"You know I'd like more . . ." he began.

"What's stopping you?"

"Dani . . ." he warned.

It was her turn to give him a hug, brief but strong, before she broke from his embrace. "It's all right, Fontaine. I know you have work to do. 'Sides, I think it's time I saw this island of yours."

She collected her gun and was out the door and moving along the hall when Troy called out behind her, "Take Hercules along!"

Dani shook her head and left the house. Moments later she slipped silently past the servants' cabins and disappeared into the moss-strewn forest.

The day passed all too quickly as Dani roamed the island, acquainting herself with the piece of land that rose far enough above the swamp to remain relatively dry. She found the heavy growth a hindrance, but she marked a trail as she went along, careful to stop and take her bearings more often than usual. It was not until noon that she felt hungry and so set up a snare made of hastily woven vine and caught a swamp rabbit. The skinning took only moments, for it was a task she'd performed for as long as she could remember. The succulent meat roasted over an open fire was more than welcome after the exotic fare she'd consumed the previous night.

Dani spent the afternoon watching and learning about the bayou inhabitants that were so elusive. Swamp rabbits, even half grown, could swim. She spotted a white-tailed deer with a winter coat of thick gray hair camouflaged against the background of dark tree trunks. When it lifted its tail, the white fur on the underside stood out like a flag. Dani did not raise her gun to fire, intent only upon exploring her new surroundings. She nearly stumbled over an opossum as it feigned death, lying limp in the dense mulch beneath the trees, eyes clamped shut, tongue lolling. Dani laughed and moved on. Troy claimed that black bears, bobcats, pumas, and cougars inhabited the swamp, but she saw none of them, for they were nocturnal creatures.

Finally, her pent-up anger spent, Dani began to make her way back toward the house. She did not become alarmed when she was unable to find the trees she had marked along her trail. Deciding she had merely taken a wrong turn, Dani gauged the position of the setting sun and backtracked to the place where she had made her noon fire. She thought she would easily locate the remains of her campfire beneath the tall, leafless tupelo gum trees, but she was unable to find even that familiar place.

The daylight was fast growing dim and in the waning light, the trees loomed larger. Still unfamiliar to her, the cypress, oak, and tupelo offered none of the peaceful security of the mountain pines she knew so well. She was surrounded by strangers.

Instinct told her to move to her right; she guessed the direction to be southeast. Her intuition failed her, though, for she soon reached the edge of solid ground and found herself up to her right knee in mud. She muttered her favorite imprecation and, holding her rifle high overhead, tried to grab a low-hanging limb with her other hand.

A splash across the narrow rivulet alerted her to danger. A vision of the cottonmouth snakes Troy had warned her about flashed in her mind. She pulled hard on the limb behind her and was nearly up and out of the water when she noticed a large, dark shape floating steadily toward her.

"Shoot," she said aloud. "I was scared of a driftin' log."

Just as the words were uttered, she realized the "log" was drifting toward her with a purpose. Her foot came up out of the mud just as the "log" opened long, hinged jaws lined with rows of sharp teeth. Dani found herself facing certain death.

Years of training forced her to act even as her mind registered a fear greater than any she had ever known. The slope she was standing on was slick with mud and water; her right boot was coated with muck. Even as she tried to move back onto more solid ground, death sped nearer, gaping at her with hideous smiling jaws. One foot slipped out from under her, and she sat down on the other leg, still clutching her rifle. It was loaded and primed, and she had time to get off one shot. She hoped.

Dani aimed and fired.

Blood spattered from the creature's throat and it roared, or tried to, but the sound ended as a deep gurgle. The animal whipped its long tail in pain and fury. Blood reddened the murky water, spreading out around the thing as it continued to swim toward shore. It was nearly upon her now, and Dani could see the creature's forelegs—bent, awkward appendages with sharp talons. It clawed its way up the gentle bank toward her.

A sob tore its way out of her throat. There was no time to reload and fire. Shaking with the force of her fear, Dani held the barrel of her rifle, ready to club the beast, which charged even as it turned the earth red with blood.

Two shots rang out, so close she heard the balls pass overhead. Another wound appeared as the flesh exploded in the space between the creature's eyes. Its forward advance halted and it began to slip down the bank, dragged backwards by its own weight.

Dani felt her throat close, and she began to gasp for air. Racked by uncontrollable sobs, she closed her eyes to the sight of the ponderous lizard and cradled her rifle in her arms.

Two strong hands grasped her and hauled her to her feet. Troy spun her about and held her at arm's length. He kept his anger in check until he was certain Dani was unharmed; then he pulled the rifle from her desperate grip and, without turning, handed it to Hercules.

Try as she might, Dani was unable to control the tremors that whipped through her frame. Dry sobs of fear followed one upon the other. She reached out with shaking hands to clutch Troy's buckskin jacket and cling to him desperately.

Troy let his anger slowly simmer and replace his fear. When he realized Dani was unharmed, he began to shake her so unmercifully that her teeth rattled in her head. The sobbing abruptly ceased, and the hands that clung to him for support suddenly began to shove against his chest as Dani sought freedom.

"Let me . . . go!" She managed to spit out the words as she tried to break his hold. She twisted in his arms.

"I could shake you to within an inch of your life. Didn't I warn you not to go out alone?"

"Of course you did. But when did I ever listen to you?"

As he stopped shaking her violently, Dani's legs took over, trembling visibly by themselves. She tried to calm her racing heart. "After the friendly little 'chat' I had with your *dear* grandmother, I had to put some distance between us."

Dani dared to look over her shoulder at the carcass of the dread creature floating half submerged along the bank. "What *was* that?" She shuddered.

"Alligator. I warned you about them."

"You never told me what they *were*! That's a damned lizard! I *hate* lizards. You know how I hate lizards." Wide-eyed, she turned back to face him and found Troy trying to hide a smile.

"I forgot. The only thing you are afraid of."

"Yep. And this place is crawling with them, I suppose?"

"Sorry." He was smiling fully now, the anger brought on by his fear for her safety slowly dissipating. "Does this mean you'll be leaving?"

Dani noticed Hercules standing a few feet away, rifle loaded and eyes trained on the surrounding swamp. Darkness was rapidly gathering around them. It was time they started back.

"Leaving?" She brushed at her muddied buckskins and straightened her jacket. "Not yet, Fontaine." Smiling crookedly, Dani moved past him and began to walk away from the edge of the bayou. "At least, not till I wear out my novelties."

Muddy and tired, her nerves still on edge, Dani made her way along the upstairs hallway toward her room. As she turned the knob, Grady's door, directly opposite her own, opened and he smiled with relief when he saw her.

"Dani! Troy found you!"

Stubbornly she lifted her chin. "I was all right. Only a little lost is all."

He smiled, and she saw that he held a wrapped parcel behind his back. "I have something for you."

Her eyes lit up with pleasure and anticipation, and she tried to see around him.

"Oh, Grady, what is it? Let's see."

He drew the flat package from behind his back and handed it to her. She could tell by the weight and shape that it was a painting.

Dani glanced up at the dim lamp attached to the wall in the hallway and bade him enter her room. "Come on in here and I'll light all the lamps so I can see better."

Grady hesitated for a moment before he followed her inside,

then stood waiting just inside the doorway while Dani lit the lamps.

"Come on in, Grady. No sense standing there in the hall."

"Dani"—his voice was hesitant—"a lady never invites a man into her room."

Dani sighed, put a hand on her hip, and cocked her head. "Then come in, Grady, or stay out. Suit yourself."

He stepped inside but remained near the open door.

Dani shook her head at his show of propriety and opened the package, which she had placed on the bed. The brown wrapping paper came apart easily, and Dani stared down at the gray and indigo shades of the Tetons against a cloudless blue sky.

"Oh, Grady!" Dani found it hard to contain her excitement. "It's wonderful. I feel like I'm right there, standing in the Snake River valley looking up at the Tetons." She smiled at him warmly, recalling their journey eastward. "You see, you did remember it all."

Dani held the painting at arm's length and then set it up against the headboard of her bed and stepped back across the room. She viewed the work from every angle.

"It's really for me?"

"It's really for you." Grady smiled. "Without your help, Dani, I might not have lived to paint it."

Unexpectedly, her eyes filled with tears as she looked at the tall, blond man.

"Thanks, Grady. I'll keep it always."

Another voice came from the open doorway.

"Miz Dani, Mr. Troy said you might be needin' a bath." Hercules filled the door frame behind Grady, nearly a head and shoulders taller than the artist. The black man's halo of wild hair was backlit by the lamp in the hallway.

"I just might, at that." She smiled, glancing at the caked mud on her buckskins.

Hercules glanced at Grady and made no move to leave. Dani stared up at him, a question in her eyes, and the servant nodded toward Grady. It seemed she had more than one chaperon on the island.

"Grady just gave me this painting, Leze," she said, lifting the oil and turning it toward the big man. "This is where I come from."

Instead of looking at the picture in Dani's hands, Hercules

was staring at a spot just behind Dani with eyes as round as wagon wheels. Dani spun around and instantly spied a crudely sewn doll hanging from a noose of dried creeper vine. It dangled from the shuttered door that led out to the gallery.

She left the painting on the bed and marched over to the doll with determined strides, her boots leaving dark mud stains on the braided rug.

"What . . . ?" Grady watched as she pulled what appeared to be a child's toy from the door.

Hercules backed into the hallway, mouth gaping, hands spread protectively before him.

"That does it." Dani snapped the vine and wrapped it about the voodoo charm. She paused long enough to collect the chicken claw and feathered gris-gris from the bedside table, then headed toward the door.

"Holding court?"

Dani recognized Leial's cool tone. Her silver hair was as distinctive in its own right as Hercules's unruly mane. Swathed again in black from neckline to the toes of her shoes, Troy's grandmother stared at Dani, missing no detail of the girl's disheveled appearance, nor of Grady standing just inside the doorway.

"It seems I need to have a little talk with your cook, ma'am."

"Dani, let me take those to Troy." Grady held out his hand for the gris-gris. Obviously Grady was not cowed by the charms, but Hercules was halfway down the stairs by the time Dani reached the hallway.

Leial stepped aside.

"No, thanks, Grady," Dani said. "You know me well enough to know I fight my own fights." Her eyes met and held Leial's. "Now, where do I find your cook?"

The kitchen on Isle de Fontaine was located in a one-room building separate from the house. An enormous smoke-blackened stone fireplace took up one entire wall. Covered pots and deep cauldrons hung suspended from hooks above the fire. Knives and cut-up vegetables and seafood littered a huge wooden table in the center of the room. The surface of the table showed the wear of years of use.

A woman of undeterminable age was bent over the fireplace, stirring a bubbling pot from which emanated a mouth-watering aroma that Dani recognized as that of the rich gombo served the night before. The woman did not flinch, even though Dani attempted to startle her by throwing the door open before she stepped inside.

"You Venita?" she asked, knowing full well the crone could be no other.

The woman calmly turned to face Dani. Glittering black eyes as dark as coal and sparkling with inner light stared into Dani's. The girl suppressed a shudder and stepped farther into the room.

The cook straightened to her full height, and Dani discovered Venita was far taller than she. Dani was reminded immediately of Leial, and the longer she compared the two, the more apparent the similarity became. Both women were tall and possessed silver-white hair. Leial was slim, but Venita was thin to the point of emaciation. One had skin the color of fine translucent china; the other was as dark as a walnut.

Dani spoke first, aware that Venita seemed content to stare. "I take it these are yours." She held up the charms. In two strides she reached the worktable, and in two more she stood beside the woman near the fire. She threw the offending objects into the flames, and Venita met her stare with an equally challenging one of her own.

"If you want to scare me off, old woman, it's going to take more than a chicken leg and a child's toy." Dani squinted her eyes and leaned forward, hands on hips. "What I want to know is why are you trying to scare me off?"

"That's what I'd like to know, too."

Troy stood in the open doorway, barefoot and half dressed, his shirt hanging open to the waist, leaving a slash of dark skin visible between the edges of linen material. He brushed his open hand over his glistening hair, still wet from his bath, and slicked it back. Dani guessed that either Grady or Hercules had alerted him during his ablutions. All thought of Venita fled as Dani stood staring at the man standing in the warmth of the kitchen. His shadow on the wall was magnified by the fire's glow.

"I told you I could take care of this myself, Fontaine," Dani whispered.

Venita ignored them both and stirred the thick, steaming gombo. The smell of baking bread emanated from the small ovens built in the wall beside the fireplace.

Dani did not move.

Troy silently closed the door behind him and spoke softly. "Venita . . . ?" The quiet question held a demanding tone.

In a gravelly, rasping voice, Venita began to speak. The words kept time to the movements of the long-handled spoon that circled inside the cauldron. Her accent was as thick as the spicy mixture, a blend of Creole French, English, and one of the languages of Africa.

"Venita *faire un gris-gris* until she go. Make magic to fight her. Girl bad magic. Not woman, not man. Wrap in skins. Venita *ouangateur*, make *ouanga*, make her go. Girl take away your power, Fontaine. Drain you of your fury. Need power, not need girl. Bes' she go."

Stunned by the little she could understand of the old woman's words, Dani held her breath and looked at Troy. His bare chest glistened bronze in the firelight. Water droplets beaded on his raven hair. *Take away your power, Fontaine*— what did the old one mean by those words? The memory of last night in her room flooded Dani. She had felt a power over Troy then; he would have given in to her needs if she had not fallen asleep. Was she draining him of his power with her need for him?

"Voodoo can only hurt those who believe in it." Troy stared hard at Venita as he spoke. "Obviously, Dani doesn't believe in it. Leave her alone, Venita."

The cook ignored Troy and glared at Dani. She walked to the cutting table. When she picked up a long butcher knife, Dani readied herself. Venita raised the knife and cleaved an onion in two as she mumbled to herself.

Dani saw the dramatic move for what it was, an open threat. Bits of bone and stuffed dolls she'd never dealt with before, but weapons she knew well. Dani crossed the room and stepped up close to Venita. "Listen, old lady, I have had just about all I can handle here for one day. Between you and your geegaws and that overgrown lizard out there"—she pointed toward the door—"my temper's getting a bit short." She didn't mention Troy's grandmother's verbal attack. "If I find any more of your trash in my room, I intend to throw it back in your face till it stops showing up. Do you get my meaning?"

Venita met her stare but failed to utter a sound.

"Good." Dani nodded and stepped around the woman.

"Dani." Troy's voice halted her at the door, "Grandmother

has planned a late dinner this evening. It will give you a chance to wash and change."

Dani thought of last evening's affair, of the houseguests she'd luckily not seen today but knew she would face at dinner, and of the morning's exchange with Leial. Coupled with the alligator attack and Venita's ominous words, the thought of yet another charade in the dining room quelled her appetite.

"Don't wait for me," she said softly, her voice growing stronger as she met Troy's dark eyes across the room. "I think I'll just go to bed . . . alone." Dani emphasized her last word with a hefty slam of the door.

Chapter Nineteen

Leial dipped the quill pen into the inkwell one last time and then completed her work with a flourish befitting a queen. She reached for the wooden-backed blotter and rolled it across the curling, evenly spaced letters, then stood and disentangled the folds of her heavy black skirt from the leg of the chair pulled up before her escritoire. Intent on finding Dani, she lifted the page from the desktop and walked out of the sitting room. Leial thought of their first confrontation, now nearly two weeks past. Leial had decided then and there that Dani was the perfect match for her grandson. The girl was as strong-willed as she had suspected. Just now though, as Leial slowly made her way up the stairs, she feared that the girl's obstinancy might stand in the way.

Nothing occurred on Isle de Fontaine that Leial did not learn of sooner or later. Hercules had been all too willing to inform her of the alligator attack and Dani's near escape. Troy himself had proudly related Dani's confrontation with the ruler of the kitchen. Voodoo. Leial shook her head and paused to catch her breath at the upstairs landing. It seemed that Venita had taken it upon herself to drive Dani away. It was no secret to Leial why the old cook felt threatened by Dani's presence.

War had been declared between Leial and Venita the day Philippe brought his new bride to the island. There had been no grand house then, just a hip-roofed cabin fronted by a porch. It was little better than the ones provided for the few slaves Philippe had owned. Venita's regal African beauty had once given her power over Philippe. But Leial had been just as beautiful, and as Philippe's wife, she became the undisputed mistress of the island.

They had maintained a silent truce over the years as Venita ruled the kitchen and Leial the house. As Venita's beauty began to fade, she had relied on voodoo to maintain the adoration of the slaves working the cane fields.

Venita had doted on Merle Fontaine and then Troy after him. Her need for revenge against Merle's murderer still smoldered. Leial suspected that need helped to fuel Troy's own obsession. She could understand how the former slave might see Dani as a distraction, one who might turn Troy away from his quest for Reynolds. Leial had hoped with all her heart Venita's fear might subside. Then, after Troy left to see to his business and make preparations for his departure to the Caribbean, Dani had remained in her room when she was not prowling the bayou with Hercules.

Leial prayed it was indecision she had read in Troy's eyes when he came to ask her to care for Dani and to help the girl feel at home. He had hoped to be gone a week at the most, but now it had been nearly two and Dani had made little visible progress adjusting during his absence. The girl rarely took her meals at the table. She preferred to eat alone in her room or outdoors with Hercules. And she still refused to don suitable clothing.

In the narrow hallway, Leial paused and listened to the sounds of Grady Maddox moving about in his own room across the hall. She shook her head. A slight smile curved her lips. The young man had sequestered himself in his room, barely pausing for meals, intent on recapturing the West on canvas.

Not a sound issued from behind Dani's door. Leial raised her hand to knock and as she did, she found herself staring at the blue veins that pulsed beneath the thin white skin stretched across the back of her hand. When had she grown so old?

"Come on in, it's open."

Dani did not bother to stand and answer the door to her room. She was seated cross-legged on the braided rug, dressed in her usual buckskin garb, working over her long rifle. Her strong young hands stroked the weapon with familiarity as she rubbed the stock with an oiled rag. When Leial entered, Dani spared her a cursory glance before returning to her task.

The welcome was nearly as frigid as the temperature in the room. Both doors stood open to the gallery, for Dani enjoyed watching the steady curtain of rain that had been falling since just before dawn. The eaves and spouts dripped heavily, filling the room with the sound of rain.

While Dani chose to ignore her, Leial stared about the room. Dani wondered what the woman thought of the changes. In the two short weeks since her arrival, Dani had transformed the place, with Grady's help. A mountain range worked in brilliant blues and grays replaced the pastoral scene that had once hung above the bed. Portraits and sketches of trappers and Indians adorned the walls and were propped up on the bureau and washstand. A thick fur of some sort covered the floor beside the bed, and prime red fox pelts had been sewn together to form the coverlet that graced the foot of the bed. A powder horn, a shot bag, and what appeared to be a bear's head shaped into a bag hung from a four-hooked hat rack above the washstand.

Two young palmetto trees planted in buckets flanked the gallery doors. Tall vases previously stored in the attic were filled with long branches of dried red maple leaves. Dani had succeeded in bringing the outdoors inside.

"You like the rain, I see, Dani," Leial said.

"Yes, ma'am."

Leial pulled up a chair and sat, despite the fact that she was uninvited. Even in the dull light of the cloudy day, the girl's hair shone. Of a rich brown, it was streaked with the fire of sunlight and hung just above her shoulders, swaying gently forward to hide her radiant complexion. Leial ached to see Dani dressed in the finery such loveliness deserved, but knew the transformation would have to come from the girl herself.

"I, too, love the rain," Leial said. "I believe that's the only way I could have stood it here on the island all these years. We have very wet winters."

"I like rain a lot. It reminds me of springtime." Dani surprised herself as she entered into conversation with Leial. After Troy left, life on the island had settled into a placid routine that Dani found annoying. He had promised he would return before the New Year, but Dani found little consolation in being left behind with his promise.

Grady spent hours locked away in his room, and thus far Dani had avoided any unnecessary contact with Leial. She half suspected the woman of encouraging Venita's attempts to frighten her into leaving, and after Leial's earlier warning that

Troy would tire of her, Dani had no wish to spend time in her company.

Hercules called upon her daily and, when the weather permitted, took her hunting. More often, though, he begged her to allow him to alter one of Jeanette Fontaine's gowns for her.

"Miz Dani," he said more than once, "I know I could make them ol' dresses 'pear good as new. Jes' think on how Mr. Troy would like to see you all dressed up. Miz Leial, too. Why I bet you'd take to eatin' in the dinin' room again stead o' always hidin' out up here or in the bayou."

But she always refused. If Troy wanted her, it would be as she was, not as something she was not.

What of the women in Baton Rouge? she wondered. Dani had seen Erantha blush and invite Troy to the Devereaux home for dinner before she and Leverette departed for town. Surely Troy knew other women as well.

"I would like you to be the first to know . . ." Leial was speaking again, watching her like a hawk ready to swoop. Dani had nearly forgotten she was in the room.

"Know what?"

"I've planned to hold a New Year's celebration, a small *soirée dansante*, while all three of you are here. I feel it's time to open our home to guests." She looked out toward the falling rain. "It has been many years since we have had a gathering of any import. I'd like you to read the invitation." Leial stood and crossed the room until she stood over Dani.

Dani stared at Leial's silk slippers. She gazed slowly up the long black skirt and noticed, for the first time, the rolled piece of paper Leial extended toward her.

Reaching out hesitantly, Dani took the paper from Leial and unrolled it. Spidery script was etched across the page. Dani squinted. She opened her eyes wide. She shifted the page toward the light. Nothing helped. The squiggles were meaningless. She looked up at Leial again.

"I can't read it."

Leial immediately masked her surprise and dismay. She had not meant to hurt Dani. Now she knew it must seem as if she had intended to humiliate her. Quickly trying to make amends, Leial took the page from Dani's outstretched hand. Smoothly she said, "Then I'll read it to you."

Dani did not look up while Leial read the invitation. She was certain Leial was shaming her again, calling attention to the differences between Troy and herself. The woman would no doubt invite a host of beautiful women to the island, women Dani could never compete with for Troy's favor. Leial stood waiting for Dani to comment.

Dani tipped her head back and her eyes, as cloudy gray as the rain-filled sky, met the shining black depths of Leial's. The war was on again.

"There will be dancing, of course," Leial said.

But I never danced before.

"And *un dîner carabiné*, a dinner complete in every detail. New Year's is a time of great celebration here. You will sing for us, perhaps? Troy said you have a most pleasing voice."

"Maybe." Dani set her rifle aside and stood up quickly. She walked to the open gallery windows and looked out at the rain. How long had it been since she'd felt like singing? She asked Leial over her shoulder, "Will there be many guests?"

"Not so many. No more than fifty."

"Fifty?" Dani felt her heart sink and spun to face Leial. "You're doing this to make me look the fool, aren't you?"

Leial paused and met Dani's hard stare. She drew herself up to her full, regal height. "No, Dani, I am not. One cannot be *made* to appear the fool."

Dani watched the woman walk toward the door.

Leial paused and said, "I hope to provide entertainment and an opportunity for you to meet Troy's neighbors and friends."

"So he can compare me to them and find me lacking?"

"Not at all," Leial countered. "I only thought to offer help, Dani. I am willing to tutor you in the ways of a lady worthy of my grandson. We have a good two weeks remaining. I will be happy to help, to teach you how to walk, how to dress, how to conduct yourself. I would also enjoy teaching you to read."

"Why?" Dani cocked her head and rested one hand on her hip.

"What do you mean?"

"Why would you be willing to do all that? Let's not pretend you hold any likin' toward me."

"But my grandson does."

Dani shook her head. "Suddenly that's enough for you, is it? Put aside the fact that I can't speak like he can, I can't walk and talk and dress like a lady? Put aside the fact that I can't read anything that isn't written in big, wide letters? Is that what you're tellin' me? That you're willing to set all that aside and help me?"

"Yes."

Dani crossed the room and stood before Leial. She caught the fresh, powdery scent of the woman's perfume.

"I don't believe you," Dani said coolly.

"I'm sorry you don't, but the offer still stands. The party *will* be held, and I *am* willing to help you. You can choose to hide like a coward in your room, or you can present yourself to my grandson's guests in a manner worthy of him and yourself. Let me know when you are willing to cooperate."

"It'd be dangerous to stand around holdin' your breath."

"Will I see you at dinner, Dani, or will you be eating up here alone . . . again?" Leial's stare was challenging.

"You won't be seein' me at dinner. I might starve trying to decide which fork to use first."

Without another word, Leial let herself out of the room.

Dani picked up one of her black leather boots and pitched it at the door. It bounced off the oak portal and then fell to the floor with an echoing thud. *Damn.* She cursed silently and walked out onto the gallery. The wind slanted the rain and sent a gentle mist beneath the overhang. It helped to cool her raging temper. What now? she wondered. Was it worth changing for any man?

But Troy was not just any man. He was the man who had taught her to love, taught her body to sing, to become as finely tuned an instrument as her voice. Dani thought of the way he'd followed her to the stream the night they met, thought of his patience and gentleness with her. She remembered the night Grady was lost on the trail, recalled the intense need they filled in each other, the comfort their lovemaking brought them. But more than that, she thought about the ways in which Troy himself had changed: his spontaneity the morning he had brought her to the island in the pirogue; his patience the day he taught her to write her name correctly; the way he was beginning to smile and share his feelings with her. Yes, she thought with a grin, Fontaine was beginning to change. Could she?

Dani knew three things for certain: She was a duck out of water, she was lonely, and she was homesick. She stared out at the sodden grounds and watched rain drip from the Spanish moss. For good measure, she kicked the wooden balustrade and regretted having let herself get treed like a raccoon. There had to be an answer to her self-imposed dilemma. She could not stay hidden in this room forever.

Another knock sounded at the door.

Out of patience, Dani called out "Come in," in too harsh a voice.

Hercules entered, his arms filled with hat boxes and packages, his springy hair glistening with raindrops. He beamed a wide smile at her. "These jes' came for you, Miz Dani. Boat jes' docked. Where should I put 'em?"

"On the bed," she directed. "Leze, what are they?"

"I don't rightly know, but I can guess. They from Mr. Troy in Baton Rouge. They come with this note." He held out a small water-spattered piece of paper.

For the second time within the hour, Dani was forced to admit she could not read. "Read it for me, Leze."

"I'm not s'posed to be able to read," he replied.

"What's that supposed to mean? Can you read or not?"

He hesitated but a second before he nodded. "Yes, Miz Dani, I can. Mr. Troy taught me."

"Then read it."

The servant sighed. He knew it was useless to explain the way things were, for this girl was unfamiliar with the slave-holders' way of life. She would not understand the reasons behind the edict that blacks were not allowed to read and write. It mattered not at all that Hercules and the others on the isle were freedmen now. Knowledge meant power, and up to now, the fact that he could read had been a secret between Troy and himself. Hercules shrugged, glanced at Dani, and read:

" 'Dani, when you are ready, these are for you. Fontaine.' "

She smiled, imagining the sound of Troy's voice as his servant spoke the words. Her smile was quickly replaced with a frown as Hercules began to open the boxes.

Dresses and petticoats, camisoles, silk slippers and stockings, ribbons, laces, and shawls poured forth. She did not touch the beautiful garments.

Hercules was not so reserved. He pulled out an apricot watered-silk dress, held it at arm's length and then against his thick frame. The dress was nothing more than a wisp of material against the man's wide bulk and bulging muscles.

"These are some of the finest dresses I ever seen, Miz Dani."

She reached out tentatively and felt the soft apricot dress with thumb and forefinger. Troy had purchased these gowns and accoutrements for her. "When you are ready," he'd written. She thought of Troy's high-handed manner in St. Louis, thought of the way she had refused to give in to his simple request that she dress like a lady. He was changing. Why couldn't she?

"Oh, Leze," she groaned, "what am I going to do?"

"Why, you gonna put these dresses on, gal, an' look dee-vine!" Clowning, he rolled his eyes heavenward.

Dani had to laugh despite her mixed emotions.

"Don't you see, I can't just put them on. I told him I wouldn't wear a dress. And I . . . I just made it clear to his grandmother that I wouldn't let her teach me to be a lady." She shrugged and held her hands out before her. "Now she's having a big fandango here and I all but told her I wasn't going to set foot downstairs."

Hercules tossed the apricot gown aside and fingered a blue day dress of muslin trimmed in lace.

"Tell her you changed your mind."

"Eat crow, you mean?"

"Some folks find it mighty tasty at times."

"Well, I don't. I'd likely choke to death." She began to pace the room. "If I could just change of a sudden"—she turned to face him again—"like a miracle . . . like a butterfly that's busted out of its cocoon . . ." Dani looked at Hercules with a glimmer of excitement in her eyes.

Warily, he backed away a step. "What you thinkin' 'bout, Miz Dani."

"*You* could do it."

"I can't." He paused. "Do what?" he added.

"You could teach me all I need to know to become lady-fied."

"Wait jes' one minute. You tellin' *me*"—he jabbed a thumb toward his chest, and the muscles balled in his arm again—"that I'm supposed to teach you to be a lady?"

"Why not?"

He stared at her and Dani could almost see his mind working.

"Why ever not?" she asked again. "You've seen more ladies in your born life than I ever have. You mean to tell me you don't know how they act? Take that Erantha . . ." Dani struck a pose, hands tightly clenched at her waist, breasts held slightly forward, and batted her long lashes. "I've seen her only once, but I can remember the way she performed. The only other prime example I ever saw was Miss Glory Hallelujah, but for some reason, Troy wasn't too pleased when I tried to act like her."

"Aw, Miz Dani . . ."

"Isn't there someplace we could be in private while you teach me? How about your cabin?"

"*No!* Gal, what you thinkin' of? Lord knows you'd be safe enough with me, but ain't nobody else gonna believe that." Hercules glanced toward the door and spoke in hushed tones. "You must be desperate for learnin', to suggest somethin' like this. When this here party to be held?"

"In two weeks."

Hercules put his hands on his hips, stepped back, and surveyed Dani from the toes of her moccasins to the crown of her head.

"We ain' got a minute to spare."

"Step, step, slide. Step, step, slide."

Hercules counted the steps of a waltz as he and Dani danced about the attic, careful to remain above the unoccupied rooms below them.

"Stop." Dani halted abruptly, forcing her partner to stop as well. "I'm so mixed up right now, I don't even know which dance I'm doing."

"The waltz," he explained patiently.

Dani moaned. "How am I supposed to keep them all straight—waltzes, cotillions, quadrilles . . . ? How will I know which steps to start out with?"

"Jes' stand and wait for the music to tell you. Watch the others. Do what they do."

"How'd you learn to do all these dances?"

"Watchin' the dancers. I never actually done 'em."

She turned on him. "You mean you've never even *danced*?" Suddenly her confidence in her dance master diminished.

"Can't be much different than what I taught you. Let's jes' get on to walkin' proper."

"Oh, Leze," she complained, "again?"

"We got two days left. This ain't no time to start moanin' and cryin'. Your dress is ready, and I'm goin' in to town to fetch it later today. This be the last chance we have to practice."

Dani's heart sank. Two days until the party and there had been no word from Troy. Grady constantly reassured her he would return on time, for Leial had sent word to him, along with invitations for Troy to deliver in town.

"Miz Dani, don't you go lookin' like that." Hercules handed her a full petticoat. She slipped it over her clothes. It fell open, and she tied the waistband closed. Her buckskins showed through the sheer muslin, and Dani laughed at the sight of her heavy moccasins peeping from beneath the petticoat hem. Hercules insisted that she wear the full undergarment so that she would become accustomed to moving in a skirt.

Dani tried to hide her smile and appear a most studious subject, but it was nearly impossible as she watched Hercules. He, too, donned a skirt to demonstrate to Dani how a "proper" lady should move. The one he had chosen was a full, faded saffron satin, generations old, part of an ornate gown complete with wide panniers. With a small knife, he had delicately slit the threads that held bodice and skirt together and then had opened the back of the skirt at the waistline. He had tied a swatch of silk about his head, imitating the *tiyons* or kerchiefs worn turban-style by many female servants. Now he slipped off his boots and stood barefoot.

"Take off your boots, too, Dani."

She complied.

"Now . . ." He took a deep breath. "This is the last time we gonna practice this, so do your best."

"I will."

The immense man moved with the grace of a finely bred lady used to years of drawing room soirees. He held his head high, his spine straight. With the thumb and forefinger of either hand, he daintily lifted the front of the saffron skirt as he began to glide soundlessly across the floor with mincing steps. A shaft of sunlight crept through the high windows at the end of the room. It set his golden looped earring glimmering as his *tiyon*-wrapped head bobbed left and right.

"How *do* you do?" he asked an imaginary guest. "How *do* you do?" There was little trace of the Gumbo, or mixed language, of a former slave in his speech as he imitated a genteel Creole lady.

What might have been an unusual sight to anyone else,

seemed perfectly natural to Dani, who followed his skirted, two-hundred-fifty-pound, six-foot-four-inch frame up and down the length of the attic, bobbing and nodding when he did, holding her skirt aloft. Finally Hercules turned to watch Dani.

"I think you're ready."

"Really?" She smiled.

"Yes. What with you eatin' all your meals in the dinin' room now . . ."

"Grady insisted." She shrugged.

"Well, I'm glad he did, 'cause now you ain't so afraid of Miz Leial—"

"I wasn't ever afraid of her!" she interrupted.

"—and you know how to eat proper—"

"Too many forks and spoons."

"—and when you wear the dee-vine dress I ordered for you in Baton Rouge, why, you're gonna put enough shock into Mr. Troy that he's not gonna be able to resist you. Wouldn't no love charm work as good as what you gonna look like at that party."

"You really think so?"

"I know so."

She had sent Hercules to Baton Rouge with notes that he had written and that she had signed with the block letters Troy had taught her to use. She was thankful that she could draw upon her own resources to pay for the gown without asking Leial or Grady to help. When Hercules insisted none of the dresses Troy bought were formal enough for the occasion, Dani had left it up to the servant to design the dress and choose the materials and accessories. Hercules assured her that his eye for fashion would not fail. He wrote out the order and Dani signed it, but to the dressmaker charged with the task, it appeared as if Dani Whittaker was possessed of the most excellent taste.

"Hercules," Dani began in a most solemn voice as the two untied their overskirts and fold them away into the trunk, "how can I ever thank you enough?"

"Miz Dani, all you have to do is walk down those stairs the night of the party lookin' every inch a lady and I'll be more than thanked. I'll be as proud as a peacock!"

She gave him a hug, and he threw back his head in laughter. He was so tall that her arms encircled him just above his waist.

It was her turn to laugh when he unwound the *tiyon* and felt with open palms the damage the turban had done to his usually untamed mane.

"There is one thing you can do for me, Miz Dani."

"Anything."

"If Mr. Troy come home 'fore I get back from town, you gotta keep where I gone a secret from him so's he don't suspect what we're up to."

Her heart tripped at the thought of Troy's imminent return. She had missed him more than she realized, missed the dark eyes that bored into hers with such heat, his touch, and his kiss. But more than anything she had missed his growing friendship. It was a moment before she acknowledged Hercules's request, a moment more before she calmed her racing heart. Dani smiled secretively.

"I won't tell him where you are, Leze. I'll try to keep him occupied."

"Holy hot shit!" Dani mumbled fiercely under her breath as she stood staring into the tall armoire. Reaching inside, she grabbed the ball formed of feathers and tufts of Spanish moss and snapped the twine that suspended it from a hook on the side wall of the cabinet.

"That does it." Dani threw the gris-gris on the bed and opened the drawer that held most of her small possessions. Pawing through the pile of goods, she finally found what she needed. Nimbly she used her long knife and a length of rawhide to accomplish her task. She then stood, grabbed up the voodoo charm, and marched out the door and down the hallway.

Grady, alerted by the slam of her door, stuck his head and shoulders out of his room and called out, "Again?"

She did not pause to look back.

"Yes!"

"Need any help?"

"Nope." She kept walking.

Near the end of the long hallway, she met Leial at the top of the stairway.

"Dani, there you are, I—"

"I'll be right back, ma'am." She held up the charm in explanation. "I've got a little business to attend to."

Leial watched her go, a half-smile curving her lips. Despite Troy's warnings to the cook, the war between Dani and Venita still raged. No one knew when or how Venita managed to secrete the charms into the house, but they appeared with growing regularity. With a shake of her head, Leial went into her own room, intent on taking a short nap. All was in order for the celebration tomorrow evening: The menu and been completed, the house prepared. Tomorrow morning the boats would begin to arrive carrying the neighbors and close friends she had invited.

Yes, she thought, all was in readiness—except Dani. The girl still stubbornly refused to discuss the affair. According to Hercules, Dani had not even tried on the lovely dresses Troy had sent her. Leial hoped Troy would not allow the girl to hide in her room while the party was under way, but could he demand that she attend? Would he force her to dress properly?

Leial stretched out on her bed and closed her eyes, determined to leave the problem up to Troy. It really was his concern, after all.

"Do you see this?" Dani held the ball of moss and feathers in front of Venita's face. The cook did not lower her eyes in shame, but stared hard into Dani's own.

Dani tossed the charm into the fire that burned in the huge kitchen hearth.

"Your magic can't touch me, Venita. Know why?" Reaching inside her shirt, Dani drew forth the rawhide string tied about her neck. A bear's claw and a piece of fox tail hung from the string along with two blue feathers and a gold coin with a hole drilled through the center. She'd kept them as trade items, but now they might work to dissuade Venita.

"This is *my* magic. This necklace will protect me from anything you care to try. I think it's about time you get it through your head that I'm not going anyplace on account of your tricks." Dani squinted at the woman, emphasizing each word. "Do you understand?"

When Venita finally spoke, her voice was but a whisper, forcing Dani to pay close attention in order to catch the old woman's words.

"It is you that understands nothing. Young master leaving here soon. Much blood, much sorrow. The past is now. Too late already for you, girl. You will go because you come too late to save him. Magic you hold is not strong enough to fight the past. You'll see."

Then the old woman threw back her head and laughed with a sound so haunting, so dry and humorless that it sent chills along Dani's spine. Dani straightened and gave the cook a final meaningful stare before she turned away.

Dani welcomed the cool rush of moist air that bathed her face as she stepped outside and left the eerie scene in the kitchen behind. She longed to break into a run. Better still, Dani wished her horse was on the island. A long ride was what she needed. She would have welcomed the chance to race with the wind and forget her worries. But Troy had insisted there was no need for horses on the small island, and so hers had been stabled with the others in Baton Rouge.

Head down, Dani lengthened her stride in an effort to put distance between herself and the house. Nervousness assailed her, her emotions caught between the excitement of tonight's party and Venita's ominous words. What had the cook meant? Was Troy really leaving? For where?

The past is now. What did it all mean?

Unaware of where she was going, Dani recognized the sound of shells crunching beneath her boots. She was on the path that led toward the river. She walked another few yards and, without warning, moved headlong into a fierce embrace. Arms as strong as whipcord held her tight against a well-defined chest clothed in the finest linen. Startled, she raised her eyes and found there was no need to struggle.

The name on her lips rushed out as little more than a breathless sigh. "Troy!"

Sweeping her off her feet, he lifted her into his arms and spun around full circle. His eyes never left hers until he lowered his head. His lips took hers, demanding she return his passionate greeting.

She clung to him as a stubborn leaf clings to a tree in a storm. Lost in the sensation of being in Troy's arms once again, Dani let go of her fears and nervous apprehension. As his tongue teased the corners of her lips, as he pressed kisses upon the smooth skin of her cheeks, over her eyelids and lashes, Dani laughed with a joy she hadn't felt in weeks. He would never know how much she had missed him.

But Troy did know, for he had experienced the same longing, the same intense need during his stay in Baton Rouge. He set her on her feet but held her close for a moment before he released her. Reaching out, he captured her face between his palms. As his gaze roamed over her perfect complexion, her still slightly sun-washed skin, Troy smiled.

She threw her arms tight about his neck and demanded another kiss and then another, each becoming more heated than the last until Troy was forced to pull away.

The sound of his laughter filled her heart near to bursting.

"I see you haven't lost your hankerin' for kissing," he teased as he brushed her lips again with his own.

"Nope. Did you think I would? Is that why you stayed away so long?" She kissed him again.

"No. I stayed away because I knew that with every passing day, you'd be more desperate for me when I returned."

She feigned a look of anger but did not release her hold. "Conceited varmint, aren't you?"

"Not at all."

"Well?"

"Well what?" he asked.

"Well, are we going to get to do it now that I'm all hot and bothered?"

Troy hesitated for a moment before his reserve gave way to acquiescence. As he held her, warm and willing in his arms, he knew that he had to have her. He wanted to give her as much of himself as he could before he went after Constantine Reynolds. He wanted to make magic of the short time left to them before he slipped away like a thief in the night after the New Year's celebration. He could only hope that he would return to find Dani waiting for him, but as yet he had not found the courage to ask so much of her.

"What about it, Fontaine?" She stared up at him, her eyes filled with longing.

"Are you down to begging?" He gave her a mock frown.

"No, I'm offering, is all."

"In that case, I know of a secret spot far enough away from the house where you can greet me properly—if that's what you had in mind."

Chapter Twenty

Scooping her up in his arms, Troy moved off the path and into the shelter of the trees along the waterway. Beneath the wide moss-draped branches of a sheltering oak, he set Dani on her feet and grasped her face between his palms. With little effort, he drew her to him and covered her lips with his, disappointed when Dani placed her hands on his shirtfront and pushed away from him.

When she began hastily to draw off her clothing, he laughed aloud and followed her example, pulling off his boots, shucking his trousers, shirt, and jacket.

"Leze won't like the way you're treating your clothes." She laughed, her gaze falling upon the discarded pile of forgotten clothing as she stepped into his arms again.

"What's this?" he paused and lifted the only item she wore, the rawhide thong with its assortment of fur, gold, and beads.

"My own voodoo charm."

"Is Venita still bothering you?"

Her eyes clouded as she remembered the words she had tried to block from her mind: *Much blood, much sorrow.* Dani was determined not to let a crazy old woman ruin Troy's homecoming—but she would be wary of Venita's words just the same.

"Nothing I can't handle." Dani lifted the charm over her head and dangled it before his eyes. "Maybe this is why you can't resist me anymore."

His own smile was secretive. "Maybe."

The charm fell forgotten to the ground as his lips traced her collarbone in toward the hollow of her throat before his tongue trailed a warm wet path to the valley between her breasts. They sank to their knees and then stretched out on the soft moss growing at the base of the trees.

Lifting them gently, he cupped her breasts in the palms of his hands and kissed their hard-budded tips one at a time, taking pleasure in the soft moans that issued from her throat. She anchored her fingers in his hair, raked her nails along his shoulders, and when she could stand the exquisite torture no longer, cupped his face in her hands and urged him to kiss her full upon the lips.

When he slid upward along the length of her, Dani felt his throbbing shaft seeking entrance to her warm recesses. Wanting him, urgently needing to feel his long hard length buried inside her, Dani opened her legs to his prodding demand. There would be time for gentle caresses later.

Dani gave herself up to sensation as Troy lost himself in her. As she lay beneath him, feeling every thrust, every teasing movement he made as he drew away and then sheathed himself deeper within her velvet core, Dani stared up into the branches of the oak and let the pleasure wash over her. Layers of gray-green moss hung down toward them, even from the highest branches, and trailed to the ground, creating an umbrella of featherlike growth that shielded them from the world. It wrapped them in a protective cocoon that even the gentle mist that had begun to fall could not penetrate.

Her skin was cooled by the mist-soaked air and the damp moss beneath her, but her blood raged with a fever that was stoked higher with Troy's every move. When he lay still and then began to suckle and tease her breasts, she lifted her head to gaze down at his glistening blue-black hair. Gently she combed her hands through it, let the tips of her fingers trace the outline of his ear and trail down his neck.

"Dani . . ." he whispered.

"I love you, Troy Fontaine."

He buried himself within her again, locked his arms about her waist, and rolled to his back. Dani found herself sitting atop him, marveling at the fact that he was still inside her. She pressed down against him, taking him deeper within her than he'd ever dared to go before. She leaned forward, bracing her palms on his shoulders, and moved up along his rigid length, teasing him as he'd so often toyed with her. As she nearly reached the tip of his shaft, she plunged down on him again and heard him catch his breath. His hands grasped her hips, his fingers dug into her skin, and he held her there, immobilized atop him.

Dani arched forward and teased his lips with her breasts. He gave her what she demanded, capturing one and then the other with his mouth. As he drew upon her breasts, heat rippled through her, coursed along her spine, and nestled in the tight bud throbbing between her legs. She moved against him then, fighting for release, fighting against his hands that tried to hold her still lest she bring him too quickly to his climax.

She rode him long and hard until they both cried out with the ultimate release of their joining. Muscles aquiver, Dani found her arms could no longer support her, and she slowly lowered herself to his chest. Troy enfolded her lovingly in his arms and then rolled her onto her back. He was in no hurry to pull away from her, not yet. There was time before they would be missed, plenty of time before the first guests would arrive. For now, Troy was content to hold Dani, as she lay warm and flushed from their lovemaking.

They lay for a time in each other's arms, naked and as free as the wild inhabitants of the bayou. Dani snuggled against Troy, afraid to break the spell that bound them together. She wished the moment might last forever, but all too soon Troy broke the silence.

"I have something to tell you."

Dani lay still against his side, wondering why his tone was so grave. "I'm listening," she said.

"I have to go away."

"Away?" she whispered. "Where?"

"It's a long story, and much of it you don't need to know, but years ago my father was murdered by a man named Constantine Reynolds. The man abducted my mother—"

"What's 'abducted'?"

"Stole."

"He stole your mother?"

"Yes. She was never found, nor was Reynolds, until recently. He's been located, and I intend to go after him."

" 'Course you will." She did not tell him that Grady had already imparted most of the details to her.

Troy was surprised by her response to his announcement.

"You're the only one who's ever agreed that I should go after Reynolds."

"He did it, didn't he?"

"Every piece of evidence we have points to it. He was engaged to my mother before she jilted him to marry my father. He was the last one seen with my parents the night they disappeared, and he left New Orleans after my father's body was found."

Although she already knew the answer, Dani asked Troy about his father's death. "How'd he die?"

"Someone—Reynolds, I'm sure—hanged him from the rafters of the old barn behind the house." He was silent again, marshaling his strength to say the words. "I found him hanging there."

Dani felt a shudder move through him. She held him tighter.

"I couldn't scream, couldn't cry out, for fear Grandmother would see him that way. So I used all the strength I could muster to lower the body to the ground, slip off the noose, and cover him with a horse blanket. Then I went for help. My father was dead. I never saw my mother again."

Suddenly Dani realized how very much he'd had to bear. She tried to imagine Troy as a young boy, tried to realize all he had suffered. It was easy to understand his dark moods, his inability to open himself to others, his quickness to anger. She would have given anything to help ease the burden of dark memories he carried. If only she knew how.

"Let me go with you."

"Absolutely not."

"Why not?" Dani pressed. "One thing I know is tracking and trapping. Don't you see, Troy? This is the reason you found me. This is why I'm here!" Suddenly she became excited at the prospect of being able to help him. "I can't read or write or do any of the things other ladies do, but I *can* help you with this, if you'll take me with you!"

"No."

"No? That's it? No? That must be your favorite word, Fontaine, 'cause you been sayin' it since we first met." She sat up and reached for her clothes. With jerking, angry motions, she pulled on her shirt and thrust one leg into her buckskin pants. She mimicked his solemn tone. " 'No, we can't make love, Dani. No, you can't wear those clothes, Dani. No, you can't go off on your own.' Now it's 'No, I can't take you with me!' No. No. No." She thrust her other leg into the breeches and yanked them up to her waist.

Damn, now I'm cryin'. She brushed angrily at the tears sliding down her cheeks. "What am I supposed to do while you go off after this Reynolds? How long will it take? Where are you going?"

Troy sat up and began to dress, pulling on his clothes as he spoke. "I know it's a lot for me to ask, but I'd like you to wait for me."

"Wait? Wait here?"

"If you will."

"Sit here with your grandmother? She doesn't think I deserve you! You want me to wait here, wearin' the wrong thing? Sayin' the wrong thing?" She had a full head of steam up when suddenly she remembered Venita's words. Stricken with fear, she knelt beside Troy. "What if you don't come back, Fontaine?"

He did not meet her gaze. "Then Grady will be here for you."

"Grady?" She was on her feet again in an instant. "Grady! You think I can just change men like I change horses? Holy hot shit!"

"There's no need to get upset. If you'll just calm down a minute—"

"You can forget me calmin' down. And you can forget me comin' to that stupid party." So much for the butterfly bursting from the cocoon, she thought.

"Hold it right there," he commanded.

When she ignored him and began to storm away, Troy grabbed her arm. He spun her about to face him. "You haven't been all that accommodating either, pet. The prerogative to say no isn't exclusively mine."

"Speak English."

"The word 'no' is your middle name!" he said. "You're the most bull-headed human being I've ever met. The only things you believe in are the immortal words of Big Jake Fisher. That and doing whatever you damn well please." He leaned forward and stared her down, nose to nose. "Lock yourself in your room for the rest of your life—I don't care. Just don't make a scene and ruin Grandmother's party. And for God's sake, forget about going after Reynolds with me. You make me sorry I told you any of this!"

Dani clenched her fists and fought down the urge to hit him. She bent and collected her boots, then turned on her heel and stalked away.

"Is the door locked?"

Hercules sighed in exasperation and gave the long, whalebone corset that encased Dani's already slim figure from midriff to below the waist another hard tug. "You jes' axed me that not five minutes ago. *The door is locked.*"

She stared at her reflection in the mirror, took a deep breath, felt the constriction of the corset, and watched tears well up in her eyes. "I can't do it."

"You can . . . and you is."

"No. Not in this thing. I'm nervous enough without you squeezing the life out of me. Take it off."

"Miz Dani . . ."

"Take it off, Leze, or I'm not going downstairs."

"You already late. Mr. Troy thinks you not goin' down at all."

"Good. That's part of the plan."

"He didn't look none too happy last time I seen him," Hercules warned.

He hadn't looked very happy the last time she saw him either. Dani sighed in relief as the corset fell away. "He'll get over it."

Despite her nervousness, she knew she had never looked more presentable. The reflection in the mirror showed her skin glowing soft and radiant, thanks to Hercules's secret concoction of melted beeswax, oil, and the few drops of rosewater he had stolen from Leial's room. He had mixed the ingredients with rich, dark mud from the swamp and then smeared the paste on her skin. She'd devoted two afternoons to the treatment after her mentor insisted it was the only thing that could be done to soften her skin and restore the natural color.

She had stayed hidden in her room for the last two days, alternately fuming and then cursing her own temper. That afternoon Troy had pounded on her door, offering her one last chance to pull herself together and attend the party. She let him know there was no way in hell she would appear downstairs that night. She had meant to keep her word—until Hercules appeared. He seemed so disappointed by her refusal to wear the beautiful gown that she finally relented. Why should all their hard work and planning go to waste?

Earlier Dani had bathed in the herb-scented bath the servant had prepared for her. The heady aroma of lavender and mint mixed with soothing chamomile helped to calm her racing heart. Now it was nearly time to face Troy. She wondered how he would react to her metamorphosis.

"Let's see if we can get this dress on over your head without messin' up your hair."

Hercules's words drew her out of her reverie. Her hair was still far too short to be swept back in a chignon or curled up on the crown of her head, so he had drawn up the thick tresses from the sides of her face and anchored them near her crown. A long royal blue ribbon, which Hercules claimed was the exact shade of Troy's satin vest, bound the locks of drawn-up hair and fluttered down her back.

He lifted the exquisite ivory crepe gown, with its satin underskirt, and helped her ease the folds of the dress over her head. As the material slithered past her shoulders, Hercules pulled it all the way down and then shook out the folds of the skirt, straightening and smoothing the crepe so as to show off the embroidery worked in colored silks around the hem. Carefully stitched flowers and forest-green vines entwined themselves around the entire skirt. A silken bouquet was embroidered near the deep, pointed waist, the threads trailing down to meet the curling vines that wound themselves around the hem. Wide beret sleeves belled out only to be gathered again just above her elbows, which were hidden by a froth of lace.

Dani glanced down at the shadow of cleavage between her breasts. The low neckline barely covered her, but a thin gauze edged with pale lace created a frothy veil of modesty. She thought of Glory Hallelujah and smiled. The perfectly fitted royal blue satin shoes were barely visible beneath the hem of the wide skirt.

Hercules nodded in satisfaction, for once awed into silence.

"Do I look all right?"

"Perfect. Except for the gloves." He handed her the ivory elbow-length gloves that Troy had had made for her.

"Why did I have to sit with my hands in bran water and dab them twice a day with all that cream you gave me if I was only going to cover them up?" Dani demanded to know.

"Because"—he leaned down until they were nose to nose—"I never seen anyone eat with their gloves on!"

Dani turned away and watched herself in the mirror once more. She spun around and faced Hercules again, her gloved hands clenched at her waist. "I can't do it," she whispered.

Hercules walked around behind her, placed an open palm on the small of her back, and gave her a none-too-gentle shove toward the door.

"I didn't go through all this sneakin' and hidin' for nothin'," he said. "You get your self on down those stairs before you have time to think about it anymore."

She walked as far as the door, then turned and looked up at him again.

"Hercules, I don't know how to say thank—"

He cut her off in midsentence. With a smile as wide as the Mississippi and a glow in his eyes as bright as the warmest campfire, he said, "Miz Dani, you don't never have to thank me for this. I ain't never had so much fun in all my life."

The drawing room doors were thrown open but even the chilled air of New Year's Eve was not enough to cool the heated interior of the room. Neighbors chatted happily together, plantation owners who saw little of one another save on such occasions now exchanged news of family and friends. Lively music was provided by a small orchestra made up of fiddle, pianoforte, and flute. Couples formed and reformed as the changing tunes dictated.

Troy Fontaine stood in the open doorway, half leaning against the frame as he watched the dancers whirl by. He raised his glass to his lips and downed the fine, smooth brandy without tasting it. After three generous helpings he no longer savored the taste. He was now drinking solely to ease his pain.

Out of the corner of his eye, Troy saw Grady approaching, but chose to ignore his friend. All too soon Grady was standing beside him, a worried frown marring his handsome features.

"Don't you think you're overdoing it a little?" Grady nodded toward Troy's glass.

"I wasn't aware that I needed a keeper."

Undaunted by his friend's cold words, Grady continued to press him. "Why are you drinking so much? What's happened?"

"Give me your drink." Troy exchanged his empty glass for

his friend's full one and winced when he tasted Grady's champagne. "Why?" Troy repeated Grady's question. "Leverette's man finally located Constantine Reynolds. He's on a small, rather unimportant island in the Caribbean. It seems he's a wealthy planter and an accepted member of society."

Troy stared without seeing at the blur of moving figures that passed before them. He finished the champagne.

"I suppose this means you're going down there?" There was undisguised alarm in Grady's tone.

Troy refused to answer.

"Do you plan to walk in and ask him if he murdered Merle Fontaine and abducted Jeanette?"

"I won't have to ask. I'll know."

"And what do you intend to do then? Murder him outright?"

"If I have to defend myself. If not, I plan to ask him what happened to my mother. Then I intend to bring him back here to stand trial."

"But you hope it won't go that far, don't you, Troy? You hope he goes for your throat so that you can murder him the way he did your father."

"No. Not that way, Grady. I plan on taking my time."

Grady placed his hand on Troy's sleeve. Fontaine shook it off. Lowering his already hushed voice to a barely audible whisper, Grady said, "And what of Dani?"

A bleak hopelessness washed over Troy, a despair he could not hide. "I'll have to leave her behind. I told her I would be going away, but not when or where I'm going. You know Dani, she—"

"Wanted to go with you," Grady finished for him.

"I asked her to stay here. To wait for me."

"That easy, is it?" Grady's tone was bitter.

Troy spun away and stepped outside onto the first-floor gallery. Grady followed. "No! Dammit, it's not easy. You have no idea how hard this is for me, Grady."

"Then why do it?"

"Because I *have* to. I have to do it for them—for my parents. I have to find out what happened to my mother. If she's alive, I want to know where she is."

"You're willing to let this ruin your life with Dani?"

"Yes. I am. For the simple reason that my life with Dani would be ruined anyway if I gave up, if I let go of the need I have to set this thing to rights and put it behind me, or die trying." Troy turned to Grady, hoping to make his friend understand. "Don't you see? I can't turn away from this now." He ran a hand through his hair and turned to look out into the mist-shrouded bayou. "I'll never be free until this is settled and behind me. As for Dani"—Troy sighed and turned pleading eyes on Grady— "I know you care enough to see to her welfare. If she refuses to wait for me, take her east the first chance you get. In time, she'll forget me."

"And if she won't go?"

"She will. She'll have no other choice, except to go back to the mountains, and if she insists, let her go."

"I can't believe you mean this."

"It's pretty obvious that she'll never fit in here, isn't it?" He would grasp at anything that might help him sever the ties that bound Dani to his heart. "We had one hell of an argument. She's locked in her room right now, refuses to open her door. Besides being so mad at me she can't see straight, she's obviously terrified of this crowd."

Grady looked over Troy's shoulder into the well-lit room. For a moment he did not speak. A slow smile curved his lips. He raised one eyebrow and turned his gaze back to Troy.

"I think you've been duped, old friend."

Troy's tone was still harsh. "What are you talking about?"

"The shrinking violet you think is hidden away in her room is just now standing in the doorway waiting to be noticed."

As Troy turned to follow Grady's admiring gaze, he heard Hercules announce to the occupants of the drawing room, "Miz Dani Whittaker."

A hushed murmur hummed through the room as all eyes turned toward the figure in the doorway. She stood alone, her silver-gray eyes glowing with triumph as she surveyed the room. Her hair hung shining to her shoulders, wisps of it tied back away from her temples by a rich blue ribbon. The gown she wore was of the finest ivory crepe, embroidered with a floral design and cut in the highest fashion of the day. Her complexion was the perfect complement to the ivory dress. Daintily, she held the front of her skirt away from the toes of her shoes with one hand. Dani looked every inch the lady from head to toe.

Troy did not move, could not move, as heat and longing flooded him. Heartsick, knowing that all he'd said to Grady was still true and that his mind was made up. He would leave on the morrow, perhaps never to return. Dani was no longer his.

He watched as his grandmother moved to take Dani's hand in welcome. Leial glowed with a triumph greater than Dani's own, pulled the girl's hand into the crook of her elbow, and led Dani into the room, where she introduced her to the assembled crowd.

Troy took a step forward, intending to go to Dani, to stand beside her and share his final hours with her. He felt Grady's hand on his sleeve as his friend reached out to stop him.

"This is her night, Troy." Grady warned, "Don't do anything to spoil it for her."

Handing his empty glass to the artist, Troy turned back toward the drawing room.

Moving as if in a dream, Dani floated through the steps of the waltz, letting the music guide her, as her mentor had suggested. Troy whirled her effortlessly through the crowd, making it easy for her to act the part of a lady. Her initial nervousness had fled soon after Leial took her in tow. Though she had been surprised by Leial's warmth, Dani had not questioned it, thinking the change in Leial's attitude stemmed from her startling appearance. Pleased by Leial's reaction, Dani had let the older woman lead her about the room. She found herself watching the other women present and once she let her natural ability to mimic their actions take over, she easily copied the manners and movements of the ladies present. Even when Erantha had approached her earlier, Dani held her ground easily, turning aside the girl's reference to her transformation with nothing more than a polite thank-you.

Troy remained at her side throughout the evening. Dani let herself relax, and for the first time at Isle de Fontaine, she even enjoyed a meal. Now, as the waltz ended and Troy released her, she paused to smile up into his eyes. For a moment she was arrested by the intense stare he gave her, but then he seemed to shake off his thoughts and smile at her easily once again.

Troy reached down and traced her full lower lip with his thumb. Her skin was as soft as the satin underskirt she wore, as tempting as ripe, lush fruit. He felt a stabbing pain in the region of his heart as he gazed down at her.

"You learn quickly, Dani," he murmured, after listening to

her as she copied the responses of the women she'd watched so intently during the meal. "You'll do fine." The last words were whispered softly so that she might not hear them.

"Would it be *proper* for us to walk outdoors for a moment?" she wanted to know.

"No. But did that ever stop us before?" he asked.

With a hand on her perfectly fitted waistband, Troy gently guided Dani through the crowd toward the gallery doors. He paused long enough to retrieve two glasses filled with champagne from a side table near the open doors. They stepped outside and found themselves alone for the moment. Dani moved close to the rail and looked out into the night. The mist was clearing, and for the first time that she could remember since she arrived on the island, myriad stars were visible in the midnight sky. She took a deep breath and recognized the familiar scent of the dampness all around.

She sensed Troy standing behind her and turned to lean against the railing. He extended a glass of champagne and she reached out for it. Tentatively she took a sip and enjoyed the sparkling drink so much so that she took another.

"There is a saying about this place, Dani." He stared out into the night. " 'Once you visit here, you never truly leave.' "

"I can see why they say that," she agreed. "There is something mysterious about this place, about the bayou and the moss-draped trees. They remind me of old women in tattered clothes." Dani turned to stare out into the night with him. "This is the first night I can remember seeing stars here. You know what I think?"

He finished his champagne and looked down at her. "No, what do you think?"

"I think the stars are a sign. This is going to be a good year, Troy. For you, for me, for everyone."

When he turned away, silent, Dani felt a small shiver run down her spine. She hoped voicing the words aloud would dispel Venita's ominous prophecy. Should she warn him? Dani looped her arm through Troy's and drew him closer to her. No. Not tonight. Tonight they would be happy and enjoy the friends who had come to share the celebration. There would be time enough tomorrow to tell him of the old woman's dire prediction.

"Troy?" A voice from the darkness disturbed their quiet moment alone.

Troy turned. "Devereaux, what can I do for you?"

"We'll be leaving soon. Before I go, I'd like to give you the details you asked for. I know this is probably not a convenient time—"

"No time would ever really be convenient, so I'll see you now. In the library."

They watched Devereaux turn and disappear into the crowd.

"Wait here, Dani, and I'll send Grady out to you. I'm sure he won't mind dancing with the most beautiful woman here."

A cold breeze blew in off the water and curled about her shoulders. Dani shivered with the effect of it, and with the coldness she heard in Troy's tone. It reminded her of the way he had treated her on the trail. Reserved, cool, yet always polite. Would she ever understand him?

"I'll wait here." She caught his hand as he started to move away without so much as a good-bye. "If you will grant me a wish."

He held himself away from her, sure of what her request would be, unsure of how he could bring himself to deal with it.

His voice nearly broke on his next words. "Your wish?"

She whispered, "A kiss."

He stared at her long and hard, sealing the sight of her upon his troubled mind. She looked innocent and serene, the way he always imagined her. Bathed in starlight, Dani had never looked lovelier to him, and yet in that moment he knew that he would have thought her beautiful even if she'd been dressed in her worn buckskins, tanned, and covered with grime as she was when he first saw her. He knew, too, that this little huntress had succeeded in capturing his heart. She would hold it forever. That was a fact that would never change, no matter what the outcome of his journey.

"Troy?" His silent perusal frightened her.

He reached out to grasp her bare shoulders and hold her tight, drawing her up against him until her lips were near enough that he could press his own to them. The kiss shook Dani to her soul with its force. Troy stepped back with her, pressing her against the railing until she felt the wood cut into her hips. Forced to cling to him, she returned his kiss deeply, hoping to give him what he sought. Abruptly, Troy released her. After a searing look, one that she could not fathom the meaning of, he turned away and left her standing alone in the cool night air.

* * *

"My feet are killing me," Dani complained in a whisper just loud enough for her partner to hear.

Grady immediately halted and sheepishly smiled down at her. "No doubt from my trodding upon your toes." He nodded toward the door. "Some fresh air?"

"Only if I can sit down, too," Dani added. "You're really not that bad a dancer, Grady." She tried to hide the pained expression on her face with a smile as he led her out onto the veranda.

He shook his head. "No need to lie. I know how clumsy I am. In fact, I think I'm a better rider than a dancer."

Dani laughed aloud at his declaration. "You're a worse rider than a farmer on a greased pig, Grady Maddox."

The gallery was no longer deserted, as it had been an hour earlier when she'd stood at the railing in Troy's arms. A couple strolled arm in arm along the long porch while a small group of planters gathered in one corner to enjoy their brandy and cigars while they talked of horses and the price of sugarcane.

Grady stood beside her until she was comfortably seated in one of the tall ladder-backed rockers. He then claimed the one beside her and matched the slow, easy tempo of her rocking to his own. They sat in amiable silence, staring out at the grounds. Alone with Grady, Dani was able to enjoy the scene before them in a way she had not done earlier in Troy's presence. Torches burned brightly, outlining the shell path that led to the bayou and glittering through the trees beyond the bend in the road. Dani knew the dock was crowded with every kind of water conveyance. As they watched, a trio of guests departed, followed by the slaves who had accompanied them. They moved slowly along the shadowed lane, their laughter and cries of "Happy New Year" ringing on the air as they disappeared from sight.

Another servant who had accompanied his master to the event appeared on the gallery carrying a silver tray laden with champagne glasses. Dani took one, grateful for something to slake her thirst. She downed the effervescent wine, then replaced her empty glass and picked up another. It was half gone before Grady, who sat staring in amazement, warned, "It's not water, you know."

Dani finished her second glassful. "I know, but I've got a

powerful thirst, as Jake would say." She then giggled and rolled her eyes in a flirtatious and quite uncharacteristic manner. "Well . . ." Dani watched Grady smugly as she reached for a third glass of champagne. "What do you think of my surprise tonight?"

He waved the servant on quickly and placed a restraining hand on Dani's.

"Wait a bit before you drink that."

"These little glasses don't hold much more than an acornful," she reminded him.

"For a reason." He touched the rim of his glass to hers as he toasted Dani. "You already know I think you are beautiful enough to be taken for a princess tonight."

"Do you really, Grady? I look all right?"

"Yes."

She couldn't see the expression in his eyes in the amber light that filtered through the window behind them, but she could sense his honest admiration.

"Do you think"—her voice dropped to a whisper—"I look enough like a lady that a certain gentleman we know might . . . well, might ask me to marry him?"

As the silence lengthened, Dani's heart sank to her toes. When would she ever learn to keep her mouth from running ahead of her brains? she wondered miserably. She took another swallow of champagne.

"I can't speak for Troy," Grady said after he cleared his throat, "but if I were in his place, I wouldn't hesitate a second to ask you to marry me."

"But you aren't Troy."

"No. More's the pity."

The comfortable silence was broken only by the tap-tapping of the rockers against the hardwood veranda. Dani set her glass on the floor, settled back in her chair, and traced the flowers on her skirt with a gloved fingertip.

"Grady, I never thanked you for being such a good friend to me, but I hope you know how much I appreciate being able to talk to you about . . . things." She leaned her head against the high back of the chair and stared out at the night.

Grady was on his feet in an instant, his square hands clenching and unclenching nervously at his sides.

"What's wrong, Grady?" She stopped rocking for a moment as she stared up at him.

"Nothing." He cleared his throat. "Nothing. I just think I'll go see what's keeping Troy. Will you be all right out here alone?"

"You and Troy act as if puttin' on a dress has loosened my mind. What makes you think I can't take care of myself?"

"It's not you I worry about, Dani; it's the guests I'm afraid to leave unprotected."

She laughed at his teasing remark. "You go on and drag Troy away from that Leverette Devereaux. They're locked up in the library."

"I'll try." With a slight bow, he walked away. She leaned on the arm of the chair and watched him over her shoulder as his tall form dressed in perfectly tailored navy moved through the crowd.

"Miss Whittaker?" A voice near the arm of the rocker drew her attention.

Dani turned to find a red-haired young man standing none too steadily beside her chair. She'd met him earlier but his name eluded her.

"You'll have to forgive me." Her accent was as smooth as Leial's as she repeated the phrase she'd heard the older woman deliver earlier. "I can't recall your name, sir."

"Jerome Chance, Miss Whittaker." He bowed over her hand. "Now that you know my name, might I ask you to stand up with me in the next dance?"

It had been easy to dance with Troy, and even with Grady, once she'd made up her mind to it. She knew them well. Perhaps, she decided, she should try to dance with another man, just for the experience. Besides, Dani thought, it might do Troy Fontaine some good to find her on someone else's arm when he finally decided to come looking.

She easily fell into the slow drawl so many of the Louisianans used. "Why, Mr. Chance, I'd be delighted."

As they walked together into the drawing room, which was still nearly full of dancing couples, she noted her partner was walking none too steadily, as if he'd had one drink too many. Dani wondered if she'd be forced to lead him through the steps of the dance.

When the musicians began to play a light, lilting waltz, she instantly regretted her decision to accept. It was one thing to be held in Troy's arms while she danced, but she found it quite another to be in such intimate contact with a stranger. Especially one who reeked of corn liquor.

Jerome Chance was not much taller than she, nor much older, for that matter. Carrot-red hair and a face spattered liberally with freckles added to his youthful appearance. Jerome's smile nearly split his face in two and revealed widely spaced white teeth.

"I can't believe I've the priv . . . privilege to dance with such a beauty." He slurred the words into her ear.

"I can't either." Dani tried to put a more comfortable distance between them, only to have him stumble into her. She felt his chest, devoid of muscular definition, press against her breast. "Watch your step there, Jerome, or I just might have to watch it for you," she warned.

Together they fought their way around the floor, Jerome leaning more and more heavily on Dani as his steps began to falter. She was looking down at the floor, taking care not to let one of her silk-slippered feet fall beneath his hard, polished boots, when she felt his hot breath against her neck. She put her hands on his shoulders and tried to push him away.

"Back away from me, Chance."

"You want me to kiss you, don't you?"

"What?" She was incredulous at the suggestion. Was he kidding?

"Kiss you." He steadied himself and took aim at her lips. Dani ducked her head and he missed, nearly throwing himself off balance completely. A quick glance told her that their clumsy attempt to dance had not gone unnoticed. The couples dancing nearest them had moved a polite distance away.

"Mr. Chance, I no longer desire to dance with you."

"What'da say?" he mumbled, still holding on to her with a death grip as he tried to slide his feet in time to the music.

She tried again, louder this time. "I said, Mr. Chance, I no longer desire to dance with you."

"Huh?" He was squeezing her tight against him now, pressing her against his hips in an insinuating manner that Dani, even in her innocence, recognized.

"I said let . . . me . . . go!" She tried to push out of his arms but found him a deadweight that was somehow still able to stand.

When one of his hands loosened, she sighed with relief, intent upon stepping away from him. When that same hand somehow snaked between them, groped for her breast, and then squeezed it painfully, Dani brought her right hand back with all the force she could muster and landed her fist dead center on the bridge of his nose. Jerome Chance went down in the middle of the dance floor with all the grace of a fallen oak. Before she could think, Dani followed her natural fighting instinct and straddled him, her beautiful clothing forgotten, her ladylike demeanor gone. She grasped his fine white cravat and pulled his face up, then delivered him another crushing blow.

"When I said I didn't want to dance anymore, I meant it, Mr. Jerome Chance," she said to the battered, unconscious man who lay beneath her.

Her words seem to echo in the silence that surrounded them. Dani looked up, suddenly aware of the awkward position she was in, sitting astride a total stranger in the midst of Leial Fontaine's guests.

The dancers who were too shocked to move away still stood staring down at her, while others tried to escape the scene by moving toward the gallery, the hallway, or the dining room where coffee and desserts had been set out.

No one offered her assistance.

Frozen, still in shock at the instinctive act of self-preservation that had taken control of her, Dani remained astride Jerome Chance, her bloodied right glove still clenched in a fist.

She closed her eyes.

"Dani . . ."

Someone was standing to her right. Someone whose voice she would have recognized anywhere. Slowly she turned her head toward the sound of that voice and then opened her eyes.

Troy stood beside her, arm extended, palm open, offering her a hand up.

Her voice laced with humiliation, Dani whispered, "What took you so long?"

Chapter Twenty-one

They moved swiftly through the small, silent crowd. Dani met no one's eye, yet she did not falter, nor did she drop her gaze. Head held high, she moved toward the hallway, Troy's hand riding gently at her waist. He paused long enough to speak quietly to Hercules, who stood near the doorway. Hercules went immediately to remove the still unconscious form of Jerome Chance from the drawing room.

Dani mounted the stairs. She was thankful for Troy's silence, grateful that he did not expect her to remain downstairs. If she was surprised when he followed her, she was even more astounded when he opened the door to her room and waited while she stepped inside. Certain he was both ashamed and embarrassed by her show of violence, Dani was stunned when, once inside her room, Troy enfolded her in his arms. She pressed her face against his crisp linen shirtfront.

"I'm so ashamed." The words were muffled against his chest.

He tucked his finger beneath her chin and forced her to meet his gaze. "Don't be." He lightly brushed her lips with his own.

She watched his eyes darken as he looked into hers.

"You aren't mad?" she asked.

"Not at all. I'm proud of you." He was still for a moment, his eyes searching her face, memorizing it. "And I'm glad to know you can still take care of yourself."

"But, Troy—"

"You have nothing to be sorry about. Jerome would probably have passed out of his own accord within the hour; he was well into his cups." Troy reached out and brushed aside a lock of Dani's hair which had fallen free of the ribbon Hercules had used to tie it back.

How can I leave her?

He pulled her close again, holding her tight against him, wishing for all the world that he could enfold her until she was somehow a part of him, a part he would never have to leave behind. Troy knew that he would carry the memory of her forever, but it would never compare to holding her close.

A soft tap against the door gave them little warning. Troy released Dani as Leial entered.

The woman looked Dani over with an appraising eye. "Are you all right, Dani?"

"Yes, ma'am." Dani straightened and stepped away from Troy. "Apologies don't come easy, ma'am, but I have to tell you I'm sorry I ruined your party."

"Ruined?" A smile eased the sternness of Leial's expression, nearly transfiguring it.

Why, she's beautiful, Dani thought as she slowly returned Leial's smile.

"The party is far from ruined, my dear," Leial said. "As a matter of fact, things were a bit dull until you livened them up. I was concerned for you, though. That young scoundrel didn't harm you, did he?"

"No, ma'am."

"Fine. That's fine." For the first time Leial looked to her grandson.

"Troy, some of our guests are departing. Will you come with me and bid them good night?" Leial did not have to tell him that Dani's reputation would suffer from his remaining so long in her room.

"I'll be right down, Grandmother."

As the door closed behind Leial, Troy reached out for Dani and took her once again into his embrace. She raised her face to his and he tasted the sweetness of her kiss.

"Will you come back to say good night?" Dani asked as she felt the familiar warmth spread through her.

"Yes."

Yes. He would come back, if only to hold her one last time.

He kissed her quickly, a feather-light kiss of familiarity and promise, squeezed her hand, and then left her to undress and wait for him to return.

By reaching over her shoulders and stretching her arms and fingers until she touched the top button on the back of her dress, Dani was able to free herself of the gown. She let it fall into an ivory puddle on the floor and stepped out of it. She blew out the lamp on the nightstand and, cloaked in darkness, dressed only in her chemise and pantalets, opened the gallery doors wide, letting in the brisk night air.

Her head had begun to pound, and as the moments passed, the pain built into a mind splitting headache. Champagne. It affected her much the same way red wine had done on the night of her arrival. She remembered Grady's words: "It's not water."

"You were right, Grady," she whispered to herself in the darkness.

She walked to the bed, shucked off her pantalets, and drew her lace-edged silk chemise over her head. The blue ribbon that swept her hair back off her face came undone easily. She tossed it on the table. She would wait for Troy in bed. Dani pulled back the sheets and checked to be certain there was no surprise waiting her, compliments of Venita. The bed was empty. She slipped between the cool, crisp sheets and let her weary feet relax. She smiled up at the ceiling. Grady *was* an awful dancer. She was certain that her toes would be bruised on the morrow.

Snuggling deeper into the bed, Dani was careful to leave ample room for Troy before she closed her eyes against the throbbing pain at her temples.

Thick fog crept over the bayou, stealing along the moss-lined banks, curling around the cypress trunks, coating the swamp in an eerie cloak of mist. From the upper gallery, Troy could see the ground fog that shrouded his world and could feel its icy dampness winding about his heart, chilling his very soul. A floorboard creaked as he stepped across the threshold into Dani's room. He moved silently, barely daring to breathe, for he knew she was asleep. He was aware that Dani usually slept with the wariness of one used to living in the wilds. The slightest noise might wake her.

The ivory gown lay crumpled where she'd stepped out of it. He crossed the room with the lithe, silent movements of a hunter and lifted the gown off the floor. After tossing it across a chair, he turned back toward Dani's bed.

He reached her bedside and realized she was sleeping much

too soundly to be wakened by a slight noise. She appeared no more than a child, her usually shining hair a dark stain spread across her pillow. Her hands were curled about the edge of the sheet she held modestly across her bare breasts as if the thin material provided protection from the night. He could just see the blue ribbon she'd worn in her hair resting on the table beside the bed. Troy picked it up and raised it to his lips before he slipped it into his pocket. Leaning his right forearm on the bedpost near her head, he gazed down at her in silence, etching her features on his memory.

It was better that she slept. There would be no need now to try to lighten his mood. Troy reached out with his free hand, no longer able to keep from touching her, and ran his fingertip along her cheek, down the length of her jaw, then across her lips.

An unfamiliar sensation overwhelmed him. It centered itself in his gut before it rose to well up behind his eyes. Forced to blink away tears that threatened, Troy pushed away from the bedpost and balled his hands into fists at his side. He had never cried—not even as a child when he had found his father's body hanging in the old barn. He refused to cry now. Troy Fontaine turned on his heel and walked out the gallery door into the fog-shrouded night.

The winter sun was high and bright, strong enough to burn off the fog and bathe the day with color. Dani woke up slowly, stretched, and then left her bed. Troy had not come to her, but she found herself feeling grateful to him as she recalled the headache she'd suffered last night. She noted the closed door and her dress draped across the chair. He'd come to her, after all, but he had let her sleep.

Glancing out the window, she realized how long she'd overslept. It was nearly midday, if she guessed correctly. The household would soon gather for the noon meal. Suddenly she was starving.

The armoire was filled with the new gowns Troy had sent her from Baton Rouge. Today she would wear one, not only to please him but to please herself as well. Realization dawned upon her that she had liked the way it felt last night to dress like a lady. She sensed that Troy would not mind her wearing her buckskins whenever she wanted. As she hastily drew on her underclothes and then the silk stockings and shoes, Dani decided on the peach day dress trimmed with velvet ribbons of the same shade. She slipped it on and fought to fasten the buttons herself. Successful at last, Dani left her room, intent upon meeting the others in the dining room.

"Good morning, Leze!" She surprised Hercules by tapping him on the shoulder as he walked toward the back door. He straightened, turned to face her, and nodded hello. No hint of his usual smile lit his face, and for moment Dani was silent. What in the world was wrong with him? Then she remembered.

"I guess even the sight of me in this dress doesn't make up for what I did last night, does it? I can't blame you for being disappointed in me, Leze, but I couldn't help myself. That worm deserved what I gave him. Even Leial said so."

His eyes were bleak. Dani sensed he was holding his tongue, unwilling to express his chagrin at her actions. "Miz Dani, I gotta go. Miz Leial wants this here letter taken into town as fas' as I can get it there." He gave her a sad nod of farewell and continued on his way.

Dani shrugged and hoped he'd soon forget or forgive, for she valued his friendship.

When she reached the dining room, Dani saw that foods left over from last night's feast nearly covered the lacy cloth. As she had expected, Grady and Leial were seated at the table. They were speaking softly, heads together. Grady was seated in the chair closest to Leial's own at the head of the table.

Grady looked startled to see Dani, and the conversation ceased. He stood immediately and pulled out a chair for her opposite his own.

"Don't you look lovely! As pretty as a peach."

Dani looked at Troy's empty place. "Isn't Troy coming to eat?"

A blind mule could not have missed the look that passed between Grady and Leial. Dani was suddenly wary.

"I'm sorry about last night . . ." she began.

Leial's eyes were sad. "It's not that, my dear."

My dear?

Things *were* serious.

"What's wrong?" Dani demanded.

"Dani, Troy is . . ." Grady looked to Leial to complete the statement.

"What about Troy?" Dani felt the blood drain from her face. "Where is he? Is he all right?"

Leial began to push her chair away from the table, and Grady moved to assist her. "I will tell her, Grady. If you'll excuse us." She turned again to Dani. "Come, my dear."

Dani was riveted to her chair. Her legs refused to move.

Startled, Dani asked, "Tell *her* what?"

Leial moved to the doorway and Dani stood on shaking legs. As if walking in a dream, she followed the tall woman through the hallway, off the veranda, and down the stairs before Leial stopped and looked back at her. The midnight black of the woman's gown seemed out of place in the vibrant sunshine. With a tender gesture, Leial drew Dani's hand through the crook of her elbow and began walking slowly down the path toward the landing.

"Troy's gone, Dani."

So soon? Dani tried to speak but only a croaking whisper escaped her. "Do you know where?"

"We aren't sure, nor do we know when he'll return."

Dani hated hearing the uncertainty in the usually strong voice. "He left a letter in my care and asked that I read it to you."

They had reached the dock. Leial sat on a bench facing the bayou. Slowly she drew a folded sheet of paper from the deep pocket of her skirt. Dani waited in silence, staring at the softly swaying moss on the trees across the water.

The page crackled as if it were alive in Leial's hands.

"'Dear Dani,'" she began, "'I am sorry to leave you this way, but I know that you would insist on going with me. I am traveling to a place I have never been, to meet a man I have only imagined in my worst nightmares. Although the future is as uncertain as the past, I will ask again that you wait for me. If you find this impossible, Grady will take you east at the first opportunity. He will help you locate any members of your family who might still be alive.

"'Grady, as you know, is a fine man and a loving friend in whom I place my confidence, indeed, my life's trust. In time, should you grow to love him, know that I will understand. I told you once, long ago, that I was not free to take your love. So now, pet, the time has come for you to choose whether to stay or go. Fontaine.'"

There was no sound from the silent, unmoving water. Mud

green, the bayou seemed to sleep, lazing away the sunny afternoon. The two women were so very still that a blinding white egret landed near them, stretched its long neck into the moss near its feet, and grubbed for bugs.

"I don't understand." Dani's voice broke on the words.

"This is something over which you and I have no control, Dani. I wish to God that I did. I wish to God that his love for you had held him here, but even that was not enough."

"His love for me?"

"Surely you know Troy loves you, Dani?"

"He's never said as much." Dani shook her head, trying to still the wild beating of her heart.

"Actions speak louder than words," Leial said. "I knew by the look in his eye the first time I saw you two together that he loved you. I just wish he'd given up this chase." Leial's eyes filled with tears. "Grady has told me you know the circumstances of Troy's past."

Still unable to find words, Dani merely nodded.

"The reason Reynolds sought to harm my son and his wife wasn't clear, but it seems Jeanette had broken her earlier engagement with him in order to marry Merle. Reynolds was humiliated. Merle gambled to excess and was easy prey for Reynolds, who was wealthy and a consummate gambler himself.

"Merle lost nearly everything to the man—everything but this island, which my husband had left to me. Constantine Reynolds was not satisfied with stripping my son of his fortune. He disappeared along with Merle and Jeanette after a gala affair at the theater in New Orleans. Soon afterward, unsigned letters arrived here, asking me to pay an exorbitant ransom for my son's life. Jeanette's release was never mentioned."

She paused, the memories draining her strength. Dani glanced over at Leial's hands and saw that although they were clenched together, still holding Troy's letter, they were shaking. Reaching out, Dani covered Leial's hands with one of her own.

"We could not raise the ransom money in time. Not many people were willing to risk their savings on my son, a known wastrel. Others thought that Merle had merely gone into hiding and that the disappearance was a hoax he'd perpetrated in order to raise money for his gambling pursuits. Soon after the deadline to pay the ransom passed, Troy found his father's body hanging in the barn behind the house." Leial shuddered, her movements shaking Dani with their force. "He was only twelve, but he wanted to spare me the pain of seeing—seeing my son hanging there. Troy lowered his own father's body to the floor and sent Hercules, who was with us even then, to summon the authorities before he came to me."

Dani had suffered the pain of losing Jake, but Jake had lived a full life. Death had come to him peacefully. She had not been forced to deal with Jake meeting such a violent end. "What happened to Troy after that?" she asked.

"I sent him away to school in the East, hoping that he would eventually forget the horror of it all. I'm afraid his absence only deepened his need for revenge. Perhaps if he'd remained here he might have been able to grieve and resign himself to the tragedy." She shrugged and sighed, "Who knows? When he brought you home, I thought my prayers had been answered. I was harsh with you, Dani, but I was only testing you. I had to know whether your love could stand up to Troy's temper and his black moods. I thought his feelings for you would force him to put aside his plans to find Constantine Reynolds. If you and Troy could have had more time together, perhaps he would have stayed and let the past rest."

As the woman fell silent, Dani thought about all Leial had revealed. Musing over the tale, she realized Leial was wrong. She shook her head.

"Troy isn't one to sit by and let a killer go free, no matter how much he eventually might have come to love me." She looked at Leial for a moment, searching the other woman's dark, expressive eyes. "I couldn't live with knowing I was the reason he'd given up. Troy would have lived his life wondering, feeling like a coward. Eventually, he would have blamed me."

She looked down at the soft material of her skirt and stared at the smooth skin on the backs of her hands and the even fingernails. Even as she recognized these outward changes, Dani fought to understand the feelings that assailed her. The devastation that swept over her as Leial read Troy's letter to her was swiftly and surely being replaced by something stronger. She was more angry than hurt that Troy had left her behind. That anger would sustain her through the next days and weeks, help her to hold on to the dream she had nurtured since the day she and Troy had ridden out of the hollow together.

"I wish you'd told me earlier that you thought I might be able to help Troy. I spent a lot of wasted hours up in my room thinkin' you were wishin' I was gone," Dani admitted. "I wish Troy had told me how he felt about me, if he loves me like you say."

"My dear, I know how upsetting this must be for you," Leial began.

"Upsetting?" Dani straightened and patted Leial's hand before she let it go. "I'm not upset. I'm horn-tossin' mad and gettin' madder by the minute." She stood up and began to pace before Leial. "Does Troy Fontaine think that just 'cause he writes me some civilized letter askin'—no, *tellin'* me to wait or just forget about him, that I'm about to do like he says? He knows me better than that!"

Dani stopped pacing in midstride, planted her fists on her hips, and stood facing Leial. The hem of her gown swirled about her legs with the sudden cessation of movement. "Where did he go?" she demanded of the older woman.

"What are you thinking of, Dani?"

"I'm thinking he was a fool to go off alone, what with Grady and me here and willing to go with him. At least *I* am willing."

Leial slowly stood, her brows tightened together as she stared at Dani with a mixture of admiration and curiosity. "You aren't serious."

"Oh, but I am. We fought about that the day he came home from Baton Rouge. He said he planned to go after Reynolds, and I said I would go with him."

"What will you do now, Dani?" Leial asked gently.

"I sure as hell don't intend to sit idle and do nothing. And I'm not going east, either." Dani stepped closer to Leial. "I'd like to wait right here—with your permission, o' course, ma'am—until you get some word from Troy or we figure out where he is."

"You may stay here as long as you like."

"When we find out where he is, I intend to follow him."

"Dani, you can't possibly mean—"

"Oh, but I do. I want to march right up to Troy Fontaine and ask him what he meant by running off and leaving me no more than a piece of paper and telling me to go and fall in love with Grady Maddox." She blinked furiously as she fought to hide the tears that threatened to fall. "As if I could," she grumbled to herself. "Besides, he's likely to need help. Maybe he's started to believe he really does have Fontaine's Fighting Forty behind him."

Taking a deep breath that ended in a frustrated sigh, Dani reached out and took Troy's letter from Leial. Gently she slipped her arm through the older woman's and smiled. A cool breeze brushed against her, chilling her slightly, and Dani turned toward the lane that led to the house.

"You sure you don't mind my staying here until we get word of Troy?" Dani asked again, wondering at her new affection for Troy's grandmother.

"As I said before, Dani, this is your home for as long as you wish. I'm not sure that Troy will send word of his whereabouts"—Leial seemed to falter on her next words—"or if we'll hear from him at all before . . . before this is all over."

"You are not going after Troy." Grady Maddox's words were emphatic.

Dani squared off, hands on hips, squinting fiercely at Grady as they faced each other across Troy's desk in the library. "I *am* going after him. I'm leaving just as soon as I can find out how he learned about Constantine Reynolds."

Grady's voice rose, not for the first time that afternoon. "You are *not* going, and that's final!"

"Why didn't you go with him?"

Grady shifted his shoulders as he tugged at the lapels of his green jacket. "I've tried to talk him out of this for years. Troy was well aware of my feelings."

"Who *can* tell me where he went?"

Grady fell silent, his expression one of worried contemplation. He turned away from her and stared at Troy's maps and scrolls, which protruded from one of the bookshelves. Dani knew that he had the answer to her question and was fighting to hide it from her.

"Tell me."

"No."

"Do you know where he is?"

"No."

Dani turned her back on Grady and walked to the fireplace opposite the doors to the gallery. This room was Troy's sanctuary, a retreat where he worked or lost himself in his reading. She envied him that ability to escape into another world just by opening a book and deciphering the tiny marks that marched across the pages. A portrait now hung on the wall opposite the bookshelves; it had not been in the room the day she learned to write her name. Dani looked up at the face of a beautiful woman and knew without asking that she was Troy's mother, Jeanette.

The eyes of the woman in the portrait were nothing like her son's. Troy had Leial's obsidian eyes, and so must have inherited them from his father. Jeanette Fontaine's eyes were warm and brown and knowing. They gazed out of the portrait with serenity and love, and although Dani was raging inside with impatience and frustration, she knew a sense of calm while staring up at the dark-haired beauty's portrait.

That sense of quietude helped Dani to think clearly. Grady refused to help. She would have to depend on herself and, for once, think before she acted. Suddenly the answer was as clear to her as a bolt of lightning flashing across a night sky.

Leverette Devereaux.

Troy had spent over an hour closeted with the man last night during the party. There was no need to ask herself what Troy found so important to talk about that he could not have done so any other time. Devereaux was the name Grady mentioned the night he first told her the story of the murder. Devereaux knew where Constantine Reynolds was and had carried the news to Troy. She would have remembered it sooner if she hadn't let her impatience get in the way.

Dani nodded slightly, thanking the silent, lifelike image of Jeanette Fontaine. Her mind was racing as she planned her escape. It was certain that neither Grady nor Leial would sanction her leaving. It was just as certain she could not remain here another moment while the distance between her and Troy grew greater. Dani took a deep breath and in a contrite tone, spoke to the man who stood staring at Troy's books.

"Grady . . ." She paused and waited until he looked at her. "I'm so sorry." Blinking her eyes rapidly, she hoped her face expressed sorrow and melancholy. "I just can't believe Troy would go off and leave me this way." Dani sighed and gazed up at Grady from beneath lowered lashes and hid the smile that threatened to give her away. The act was working. He crossed the room toward her. She let her eyes fill with unshed tears and lifted them to meet his.

"I won't bother you again," she murmured. "Troy's your friend, and I'm certain you think you're doing the best thing for both of us."

"Dani, if I thought telling you would help . . ."

She raised her hand as if the very movement was an effort, and he waited for her to continue. "I'm going up to my room now, Grady. If you could be kind enough to tell Leial that I don't feel like having any dinner, I'd be obliged."

"Of course." He nodded, then reached for her hand. "Some rest will do you good, Dani. Try not to worry."

She sighed again. "I will."

Willing herself to move slowly, she gave him a weak smile and walked out of the library. It was all Dani could do to refrain from lifting her full, soft peach muslin skirt and running up the stairs to her room. Patience might be a virtue, she thought, but not when there was little time to waste.

Intent on leaving as soon as possible, Dani confronted Hercules, demanding to know why the servant had not accompanied Troy.

Leze's face reflected his despondency as he explained, "I offered to go with him, Miz Dani. The Lord knows I begged to go, but Mr. Troy, he say no. He tol' me he was goin', but not a word about where. I says, 'Let me go, too, 'case you need me,' but he say I was to stay here with you."

"I'm going after him, Leze."

"If you be goin', then I 'spect I be goin', too." He smiled broadly, happy with her decision.

"I need you to do one thing for me first. Go into town and tell Leverette Devereaux I'll be in tomorrow to talk to him."

She dictated a note to Devereaux, which Hercules penned for her. Then she waited on edge until he returned late that evening. Leverette Devereaux, Hercules reported, was in New Orleans and would not return for two weeks. There was nothing they could do but wait.

Chapter Twenty-two

Dani took a deep breath and let her clear, strong singing voice fill the sitting room. The words flowed so effortlessly that neither Grady nor Leial, who played the pianoforte in accompaniment, suspected that Dani's thoughts were not on the music. Leverette Devereaux had finally returned to Baton Rouge and the longest two weeks of Dani's life were nearly over. She had been so anxious to leave that the days had crawled by as slowly as a turtle on a cold day.

The thought of leaving set her nerves on edge, and she pressed the palm of her hand against her midriff to still the jumpiness there. Tonight she and Hercules planned to slip away to Baton Rouge. By tomorrow they would know where Troy had gone and, if all went smoothly, would be on his trail before the sun set.

As the song ended, Leial smiled up from behind the pianoforte and nodded to Dani. "That was lovely, dear. Would you sing my favorite now? Do you remember the words?"

Dani gave Leial a sparkling smile of affection. It was hard not to care for this woman who had lately treated her with such kindness. Leial's silver hair glistened in the dancing candlelight, her long, elegant hands poised above the keys in readiness. Leial had taught her the song "Greensleeves," claiming it was her favorite. She told Dani the song had been sung for centuries. Dani, too, loved the lilting melody and especially found the opening words near to her own heart and circumstance. She nodded to Leial, smiled at Grady, who sat comfortably ensconced in a wing chair beside the fire, and took a deep breath: " 'Alas, my love, you do me wrong, to cast me off discourteously, And I have loved you so long delighting in your company.' "

The song was not all she'd learned in the past two weeks, for Leial was determined that Dani should read and had worked with her each afternoon. The first task was to review the alphabet, and Dani found it had not changed since Jake had tried to teach it to her long ago. She discovered, too, that when Leial wrote out the letters in large block form rather than tight script, she was more likely to recognize them. After they read the letters and a few simple words that Dani was learning to recognize, Leial often left her alone to painstakingly copy the words on a sheet of paper.

Dani found the work tedious for it demanded much concentration. The letters seemed to want to reverse themselves as she transferred them from her mind to the blank page, and when she complained to Leial at last of her headaches and frustration, the woman assured her that she could learn, but perhaps she was in need of glasses.

"Spectacles?" Dani had shouted, her outburst nearly unseating Leial. "How am I supposed to go around in spectacles? That's all I need. What if I end up in a tussle and . . . and they break and stab me in the eye?" she wanted to know. "My aim is near perfect. Why, I can hit a squirrel from as far away as the gun will shoot, ma'am. How can there be anything wrong with my eyes?"

They had let the subject drop, but the lessons continued. Tomorrow, though, Dani knew her schooling would end when she left the island. For tonight, she was determined to act as natural as possible so that neither Leial nor Grady would suspect that she was leaving before dawn.

"That was wonderful, Dani." Leial complimented her again when the song finally ended. "You are such a treasure."

Dani felt a deep sadness wash over her at the woman's kind words, and her feelings were impossible to hide. She looked down at the toes of the silken shoes that peeped from beneath the hem of her navy blue gown and took a deep breath to help choke down the heaviness in her throat. When she looked up again she found Leial standing beside her.

"Are you all right?" the woman asked.

Dani nodded. "Yes, ma'am. I was remembering something Troy once said to me is all."

There was a silence between them for a moment before Leial took Dani's hand.

"You're doing the right thing, Dani, waiting here for word of Troy."

"It's been two weeks, ma'am. Do you really expect to hear from him?"

Leial's eyes met hers without faltering. "No. I suppose not. Not until he comes home."

If he comes home.

Although they shared the same thought, neither of them dared to speak the words aloud.

Dani shrugged off haunting thoughts and forced another smile.

"Have I ever told you two about Irish Billy?" she asked, her eyes alight with mischief.

Leial shook her head, and Grady sat forward in his chair, motioning Dani to the center of the rug before the sitting room fire. "No, you haven't," he said, "but I'm sure there's a story coming."

Dani stepped forward, a bounce in her stride. "There is, there is indeed. Have a seat, ma'am." She pointed to a chair that was a companion to Grady's. It had become a nightly custom for her to entertain them by acting out stories of the mountain men she'd left behind. Dani put her hands on her hips and swayed back and forth as the tale settled in its proper sequence in her mind. When she had the bits and pieces in place, she began speaking, this time in the heavy Irish brogue she'd heard the redheaded trapper use time and time again.

"Irish Billy liked his whiskey thick and his women thin . . ."

Under the cover of darkness, Dani made her way along the footpath that stretched between the house and the small kitchen outbuilding. She was careful not to make any sound that might carry on the still night air. It felt good to be in buckskins again. Every muscle seemed alive, attuned to the danger of the adventure on which she was about to embark.

She was starving, or so it seemed as her stomach rumbled hungrily. She'd been far too excited to eat much of the dinner that had been before her. Dani slowly turned the knob and let the kitchen door swing inward. The room was gilded by the orange glow of the dying fire. Pausing for a moment, she

listened intently. The only sound in the room was the soft hiss
of the fire as embers fell into the ash. She stepped inside and,
moving with the graceful silence of a stalking cat, found a loaf
of bread, still warm, on Venita's workbench. Tearing away a
large portion, she stuffed it into a cloth bag she carried, then
looked around the room for other bounty. Dani froze when she
spied the tall, gaunt form of Venita outlined in the open
doorway.

The glow of the fire cast Venita in a blood-red wash of light.
Dani tried to still the heavy pounding of her heart. She let the
old woman speak first.

"You are leaving."

Dani knew Venita was not asking a question. "Yes."

"You go to him."

"Yes."

The old woman merely nodded. "I make *ouanga*— magic—
and pray you not too late."

The words chilled Dani to the bone. *Too late? Too late for
what?* She tried to speak, but when she opened her mouth the
sound that issued forth was a mere croak. "What do you
mean?"

Venita stared at her across the rapidly darkening room.

"You know where he is!" Dani's voice gained strength as
her excitement mounted. As she stepped around the workbench, intent upon gaining answers from Venita, she caught
the toe of her moccasin on a heavy bag of rice and was pitched
headlong into the center of the room. Lightning-swift reflexes
halted her forward momentum and Dani was able to right
herself before she slammed into the floor. Squarely on her feet
again, she turned toward the doorway.

Venita was gone.

"Damn," she muttered. Moving as quickly as silence would
allow, she closed the door behind her, still clutching the bread
bag in one hand.

There was no sign of Venita outside, nor had there been time
for the cook to reach her cabin across the clearing. Frustrated,
Dani shook her head and hurried toward Hercules's slant-
roofed cabin.

He was waiting on the low porch that fronted the small
house, leaning against one of the slim posts that supported the
sheltering overhang. Beside him lay a small bundle of his
possessions as well as Dani's pack of clothing and her rifle and

shot. She had secreted a dress and other goods to him over the past weeks while they awaited Devereaux's return.

"Did you see Venita?" Dani asked.

"No. I seen nothin' o' that ol' crow. Why you ask?" As he spoke, Hercules hefted both bundles, leaving Dani to carry her rifle.

"I saw her in the kitchen. She knows where Troy is, I just know it. She says he's in trouble."

"She don' know nothin'." His expression belied his words.

Dani looked back toward the kitchen. "Should we try to find her?"

"Even if she know somethin', Venita won't be tellin'. Not that one." Hercules shuddered visibly. "She be evil, Miz Dani."

"Posh. She doesn't scare me with all those wangas of hers." Dani stared out into the darkness, debating whether to waste time trying to find Venita. She decided against it, knowing the woman was so familiar with the island that she could evade them for hours. "Let's go."

Hercules silently obeyed and stepped around Dani to lead the way to the bayou.

As they paddled the pirogue through the still water, Hercules outlined the plan he'd carefully formulated. Before they reached town, Dani would change clothes. Once they arrived at Baton Rouge, she would withdraw funds from the bank and then continue on to Devereaux's office. As soon as she gained the needed information, they would be on their way. It all sounded simple.

Too simple.

The moss-draped trees hung out over the water like huddled, shrouded mourners as the swamp closed in around them. As long as Hercules kept talking about the role she was to play, Dani was able to keep doubt from clouding her mind. But when he became silent as he concentrated on guiding the pirogue through the twisted waterways, she felt her nervousness mount.

She wished she had watched more carefully, listened more intently, when Troy and Grady obtained lodging or booked passage on the steamboats. As they grew ever closer to Baton Rouge, Dani realized that she knew nothing of such things.

"Leze?" She continued paddling as she called back over her shoulder.

"Miz Dani?"

"I know ant's piss about moving around in town alone."

She heard what amounted to a sigh of exasperation escape the giant.

"Miz Dani, the first thing—the very *first* thing—you gotta recall is that ladies don't go 'round sayin' 'ant's piss,' 'damn,' or any of them cusswords you been using. You understan'?"

Contrite, she answered softly, "Yep."

"An' second, you don't have to worry too much about conductin' yourself in town. I know all we have to know. You jes' take care to watch the other women and do like they do an' leave all the rest to me. Hear?"

"Yep."

"An' one more thing. When we get to town, ya'll can't be actin' like I'm your bes' friend. That's the one rule you gotta remember, 'cause I'm black, an' I'm a man—an' bigger than most. You gonna find some folks don't cotton much to the combination. You hear me, gal?"

"Yep. I hear ya."

But she wasn't sure she understood it at all.

"No need to knock at an office door. Ya'll jes' go on in."

Hercules nudged his charge as they stood outside Leverette Devereaux's office. She glanced up and read the sign above the door: "At-tor-ney-at-law." Dani shrugged. "You sure you can't go in with me?"

"No, I can't," Hercules insisted. "It wouldn't be right. You be a lady here to conduct business, and I mean for you to do it proper."

"But every time I've seen this man he's been looking at me the way a coyote looks at a lame rabbit."

"Get."

"Leze . . ." she pleaded.

"Go. You want to find Mr. Troy or not?"

She mumbled an imprecation under her breath, and he shook his head in warning. The man was as hard on her as Leial had been during their reading lessons.

As Dani opened the door and stepped into Leverette Devereaux's well-appointed waiting room, she wondered how she had become so far removed from her simple mountain life. Her gloved hands clutched a small drawstring reticule, which was filled with the money she'd just withdrawn from the bank. She

felt virtually helpless in her peach gown and tried to pull the
soft cashmere shawl tighter about her shoulders. Unarmed,
Dani felt vulnerable, and if it hadn't been for the buffalo knife
strapped to her right thigh, she might not have ventured out
onto the streets at all. It was one thing to be outfitted in the
restrictive skirts at home, but quite another to know that any
attempts to run would be hampered by the yards of cloth about
her legs.

She waited but a moment before Devereaux, alerted by the
chiming of the bell above the door, walked out of the inner
office to greet his visitor. His glistening brown hair was
perfectly smoothed away from an even part on the left side of
his head. Eyes as green as springtime quickly assessed her
from head to toe. Dani stood her ground, determined not to
squirm, for she needed information from this man, and she
intended to get it.

"Miss Whittaker, what a delightful surprise. What brings
you into town?"

As if you didn't know. "I wish to speak with you about a
private matter, Mr. Devereaux."

"Please," he said as he ushered her into his inner office,
"call me Leverette. All my friends do."

The door closed behind them with a ring of finality, and
Dani felt every muscle tense.

"Sit down, Miss Whittaker, sit down."

She sat. He chose to perch on the corner of the desk nearest
her chair. Dani leaned back, forcing herself to appear comfortable in his presence, but she could almost feel the heat
emanating from the emerald shards that pinned her to the chair.
This was a bad idea, she decided. Bad from the start.

"How may I help you?"

She remembered to let go of her shawl as Hercules had
directed. Devereaux leaned forward.

"You can tell me where Troy is."

He did not so much as blink at her forthright statement.
"What makes you so certain I know where he is?"

"You talked to him for over an hour the night of the party.
He left soon afterward."

"Perhaps if you let me know why it's important to you to
find out, I might be able to shed some light on his whereabouts."

"I need to know."

"You aren't thinking of going after him, are you?" Devereaux shifted his position on the desk.

"Not at all," she lied. "It's just that his grandmother has had no word of him and she is beside herself with worry."

"You are not a very gifted liar, Miss Whittaker. I can't imagine Leial Fontaine being beside herself with worry over anything. The woman is too strong to show fear even if she feels it."

"Then you guessed right." She decided to tell him the truth. "I am going after him."

"That's the very reason Troy made me promise him I would not tell anyone where he went. It's out of the question."

"Why?" she demanded. A slow, frustrated anger began to simmer inside her.

"You would only be in his way."

He was blatantly staring down the front of her dress now, enjoying the rise and fall of her breasts as her fury made her breathe that much faster. She curled her fingers around the arms of her chair and held on tight, determined not to stand and take a swing at him.

"Will you allow me to call on you sometime, Miss Whittaker? Now that Troy will be gone for an indeterminate amount of time, that is?"

"What would you want to call on me for?" She tried to smile, to be patient, to extract the answer she had come to get.

"As a suitor."

"I don't need a suit."

"How humorous you are, Danika."

"I'm not laughing. Where's Troy?"

Before she was aware that he had moved Leverette was leaning over her, his hands atop hers on the arms of the chair, holding her immobile. He was so close now that she could smell the spicy scent of his cologne and count the tips of his eyelashes. Wariness made her alert to his every move and she kept her eyes on his lips, for they seemed to pose the biggest threat at the moment. She watched them move with his next words.

"I think my friend Troy was a fool to leave such a lovely lady all alone. I'd have never done so."

She pressed against the chair back and found herself trapped. Slowly, emphasizing every word, she warned him, "I think your friend Troy would politely remove your arms and legs from your body if he could see you leanin' over me like this, peerin' down my dress the way you are, *Mister* Devereaux. But since he isn't here, I'll just have to remember to tell your *friend* when he returns."

Devereaux colored but made no attempt to move until a sharp knock sounded upon the door. He sat back and called out an irritated "Come in."

Dani nearly laughed with relief when she saw Hercules in the doorway, shuffling his feet uncertainly and nodding in her direction.

"Miz Dani, I tol' Miz Leial I'd see you was back to the islan' before dinnertime."

The man who called himself Troy's friend looked as if he might object to the servant's timely intrusion, so Dani seized the moment to stand and move away from him.

"I guess you won't be telling me what I need to know, then. Am I right?" she asked him.

"That's right, Miss Whittaker—unless you assure me that I will have an opportunity to get to know you better if I tell you where Troy is. Perhaps then I might see that you have no intention of hampering my friend's mission by following him."

In a voice that was as soft as a whisper Dani said, "I think I know you as well as I care to already, Mr. Devereaux. So if you'll pardon me, I'll be leaving."

Without so much as a good day, Dani lifted her fashionably wide skirt and turned toward the door. Hercules stepped aside to let her pass and then followed her out of the office and onto the street. Leverette Devereaux, she noticed, did not offer to see her to the door.

Dani wanted to curse in frustration but held her tongue, all too aware of Hercules following her at a polite distance like a watchdog. They hadn't taken more than twenty paces when she nearly bumped into Erantha Devereaux walking toward her brother's office.

"Why, Danika," the woman called out, knowing full well the use of her name infuriated Dani. "I'm so surprised to find you in town. I hear Troy has left you out on that dreadful island all alone. What happened to your Indian clothes?"

"I only wear them for special occasions."

"Well, it's really too bad about Troy up and leaving you like that."

Dani could not stand to let the other woman best her,

especially by mentioning Troy's abandonment. "He'll be back shortly."

"That's highly unlikely." Erantha tossed her carefully curled and beribboned yellow hair. "After all, that little island he sailed to is off the coast of Venezuela. It isn't the easiest place to get to."

Dani nearly stopped breathing when she realized that standing before her in the guise of Erantha Devereaux was the answer to her question. "Really?" Dani feigned the innocence of a child, all the time aware of Hercules listening intently a few paces behind her. "I don't know too much about islands."

To Dani's satisfaction, the other woman puffed as visibly as a toad. "I don't suppose you would. Tobago is one of the southernmost of the Caribbean Islands, and as I told you, Troy won't be there and back any too soon. How long do you plan on keeping yourself amused? Or will you be leaving for home soon?"

Dani was not at all surprised by the wishful tone in Erantha's voice. "I'm sorry I'm going to have to disappoint you, Erantha, but I don't have any plans that include leaving Troy to the likes of you. Coming, Leze?" she asked over her shoulder as she sidestepped Erantha and moved on down the street.

"Well, I never!" Erantha's words drifted back to Dani.

"Nope. I don't reckon you have, and unless you meet some poor soul who's both deaf and blind, you probably *won't* ever, either."

Dani heard Hercules's deep chuckle in response to her comment as they hurried toward the river.

Chapter Twenty-three

At Hercules's suggestion, Dani agreed to pose as a widow. He assured her that a bereaved widow accompanied by her faithful servant would not be questioned as to why she was traveling two thousand miles to Tobago. Miraculously, before they boarded Captain Jeremiah Howath's ship bound for the Caribbean, Hercules produced two of Leial's oldest black dresses for Dani to wear.

"How'd you get these?" she wanted to know.

"They was in the back of the closet, an' I knowed they wouldn't be missed. Miz Leial got so many black dresses she don' know one from t'other."

Dani shook her head. "There's nothing she doesn't know about, Leze, believe me. You were mighty sure of me approving of this plan, weren't you?"

He smiled. "You got one of your own?"

They had seen each other rarely on board ship, for their station did not allow for communication other than that of mistress to servant. Dani found she missed the close camaraderie they usually shared, but for the sake of his safety, she treated Hercules like a servant during the extended voyage.

Not only did the ship stop at various Caribbean ports of call, but a lack of wind held the crisp-sailed schooner in irons for more than a week. They had entered the doldrums, the captain explained. There was nothing to do but ride out the lack of wind. During that time Dani paced the deck, a stifling captive in her high-necked, long-sleeved black gown, anxiously watching the cloudless sky for any break in the sultry weather.

The craggy-skinned Captain Howath was equal to Dani in height and possessed a storehouse of oaths that even she admired. Well into his fifties, he was touched by the plight of the young widow Whittaker. He had even offered her accommodations with his spinster sister, Mildred, once Dani reached Tobago. Mildred, he said, would be happy to introduce Dani to the small but welcoming circle of island society. Dani accepted his offer immediately, happy to be relieved of locating suitable quarters for herself and Hercules.

Each evening she and the handful of passengers bound for islands with exotic names dined with Captain Howath. Stifling the urge to fan her face with her skirt, Dani sat with the others in the stuffy main salon, thankful for the colorful conversation that helped take her mind off the heat.

"Always, always bathe in the early morning," the captain advised the group gathered about the table. He did not expound upon why they should do so, but continued, "And above all, drink copious amounts of coffee and ginger tea. If you'll take the advice of an old man"—he leaned forward, both elbows propped on the table, his heavy brows arched high— "go lightly clad."

Dani nodded and smiled, stuffing a forkful of potato into her mouth. She had already done away with any form of underclothing except a petticoat. A woman would have to have lost her mind to want to wear anything more in such heat, she thought.

The ship finally docked in Rockly Bay on the leeward side of Tobago. The voyage had taken nearly a month and a half, and to Dani, who had never seen the sea, they landed not a day too soon. She did not like "the big pond," as she called the Caribbean.

Captain Howath personally escorted Dani and Hercules to his sister's home where the rotund Mildred, who possessed the same azure eyes as the captain, greeted her surprise guest with open arms. Mildred escorted Dani into the whitewashed wooden cottage that sat on a hill overlooking the village below.

"I've far too much room here just for myself, and since Jeremiah refuses to stay anywhere but on that bobbing wooden cork he calls a ship, I'm more than happy to have your companionship."

Dani liked the cheery woman immediately, taken by both the open welcome and the breezy outdoor look of Mildred's glowing skin and pink cheeks. Here was a woman who did not bother with the convention of hiding herself from the sunshine.

When Dani said she would gladly pay for her lodgings, the woman promptly protested. "That's not necessary, Mrs. Whittaker. Not at all. I 'make garden,' as the natives say, and the fruits of my labors are many! Why, I have more than enough food for you and your servant." The woman eyed Hercules's massive frame as he lingered near the doorway where he kept a wary eye on the fine long-tailed parrot preening on a perch near the open windows.

Dani was settled in with graciousness and ease. She ignored Captain Howath's advice and bathed that very evening. As she sat in the tin tub that Hercules had carried into the guest room, Dani looked out of the open window into the dark night and listened to the rustling palm fronds as they moved in the gentle night breeze. After depositing the tub, Hercules had gone into town in search of Troy.

She paused, washcloth in hand, and wondered what Troy's reaction would be to her arrival. Not likely a pleasant one, she guessed. But here she was and here she'd stay whether he wanted her to or not. Then, as she recalled how he had sneaked away from Isle de Fontaine, she began to scrub herself with a vengeance. By the time she was finished and had stepped from the tepid water, Dani had to talk herself out of going off in search of Troy immediately.

After toweling herself dry, Dani slipped into her nightshift. She was just about to crawl into bed when she heard a husky whisper just beneath her window. Recognizing Hercules's voice, she hiked up the long shift and climbed out the window into the garden.

"Did you find him?" she wanted to know.

"No, but I foun' where he was stayin'. The Hotel Royale."

"Where is he now?"

"He ain' been there for near three weeks. But he left his things there. The owner didn't seem too concerned. Thinks maybe Mr. Troy's travelin' aroun' the island seein' the sights."

"What do you think?" she asked Hercules, trying to ignore the knot of worry that was tightening inside her.

He shook his head. "I think he's either out lookin' for the man Reynolds, or he already foun' him."

They were both silent as they considered the possibilities. The night sky was crowded with stars, more than Dani had ever

seen before, even in the Rockies. The rainbow of bougainvil-
lea, hibiscus, and oleander blooms that surrounded them was
hidden by a cloak of darkness. Dani glanced back to her open
window. The house was quiet except for the soft sound of
Mildred's snoring. The parrot, King George, who was named
for the fort built on the hill above Scarborough, called out
sharply from his perch on the veranda. Hercules stepped back
into the shadows and shook his head in warning as Dani began
to speak.

"Don' say nothin' in front of that bird," he warned.

"Why?"

"He understands. Might talk about it, too."

"Are you serious?"

His voice remained a mere whisper as he glanced toward the
veranda. "I ain't foolin', Miz Dani." She watched the outline
of his wild mane move in the shadows. "The Negras here hate
parrots. Claim those birds can understand every word you
say."

She found herself glancing back uncertainly and lowering
her voice. "You think Troy's still on the island?"

"Why would he leave his clothes? I don' like the idea of Mr.
Troy's things just settin' there."

"I don't like the idea of Mr. Troy just settin' somewhere on
this island and us not knowin' where," she added. "What do
you think we should do now?"

Dani heard him sigh.

"I don' rightly know, Miz Dani. I'm plumb outta ideas."

Hands on hips, she thought for a moment as she began to
pace back and forth in front of him.

"It seems to me," she began, "that if Troy set out to find
Constantine Reynolds, then we should find him, too, and then
work our way back to Troy. The trouble is, how are we gonna
find out about Reynolds without being too obvious?"

"I don' rightly know, Miz Dani, but I got the feelin' we best
be gettin' about it right quick."

As Dani looked around the darkened hillside and listened to
the sound of the sea below, she tried to quell her growing fear.

"I do, too, Leze. I do, too."

Troy thought it was dark, but he could not be certain. The
small window in the door of the one-room prison was on the
wall behind him and he could not see the sky. Most of the men

crowded into the building were asleep now. Only Jebba, the injured man, was still moaning.

During his first week in hell, the foremost thought in Troy's mind had been of escape. Now, at the end of the third, Dani was all he thought of—Dani, and staying alive. He never stopped watching and waiting for an opportunity to break free, but as the days passed, Troy hoped that when the chance did come, he would still be strong enough to take it.

He had only himself to blame for his predicament. After his arrival on Tobago, Troy had set out to find a way to meet Reynolds face to face. The opportunity came to him during the first week of his stay. He learned that the Hotel Royale was a gathering place for the island's planters when they ventured into town. Passing as a newcomer interested in acquiring land and becoming a planter himself, he had easily made the acquaintance of many well-established plantation owners. From them Troy had learned that Constantine Reynolds rarely traveled into Scarborough, but he had soon found a way to meet him.

After a slave uprising on the northeast end of Tobago, the planters had met to discuss tighter controls on slave movement about the island. The meeting was held at Golden Palms, Reynolds's plantation near Mount Saint George, and Troy, in his role as a would-be planter, had been in attendance. All had gone well until some of the guests departed and those who were staying the night had gone to bed. It was then, as Troy was about to leave, that Reynolds had called him aside.

"Mr. Fontaine," Reynolds said, assessing him coolly as they stood alone beside one of the tall columns fronting the mansion, "I want to speak to you alone."

Troy had watched Reynolds warily, trying to hide the tension he felt knowing he was face to face with the man he believed to have killed his father. "Reynolds." He nodded.

"How do you like Tobago?" Reynolds asked.

"Fine." Troy was willing to play cat and mouse for a while.

"It is a beautiful place, is it not?"

"Quite."

"Almost as beautiful"—Reynolds paused and turned to face the long drive that led to the house—"as your mother was."

A shock as cold as ice and then as searing as fire reverberated through Troy. He collected himself before he spoke, maintaining his cool exterior.

"You weren't even wise enough to change your name, Fontaine. Did you think I wouldn't recognize you?"

"I've never seen you before in my life," Troy admitted truthfully.

"That's true." Reynolds stepped nearer. "But you are the image of your father. Even had you assumed another name, I would have known you on sight."

"Then we can dispense with all pretense."

"By all means. What are you doing here?" Reynolds demanded, his voice as smooth as expensive bourbon.

"I've come to take you back to Louisiana to stand trial for the murder of my father."

"Is it as simple as that?"

Troy shifted his weight, sure of himself, sure of the weapon tucked in the waistband of his trousers. "We can make it complicated if you prefer."

"I don't think that will be necessary." Reynolds looked over Troy's shoulder, but Fontaine refused to be caught by such an old trick. He kept his eyes on Reynolds. "Escort Mr. Fontaine to a safe place, Garth. I'll deal with him later."

A light footfall behind him alerted Troy. He drew his pistol as he spun around, only to find himself facing a tall, thin man armed with a rifle. The gun was pointed directly at Troy's midsection. Four slaves armed with clubs stepped out of the shadows, their bare feet soundless on the veranda.

Troy had been locked away for four days before he saw Reynolds again. By that time, all the visiting planters had departed. Troy was escorted to the dining room, and the two men dined alone, Reynolds impeccably dressed in white linen, Troy bearded, barefoot, and dirty. Reynolds paid Troy's appearance no mind.

"I loved your mother," Reynolds said at the end of the meal. "But she betrayed me. After twelve years in France I still could not forget her or what she'd done. So I returned to New Orleans for her."

"And you killed my father."

Reynolds shrugged. "It was necessary. Even if the family had obtained the money I asked for his release, I would have had to kill him. He was no good for Jeanette. No good to anyone. In fact"—Reynolds toasted Troy—"your life probably turned out much better because you were rid of him."

Troy pushed away from the table and was immediately

shoved down into his chair by the guard stationed behind him. He forced himself to swallow, to calm his seething rage. "And my mother?"

"She went with me willingly. Jeanette realized what a mistake she'd made. We lived in Italy for a time, then in France. When she died, I came here."

When she died? "You're lying." Troy ground out the words.

"Why would I lie about something so painful? I miss her. She meant everything to me, and I to her."

"No!" Troy shouted as he leapt from his chair. With a strength born of madness he shoved aside the guard and lunged at Reynolds.

"Garth!" Reynolds's voice rang out. The slave who acted as guard subdued Troy, who strained to free his arms from the man's iron grasp. "Get him out of here." Reynolds pointed at Troy. "Lock him up with the others. I'll take care of him once I'm certain he's working alone."

They had taken his clothing and given him a pair of ragged calf-length pants of the type worn by slaves. He was not given a shirt or shoes, and even now, three weeks since the day he had been placed in chains, his feet were still raw and bleeding.

He was chained together with runaways, disobedient slaves, and a few men who claimed they were as innocent as he. Each day they were forced to work the fields or marched to the high wooded ridges to fell lumber used in building. Rain or shine, they cut cyp and mahogany trees and hauled them downhill with a series of ropes and levers. McCarthy, an overseer with a penchant for stripping the skin off the backs of the lazy with a cat-o'-nine-tails was the first white man Troy saw in the morning and the last at night.

The slave named Jebba moaned again, but the sound of his breathing told Troy that he would not last much longer. That afternoon the man had been pinned beneath a massive log that had broken free. The huge mahogany log had crushed the man's legs before anyone could warn him of the danger. McCarthy had unfettered the injured man and told the others to leave him, but one of the runaways—a short, muscular man named Carlos—had carried Jebba's broken body back to the prison.

The dank, nearly airless stone cell afforded no comfortable surface for sleeping, but the exhausted, half-starved men did not seem to notice as they lay like the dead in the small space.

Reduced to living a life unfit for animals, they became as such, fighting over every worm-infested scrap of food that was thrown to them.

Determined to live and to escape, Troy closed his eyes and leaned back against the rough, cold wall of stones. He would need all of his strength to fight for his morning ration. He pictured Dani, silhouetted against a wide blue sky, standing in a mountain meadow. Her smile was warm and welcoming; her gray eyes were lit with love and merriment. The air around her was crisp and clear, nothing like the thick, humid darkness that suffocated him now. He thought of her and smiled, and then slept.

It had rained all day. Mildred assured Dani that February was the end of the rainy season. The woman spent her time indoors, happily making papaya jelly while Dani became as restless as a caged cat. The rain kept Hercules at home, although he had offered to walk to town to see if Troy had returned to the hotel.

Dani paced the veranda and watched the curtain of rain that fell from the pitched roof into the ferns and crotons planted under the overhang of the porch. Gray clouds hung over the island as streams of water carried brown mud down the hillside toward the bay. Impatient with the delay, she crossed her arms and walked to the kitchen where Mildred had taken over the cook's duties for the morning.

"Would you like to try some jelly, Dani?" Mildred offered kindly.

"No, thanks."

"You seem a bit out of sorts today, dear. Could it be that your woman's time is upon you?" The blue eyes showed concern and sympathy.

"No." Dani shook her head. Come to think of it, she hadn't had that problem since she left Louisiana. Perhaps it was the heat.

"Then it's just the rain that's bothering you. We islanders are used to it. Lord knows, the planters need all the rain they can get to grow sugar. Still, I know how hard it can be for visitors when we have too many wet days in a row."

Dani sat on a high stool beside the chopping table where Mildred was mashing papaya. She watched the soft, golden pulp spread out beneath the spoon and squish up the sides of the bowl. "Are there many planters on the island?" Dani asked.

"Nearly eighty sugar plantations now. Of course, there were more when sugar was first cultivated, but some years are better than others, some planters move on to other places. There are cocoa and coconut plantations, too."

Dani nodded. Wondering how to broach the subject of Constantine Reynolds. "Do you know many planters?"

"Oh, my, yes. Many."

Do you know Constantine Reynolds?

Afraid to ask, afraid she'd have to explain why she wanted to know, Dani fidgeted on the stool and tapped her fingers against the tabletop. Mildred poured sugar into the bowl of papaya. Dani suddenly felt the overwhelming urge to cry and wondered where it came from. After all, she wasn't the type to turn into a waterfall at the first sign of disappointment. It had to be the rain, she guessed. The rain, and worry over Troy's safety.

"We've been invited to a picnic on the beach tomorrow, Dani. That should help lift your spirits." Mildred stirred the sugary mixture, glancing up at Dani now and again. "You haven't yet had a walk on the beach, and Tobago has the finest. Did you ever read Defoe's novel, *Robinson Crusoe*?"

Dani shook her head. *Best not to get into that.*

"Everyone is certain that the story was set on Tobago. Crusoe's cave is located on the Milford Bay shore. Would you like to see it? It's quite a popular spot for visitors."

Dani shrugged. What did she care for an empty cave? Who was Robinson Crusoe anyway? She stood up and excused herself, then wandered back out onto the veranda. King George preened and called out, "Hello! Nice day!"

She glowered at the shiny-feathered bird and sank into a plush-cushioned chaise on the veranda. "Hush up, George, or you'll find yourself plucked and spitted. I've a hankerin' for something besides pork."

The following day, the sun shone brightly, creating thick humidity as it dried the rain-soaked land. Despite her unwillingness to attend the beach picnic, Dani was finally persuaded by Mildred that she should not mope about the house on such a lovely day. Dani agreed to go, hoping that Hercules might finally gain information regarding Troy's whereabouts.

She relaxed on the long drive to the beach, letting the bright blue sky and the warm sun cheer her. Mildred had been right to insist she attend the outing. Once she was on the beach, Dani lifted her long skirt above her ankles, stood barefoot at the shoreline, and let the sea wash over her feet. The wide crescent-shaped bay sparkled in the sunshine, and the air was heavy with salt and spray. Dani walked alone along the curving shore, aware of the constant sound of the waves that came in timed succession to the shore and pulled back out again.

There were nearly twenty guests at the picnic. The group was still assembled under the palm-frond shelters that had been hastily set up by the slaves to guard the women from the sun. No one was paying Dani any mind.

Dani scooped up the back hem of her skirt and drew it between her legs. She pulled it up and looped it over the sash at her waist, copying the peasant women she'd seen walking along the roadside. She moved freely along the surf line and kicked at the receding foam. Much better, she decided. The next best thing to britches.

She walked the length of the bay before hunger forced her to turn back. Nervousness had kept her from eating much the day before, and she decided the diet of island pork did not agree with her. Lately she had awakened to bouts of nausea. But just now she was starving as she made her way back to the open-sided shelters.

The party guests had carried in cooked food and Madeira wine and had brought along tables, chairs, and crockery in a wagon that followed the line of carriages. Everyone was seated when Dani reached the shelter and took her place beside Mildred. Dani filled her plate from the various dishes the slaves carried to each guest.

"Why, look!" a man in a wide-brimmed hat called out. "It's Connie come to join us."

"Don't let him hear you call him that, old man," another said in warning. "He doesn't take kindly to it."

"No. I don't suppose he would, at that."

The discussion ended abruptly, and Dani asked Mildred about the new arrival. She could see the shiny black carriage on the ridge and watched as a man in a white coat and trousers made his way down the narrow path to the beach. He walked slowly, with an air of nonchalance, as if he didn't really care whether or not he joined them. As he drew near, she saw him smooth his fingers over his gray mustache and goatee.

"Who is he?" she whispered to Mildred. Everyone present seemed to know the man, or at least his disposition, for the happy chatter had ceased with his approach.

"Him?" Mildred smiled, shaking her head. "A planter. His name is Constantine Reynolds."

Dani's fork clattered loudly as it fell onto her china plate. *Reynolds here?* The coincidence was too great. She couldn't believe her good fortune and so asked Mildred again. "Who?"

"Constantine Reynolds. He lives above Mount Saint George in a mansion in the middle of his land. He grows sugar as well as coconuts. He's extremely wealthy, rarely visits town, and keeps to himself. I've only seen him a few times. Why, Dani"—Mildred stopped speaking, and Dani found her watching her intently—"would you like to meet him?"

Dani stared at Reynolds again. Could this thin, well-dressed man in his mid-fifties be Troy's adversary? If Reynolds was here, then where was Troy?

She nodded in answer to Mildred's question. "Yes. I would very much like to meet him."

Dani had not realized how easy it would be to bat her eyes and flirt with a man the way she'd seen Erantha perform on Isle de Fontaine. But flirt she did, and she did it well, it seemed, for Constantine Reynolds hung upon her every word. Mildred introduced them once the meal was complete and then stayed close to Dani's side while they talked. It was not easy to study the man while she was occupied with all the eye fluttering, smiling, and agreeing she was forced to do, but Dani tried. The man's eyes were a nondescript brown flecked with yellow. They never smiled, not even when his mouth did. His clothing was impeccable, reminding her of Grady and the way he fought to stay clean even on the trail. Reynolds sat perfectly still beside Dani, and she tried to project the same nonchalance.

She found herself staring at his gray goatee as it bobbed with his every word. *Where was Troy?* If she'd come across Reynolds so easily, she had to think that Troy had, too. What had happened after that?

"You have quite an elegant home, I hear," Dani said, trying hard to mimic Mildred's inflection.

"I like to think so." He nodded. "It's not far from here, but far enough from town that I don't get into Scarborough often enough. My home isn't half as lovely as you are, Mrs. Whittaker."

The heated look in his eyes chilled her, but she forced herself to smile. "Thank you, Mr. Reynolds."

"Might I be so bold as to invite you to visit my home at Golden Palms?"

"Why, how *kind* of you," she oozed and hated herself for it. "I'd be delighted."

"So would I," Mildred intruded. "After all, Dani should not travel alone, Mr. Reynolds. What day will you expect us?"

Dani smiled, this time a genuine smile, as she listened to Mildred make the final arrangements for their day trip to the plantation Reynolds called Golden Palms. She looked out at the sea from beneath the palm-roofed shelter. For some mysterious reason, she suddenly felt closer to Troy than she had in a long while.

The plantation Reynolds had named Golden Palms appeared to be a quiet, elegant retreat situated on a ridge surrounded by the mountains that ran like a spine down the center of the island. As the open carriage driven by Hercules entered the long, narrow drive bordered by giant coconut palms, Dani stared toward the massive white house at the end of the lane. A sense of foreboding came over her, one she could not dispel as the carriage drew nearer. The house itself seemed to call out a warning, but it was too late to turn back now.

Mildred straightened and shook out her skirt, smoothed back her hair, and chattered nervously. The woman had taken it into her head that Dani was attracted to the planter, and as Dani's friend, she was determined to play matchmaker.

"Now, you just give me a sign if you care to be alone with Constantine, dear, and I'll request a moment to rest or walk in the gardens."

"Mildred, I don't think I'll want to—"

The woman cut her off. "Nonsense. I'm not really here to chaperon you; I was only curious to see the mansion. I've heard so much about it."

Hercules pulled the hired carriage up to the door and glanced back at Dani. The look that passed between them went unnoticed by Mildred, who sat staring at the massive front of the two-story house. Made of wood and stone, it was unlike any other on the island. Tall columns lined the veranda. The windows of the upper story were all covered by jalousied shutters that allowed air to enter, but no light. Dani wondered what lay behind them.

She gave Hercules her hand as he helped her alight and then stood beside the carriage waiting for Mildred to step down.

"Leze, you may go around to the kitchens and see if the cook will be kind enough to give you refreshment." She had rehearsed the line he'd taught her until she did not even hear herself repeat the words.

"Yes, Miz Dani." He made a half-bow to the ladies and, with a grace that belied his bulk, rounded the corner of the house and was out of sight before Dani had moved toward the wide veranda. She hoped Hercules would be able to speak freely to the servants. If their luck held, he would learn something of Troy, a task he'd been unable to accomplish thus far.

They were admitted by a servant and ushered into a parlor that looked out over the immaculate front drive and gardens. Too nervous to sit, Dani chose instead to stare out the window as she waited for Reynolds to arrive. Mildred, who sat perched on a small chair like a quail ready to be flushed, gazed about the room at the plush furnishings and the ancient tapestries that lined the walls.

"Please forgive me for keeping you waiting, Mrs. Whittaker."

Because she had not even heard him approach, the sound of Reynolds's voice startled her. She chided herself for her show of nervousness.

"I'm delighted that you could join me for dinner this afternoon," he said, and although his eyes never left Dani's he added, "both of you."

"Thank you, Mr. Reynolds," Dani said.

"Would you be so kind as to call me Constantine?"

"Only if you will call me Dani," she said, but dreaded hearing her name on his lips.

His eyes were hooded as he looked down at her. "I'd be happy to, Dani." Constantine glanced at Mildred who hovered nearby, awaiting a greeting. "Good day to you, as well, Mistress Howard. Since I've been amiss in my duties as host up to now, please allow me to show you ladies the house before we dine."

They walked through a succession of rooms that were
equally elegant, and although she had little experience on
which to base her knowledge of such things, Dani recognized
the fine quality of the furnishings and draperies, the huge
paintings that adorned the walls, and the touches of gold here
and there. She found the house cold and unwelcoming,
however, as if the rooms were only fit to look at and not a
proper place in which to live. She thought of the comfortable,
lived-in appearance of the old house on Isle de Fontaine and
was surprised by the sudden wave of homesickness that swept
over her.

The tour continued. Mildred babbled. Dani tried to add to
the conversation but the pall of evil that hung over the house
stilled her tongue. Troy had been here. She knew it now.
Somehow she felt it clear through to her bone marrow. Dani
thought of Venita's startling words and prayed silently that she
was not too late to save him. She prayed that she could keep
her wits about her. *Help me, Jake. Don't let me make the
wrong move.*

The dining room reflected the opulence of the rest of the
house. The meal was light and much to Dani's liking—tender
chicken, fresh vegetables and fruits, and a moist, rich cake.
Hungry despite her nervousness, she emptied her plate and
then leaned back in her chair.

"Do you have many visitors, Constantine?" she asked.

He lifted the long-stemmed glass of ruby wine and looked
through it before he took a sip. His brown hair was evenly
streaked with the silver that marked his mustache and beard.
He looked at her through close-set, narrow eyes and smiled.

"Not as many as I would like, Dani. You see, I have no
hostess. It's hard for a man like myself to entertain properly."

Mildred twittered and Dani fought the urge to shake her.

"I noticed the buildings behind the house as we came up the
drive," Dani said. "You must have many servants."

"Slaves, Dani, not servants."

"I see."

"You are not one of those who abhor slavery, are you?" His
eyes narrowed almost imperceptibly.

Dani held her tongue for a moment before she blurted out the
answer to his question. "Of course not," she lied.

Before she could request a tour of the ground and the small
village of workers that made the plantation self-sustaining,

they were interrupted by booted footsteps ringing against the polished wood floors. The sound came closer and stopped just outside the dining room door. A tall man clothed in sweat-stained clothing stood in the open doorway, impatiently tapping a riding crop against the top of his knee-high black boots. He had not bothered to remove his flat-crowned black hat, nor did he look as if he intended to wait long for Reynolds to join him.

"Excuse me, ladies. I shall speak to my overseer, McCarthy, and return shortly." Reynolds pushed back his chair before the hovering servant could assist him. He stepped out into the hallway, closing the door behind him.

"I believe he hinted to you that he needs a permanent hostess—" Mildred began but was shushed by Dani who held up her hand and stared intently at the closed door. She strained to hear the men's words as Mildred stared at her, unused to her commanding tone.

The men's words were muffled but audible. ". . . having some trouble down at the rock house. The one you sent down a couple weeks ago."

She heard Reynolds whisper but could not make out his words.

"Yeah, him," McCarthy said.

Reynolds whispered again and then McCarthy's footsteps echoed along the hall again.

The door swung open and Constantine Reynolds entered. His mud-brown eyes burned with fury that was quickly suppressed when he glanced at the two women. He walked to Dani's side and pulled back her chair while the servant moved to assist Mildred.

"Ladies, I'm afraid you must excuse me. A minor problem has arisen that needs my immediate attention. I will return in little over an hour, and it would please me greatly if you would use the time to rest until I return. Thomas here will show you to a guest room."

"Why, how considerate of you, Constantine," Mildred chirped. "I'm certainly ready for a nap after that delicious meal, aren't you, Dani?"

"It's a wonderful idea," Dani added, thankful to be relieved of his presence for an hour. She remembered to smile as he excused himself and left the room.

The slave led them up the winding staircase to the upper

floor where they were given a room decorated in cool green and white. As soon as the door closed behind him, Dani walked to the window and opened the shutters. She caught sight of Reynolds and his hired man bent close to the necks of their mounts as they rode off toward the northeast.

"The room will stay cooler if you keep the shutters closed," Mildred reminded her before she stretched out on the bed, ready to sleep away the hour.

"Mildred," Dani said, turning to face her friend, trying not to appear too anxious to leave, "I'm not tired at all. In fact, I need a little fresh air. I'm going to walk through the gardens, if you don't mind me leaving you alone?"

"Not at all. As long as you don't mind if I remain here. This bed feels heavenly and I'm afraid I'm too full of food to move."

"Well, then, I'll see you later." Dani wished the older woman good sleep and stepped out into the hallway. Silently she slipped along the corridor, then paused and listened, but heard nothing. With a stealth born of long hours of tracking, Dani crept down the wide, curving staircase and made her way across the polished stone floor of the entryway. Staying close to the outside wall of the house, she slipped along the veranda to a path that led toward the expansive gardens behind the house.

She stood still for a moment when she suddenly heard the sound of gently falling water. It seemed to be coming from behind the high wall that surrounded a small cottage in the middle of the formal gardens. Dani moved off of the graveled path to walk in the soft grass along its edge so as to keep her footsteps silent. A tall, weather-worn wooden gate that had once been painted green stood open just wide enough for Dani to catch a glimpse of a small, sparkling fountain in the center of a quiet garden.

She pushed the gate open far enough to see fully what was hidden behind the wall.

Chapter Twenty-four

Dani was not prepared for the sight that met her eyes.

The garden was alive with flowers of every color imaginable. Crowded one upon the other, the plants seemed to thrive in the small space within the high walls. From where she stood in the open gateway, Dani could just see the corner of a small cottage. The sight of a slender woman seated upon a stone bench near the fountain drew her attention. Her back was turned to Dani, her head bent forward, as if she was reading or staring at the ground.

"Excuse me . . ." Dani spoke softly as she walked slowly toward the woman draped in emerald green silk.

Startled amazement showed on the woman's face as she turned at the sound of Dani's voice. Her hand went to her throat in a gesture of surprise, and she returned Dani's wide-eyed stare. Her skin was of the purest ivory, her hair a warm chocolate brown, the same color as her eyes.

Rimmed with lush mink lashes, her eyes arrested Dani's gaze and held it as the two women stared at each other. Dani ceased to breathe for a moment as she tried to recall the name of the woman in the garden, for surely she knew her. Somewhere she had seen this woman before.

"I'm sorry if I'm bothering you, but . . ."

Dani stopped, unable to say more. The feeling that she knew this woman haunted her. The woman's eyes had looked down at her once . . . *from the portrait in Troy's study!*

Dani stepped forward tentatively, afraid of frightening her

away. Afraid that if she moved forward too quickly the
dark-eyed woman would bolt like a frightened doe.

"Are you Jeanette Fontaine?"

The woman's face drained of all color, the ivory skin
becoming deathly white. The hand at her throat dropped to
clutch at the edge of the stone bench as if she feared she might
topple to the ground.

"You *are* Jeanette Fontaine, aren't you?" Dani's heart began
to pound with excitement. She crossed the space that still
separated them and knelt before the bench, taking the woman's
ice-cold hands into her own warm ones. The hands felt lifeless,
unprotesting, as Dani rubbed them without thinking. The dark
brown eyes showed intense fear. They darted to the open gate
and then back to Dani.

"Go away." It was a harsh whisper.

"Have you seen Troy?"

Dazed, the woman stared at Dani. "Troy?"

"Yes. Troy came to find Reynolds. And you. Did Reynolds
kill your husband?"

The woman's expression mirrored shock at the blunt questions. She blinked and then looked away. "You ask too many
questions. Go away."

Dani clutched the hands tighter and tried to shake the woman
out of her benumbed state. "I have to ask questions. Troy's life
may be in danger."

The woman stood, and Dani released her hands. She walked
away from the bench, moving like a shadow toward the
fountain. Her eyes were vacant.

"It's been more than seventeen years."

Dani strained to hear the words. She rose and moved to stand
behind Jeanette Fontaine. The woman was at least four inches
shorter than Dani, who was trying to imagine how such a tiny
woman had produced a son like Troy. Glancing toward the
open gate, she surmised quickly that the woman was not a
prisoner.

"Why didn't you go home?" Dani asked.

"Home?"

"To Isle de Fontaine."

The silk rustled against the gravel path that surrounded the
fountain as the woman turned to face Dani again.

"Jeanette Fontaine is dead. I am not Jeanette Fontaine."

"Yes. Yes, you are, as sure as dogs have tails you are!" Dani was suddenly angry to think that Troy might have risked his life for a woman who cared nothing for him. "How could you leave Troy thinkin' all these years that you had died, too? Or worse yet, wondering if you had run off and left him? Did you know he found his father's body hangin' in the barn when he was no bigger'n a bean sprout?"

The woman covered her face with her hands. "God, no!"

"God, yes." Dani peeled Jeanette's hands away from her face and held them tight by the wrists. "Yes, he did. And he's suffered all along, wondering where you were, thinkin' you might have died with your husband. He came here because he was certain Constantine Reynolds was the murderer." She dropped Jeanette's arms when the woman winced at the force of Dani's hold. Angry enough to strike Troy's mother for seeming so insensitive to her son's plight, Dani stepped back. She stood silent as her anger cooled and turned to sorrow. "Now he may be dead."

"My son," Jeanette whispered.

Dani brushed at the tear that slid down her own cheek and let anger rid her of her weakness.

"Yes, your son!" Unable to contain her fury, Dani reached out and shook the woman by the shoulders. "Tell me what you know about Constantine Reynolds and what you're doing here. I have to get back to the house before he returns." Dani released Jeanette and dropped her hands.

"Please . . ." Jeanette looked away, staring at the ground. "It's so hard."

"Lady, I don't have *time*."

"Tell me who you are. What are you to my son?"

"I love him. And I'm sick with worry about him. And I'm running out of patience. My name is Dani Fisher, but I go by the name of Dani Whittaker now—the widow Whittaker."

Jeanette rubbed her forehead with the fingertips of one hand and sighed. She walked to the stone bench and sank down upon it. Dani sat beside her, straining to hear her words.

"Before I married . . . Merle, I was engaged to Constantine. I ran away with Troy's father, disgracing Reynolds by leaving him just days before we were to be wed. Constantine left Louisiana and traveled on the Continent. He moved to France and married a countess. She died, or so he said, and he conveniently inherited her fortune. It had been more than twelve years since I'd seen him. He returned to New Orleans and began to move in our circle of acquaintances.

"My husband gambled. It was a sickness with him. He lost money to Reynolds, and I know now it was because Constantine cheated in order to strip Merle of his land, his home, his slaves. In some twisted corner of his mind, the man thought he could win my love again if Merle lost everything."

Jeanette looked even paler now, and Dani feared the woman was about to faint. Even so, she pressed her for more details.

"What happened then?"

"We traveled to New Orleans to attend the theater and then a party at a friend's home. Constantine was present, of course, and he cornered me in the garden. He told me I could have everything I had ever dreamed of if only I would leave Merle and my son and go with him. I refused, and he became incensed."

Her eyes were focused somewhere in the distance as if she were seeing the entire scene again.

"That night Merle drank heavily and lost heavily. He even gambled away the servants and livery we'd used to drive to the affair. Constantine offered us a ride to the town house we had rented and I tried to decline, for Merle had no notion of how much Constantine wanted me. He was obsessed."

"And you never made it to the town house?" Dani surmised.

Jeanette shook her head. "No," she whispered. "Constantine took us to an abandoned mill and held us there for two weeks. During that time I was not allowed to see or talk to Merle."

"That's when he asked Leial for money, but she couldn't raise enough in time?"

The woman shuddered and nodded. "Yes. Then he took Merle away. I never saw him again."

"How did you get here?"

"Reynolds took me to Jamaica first. I refused to become his wife. Nor would I agree to be his mistress. I fought him with every ounce of my strength."

From what Dani could see, that was not much.

"He's quite mad, you know," Jeanette said. "No one even suspects."

Dani shook her head. "He seems so normal."

Showing the first indication of anger, Jeanette turned and stared into Dani's eyes. "He's not. He is the devil incarnate.

You ask me why I never returned to Troy? Because in Jamaica, Constantine gave me over to a whorehouse madam with instructions that I was to experience every form of perversion. I spent a year as a captive there, and during that time my soul died." She no longer met Dani's eyes. "I was so filthy, so tainted, by what I'd been forced to do that my son was better off thinking me dead."

"Reynolds came back for you?"

Jeanette nodded. "At the end of the year he returned and asked if I would prefer life as his mistress to life in the whorehouse. I chose Reynolds and gave up all hope of going home again. There was no longer any reason to escape."

Dani tried to show understanding, still unaware of the perversions the woman had endured.

"You might wonder why I did not kill myself."

"No, I—"

"Because of my faith," Jeanette explained. "My only hope of salvation is in the next life. I will not give that up, even to escape Reynolds."

The fountain continued to splash and play before them. Dani watched a brightly colored bird light on the rim of the lowest tier and dip its head for a drink. It spread its brilliant red wings and sailed effortlessly over the garden wall.

"Now I have told you my story." Troy's mother turned and grasped Dani's hands. The brown eyes pleaded for understanding. "I have not seen my son here. So please go. When you find him, never tell him about me."

"I can't leave you here," Dani protested.

"Yes. This is my home. Not the other. Not the island in the bayou."

The woman's hopelessness was so deep, so all-consuming that Dani wanted to hold Jeanette Fontaine close and comfort her. She could not leave Troy's mother here.

"I'll be back," Dani whispered. She drew away from the woman in emerald. As she crossed the fragrant garden, she heard a single whispered word.

"No!"

"You could have knocked me over with a feather when I found out Troy's mother was alive. Think on it, Leze. She's been here all this time."

The big man shook his head in wonderment.

"That's my story. Now, what did you find out?"

Dani sat beside Hercules on the low stone wall that protected Mildred's vegetables and fruits from the island pigs, which ran wild and raided gardens and cane fields. The opportunity for them to talk alone had not come until Mildred retired for the night. Once she began snoring softly, Dani had escaped the house and met Hercules near the wall. They were seated beyond a stand of banana trees that hid them from view. The breeze had died away that afternoon, leaving the island sweltering in the close, humid heat.

Dani lifted her long black skirt up to her knees and fanned it open and closed in an effort to cool off. She left it bunched at mid-thigh and swung her legs as she talked to her companion.

"Reynolds? He's a bad one," Hercules said. "The slaves wouldn't talk much, but the cook, she's an uppity woman if I ever saw one and jes' so's she could act like she weren't afraid o' him, why, she be talkin' plenty. All's I had to do was smile big and let her touch my hair." He turned toward Dani in the darkness, patting the ends of his natural halo. "You think I should cut my hair, Miz Dani?"

"I think I'm gonna take it off personally with my buffalo knife if you don't stick to the story. What did you find out?"

"Seems Reynolds got a hate streak in him a mile long, but it don' always show. That's what's got 'em all scared o' the man. One minute he might be talkin' jes' as smooth as you please, an' the nex', why, he off beatin' the life outta one of his slaves. His meanness jes' sneak up on him like a snake. The women are all afraid of him. Seems like he likes it pretty rough."

"What?"

"I say, 'Seems like he likes *it* pretty rough.' "

Dani swatted at his shoulder. "I know what you said. I meant, *what* does he like pretty rough?"

He turned slowly from the waist to face her, trying to read her expression in the darkness.

"Never mind."

It was an answer she could not accept. "He likes *what* pretty rough?"

Hercules squirmed where he sat and ducked his head. Although he mumbled the word, Dani was able to hear it. "Lovemakin'."

"Poor Jeanette," she whispered.

"An' he likes it with men, too."

"Men? How—"

He cut her off before she could ask more. "I ain't gettin' into *that*. No, sir. No, ma'am. No way I be tellin' you all this. You bes' ask somebody else."

Dani set her curiosity aside and asked the one question hanging over her heart. "Do you think Troy's still alive?"

"He jes'-got to be, Miz Dani. Seems Reynolds got slave camps all over the property. He even got one particular place that's like a prison, jes' for the bad ones dat try to run away." He leaned close, as if sharing a deep secret. "The cook say she hear they be some white slaves there, too, but she never seen any."

Dani hopped off of the wall and started pacing up and down as she tried to formulate a plan.

"That's where we're going. The prison. Where is it?"

"I don' know, but it's made o' stone, with no windows, only a door."

"The rock house."

She'd overheard the words during the hurried conversation between Reynolds and his overseer, McCarthy.

"We have to go tomorrow night," she decided.

"Tomorrow?"

"Yep. We can't wait a day longer."

"How we jes' gonna walk in there and walk out with Mr. Troy? *If* he there?"

"How? I don't know how. I'm still thinkin' on it, but one thing's sure. I can't go out huntin' for Troy in this"— she raised her skirt again—"and I'd roast alive in my buckskins. You'll have to go into town tomorrow and get me some pants and a shirt. Something dark, if you can. Have you got anything left of that money I gave you?"

"Yes'm. I hid it out behind the servants' cabin."

"Use it," she instructed, "and get us somethin' to ride. I'll meet you out here tomorrow night as soon as Mildred's asleep."

As nervous as a treed coon, Dani spent the day checking and rechecking her pistols, shot bag, and medicine pouch. The rifles she'd carefully wrapped in hide and brought from Louisiana needed to be oiled, a task she was forced to hide from Mildred.

Hercules disappeared, leaving for Lower Town at sunrise. She was anxious to talk with him again, but knew that he would meet her at the appointed time, so she tried to calm the jumpy sensation in her stomach.

Finally, the sky began to change from brilliant blue to flaming oranges and golds, then pinks and twilight violets. Darkness crept over the island and Mildred finally crept off to bed. Dani cut the ermine lining out of her high moccasins, put them on, and slipped her sheathed knife down inside the right boot. The long black dress hid the moccasins completely. Next she drew pouches of shot and powder over her shoulder, picked up her weapons, and soundlessly left the room.

Hercules was waiting behind the banana trees.

"Where are the horses?" She glanced over the wall toward the jungle growth beyond Mildred's carefully cultivated garden.

"Ain't no horses."

"What?" She grabbed the bundle of clothing he handed her in exchange for the guns. She shook out the clothes and held up a pair of short cotton trousers. They were dark blue and blended well with the darkness. Dani stepped into the pants, pulled them up under her skirt, and tied them at the waist. They were far too large, but she cinched the waistband as tight as she could. "If we don't have horses, what do we have?"

When Hercules saw that she intended to take off her dress right before his eyes, he turned around.

"We got mules," he said.

"Mules."

"Two of 'em."

"Might I ask"—she used Leial's most haughty tone—"where they are?"

"Back a ways behind that thick growth there. I found a path through the woods and left 'em out of sight."

"Why are you talkin' to those trees? You lost your mind?"

"Is you dressed?"

"Yep."

He turned around as she balled the hated black dress into a wad and hid it on the other side of the wall. The loosely woven white shirt was large enough for two of her. Dani gathered the hem and quickly tied it into a knot at her waist.

"Let's go."

* * *

They miscalculated the time it would take them to travel across the island on two stubborn mules, negotiating the road in the darkness while trying to avoid being seen. Finally, irritable and sore from riding bareback, they reached the edge of Reynolds's plantation.

"Let's ride past the main house and circle around. That should put us above the slave quarters." Dani pointed to a dark silhouette against the night sky. "From the top of that ridge we'll be able to see for miles and get the lay of the land. We should be there before dawn."

"Doesn't soun' so easy."

"This isn't a pleasure trip," she reminded him.

Working their way through the canebrake was no easy task. The humidity was as heavy as a thick cloak. The fields were alive with mosquitoes that seemed to take pleasure in Dani's thick mountain blood.

The dense foliage forced them to leave the mules tied at the bottom of the ridge. As they began to climb up through the tangled undergrowth, Dani was thankful that they were not forced to battle mud. As it was, the ground was damp and slippery, and in many spots the slick soles of her moccasins caused her to lose her footing.

"Damn," she muttered under her breath as her foot slipped. They were working their way up a steep deer trail, the narrow path barely discernible in the dark. Twisted vines hung from the dense growth that clung to the side of the hill, and far overhead in the branches of the trees, wild parrots, disturbed by their passing, screeched their warnings.

"We're almost there." Trying to encourage Hercules, she spoke to him in a hushed voice from her position in the lead. She was using her hands now to help propel herself up the steep ascent.

Once they reached the top of the ridge, they threw themselves on the ground and gasped for air. The sun was just beginning to light the dawn sky. They heard a mountain stream flowing downhill in the nearby undergrowth and decided to remain where they were.

"It must be the heat," she declared. "I never had so much trouble climbin' before."

Hercules stared at her in the darkness and started to laugh.

"What's so funny?"

"Look at your legs. They as black as mine."

She looked down. Mud covered her legs from knee to ankle.

"That's not a bad idea." She sat up straight and scooped up a handful of the soft, moist earth. She rubbed her hands together and then spread the mud over her forearms, hands, face, and neck. "Now I won't be so easy to see against the trees and the mountainside."

They watched from the ridge as the plantation came to life. Male workers left for the fields at sunup while the women tended the small gardens behind the cabins. The grouping of buildings reminded Dani of a small village with its blacksmith, mill, and outbuildings. She recognized Reynolds's man, McCarthy, by the high-stepping horse he rode, as well as by his black hat and riding crop.

"That's the one we want to watch." She pointed the overseer out to Hercules. "Be sure to see which way he goes."

There was no sign of Reynolds until later in the day. Dani saw the sunlight wink against the silver streaks in his hair as he stepped out of the main house and walked through the gardens toward Jeanette's cottage. She nudged Hercules and pointed again. Reynolds entered the cottage, but did not walk out for at least an hour.

They took turns resting after midday. The strain of constant vigilance as well as the heat exhausted them quickly. There was no sign of McCarthy for the rest of the afternoon, but they had noted the direction he had taken, and they planned to explore the trail as soon as darkness returned.

"I'm starving," Dani finally admitted as they watched the sun set behind the mountain.

"That's why I brought some vittles with me," Hercules said, pulling an oilcloth bag from around his neck.

"Just when were you planning to eat?" she wanted to know.

"Look!" He pointed to McCarthy who was returning to the slave quarters. After riding back from the same direction he'd taken at dawn, he dismounted and walked to the main house.

"He came from that ravine. That's the first place we're headed," Dani told Hercules.

"I shoulda known it wouldn't be close."

Chapter Twenty-five

Troy stared at the tiny barred opening, the only window in the stone building that was his prison. He tried to focus, but when the small square high in the door blurred he closed his eyes. He couldn't remember when he'd eaten last, but his stomach told him it had been far too long ago.

The man beside him, a habitual runaway named Raymond, rolled in his sleep. The movement tugged on the chain that linked the two men together at the ankles. Troy fought against crying out as pain seared his leg from ankle to groin. He rolled to his side rather than resist the pull of the chain against his injured ankle.

It was impossible to see in the pitch darkness, but he knew his ankle was swollen as far as the iron around his leg would allow. Before his foot went numb, Troy had felt blood seeping from the wound he'd suffered three days ago when he slipped on the way down the mountainside. Unable to hide the injury for more than a day, Troy had been left behind in the "rock house" instead of being taken up the hill to work.

"You don't work, you don't eat"—that was McCarthy's motto. It had been two days since he'd been allowed any of the slop they called food. Troy knew that without nourishment he would become too weak to fight off the infection settling in his leg.

It was raining again. He longed to step outside and throw his head back to drink of it. He was filthy. What he wouldn't give for a chance to swim in an icy mountain stream. He knew he would be content with a bucket of water that wasn't green with algae.

Pain shot along the inner length of his leg and up to his groin. Dizziness swept over him accompanied by a wave of nausea that made him retch. His empty stomach contracted and then quieted. He began to shiver and wrapped his arms about his bare upper body, then tried to still his chattering teeth.

Suddenly the image of Dani stood before him. He saw her clearly, dressed in the pure white doeskin dress, her hair tied up with feathers and beads. She held out her arms and smiled, tempting him, teasing him, offering him all of her love.

"I'll keep you warm . . ."

Troy thought he heard her say the words and reached out into the darkness.

He grasped nothing.

He rolled to his back and lay flat upon the cold stone floor. Somewhere in a lucid corner of his mind he knew that he was hallucinating, but even a vision of Dani was far better than having none of her at all.

There was nothing of her left to him now. When they stripped him of his clothing, they had taken away the only tangible reminder of her—the sky-blue ribbon he had stolen from her room the night he left home.

Where was Dani? he wondered. Where was the warm, caring, laughing girl who had invaded his heart with her candor and undisguised love? Would she be waiting for him on Isle de Fontaine, or had she already gone back to the mountains she held so dear? He fought against the despair that threatened to choke the life from him. The thought that he might live to see her again was all that had kept him one step away from madness. That thought had kept him alive through beatings, starvation, and excruciating pain.

He wondered when Reynolds would finally tire of the game and have him killed. Troy had given up blaming himself for walking into a trap, since regret served no purpose. It only plunged him deeper into self-pity.

Troy smiled into the darkness.

He smiled at the dream version of Dani and then laughed out loud in the darkness. It was a harsh, rasping sound that might have been mistaken for a sob.

It took Dani and Hercules two hours to work their way around the ridge. Below them, a river wound its way through the valley, creating a deep crease in the land. If there was a building in the ravine, it was invisible in the growing darkness. They climbed down and found the vegetation so thick along the river that Hercules used Dani's long knife to hack a path through the vines and tangled undergrowth. Wild cane had taken root in many places, creating a nearly impenetrable barrier that had to be skirted.

As they worked their way along, Dani stayed well behind Hercules, her eyes and ears alert to every sound. They had to find the rock house before McCarthy returned at daybreak.

What if we're nowhere near it?

Dani pushed the thought from her mind. They would look elsewhere, she told herself. Search until they found Troy. She refused to give up after coming so far.

Hercules stopped abruptly. Because she was staring at the ground, fighting to see the path, she ran headlong into his back.

"Damn!"

"Don't swear, Miz Dani."

"You big oaf, I just about killed myself. You're harder than a tree trunk." She tried shoving him aside, but he wouldn't budge.

"Do you see anythin' up there?" He squinted into the darkness.

"Where?"

"There." He pointed through the trees to a small clearing beside the river dead ahead of them. A low fire, no more than glowing embers, illuminated a rock structure in the clearing.

"That's it!" Dani whispered excitedly. She pounded a fist on Hercules's shoulder as the two crouched and stared ahead. "That's the rock house!"

"They mus' be pretty sure no one can escape that place. Only lef' two guards, and one's asleep."

Dani strained to see the men sitting against the wall of the building. They were obviously Reynolds's slaves, but they were trusted with weapons, for they cradled rifles in their arms. One was asleep, his head drooping against his chest. The other stared out into the night.

Dani gave Hercules a silent signal to circle around to the left of the building while she went to the right. She kept herself low to the ground and slowly worked her way through the dense jungle until she was behind the right wall of the building.

Silently, barely daring to breathe, Dani crept up on the

sleeping guard. She eased the pistol from her waistband and raised it high, butt end forward, over the man's skull.

As she swung downward with all her strength, aiming to knock the guard cold, he leaned forward and stood. Dani found herself swinging at dead air, pulled forward by the force of the intended blow.

Alert to the commotion, the guard swung around, his eyes wide in the darkness. Unsure of the weapon in his hands, he nervously fumbled, trying to sight the rifle. Dani instantly aimed her pistol at his chest.

"Stop!" she cried out.

An immense shadow appeared behind the guard, and before she could fire, the guard toppled forward. Hercules stood behind him holding a stout length of wood.

"Thanks."

"The one I hit first didn't have no key on him."

Dani bent and quickly searched the guard who'd fallen at her feet. Nothing. She checked to see if there was a key about his neck or in his pockets, but was unrewarded. She stood and shook her head to let Hercules know her search had proved unsuccessful. They hurried to the door of the prison Reynolds's cook had told Hercules about.

"What if he's not in there?" she asked.

Hercules, suddenly wary of uncaging whatever lived behind the iron-trimmed wooden door, paused for a moment and looked down at her.

"Only one way to find out."

He stepped up to the high window and pressed his face against the bars. The hole was no bigger than a man's face. Hercules's hoarse whisper sounded as loud as a shout in the still jungle night.

"Mr. Troy, you in there?"

The only sound that issued from within was the metallic chink and rattle of chains. A man groaned. Dani tried shoving Hercules aside, but he wouldn't budge. Even on tiptoe she could not see through the window.

"Mr. Troy?"

Troy covered his ears with his hands, shutting out the whispered words. His mind was gone, he was sure of it now. There was not a chance in hell that his friend was standing outside the door.

I'm insane.

He was too weak to raise his head off of the floor and drag himself to a sitting position. His entire right leg was throbbing now, an incessant pain that kept time with his heartbeat.

"Mr. Troy Fontaine!"

His hands could not shut out the hollow pounding on the door. Troy tried again to sit up but his limbs would not obey.

"Leze?" He spoke, but no sound issued from between his cracked lips. He cleared his throat and tried again. "Leze?" Louder this time, the sound carried to the door.

"Mr. Troy!"

He heard Hercules call again and then speak hurriedly to someone outside.

"Mr. Troy, where's the key?"

The others in the cell were stirring now. Troy sensed a wariness in the men who'd been caged so long. Chains rattled against the stone as prisoners came awake, sat up, and stared at the portal.

"Stan' up, Fontaine."

Raymond was shaking him now, barely awake himself, drugged by the deep sleep of exhaustion that nightly spared the men awareness of their discomfort. He stood and pulled Troy to his feet. The pain was more than Troy could bear, and he fought to remain conscious. He shook his head and tried to step toward the door. Raymond looped Troy's arm over his bare shoulder and half dragged, half carried him to the door.

"Ain' no key," Troy heard Raymond tell Hercules. "Mc-Carthy keep it on him."

"Stan' back, then, we gonna blow the lock off."

There was more pain as Raymond dragged Troy back away from the door. They bumped against the other men who were standing in anticipation, waiting for the sound of the explosion that would set them free.

"Move out of the way and give me some room." Dani shoved at Hercules and he granted her a few inches of space between himself and the doorway. She tamped gunpowder into the lock that held the bolt secure on the door and then stepped back and took aim. The sound of the shot cracked the air and was followed by the acrid smell of gunsmoke. Hercules jumped away from the door and swung around to face her.

Dani ran forward to flick the remains of the blasted lock off the bolt.

"Dammit, Miz Dani, you near shot off m' toe!"

Ignoring him, she slid back the heavy iron bolt and clawed at the door, fighting to open it. As it swung wide, she reeled against the overpowering stench of human waste and sweat that swept out into the night air.

For a moment the men inside stood paralyzed, as if unwilling to step out of the security of their prison. Dani watched as a black man stepped forward. An equally tall man slumped against his side, his head hung forward, dark hair hiding his face. He was thinner now, dirtier, and from the looks of him, near dead.

"Troy!"

She rushed forward to grab him as the big man shackled to Troy lowered him to the ground. As Troy battled against unconsciousness and tried to raise his head, Dani felt unbidden tears begin to flow down her cheeks. She knelt, cradling his head against her thighs, smoothing back his matted hair, letting her fingertips explore his face. His eyelids fluttered and then opened. Troy focused on her for a moment, and she watched his lips twist into the crooked, endearing half-smile she knew so well.

"What took you so long?" he whispered.

The freed prisoners led Hercules to the woodpile behind the prison, where he found the hammer and chisel McCarthy used to open the chains. He released the other men first and then took his time freeing Troy without further injuring his swollen ankle. The prisoners began to scatter, some arguing among themselves before taking to the hills. Others opted to wait and turn their hatred on McCarthy when he arrived at dawn.

Dani and Hercules moved Troy a mile downriver before they stopped. Hercules carried the lighter man as easily as he might a child. They chose an area near the bank, out of sight of the prison and hidden by lush vegetation. Dani stayed with Troy, dribbling water onto his parched lips while Hercules left to fetch the mules. She rolled Troy closer to the slow-moving water in order to soak his injured ankle and foot in the river. While his foot was soaking, Dani extracted some barberry root from the medicine bag hanging at her waist and began to chew it to a fine pulp. She used the mashed root and water to wash his abrasions. Then, lacking other material, she slashed the hem of her shirt and tore off a wide swatch of its tail. Soon she had the material she needed to wrap Troy's swollen ankle. Her tasks completed for the moment, she took a long drink of the crystal water and then settled back, once more holding Troy's head in her lap.

Weary but alert, Dani leaned back against a tree trunk and closed her eyes to the surrounding darkness. She absently stroked Troy's forehead with her fingertips and then raked her fingers through his dark hair. His lips parted, and she lowered her head to catch his whispered words.

"I'm sorry for everything I've put you through, pet."

She leaned forward and pressed her lips against his for a brief kiss. His lips were warm and dry. "I wouldn't be here if I didn't want to be," she said.

"If I didn't feel so lousy, I'd be mad as hell right now."

"Don't I know it?" She smiled. "I like you helpless."

"Finally have me right where you want me?"

She kissed him tenderly, careful not to demand too much as she sought to comfort him.

"Will you marry me?" he whispered.

Her heart soared. With shaking fingertips, she smoothed his hair away from his temple and smiled down at him. "I'll answer you tomorrow, when I'm certain it's not just the fever that's got you talking about marriage."

Troy closed his eyes and slipped back into the healing sleep his body required.

Dani held Troy close and rocked him gently. She feared her heart was beating as loud as a Sioux war drum, loud enough to wake him, but still she held him close. Fever or not, Fontaine had asked her to marry him, and as soon as they saw their way clear of the mess they were in, she intended to tell him that she would.

She knew there would be rough times ahead, for Troy Fontaine was a man of many moods. Hot and cold. Light and dark. But the one undeniable truth was that she loved him, and had since the night he'd first made love to her beside the mountain stream. She'd crossed half a world to be with Troy Fontaine. There was no way she would let him go now.

Dani closed her eyes and listened to the sound of rain that the trade winds brought to the valley.

* * *

With a start, Dani straightened and earned a groan from Troy, whose head was still nestled on her thighs. The tree provided slight shelter from the constant light drizzle that had begun to fall an hour ago. It was near dawn now, or at least she thought it must be, and Dani anxiously began to scan the forest for some sign of Hercules. They needed to leave the valley and head for the main road before McCarthy rode into the ravine and found the prisoners missing. She wished she could hide and see how he made out against the freed prisoners, but Troy's safety came first.

When a twig snapped behind her, Dani pulled her rifle closer and listened intently, staring back at the twisted shadows of trees and vines. She watched through the monotonous drizzle as Hercules moved into view. He led no mules behind him.

"That took you long enough. Where are the mules?"

His expression was glum. "They got hungry. Took off, I guess. The lead mule chewed through the rope."

"You'll have to carry Troy."

"Give him over." He knelt down to lift the lighter man.

Troy roused himself and tried to sit up. "I can walk."

Dani glanced at his bandaged ankle. "And I can fly. Pick him up, Leze."

They started toward the main road, hiding amid the undergrowth. Dani took the lead this time, carrying her rifle, her pistol in her waistband, her long knife in hand. Feeling like a pack mule burdened by the weapons, shot bag, and powder horn, she slashed at the bushes that slapped at her arms and face, hacking them down without mercy to cut a path for Hercules. The rain was a constant source of irritation as it ran down her hair and into her eyes, and muddied the ground beneath her feet. She slipped more times than she could count as they traveled up the gentle incline toward the road.

Dawn slowly lightened the sky to gray, but the rain continued. As Troy's strength slowly returned, his impatient grumbling increased and he insisted on walking. Hercules refused to put him down. Finally, just about the time Dani was certain that Hercules would not be able to take another step, they saw the road ahead of them and found a place to hide beneath the thick growth alongside it. Dani reckoned they were far enough away from the prison to take another much needed rest.

"We'll stay here until late in the day and then start moving. Once we're farther along the road we can stop a carriage headed toward Scarborough." Nearly exhausted herself, she halfheartedly slapped at a mosquito and then left the men long enough to hack down a banana tree so she could reach a bunch of ripe yellow fruit.

"Here. Better fill our stomachs with these. That's all there'll be for a while." She handed some to Hercules, then sat down beside Troy and peeled one of the soft bananas for him.

"Troy?" she asked softly, afraid to rouse him, but aware that he might be listening with his eyes closed against the pain in his leg.

"I'm awake," he announced.

"Eat this." She held a banana out to him.

He raised himself, one elbow pressed against the soggy ground, and ate the fruit hungrily.

"I think that's just about the best meal you've ever made me."

"Thanks." She glanced at him from beneath lowered lashes and wondered if he remembered proposing marriage to her. Had he been delirious?

Hercules ate his bananas in silence and then wiped his mouth with the back of his hand. He stretched out unceremoniously in the dirt and crooked an arm beneath his head. Within seconds he was breathing deeply, rhythmically.

"Dani?"

"What?" She met Troy's eyes.

He reached out and took her right hand in his own. With his thumb, he rubbed the tips of her fingers before he carried them to his lips and kissed them gently.

"Thank you." His voice was gentle. It sent a chill along her spine.

Weary to the bone, she smiled down at him then wiped the rain from her forehead with the back of her arm.

"You'd best get some sleep," she advised.

"You, too."

"I'll watch awhile," Dani volunteered, drawing her knees up and crossing her arms over them.

When Dani woke next, the rain had stopped but the sky had

not yet cleared. She figured it to be near noon when the clouds parted for a moment and she got a glimpse of the sun riding nearly overhead. The burst of sunlight between the clouds turned the steaming undergrowth into a humid sweat house that sapped her strength. She shook her head to clear it and then reached out to feel Troy's forehead. It felt cooler than it had during the night, and so she let him be. Hercules snored softly.

She sat up and brushed her damp, matted hair out of her eyes, wishing she had some water to rinse out her mouth. The rough-woven blouse clung to her, outlining the contours of her breasts and nipples, the material spattered with rich island soil. She held it away from her body so that it might dry, but gave up the task when the sky darkened again with a passing cloud and the rain began to fall once more.

Dani stared at Troy who was still sleeping peacefully. She was preoccupied with a thought that had been with her ever since she had awakened: Jeanette Fontaine was still in Reynolds's house.

Earlier, as she had cleared the way through the jungle, a plan had slowly taken shape in her mind. She would make her way back to the house, slip into the cottage, and collect Jeanette Fontaine, then rejoin the men before darkness fell. It would be a simple enough task, provided she was not discovered. Her skills in hunting and tracking included hiding and stealth as well, and Dani was certain she could easily accomplish her goal.

Silently she laid the rifle next to Hercules. She slipped the powder horn and shot bag over her head and stealthily loaded and primed her pistol. She slipped the weapon back inside the waistband of her britches. The long knife was safely tucked inside her moccasin. She would take nothing else.

Dani rose to a crouch and, without so much as rustling a rain-beaded leaf, slipped away from the men and let the jungle close in around her.

Chapter Twenty-six

—→•❋•←—

The rain Dani had cursed all morning proved to be a blessing, for the usually busy grounds around Reynolds's mansion were all but deserted. Staying away from open areas, Dani worked her way close to the house by slipping alongside the buildings, taking care not to move too near the open windows. Her soft-soled moccasins made no sound as she moved toward Jeanette Fontaine's cottage.

The gate stood open as if in welcome, and Dani silently slipped inside. The garden appeared unchanged, except that today crystal rain beads hung like jewels from the leaves and flowers. Petals littered the ground beneath the bushes, the blooms scattered by the heavy morning rains.

With the stealth of a cat, she moved to the door of the cottage and tried the knob. It turned freely. She let the tall wooden door swing inward and paused to look around the quiet room before she stepped inside.

"Mrs. Fontaine?" Her whisper echoed hollowly in the large deserted sitting room.

Dani moved farther inside, pausing every few steps to glance over her shoulder. If Jeanette Fontaine was in the cottage, she had to be in the adjoining room. Dani walked directly to a second door and rapped gently upon it.

No one answered her knock.

She turned the knob and stood in the doorway, staring at Troy's mother's room.

The place was tidy and welcoming, the high bed lush with embroidered pillows and lace-edged linens. The mosquito netting was invitingly draped back on one side and for a moment Dani was tempted to lie down and rest. A window on the opposite wall looked out onto the garden with its ever flowing fountain and soft colors.

Quickly Dani turned and retraced her steps through the sitting room to the front door. She hid behind the garden gate until one of the house servants had walked by, and then she peered around it. No one else was in sight. Walking quickly, Dani moved along the garden paths to the wide veranda and scooted along the wall of the main house. She reached the kitchen and pressed her back against the wall, listening for what seemed like hours to the sounds inside. Footsteps approached the open door, and she held her breath as a middle-aged woman in a *tiyon*, much like the one Venita always wore, stepped out onto the veranda. If she turned to reenter the house the woman would be staring at Dani face to face.

But the cook stepped off the veranda and moved through the garden toward the slave cabins beyond Jeanette's cottage.

Dani crept through the open doorway and went through the kitchen. She was about to enter the dining room when she noticed a narrow stairway beside the stove. She pulled the pistol from her belt and slowly began to ascend the servants' staircase to the second floor.

There had been no sign of Reynolds. If McCarthy had lived to spread the alarm that the prisoners had been freed, Reynolds and the men were no doubt out searching for them now.

The servants' stairway led to a closed door that, once opened, revealed the upper hallway. Moving along the hall, she stopped before each door and listened for the slightest sound. Finally, at the end of the long passageway, she stood before Reynolds's room. Dani thought she heard the soft, muffled sound of a woman sobbing. She took a firm grip on her pistol and then opened the door.

Jeanette Fontaine stood at the window staring toward the rolling green hills in the distance, her shoulders shaking with the force of her sobs. One hand held a handkerchief against her lips.

"Ma'am?" Dani whispered as she moved across the room toward the figure near the window.

Jeanette whirled about at the sound, her eyes wide with alarm. "You!"

Frantically, Jeanette glanced behind Dani to the open doorway.

"I'm here to take you to Troy."

"It's too late." Tears washed down Jeanette's face, tears that she did not seem able to control.

"What do you mean?" Dani stepped closer.

Jeanette drew a deep, shuddering breath. "Constantine is having him killed today. My son was here, the prisoner of that madman."

Dani reached out to offer a gesture of comfort until she noticed her muddy hand and let it drop.

"You're wrong about that." Dani smiled. "Troy's safe; we got to him in time."

"Safe?" The woman's eyes mirrored the disbelief in her tone.

"Yep. And you are, too. Come with me."

Jeanette Fontaine shook her head, refusing to step toward the open door. "No, I told you before, I can never go back."

Dani glanced toward the open doorway. Had she heard a sound in the hallway? She was unsure, but took the precaution of lowering her voice to a whisper again. She reached out for Jeanette's wrist.

"I'm tellin' you, you're comin' *now*, even if I have to knock you out and drag you."

With a resounding echo, the door slammed shut behind Dani and she whirled about in time to see Constantine Reynolds lean against it, a sinister smile on his face.

"Isn't this a touching little scene? The widow Whittaker." He stepped toward them, one hand stroking his goatee. "Now, what brings you here?" He glanced down at Dani's bare legs and let his eyes slide up the calf-length britches until they paused on the short, sodden shirt that clung to her breasts, revealing far more than they concealed. "And in such a state of undress?"

Dani tried to stare him down.

"Might I take this as a sign of your passionate affection for me, Mrs. Whittaker?" He took another step forward.

"Stand back," Dani warned as she leveled the pistol at his heart.

He took another step.

"I'm warning you."

She took aim.

He reached out toward her, still an arm's length away.

Dani pulled the trigger.

The hammer fell and clicked. There was no flash of powder, no explosion.

The only sounds in the room were Jeanette's gasp of fear and Reynolds's silken laughter.

Dani cursed and stared at the useless weapon in her hand. Reynolds stepped close to her and reached out for the pistol. Reluctantly, she handed it to him, biding her time while she thought of ways to escape. It would not be easy if she had to drag a reluctant Jeanette Fontaine in tow, but she had no intention of leaving without her now.

"I could tell just by looking at you, Mrs. Whittaker, that your pistol was likely to be just as damp as you are. How foolish of you."

"Can't blame a girl for tryin'." Dani tried to shrug off his comment.

"Not at all. What I want to know is why?"

Dani glanced toward the open window.

"I wouldn't suggest it," he warned. "Unless you want to end up on the stone walkway below."

He was nearly standing against her now, and Dani was forced to look up into the cold brown eyes.

"Leave us, Jeanette," he ordered without looking away from Dani.

"Constantine, no! Let her go. You must not harm her!"

He continued to stare down into Dani's eyes. "Why not?"

"Please . . ." Jeanette pleaded, tugging at his sleeve.

"I only intend to find out what she wants with you."

Dani finally found her voice. "That's my business."

"And I believe that, since you are in my room, it's my business as well, Mrs. Whittaker."

A quick knock on the door made Reynolds spin around and call out, "Enter!"

A servant bowed politely and then announced that Reynolds had a caller waiting below.

"Who in the hell is it?"

"Don' know, sir. A gent'mum in a fine carriage. Nevah seen him before."

"Have him wait, Thomas. I'll be right down." Reynolds then turned to Jeanette. "Bring me the sash from my robe."

"Constantine, no!"

His eyes flamed with fury, and he swung around, slicing the back of his hand across the woman's cheek. The force of the blow nearly sent her to her knees.

"Bring it, damn you!"

His face was mottled with fury. "Sit down." Reynolds pointed to the floor, commanding Dani to lower herself onto the polished wood surface. "I don't intend to have anything else soiled."

She smiled with cold satisfaction as she noticed the muddy trail her moccasins had left on the thick, patterned carpet in the center of the room.

Jeanette handed him the black silken cord to his dressing gown and stepped back as Reynolds crouched behind Dani, jerked her arms behind her, and swiftly bound them at the wrists.

"Get back to the cottage and stay there," he warned Jeanette as he held the door open for her. "No matter what you hear."

He turned to Dani, his face again a smooth mask that hid all emotion. "Make yourself comfortable, Widow Whittaker."

Troy awoke to the raucous cries of parrots in the canopy of tree limbs overhead. He sat up slowly and stared about at the undergrowth, trying to piece together the events of the previous night. Gingerly he inspected his injury. The bandage hung loose where the swelling had decreased. He rewrapped the wound and marveled at the healing that had already taken place. Dani's handiwork, no doubt.

Hercules lay beside him, stretched out and snoring loud enough to raise the dead, but Dani was nowhere in sight. Reaching out, he shook his friend hard, for experience warned him that Hercules would not awaken easily, or cheerfully.

The big man swatted his hand away.

"Get up, Leze."

An incoherent mumble was the only greeting Troy received.

"Dani's missing," Fontaine added.

Hercules slowly pulled himself up and shook his head from side to side to clear his sleep-fogged mind. "Missin'? She ain't on watch?"

"No. And from the looks of it, she's been gone awhile."

The ground around them was slowly drying, but spongy, humid air surrounded them in the thick undergrowth beside the main road. They waited for a few minutes, but when there was no sign of her, Troy turned a worried frown to Hercules.

"Where is she?"

"If I'm thinkin' clear," Hercules began, his voice hesitant, "she went on back to Reynolds's place."

Troy looked startled. "Back? Why?"

"Jus' a notion I got," Hercules admitted somewhat vaguely. "How you feelin' today, Mr. Troy?"

"Like I'll live, thanks to Dani." His eyes searched the brush around them as his mind tried to imagine Dani facing Reynolds. Why had she gone back there?

"My ankle seems to have lost most of the swelling. The fever's gone, too."

"Can you walk?"

"I don't know yet, but if I can, it won't be far."

Hercules glanced toward the roadway that bordered Reynolds's plantation. It was late afternoon now, and there was no sign of anyone traveling in either direction.

"Mr. Troy, if you don' mind, I'm gonna try and stop the next carriage that passes by. You ain' gonna make it back to town, an' I don' think we can lose any more time gettin' to Miz Dani."

"Use the rifle if you have to. No one is going to politely stop for us, looking the way we do." Troy glanced down at his ragged pants and shirtless, muddied torso. He tried to slick his hair back with his fingers, but the tangled mass wouldn't move. Worry began to fester in him worse than his wound. If anything happened to Dani, Troy knew he'd never be able to live with the guilt.

"The next carriage that comes along this here road is gonna stop." Hercules patted Dani's long rifle. "I'll see t' that."

They turned to face the lonely stretch of road, and Troy began to pray silently that the wait would not be a long one.

"Don't tell me you don't appreciate my hospitality?"

Dani froze where she stood. Having worked her way to a standing position, she had just reached for her long knife when Reynolds reentered the room. Hastily, she straightened and wiped all expression from her face, silently admonishing herself a second time for not listening more intently for his footsteps. If he suspected that she had a knife, he gave no indication of it.

Once again she found herself the object of his curiosity.

"Now I suggest you tell me what is going on. Why are you here? What do you want with my mistress?"

She raised her chin defiantly and gave him her best squint-eyed stare.

"Just out for a stroll?" He reached for her left breast, outlined beneath her damp garb, and grasped her nipple.

Dani gasped in pain but refused to cry out as his fingers pinched the sensitive bud. Tiring of his game, Reynolds let go and then raised his hand, bringing it down with ringing force against her cheek and mouth.

"Tell me!" he thundered.

Dani reeled with the force of his abuse and felt blood stream from her lower lip. She was not afraid to meet his stare with one of her own as she slowly licked the blood away. His eyes were riveted on her tongue. She sensed a new tension in him that had not been there before. His breathing was faster and shallower now.

"You liked that, didn't you?" she taunted. "Causing pain makes you feel like a man." She was afraid. So afraid she knew he would see her heart pounding if he chose to look, but she continued to hold his eyes with her own. "But you aren't a man, Reynolds. You aren't even fit to be called an animal."

This time when he raised his arm, he backhanded her across the other side of her face.

Dani was ready for the blow and moved with it, her knees absorbing much of the shock as she swayed to the right.

"How dare you?" he whispered.

Her answer was brazen. She had to keep him arguing until she found a way to escape. "I know what I see."

"Did you hear the carriage that left moments ago? Perhaps you might care to know that the gentleman who called on me was a friend of yours. At least he claimed to be. He was inquiring as to your whereabouts."

She knew that Reynolds would easily recognize Troy and would never let him drive away. Besides, as far as she knew, he and Hercules were still waiting beside the road. Who was the man asking for her?

"I see your mind turning as you search for an answer, Widow Whittaker. Do you recognize the name Grady Maddox?"

"Grady?" she whispered.

"Another scorned suitor, perhaps? I see the mention of his name startles you."

Dani refused to give in to his questioning. Let him guess. Perhaps Grady would come back.

"It seems," Reynolds volunteered, "that he arrived on Tobago at dawn. He surprised your hostess, the plump and ever smiling Miss Howath. She was alarmed to discover you missing and suggested he look here. Why? Is your passion for me so great that the entire island knows of it, Danika?"

Reynolds grasped her chin between his thumb and forefinger and forced her to meet his gaze.

"I will have the answers from you, one way or another. But before we get to know each other more intimately, I would like you to bathe. You see, despite what you believe to be my origins, I do not relish touching a woman who's as muddied as a wild pig. I'm sending a servant up with water."

"Don't bother."

"You may bathe yourself, Danika, or I will have someone do it for you."

"Some choice."

"We'll see how sharp your tongue is later." He grabbed her bound wrists and pulled her toward the bed. Quickly untying her bonds, he secured her anew to the bedpost.

The knife was out of reach, but still in her moccasin. She intended to use it.

When he reached the bedroom door, Reynolds paused, one hand on the knob. He smiled at her again with the cold, malicious smile of a snake about to strike. "Until later, Danika."

As she heard the sound of a key turning in the lock, Dani let her shoulders slump and then leaned heavily against the bedpost. She ran her tongue over her swollen lower lip and blinked back tears as she stared up at the ceiling.

Gaining strength by the moment, Troy Fontaine sat awkwardly crouched in the bushes awaiting the approach of a carriage bound for Scarborough. Hercules stood beyond him, planning to step out before the driver could turn the vehicle around at the first sign of trouble.

The black, covered vehicle drew ever nearer, and Troy knew a moment of concern for his servant and friend as the big man made his presence known. A black man carrying a gun on

Tobago would more than likely be shot first and questioned later. Troy held his breath as Hercules tried to shout above the sound of carriage wheels and horses' hooves.

"Stop your carriage an' throw down your gun."

Troy heard the carriage stop and could no longer leave Hercules to his own fate. Pulling himself up to a standing position, Fontaine stiffly tried to walk out to join his friend on the road when he heard Hercules's deep voice cry out in recognition.

"Mr. Grady? Is it really you?"

Troy struggled forward and winced at the sharp pain that tore at his ankle. He slowed his pace and watched as Grady swung himself down from the driver's box on the high-slung carriage and began to race toward him.

"My God, Troy! What happened?"

"What are you doing here?" Troy asked, shaking his head as Grady slipped a supporting arm beneath his friend's.

"Watch his leg," Hercules warned as Grady led Troy to the carriage.

"I came looking for Dani. Did you know she followed you?" Grady glanced at Hercules. "I guess you must."

Troy tried to save time by explaining briefly. "She found me. Saved my life, too. But right now, we don't know where she is for certain. Leze thinks she went back to Reynolds's house."

Grady tried to help Troy into the carriage but only succeeded in bumping against the injured ankle and earning a muffled curse from his companion. Hercules took over and easily lifted Troy up into the carriage seat.

"I was just there asking about her. Reynolds told me he hadn't seen her, but now that I think back on it, he seemed highly anxious for me to leave."

"What's she up to?" Troy mused.

"She went back for somethin'," Hercules volunteered.

Troy shook his head, visibly angered. "What in hell's name would she go back for? I hope to God she didn't take a notion to finish what I started."

"I can't say for certain what it was she went back for," Hercules said evasively, "but I know she's there."

Grady voiced his decision. "Then we must go back."

"You'll have to hide us in the carriage or you'll never get up the drive." Troy gingerly lowered himself to the carriage floor.

"I'll go back in and say I lost something," Grady began. "I'll say, 'Hello, Reynolds, sorry to bother you, but—"

"Just drive, Grady. And try not to carry us off the road," Troy warned with impatience.

Grady climbed up on the driver's seat and picked up the reins while Hercules climbed inside with Troy. The two of them tried to flatten themselves against the floor.

A frightened female slave accompanied by three burly men who made better guards than water bearers had warned Dani that she was to bathe or the men would see to it that she did. Dani had complied on the condition that they all turn their backs. Hastily, she had stripped off the moccasins, leaving the knife hidden inside one of them, and laid them atop her muddied clothes. She had set the pile aside, hoping the woman would overlook it when she tidied up the room.

Clean now, her hair damp but neatly combed, Dani wore Reynolds's black silk robe as she awaited his return. The servants used the sash to bind her hands to the bedpost again and then, accustomed to obeying orders, left Dani's clothing alone after she curtly warned them not to touch it.

When Reynolds reentered the room, Dani was hard-pressed not to stare at the moccasins.

"This is much more to my liking," Reynolds admitted, openly admiring the exposed flesh beneath the gaping front of the silken robe.

She accurately read the menace in his eyes. "Keep away from me."

"You invited yourself into my bedroom. Now tell me why."

Dani took a deep breath, stealing herself against the hideous feel of his moist palm as he reached beneath the robe to stroke the underside of her breast. She shuddered in disgust and relied upon shocking him to stay his hand.

"I came for Jeanette Fontaine."

His face paled visibly. "How do you know her name?"

"I'm in love with her son."

Unexpectedly, Reynolds threw back his head and laughed heartily. Just as suddenly, he was deathly quiet. He leaned so close to Dani that she could feel his hot breath on her face as he rasped out his next words. There was no flicker of life behind his eyes.

"Please accept my deepest condolences. He's dead."

She smiled and knew a sense of heady triumph. "I hate to be the one to tell you this, but he's not."

"I can't believe you," he said coolly.

"Would you if I told you I've seen the rock house prison in the valley over the hill? Would you believe it if I told you the two stupid guards your man left there were easily disarmed and all the prisoners have escaped, including Troy? If you're real lucky, Reynolds, they aren't on their way here to give you a taste of your own hospitality."

"It's all a lie. McCarthy would have come back to tell me of the escape."

"Not if they killed him."

His fists clenched as he tried to contain his rage. Dani watched the skin above his collar redden, saw the stain spread upward until it reached his hairline. Suddenly his temper cooled, his eyes cleared, and his lips set in a taut line. His fingers relaxed.

Constantine Reynolds reached out and untied her. He curled his hand tightly around her left wrist, his fingers cutting into her skin. "Get on the bed," he commanded.

Dani glanced toward her moccasins. "There's no way in hell—"

"I'll bring hell to your very doorstep, Danika. I'll show you its flames. You'll beg me to kill you before I'm through."

She glanced down, trying not to alert him to the fact that a weapon was hidden not halfway across the room. Her eyes widened when she saw his engorged member pressing against the front of his white linen britches. Dani began to back toward the bed, hoping to put distance between them. She had to stay alert, had to think of a way to get to her knife.

When the backs of her legs came in contact with the edge of the bed she nearly cried out.

Reynolds reached out with his free hand to further open the front of the robe. He licked at the corner of his lips and stepped forward, grasping her waist with his free hand. He pulled Dani to him, fighting to press her hips against his own.

She tried to twist away, jerking at the hand that held her wrist with fingers that gripped like iron bands.

For a moment, as Reynolds released the hand he held pressed against her hip, Dani thought she might break free. It was then he shoved with all the force he could muster and threw her onto the crimson bedcover.

Chapter Twenty-seven

"Dani?"

She thought she heard someone call her name. Struggling valiantly against Reynolds's greater strength, fighting his hands as they grasped her tender flesh, she was unable to respond to the call. When she sought to roll away from Reynolds as he pressed her down against the bedclothes, she heard the voice again. Closer, clearer, a man called out.

"Dani!"

This time Dani was certain. Someone was searching the house for her. She tried to butt her head against Reynolds's and succeeded in ramming her forehead into his teeth. For a moment, she was stunned. When Reynolds reared back, roaring in pain and rage, his hand pressed against his bleeding lip, Dani managed to escape his hold.

"Here!" she shouted toward the door as she scrambled off the bed. "I'm in here!"

When she reached her moccasins, Dani pulled out the buffalo knife. Reynolds started toward her. On the opposite side of the room, the bedroom door swung open and crashed against the wall.

A solid two hundred pounds of Grady Maddox stood framed in the doorway.

Constantine Reynolds turned toward the intruder. Lifting a heavy cloisonné vase off the table, Reynolds charged the man in the doorway.

Dani pulled the gaping robe closed with one hand while she

brandished the knife with the other. "Look out, Grady!" she screamed.

"Don't worry," Grady smiled back with almost boyish gaiety. "I brought Fontaine's Fighting Forty with me."

The smiling blond man then made the mistake of trying to outmaneuver his lighter, quicker adversary. Just as Reynolds swung the vase above his head, Grady stepped forward. The heavy cloisonné piece clipped him squarely beneath the jaw, and Grady crumpled like a wilted leaf to the polished wooden floor.

Moments after Troy Fontaine watched Grady gain admittance to Constantine Reynolds's home, he heard his friend call out Dani's name. After a quick glance at Hercules, Troy grabbed the rifle and climbed down from the carriage.

"Go on, Leze." Hampered by his injured ankle, Troy urged the man ahead.

Hercules took the steps two at a time and shouldered his way through the door. The sound of his heavy footsteps reverberated through the high-ceilinged hallway as he charged toward the curving staircase. At the sound of a crash from the second floor, Troy limped to the stairs. Hand over hand, he used the banister to work his way up the staircase. Troy could see Hercules wrestling with one of Reynolds's servants until the sound of a pistol shot exploded around him, echoing off the walls of the stairwell.

"Leze!" Troy shouted when he saw the big man recoil from the blow of a wound to his shoulder.

Still on his feet, Hercules used his mighty fist to flatten Reynolds's only defender. He then stepped over the man's body and rushed headlong toward the nearest open doorway.

Troy spotted a trail of muddy footprints on the carpet runner. Small footsteps marked a path to the nearest open doorway. Dani's footprints.

He entered the room, his heart lodged somewhere between his chest and his throat, not even daring to think of what he might find inside. He saw Hercules bent over Grady's fallen form.

"Where's Dani?" Troy leaned against the door frame, his limbs shaking from exertion. At the sound of a low moan from Grady, Troy glanced down at his friend. "Thank God," he said.

Hercules stood, blood streaming from a flesh wound on his shoulder. Eyes wide and wild, he said, "Reynolds's got Miz Dani."

A connecting door to the room beyond gaped wide, and as Hercules ran toward it, a scream echoed through the hallway. Troy spun toward the sound as Hercules charged through the adjoining room and flung the hall door wide. Both men stood in the open doorways and faced Reynolds. The man held Dani against him, using her body as a shield as he pressed the lethal point of her hunting knife against her jugular.

"If you take one step into the hallway, I'll kill her," he shouted at Troy and Hercules.

Dani struggled against the man's hold, the silk robe gaping wide. It was not until she felt him press the tip of the knife harder against her throat that she quieted.

"Kill him, Troy," she commanded. Head high, her eyes flashed with anger. "Do it!"

"Kill me and you kill her, too, Fontaine. After all these years, is it worth it?"

Troy stood motionless in the doorway, the rifle hanging primed but useless in his hands.

"Do it, Troy!" Dani yelled again.

"Shut up!" Reynolds jerked her higher against him. She lashed out with her foot and hit him squarely on the kneecap. When he staggered, Dani jabbed an elbow beneath his ribs.

Hercules stepped into the hallway.

"I'll do it," Reynolds screamed, as he backed away from the men and fought to maintain his hold on Dani. "I'll kill her just as I killed your mother and father."

"No, he won't," Dani argued. "He's lying. He knows he'll never get away now."

"I'd like to stay and argue, but . . ."

Troy watched Reynolds drag Dani closer to the stairs, watched and waited for the man to drop his guard. A deathly calm pervaded his senses as Troy witnessed the unfolding scene with a sense of detachment. His whole life had culminated in this one moment, and now he was faced with the ultimate decision. Reynolds made an easy target. All he needed to do was aim and fire and justice would be served.

But there was no way he would risk Dani's life.

Reynolds stepped back, carefully feeling his way toward the top step. Dani had ceased struggling while she waited for an opportunity to break free. She stared hard at Troy, trying to communicate her thoughts, focusing her eyes on the rifle, then meeting his. She was willing him to raise the gun and fire.

Hercules took another step forward.

"Call your man back, Fontaine," Reynolds warned, switching his attention from Troy to Hercules.

In the split second that followed, Dani shouted "Now!" and pulled as far away from the blade as Reynolds's grasp would allow. The movement unbalanced the man as he stood above the stairwell. He let go of Dani as he fought to maintain his foothold. His hands groped the air as he sought the banister. Dani flung herself to the floor. Troy raised his gun and fired at Reynolds.

Gunpowder exploded. Blood burst forth in a crimson shower from Reynolds's forehead. The explosion reverberated in the hallway, followed by the clatter and pounding of Reynolds's body as it toppled lifeless down the stairs.

Dani pulled herself to her knees as Troy limped toward her. Hercules rushed past them both, intent on making certain Reynolds no longer posed a threat. As Troy knelt and clasped Dani to him, Hercules called out, "He's dead, Mr. Troy!"

Dani hid her face against Troy and tried to still the quaking that shook her frame. He raised her lips to his as he placed a gentle finger beneath her chin and then brushed her mouth with his own.

"It's over," he whispered.

As her silver-gray eyes searched his, Dani discovered an emotion reflected in Troy's eyes she'd never seen there before—a look of overwhelming peace.

Inside Reynolds's room, Grady moaned and Dani slipped from Troy's embrace to go to their friend. She knelt by his side, fighting to keep the oversized robe closed about her.

"Did they get here?" Grady wanted to know as he sat up slowly, focusing his vision while carefully moving his jaw back and forth.

"Who?" Dani asked.

"Fontaine's Fighting Forty."

Dani felt Troy's presence beside her and looked up at him with a glow in her eyes.

"They got here."

Grady returned her smile, and looked relieved in the bargain. "Good. Now can we go home?"

"We have a few things to clean up here," Troy said gravely.

Dani sat back on her heels and stared up at Troy, weighing her choices. She decided that surprise would be the best tactic and so held out her hand for his assistance. He obliged by pulling her up to her feet.

He didn't release her hand. Instead, he continued tugging until she was close enough for him to rest his weight against her.

"Now I know you love me," he said.

"I never tried to hide it," she answered.

"But now I'm sure of it. As filthy as I am, no one else could stand to be this close to me."

She tipped her head and smiled up at him with mischief in her eyes. Her robe hung open between them, her nakedness hidden against Troy's length. The feel of her breasts brushing against the hard wall of his chest nearly drove all else from her mind. Suddenly Dani found herself wishing away Grady, Hercules, and the hideous knowledge that Reynolds lay dead at the foot of the stairs. She conjured up visions of herself and Troy, wrapped in each other's arms, the way they'd been before, the way she was certain they would be again.

"I wasn't exactly clean when we met, but look how you took to me," she teased.

"I can vouch for that," Grady said from his position on the floor at their feet.

Suddenly embarrassed by Grady's presence, Dani tried to pull the silk robe closed. Troy, aware of her predicament, reached between them and slowly drew the edges together, then turned her away from Grady. They walked slowly toward the connecting door to Reynolds's dressing room, Troy leaning on Dani's shoulders for support. She helped him sit down on the edge of the bed.

"Find yourself something a bit more modest to wear and then we'll have Grady drive us back to town."

Dani smiled up at him. She had one more task to accomplish.

The garden surrounding the tiny cottage was far from quiet. The fountain splashed merrily, drops of water shining in the bright late-afternoon sunshine. Birds of riotous colors, far more splendid and shining than any of the flowers, sang gaily overhead. Dani led Troy through the faded gate and along the path that wound through the walled secret garden to the front door of the cottage. She halted there, took a deep breath, and raised her hand to knock.

"What are you up to?" he asked.

Dani looked at Troy. He'd washed and changed into one of Reynolds's shirts; he had been forced to leave the white silk open down the front, for the smaller man's clothing barely fit. The cook had been happy to oblige him by rounding up a pair of pants from one of the taller house servants. They had found Reynolds's slaves far from distressed over the man's demise and more than happy to assist their liberators.

Smiling up at him, Dani tried to quell her nervousness. She hoped she was doing the right thing. Her intuition told her to go ahead; she just prayed that the woman inside the cottage would forgive her.

When no one answered her gentle knock, Dani tried again. Still no one responded.

"I know you're in there," Dani said softly. The windows were open wide, and her voice was carried in on the breeze.

Dani tried again. "Please come out."

She knocked once more. "You may not want to see me, but I think you'll want to see the man with me."

"Who are you talking to?" Troy asked, bending to whisper in Dani's ear.

The door slowly opened from the inside.

Dani felt him straighten. She heard Troy's breath catch in his throat and listened to the hoarse sound of the word he uttered in a hushed whisper.

"Mother?"

When Troy's eyes flooded with unshed tears, Dani's own eyes burned and she looked away from him to face the woman in the doorway.

Jeanette Fontaine held shaking fingers to her lips as if to stop the words, but she was unable. "Oh, Troy. Oh, my son!"

Without a word, Troy opened his arms and stepped forward to enfold the petite woman in his embrace. Jeanette's arms slipped beneath Troy's to clasp him to her. When Dani heard Jeanette's broken sobs and saw Troy bury his face against the woman's neck, she turned away from the heart-wrenching scene and walked toward the welcoming bench beside the singing fountain.

Wearily Dani sank down to the cool marble bench and let her

fingers trace the pattern on the pants she'd confiscated from Reynolds's closet. Dani let her open palm rest against the bulky material cinched at her waist. She'd donned one of Reynolds's shirts as well, a cool saffron silk that felt as light as air.

Sighing, she thought of the two people in the cottage who needed time alone to heal old wounds. She thought of Grady and Hercules, the two other men who had become so dear to her. When last she had seen Hercules, he was in the kitchen being fussed over by the housemaids while Grady, nursing a headache, was on his way to Fort George to report Reynolds's death to the authorities.

Dani braced her arms behind her on the bench and lifted her face toward the lowering sun. The sound of the bubbling fountain soothed her soul. She knew she was carrying Troy's child; the realization had come to her at the oddest time—while she was bathing in Constantine Reynolds's room. Because of the discovery she had fought that much harder to escape his hold. She could no longer blame her fatigue on the heat, nor could she shrug off the lack of Eve's curse. All the signs pointed to only one answer: she would have Troy's child before winter came again.

The sound of limping footsteps on the gravel path behind her alerted Dani to Troy's presence. But she did not turn to welcome him. She let him come to her. The footsteps halted and then Dani felt his hands on her shoulders. His fingertips began kneading the tension from her muscles. She rubbed her cheek against his knuckles and then peered over her shoulder and met his eyes.

"Will she go back with us?" she asked softly.

He sat down beside her and took her in his arms.

She felt him nod as he rested his cheek against the top of her head. "Because of you, I'm not only alive, but I have my mother back. Thank you, Dani."

She recalled the way he'd thanked her last night in the jungle. "I'd do it again."

"So would I," Troy said. "All of it. If it was the only way I could have you." He kissed her, then traced the outline of her lips with his tongue. Troy pulled back and stared into her eyes.

Wanting to share her newfound secret with him, Dani dropped her head and hid her eyes against his shoulder. Her words were muffled, but he heard them all the same. "I guess I'm paying for all that loving I begged you for."

He rubbed his open palm along the length of her spine. "How?" he asked.

"I never did this before, so I'm not real sure what's going on."

"Do you think you might make this just a bit clearer for me?"

She took a deep breath and looked up at him. "Last night you asked me to marry you."

"I know. You've yet to give me your answer."

She let out her pent-up breath and smiled. "I thought maybe you were delirious with fever."

"I was never so lucid in my life. I do my best thinking when I'm feverish."

Dani smiled. "I'll agree with you there." She dropped her gaze again. "You won't mind being tied to—someone like me?"

"I don't deserve you, Dani. All I've ever done is take from you."

She looked up again and shook her head, denying his words. "Funny, but the way I see it, you're getting the short end of the trade. I can't cook, I can't sew anything fancy, and I never had a grand place to care for, so I can't even help with that."

Troy couldn't resist planting a kiss on her pouting lips. "You can make love and have babies. I'll do the rest."

"All I have to do is make love with you and have babies?"

He nodded.

"How about hunting and fishing and getting into trouble right and left?"

He feigned a resigned sigh. "I'm sure you'll be doing that, too. I didn't feel the need to bring it up."

"About the babies . . ."

"Forget I said that." He smoothed the hair away from her face. Thinking he saw fear in her eyes, he added, "That'll come when you're ready."

"Maybe a lot sooner than you think." She shrugged and smiled crookedly.

Troy grasped her shoulders and forced her to face him. He searched her eyes for the truth and then broke into a smile. He pulled her close and held her against his heart.

"Then I had better make you pay for your mistakes as soon as possible," he said, his cheek resting against her hair.

She pulled away and sat up straight. "I keep forgetting that I have money of my own. What if you just forget the shipping business and stay home with me?"

Troy kissed the tip of her suntanned nose.

"I could be tempted."

Dani reached down and toyed with the shirt button between her breasts. "I'll work on it."

Epilogue

The inhabitants of Isle de Fontaine, old and new, gathered in Leial's comfortable parlor to listen to Grady relate his part in Troy's adventure. Warm spring sunshine bathed the land outside the open windows behind the storyteller, while a slight breeze gently rustled the lace curtains. Leial, regal in a rich wine-colored gown, sat beside Jeanette Fontaine on the curved-legged settee and held tight to her daughter-in-law's hand. Jeanette was becoming more at ease around them now, but Leial knew it would take time for her emotional wounds to heal. As soon as Jeanette was ready, Leial intended to invite a few close friends to the island for a small gathering to reintroduce her daughter-in-law to Baton Rouge society. Nothing grand, she assured herself. No more than fifty guests.

She glanced across the room at Dani. The girl sat comfortably in a wing chair, her feet resting on a small, needleworked footstool. Troy lay stretched out beside Dani's chair. He toyed with her fingers, his eyes on his new bride.

Leial then turned her concentration to Grady, who straightened the already perfect lapel of his forest-green coat and then pulled at his shirtsleeve.

"I wrote to my father when we returned from the expedition west, but it was weeks before he could respond to let me know what his lawyers had learned about Dani's family, the Whittakers of New York." He cleared his throat and puffed visibly with his own importance. "Finally they were able to locate a second cousin of Dani's who could relate the story of her origins. It seems that her father, the sole heir to a fortune, fell

358

from grace when he married one of the family serving girls, a Danish immigrant. When Whittaker's father threw him out without a cent, the man left to become a missionary. The couple had a child before they left the East; that child was Dani, of course." He nodded in her direction. "Her grandfather knew about the little girl, but he still would not let his son back into his good graces."

Grady glanced around the room to be sure they were all listening, although everyone except Leial already knew the story quite well. "The son left home and took his wife and little girl west. The two of them died, leaving Dani all alone. It seems her grandfather spared no expense searching for them, but never found a trace. Ironically, he died shortly before Dani rode into St. Louis. But," Grady added, smiling triumphantly, "he left the bulk of his estate to any children who might have survived the son and his wife. The information in Dani's family Bible proves who she is and that she's entitled to the money. My father's lawyers are working on securing the funds for her now."

Leial began to piece the information together for herself. "When the letter from your father arrived, Dani had already left for Tobago with Hercules."

"That's right." Grady nodded. "So I followed her, hoping to find her before she got herself killed. I also intended to talk your stubborn grandson into coming home with me before he ruined his life." Grady smiled at Troy. "I was going to tie him up if I had to."

"I'd like to see you try." Troy smiled back.

"Let me get back to my story." Grady ignored the man on the floor and turned to Leial. "So, when I got to Tobago . . ."

Troy tugged on Dani's fingers, drawing her attention away from Grady. She glanced down at him, a slow, contented smile curving her lips.

He mouthed the words "Follow me" and nodded toward the door, then stood and quietly slipped out of the room. Dani waited to the count of ten and then did as he had asked. She tried to still the rustle of her peach silk gown as she moved toward the hallway, but Leial glanced her way, alerted by the sound. Dani shrugged and Leial winked; then Dani slipped out of the room. She raced down the hall toward Troy, who stood waiting for her at the foot of the stairs.

"Tired?" he asked.

"A little." She looked up at him through lowered lashes. "I could use a nap. It's not that easy dragging around the weight of all this clothing all day." She shook her skirt for emphasis.

"Your buckskins are in the closet, pet. Don't blame me."

"I do blame you, Fontaine. You know damn well I can't fit in them anymore." She gave him a sideways glance. "But you can bet I'm going to as soon as I can."

Without another word, he took her hand and led her up the stairs. The master bedroom was theirs and had been since their return from Tobago. Leial insisted that she'd kept it far too long and that Troy, as head of the household, and a newlywed, deserved the master's room. The walls and furnishings that once reflected Leial's occupancy were now covered with Troy and Dani's belongings. Grady's Rocky Mountain scenes graced the walls while Dani's buffalo hide covered the floor near the bed. Their clothing hung side by side while their shoes and boots vied for space on the closet floor.

Troy did not hesitate to turn back the bedding before he bent to remove his boots. Dani sat on the edge of the bed and drew off her silk slippers, then tossed them toward the closet.

"No stockings, Mrs. Fontaine?" Troy asked with a teasing glint in his eye.

"My husband won't let me wear them," she informed him.

"No?" He tried to look skeptical.

"Nope. No 'unders,' either."

He looked aghast. "*No* underwear?"

"Not a stitch."

"What a strange man your husband must be." Troy shook his head.

She laughed and hooked her arm through his, pulling him back until they were stretched out across the bed. "My husband is a very practical man. He knows what I need."

"From the looks of the plate of petticoat cookies on the side table I'd say Venita knows what you need, too."

"I think she's trying to make up for the voodoo gris-gris I used to find in my room. Now all she leaves is food. I still can't figure out how she gets in and out without me seeing her."

"The mysteries of the bayou are staggering."

Dani was content to lie beside him and stare up at the *baire* draped above them. She decided that afternoon was fast becoming her favorite time of day. Since their return, Troy had not only insisted she rest but had invited himself to rest with her. And sleep was usually the farthest thing from their minds.

"How long will it be before Devereaux gets back from Tobago?" she asked.

"At least a month. I still can't believe he might be able to persuade the authorities that Reynolds's holdings should belong to us."

"Why not?" She sat up again, ready to argue. "You deserve to get everything that man had. After all, he did kill your father, and he held your mother prisoner for years. He has no children to pass everything on to, so I think you and your mother deserve every cent that plantation will bring!"

"Calm down, pet." Troy reached for her and pulled her back down beside him. "Let's talk of something else." He thought for a moment before he said, "Grady will be leaving soon."

"I'll miss him," Dani admitted. "He's a good friend. I sure wish I could find a decent woman for him."

Troy laughed aloud and rolled on his side to face her. He propped his head on his hand. "And what kind of a decent woman would you find for Grady?"

She mused over her answer for a moment. "Someone shy. Definitely a woman who blushes."

"Why?"

"Well, she can't be a woman who cusses a blue streak, that's for sure. Grady's heart couldn't take it. She'll have to be somebody who thinks the sun rises and sets with Grady. Someone who will make him feel strong, sure of himself, too."

"You mean someone who'll keep him from stumbling over himself?"

She nodded. "Yes. Someone who will appreciate him for what he is." Dani bit her lower lip, then added, "He's sure handsome enough." It was her turn to roll to her side and face him, nose to nose. "After his exhibition in New York, he plans to go west again."

Troy searched her eyes for any hint of homesickness. "Would you like to go back?"

Without hesitation, she shook her head. "Nope. I lived there once, but I guess I'm like Robinson Crusoe in that book Leial's been reading to me. My life's stretched out in a lot of different chapters, and now I'm starting a whole new one here in the bayou with you and your kinfolks, and the baby."

Troy thought of his own life and how much it had changed since he found his Rocky Mountain wildflower. His life was no longer overshadowed by the mystery of the past; his mother had returned to the island. The man responsible for his father's death had paid for his crimes. Troy was able to accept all the love Dani offered and return it in full measure. Where there had been darkness, now there was light and love and laughter. He smiled into Dani's eyes, eyes shining with love for him, and was satisfied by her clearly defined perception of life. He, too, was ready to write new chapters of his own.

"No regrets, pet?" he asked.

She put her arm around him and whispered against his lips, "Just a small one."

Troy's eyes darkened and he frowned. "What is it?"

"You still talk too much when you ought to be kissin', Fontaine."

"Then I'd best get to it," he said, and drew her into his embrace.